Our Melody

Claire Hollis

Published by Claire Hollis, 2024.

This is a work of fiction. Similarities to real people, places, or events are entirely coincidental.

OUR MELODY

First edition. October 8, 2024.

Copyright © 2024 Claire Hollis.

ISBN: 979-8224179411

Written by Claire Hollis.

Chapter 1: Echoes of Yesterday

The notes rise and fall, each one a haunting reminder of the joy that once filled my life. I can almost see my mother's face, lit up with pride as I fumbled through my own attempts to play the piano. Music was our shared language, an unspoken bond that tied us together. But here, at the edge of Crescent Lake, that bond feels frayed, the chords out of tune. I take a step closer, my heart racing as if I might interrupt a sacred moment. The boy doesn't seem to notice me at first, lost in his melody, pouring out his soul through the saxophone.

"Hey," I finally call out, my voice barely above a whisper. It sounds foreign to my ears, fragile like the autumn leaves drifting from the trees above. The music stops, and he turns, eyes wide, as if I've startled him from a dream. His gaze is a deep shade of blue, reminiscent of the lake, shifting like the water beneath the fading light.

"Sorry if I was too loud," he says, a playful grin spreading across his face. "I tend to forget the world exists when I'm playing. I'm Jace."

"Not too loud," I reply, forcing a smile that feels more like a grimace. "Just... unexpected." I'm not sure if I'm more startled by his sudden presence or by the way my stomach flips at the sight of him. He looks like someone who walks straight out of the summer sun, with an effortless charm and an air of confidence that only amplifies the awkwardness I feel in his company.

"Unexpected can be good," he counters, tilting his head in a way that suggests he knows secrets about the universe. "What's your name?"

"Lily," I manage to say, my voice steadier now, as if I've crossed some invisible threshold into this new reality where the air is charged with possibility. "You play really well."

"Thanks," he replies, shrugging as if it's no big deal. "I've been at it for a while. The lake has the best acoustics. I come here to practice when I need to clear my head."

There's something about the way he talks, so unguarded and open, that makes me want to peel away the layers of my own grief and reveal the messy, raw parts of me that I keep hidden. But instead, I stay silent, letting the moment stretch between us like the fading sunlight, warm yet fleeting.

"Are you new around here?" he asks, glancing at the old wooden dock where I usually sit, taking in the tangled brush and vibrant wildflowers that edge the shore. "I don't think I've seen you before."

"Kind of," I reply, rubbing the back of my neck, a nervous habit. "I mean, I've lived here my whole life, but..." I trail off, unsure of how to explain that I've only recently started to emerge from the cocoon of my grief.

"But you haven't really lived," he finishes for me, his tone softening as if he understands more than he lets on. "I get it. Sometimes, the world feels too heavy to bear."

I look at him, surprised. "How do you know?"

"Trust me, I know." His voice drops, revealing a vulnerability that contradicts his earlier confidence. "Life can throw curveballs, and it's easy to get lost in the chaos."

A moment hangs between us, heavy with unspoken truths. I can feel the weight of my own sorrow pressing down, and for a brief flicker, I wonder if sharing it with this stranger might lighten my load.

"I lost my mom two years ago," I say, the words tumbling out like stones thrown into the still water. The moment they leave my lips, I realize how long I've kept that truth hidden, how tightly I've clutched it, afraid of the reactions it might invoke.

"I'm sorry," he says, his expression turning serious, a flash of empathy in his eyes. "That's... rough."

"It is," I admit, surprised by how much lighter it feels to say it out loud. "Some days are better than others, but the pain just lingers like a ghost."

"I get that," he replies, his gaze shifting back to the lake, where the last light of day begins to dissolve into twilight. "Music helps me cope. It's like therapy, you know? I can pour my heart into it and find a little bit of peace."

"I used to play," I say, feeling a tug of nostalgia. "Piano. But it's been a while. I haven't been able to touch it since..." I pause, the words catching in my throat.

"Since you lost her?" He finishes gently, and I nod, unable to voice the truth.

He smiles, warm and inviting. "You should try again. You might surprise yourself. Maybe we can make a deal—you teach me piano, and I'll teach you how to play sax. Who knows? We could start a band."

"Right," I chuckle, but the sound is laced with a wistfulness I can't shake. "A band? With what audience, the ducks?"

"Hey, don't underestimate the ducks," he laughs, his voice brightening the heavy air. "They're a discerning crowd. They'll know talent when they see it."

The corners of my mouth twitch upward, and I'm surprised by how easily he pulls a laugh from me. For the first time in months, the ache in my heart softens just a fraction, replaced by the warmth of connection. "Okay, maybe we can perform for them someday."

"Deal," he replies, his smile infectious. The promise of the moment feels like a thread woven into the fabric of my existence, connecting me to something I thought I'd lost forever.

As the sun sinks below the horizon, painting the sky in deep purples and fiery oranges, I feel a spark of hope ignite within me. Here, at the edge of Crescent Lake, amid the echoes of yesterday, a new melody begins to unfold, one that I'm more than ready to embrace.

The moment stretches as I stand there, caught between the warmth of the fading sun and the chill of the lake's evening breeze. Jace's saxophone is a siren call, and I feel like I'm being pulled into a new world, one where grief doesn't weigh as heavily. He continues to play, each note ringing out like a pebble dropped into water, creating ripples that dance across the surface of my heart.

"Didn't mean to interrupt your moment," I finally say, taking a few tentative steps forward. "I thought the ducks were your only audience."

"They're a tough crowd," he chuckles, a glint of mischief in his eyes. "But they do appreciate a good solo. You should see their heads bobbing along." He leans back against the cool wooden rail of the dock, looking effortlessly at ease, as if this were his natural habitat.

I sit down on the edge of the dock, letting my legs dangle over the side. The water swirls beneath me, reflecting the last vestiges of daylight. "So, what's your story? You come here often to serenade the wildlife?"

"Guilty as charged," he replies with a playful smirk. "But really, I just needed an escape. My life can get a bit chaotic too. This place feels like a reset button, you know? Plus, it's way better than my room, which is a vortex of musical chaos and laundry that may or may not be sentient."

I laugh, surprised by how quickly my heart warms to him. "I can relate. My room is a museum of my grief. Exhibit A: the untouched piano covered in dust and memories. It could really use a tour guide."

"Dusty pianos are like neglected plants—they just need some love and water," he replies, a glimmer of determination lighting his eyes. "And maybe a little fertilizer in the form of inspiration."

"Or a good shove off the edge of the dock," I joke, nudging him with my elbow. "I've thought about launching it into the lake a few times."

"Hey, we can't lose such a beautiful instrument to the depths of Crescent Lake!" he exclaims dramatically, clutching his chest as if I'd just declared war on the musical arts. "How about we save the piano and get you back to playing? I promise I won't judge."

"Okay, but you might want to keep your ears covered," I warn, my cheeks warming at the thought of sharing something so personal with him. "I haven't played in ages. My fingers might refuse to cooperate."

"Then we'll stage a mutiny," he declares, grinning as he hops off the dock and lands gracefully on the ground beside me. "I'll help you find your rhythm again. We'll start a band and take over Crescent Lake's underground music scene."

"First order of business: securing a better audience than just ducks," I counter, laughing at the idea.

"Challenge accepted," he says, nodding seriously. "But first, what about you? What's holding you back from playing again?"

I glance away, the question hitting closer to home than I expect. The sunset's last rays dip beneath the horizon, leaving a soft, muted glow. "It's just… every time I sit down, it feels like I'm opening a wound," I admit. "My mom and I used to play together, and without her, it's like I'm trying to breathe underwater."

Jace nods slowly, understanding written all over his face. "That sounds heavy. But maybe it's time to let some air in. To create new memories at that piano, not just revisit the old ones."

There's something about his earnestness that makes my chest tighten. "You make it sound so easy. Like flipping a switch or turning a page."

He shrugs, his expression turning thoughtful. "Maybe it is easy—at least, the idea of it. The execution? That's where it gets messy. But messy can be beautiful too."

The air between us feels charged with unspoken possibilities, the weight of my loss sitting heavy but somehow lighter in this shared space. "You're full of surprises, Jace," I say, a smile playing on my lips. "What else are you hiding beneath that charming exterior?"

"Just the saxophone and a few killer dance moves," he replies, striking a pose like he's auditioning for a bad music video. "But I think I'll keep those moves to myself for now. The world isn't ready."

"Oh, I don't know. I think I'm ready," I tease back, my heart lifting in a way I haven't felt in a long time.

Just then, the air crackles with a sudden gust of wind, rustling the leaves overhead. I shiver involuntarily, and Jace notices, shifting closer. "Cold?" he asks, his voice low and warm.

"A little," I admit, though it's more the sudden closeness than the temperature that makes my heart race.

Without a word, he shrugs off his jacket and drapes it over my shoulders, the fabric smelling faintly of fresh grass and something uniquely him. "Here, keep warm. We can't have the next piano prodigy freezing to death on my watch."

"Now I feel like I'm in some kind of cheesy movie scene," I say, trying to inject levity into the moment, but warmth floods my cheeks nonetheless. "I should be handing you my Oscar already."

He chuckles, the sound rich and inviting. "Who says life can't be a bit cheesy? Besides, maybe one day we'll have an actual audience beyond the ducks, and they'll appreciate this moment."

"Alright, fine. Let's say I play the piano again," I say, lifting my chin defiantly. "What happens next?"

Jace's eyes spark with excitement. "We find a venue, maybe a cozy coffee shop or a park stage, and perform. Just you, me, and our gloriously unprepared selves. We'll take the world by storm, or at least the ducks."

"Sounds like a plan," I reply, feeling a flicker of hope spark within me. "But only if you promise to practice your sax a lot more."

"Deal," he laughs, his eyes gleaming as he leans back against the railing, seemingly content in the unfolding magic of the moment. "Let's make this a summer to remember."

As twilight envelops us, the stars begin to peek through the darkening sky, and I find myself staring at the night with a new sense of purpose. Maybe, just maybe, I could take those first steps out of my cocoon, and Jace—this unexpected boy with a saxophone—might just be the person to guide me.

The stars begin to emerge, twinkling like diamonds scattered across an inky canvas as the last remnants of twilight fade away. With the cool night air settling in around us, the world feels almost alive, each sound amplified in the silence of dusk. Jace sits beside me, his presence a comforting weight as the melodic echoes of his sax linger in the space between us, wrapping around me like a familiar song.

"Okay, what's the first song we should work on?" he asks, breaking the comfortable silence with an infectious enthusiasm that makes my heart flutter.

"Um, I don't know. Maybe something simple? I mean, I haven't played in forever," I reply, biting my lip. The thought of returning to the piano feels like climbing a mountain I've avoided for too long.

"How about 'Let It Be'?" he suggests, a playful smirk lighting up his face. "I promise, it's a crowd-pleaser, and even I can't mess it up too badly."

I can't help but laugh at the image of Jace fumbling his way through a classic. "You, messing it up? I refuse to believe it. But I'll take that as a challenge. It's settled then—if we're going to start a band, we need a setlist."

"Band names are equally important," he insists, a mock-seriousness replacing his playful demeanor. "What do you think of 'The Quacking Quartet'? It's got a nice ring to it."

I snort, doubling over with laughter. "Unless we find some actual ducks to join us, I'm not sold. What about 'Crescent Vibes'? A nod to our lake and all that."

"Nice! I can see the posters now—'Crescent Vibes: The Concert That Will Make Ducks Cry,'" he says dramatically, throwing his hands up as if we were already on stage.

For a moment, we both indulge in the fantasy, envisioning our names plastered on flyers with the sounds of applause echoing in our minds. But then reality settles back in, and the warmth between us tinges with something softer, a layer of vulnerability that both excites and terrifies me.

"You really think I could get back to playing?" I ask, my voice barely above a whisper, the fear creeping back into my chest.

Jace turns serious, meeting my gaze with an intensity that makes my breath catch. "Absolutely. It's about reclaiming the joy you once had. Trust me, it won't be easy, but the best things never are."

I want to believe him. I really do. But doubt flares up, reminding me of the weight of my grief and the memories tangled with the piano's keys.

"Can I confess something?" I say, nervously glancing at the lake, where the water reflects the silvery glow of the moon. "I've thought about just... giving up on it all. Selling the piano, moving away, pretending I was never here."

His brow furrows in concern. "You don't really want that, do you? You're just scared."

I nod, swallowing the lump in my throat. "Scared of everything changing, of the memories fading. It feels like a betrayal sometimes."

"It's not a betrayal," he replies softly. "It's growth. Your mom wouldn't want you to be stuck in sadness; she'd want you to live, to create, to embrace every messy part of it. We can do it together, you know."

The sincerity in his voice makes my heart swell and ache all at once. "Together," I echo, the word tasting foreign yet comforting on my tongue.

We sit in silence, the weight of unspoken promises lingering in the cool night air. The moon climbs higher, casting a shimmering path across the lake, and for the first time in ages, I feel the tug of hope—a gentle pull urging me toward something brighter.

"Hey, do you want to know a secret?" Jace asks suddenly, his eyes gleaming with mischief.

"Only if it's a good one," I tease, tilting my head in curiosity.

"I've got an old saxophone that I've been meaning to fix up. I'm kind of terrible at it, but it's a family heirloom," he confesses, his voice dropping to a conspiratorial whisper. "I could use a partner in crime for my own comeback."

"Sounds like we're both full of surprises," I reply, feeling buoyant at the thought of us teaming up. "Maybe we should add a saxophone solo to our setlist then."

He grins, the kind of grin that makes my insides flutter. "Absolutely. Just think of it—an epic piano-sax duet. The crowd won't know what hit them."

"I can already picture the ducks throwing roses," I say, laughing again. The laughter feels different now—lighter, freer.

"Now that's an audience I can get behind," he says, his tone teasing but laced with genuine enthusiasm.

The moment feels electric, and I can't help but wonder where this strange connection might lead. Maybe it's the magic of the lake or the way Jace's laughter dances in the air, but my heart races with the promise of something new.

Just then, my phone buzzes in my pocket, jolting me from our whimsical exchange. I pull it out and frown at the screen.

"It's Mia," I say, glancing at the message. "She wants to know when I'm coming home. I told her I'd be out for a bit longer, but she's probably worried."

"Does she know about me?" Jace asks, a hint of apprehension in his voice.

"No, not yet. I think she'd be thrilled that I met someone who seems... interesting," I reply, gauging his reaction. "But I think she might also grill me about you. You know, like an interrogation about your intentions."

"Ah, yes, the classic 'meet the best friend' scenario," he laughs, feigning dramatic dread. "Should I be practicing my innocent face?"

"Definitely," I giggle, the lightness of our exchange lingering in the air. "And my 'please don't scare him away' face."

"Right, we'll prepare for battle." He leans closer, lowering his voice as if sharing a conspiracy. "Just tell her I'm definitely not a duck in disguise, and we'll be fine."

I roll my eyes but can't suppress a smile. "Noted. No ducks, just a charming saxophonist with questionable fashion choices."

His laughter mingles with the soft rustling of leaves, creating a symphony of unexpected camaraderie.

"Hey, before you go," he says, suddenly serious again, "can we meet here tomorrow? Same time?"

"Absolutely," I reply, my heart racing with excitement and fear. "I'll bring my courage, and you bring the sax."

"It's a date," he says, a hint of mischief returning to his eyes.

As we rise to leave, a sudden sound disrupts the calm—the crack of a branch snapping behind us. I turn quickly, adrenaline rushing through my veins. The water of Crescent Lake ripples violently as shadows dance on the shore, revealing something moving swiftly through the trees.

"What was that?" Jace whispers, his earlier lightness replaced by concern.

"I... I don't know," I stammer, my heart pounding. The hairs on my arms stand up as the feeling of unease settles over me.

Suddenly, a figure emerges from the darkened trees, and I gasp, my breath hitching in my throat. It's a tall man with a wild look in his eyes, and he steps forward, uncertainty and menace blending in the depth of his gaze.

"Lily?" he calls, his voice gravelly, as if it's been years since he last spoke. My pulse quickens as a chilling recognition washes over me.

"Who are you?" I whisper, the question lingering heavily in the air as fear grips my heart.

"Time to come home, Lily," he says, stepping closer, and in that moment, I realize that this summer night is about to take a turn I never saw coming.

Chapter 2: Unraveled Threads

The clink of ceramic cups and the muted chatter of patrons wrap around me like a familiar embrace as I settle into my usual corner at The Silver Spoon. The café is a riot of color and texture, with its mismatched furniture and walls splattered with local art that feels as alive as the people within. Sunlight filters through the large windows, casting playful patterns on the hardwood floor, illuminating the air heavy with the scent of freshly ground coffee and sweet pastries. I can hear the hiss of the espresso machine punctuating the soft melodies wafting from a vintage record player, a soundtrack that feels both nostalgic and vibrant.

Mia, my best friend and the self-proclaimed queen of spontaneity, nudges me with a mischievous grin. "Look who's here," she whispers, nodding toward a familiar figure hunched over in a booth by the window. It's Felix, the saxophonist from the lake—the one whose music wrapped around me like a warm blanket, pulling me out of my head and into a moment that felt electric. He's scribbling furiously in a battered notebook, his fingers stained with ink and his brow furrowed in concentration. There's something about him that pulls at the edges of my curiosity, an unrefined magnetism that makes the mundane seem extraordinary.

"Are you going to talk to him or just gawk like a love-struck teenager?" Mia teases, her eyes sparkling with mischief.

"I don't gawk," I retort, though my heart betrays me, skipping in a rhythm that mirrors the beat of his saxophone. It's now or never, I tell myself, summoning every ounce of bravery that I can muster. I push back my chair, its legs scraping against the floor like a reluctant companion, and walk over, my heart hammering in my chest.

"Hi," I say, my voice steadier than I feel. He looks up, and for a brief moment, our eyes lock. It's as if time freezes, the world outside the café dissolving into a blur of colors and sounds. He flashes a smile that's equal parts shy and self-assured, and I can't help but return it.

"Hey there," he replies, closing his notebook but not before I catch a glimpse of swirling musical notes and half-formed lyrics. "I didn't think anyone would come over. I'm Felix." His voice is a smooth blend of confidence and vulnerability, a mix that makes my skin prickle with interest.

"I'm Lila," I say, trying to suppress the flutter in my stomach. "I heard you playing at the lake yesterday. Your music—it was incredible."

"Thanks." He leans back, his posture relaxed but his eyes sharp, studying me as if trying to decode a complex melody. "Most people don't even notice when I'm playing. Just another ghost haunting the lake, I guess."

I laugh, the sound surprising me with its lightness. "You're not a ghost. You're a—what's the word? A muse? No, a siren! That's it. You lure people in with your enchanting music."

"Now that's a compliment I can get behind." His grin widens, revealing a dimple that deepens the moment. "You think you can handle the allure of a ghostly saxophonist?"

"Absolutely." I feel a spark of daring. "But only if you promise to play a private concert for me. Just you, your sax, and a couple of cinnamon rolls. The perfect trifecta."

"Cinnamon rolls? You sure know how to tempt a guy," he chuckles, the sound rich and warm, making my heart feel like it's dancing to an upbeat jazz number. "Okay, Lila, you've got a deal. But only if you share your secrets too."

"Secrets? I'm not sure I have any worth sharing." I lean closer, intrigued. "What do you want to know?"

"Tell me your dreams. What makes you tick?" He tilts his head slightly, his expression genuine, as if the question is not just casual banter but an invitation to unravel the threads of my life.

I hesitate for a moment, feeling the weight of his gaze. "Well, I've always wanted to be an artist—painting, mostly. But life has a funny way of throwing curveballs, you know? It's easy to get lost in the mundane."

"I know the feeling," he replies, and there's a flicker of something in his eyes—recognition, perhaps. "It's easy to feel invisible, even when you're surrounded by people."

That resonates with me. The weight of the unspoken and the ordinary often feels like a shroud, dulling the colors of our lives. I nod, wanting to dive deeper into this shared understanding. "How about you? What are your dreams?"

He pauses, looking out the window at the busy street, his expression thoughtful. "I want to make music that matters. Something that resonates, even if it's just for a moment. But sometimes, it feels like the harder I try, the more elusive it becomes."

"Maybe that's the magic of it," I suggest, my voice a bit bolder now. "The chase, the mystery. It's like trying to catch a shadow."

"Exactly." His smile is softer now, and I catch the glimmer of something deeper in his eyes. "You're not afraid to see the world differently. I like that."

The conversation flows, an effortless exchange of laughter and shared dreams that spirals into a comfortable rhythm. I learn that Felix is a senior at Crescent High, like me, but he feels like a ghost among the living, moving through the halls unnoticed while he tries to find his place in a world that often overlooks him. As we talk, I feel the warmth of connection bloom between us, an uncharted territory that hints at something both thrilling and terrifying. For the first time in ages, the weight of my own uncertainties feels lighter, almost as if I'm unravelling threads that have kept me tethered to a past I'm desperate to move beyond.

"So, Lila," he says, his eyes sparkling with mischief, "if I were to host a private concert, what would you play along with me? A duet of dreams, perhaps?"

"Only if you promise to let me handle the cinnamon rolls," I tease back, my heart racing at the unexpected levity of the moment.

"I'll bring the sax, you bring the sugar," he replies, laughter dancing between us, and in that instant, I realize that the connection we're forging is more than just whimsical banter. It's a step into a brighter chapter, an opportunity to explore the uncharted paths of possibility that lie ahead.

As the sun climbed higher in the sky, spilling golden light across the café, I felt as if a fresh chapter was beginning to unfold—not just for me, but for Felix as well. We talked about everything and nothing, letting our laughter fill the spaces between us like the notes of a jazz tune. The more we conversed, the more I could sense the subtle complexities woven into the fabric of his being. He was not just the saxophonist from the lake; he was a tapestry of dreams, disappointments, and a passion that flickered just below the surface.

"I'm not really a fan of the spotlight," he admitted, running a hand through his tousled hair, making it stand up even more. "I prefer being behind the scenes, letting the music speak for itself."

"Ah, the classic artist move," I teased, leaning in conspiratorially. "Always hiding in the shadows while the world dances in your light. What's wrong with a little attention? You have a gift, Felix. You should share it."

He shook his head, a rueful smile tugging at his lips. "I'd much rather let my sax do the talking. It's easier that way. I'm not great at words."

"Trust me, you're doing just fine," I replied, my own words flowing more freely than I had expected. "If I were a saxophone, I'd be squeaky and out of tune, but you're like the smoothest jazz."

His laughter rang out, a rich sound that seemed to make the café feel more alive. "Smoothest jazz? I might just steal that line. You're a natural at this."

With that, I felt a soft blush creep into my cheeks, and I ducked my head, feeling a delightful thrill course through me. Our playful banter continued, filled with quick-witted exchanges that revealed glimpses of our personalities. I was surprised by how easy it was to talk to him. It felt as though we had been doing this forever, exchanging secrets and dreams as if they were confetti.

But amidst the laughter, I sensed an underlying current—something unspoken that flickered behind his eyes whenever he mentioned his music. I was itching to ask about it, to probe deeper into his world, but just as I opened my mouth, the café door swung wide, and a gust of wind rushed in, scattering napkins across the counter.

My gaze flicked to the entrance, where a tall figure stepped inside, shaking raindrops from his dark hair. He wore an expression that blended annoyance with a hint of mischief. I recognized him immediately—Ethan, my ex-boyfriend. He was a whirlwind of charm and chaos, the kind of person who always seemed to be at the center of attention, his laughter resonating like a drumbeat. The last person I wanted to see today.

"Lila!" he exclaimed, spotting me before I could duck back into my conversation with Felix. "Fancy seeing you here. Are you hiding from your responsibilities again?"

A wave of irritation washed over me. "No, just enjoying my coffee. What brings you here?"

Ethan sauntered over, an air of confidence trailing behind him. "Just passing through. You know me, always on a grand adventure. What's with the saxophonist?" He glanced at Felix, his brow raised in curiosity, as if gauging whether this was a worthwhile distraction.

"Hey, I'm Felix," he introduced himself, extending a hand, but there was a tension in the air that made the moment feel awkward.

Ethan shook his hand, but the camaraderie didn't last. "Nice to meet you. So, you're the one responsible for Lila's daydreams?" His tone held a teasing edge, a playful jab that felt sharper than it was meant to be.

Felix chuckled, though there was a slight tightness to his smile. "I'm just trying to coax her out of her shell, that's all."

Ethan's gaze flickered between us, a mixture of amusement and something else, something that sent a chill racing down my spine. "Well, good luck with that. Lila here has a penchant for hiding behind her brushes. She's an artist, you know."

"Just like you're a master at dodging responsibility," I shot back, my heart racing. I didn't want this to turn into a spectacle. The last thing I needed was Ethan shining his spotlight on my life, picking apart every decision I made.

"Touché," Ethan replied, raising an eyebrow, his grin widening. "But I'm serious—maybe I should help you break out of your artistic shell. We could paint the town red, or at least, I could show you the best spots in town for inspiration. I'm always up for an adventure."

"Thanks, but I think I'm good," I replied, crossing my arms, trying to suppress the irritation that simmered just below the surface. "I'm busy exploring the world through my art."

"Right." He smirked, unfazed. "We'll see how long that lasts before you're dragged back into the chaos of reality."

The tension in the air thickened, and I could feel Felix shift slightly, as if he were preparing to take a step back from the unexpected drama unfolding before us. But then he surprised me by leaning forward, his eyes sparkling with mischief. "You know, Ethan, if you're looking for chaos, you might be in the wrong café. We prefer our chaos with a side of cinnamon rolls here."

Ethan chuckled, the atmosphere easing slightly as he glanced at me. "See? He's got the right idea. Join me on the wild side, Lila. You know you want to."

"No, I really don't," I said, feeling the weight of his gaze on me, a challenge wrapped in charm. "Besides, I think I'd rather stay here with Felix."

Ethan's smile faltered, and I caught a glimpse of genuine surprise flaring in his eyes. It was enough to send a surge of exhilaration through me. I had stood my ground. Felix's presence felt like a shield against the storm that was Ethan, and I felt a rush of pride.

"Fair enough," Ethan said, recovering quickly. "I'll leave you two artists to your creativity then. But just know, Lila, life's too short to hide away."

With that, he winked and turned to leave, the door chiming behind him as he stepped back into the street. I released a breath I didn't know I was holding, the weight of tension lifting, though I could feel the energy shift between Felix and me.

"Wow," he said, breaking the silence that lingered in the aftermath of Ethan's departure. "That was... something."

"Yeah, I'd say so." I couldn't help but laugh, shaking my head. "He has a knack for making everything feel like a performance."

"Well, it's his loss if he can't see how brilliant you are," Felix said, his tone serious, but a playful glint sparkled in his eyes.

"Thanks, but I'm not sure I want him to see me that way," I admitted, feeling the remnants of frustration fade, replaced by the warmth of camaraderie that had been growing between us. "I'm just trying to find my way, you know?"

Felix nodded, his expression shifting from amusement to sincerity. "Then let's find it together. You can show me your world, and I'll share my music. Deal?"

"Deal," I said, feeling a surge of hope blooming within me. Our laughter bubbled up again, a melody that echoed against the café walls, weaving together the threads of our conversation. In that moment, I knew I was exactly where I was meant to be, wrapped in the possibility of new beginnings, each note a step closer to discovering the music in my own heart.

The scent of fresh coffee mingled with the buttery aroma of pastries as Felix and I settled into a comfortable rhythm at our little corner table. The sunlight bathed us in a warm glow, transforming the café into a sanctuary away from the chaos of the outside world. Our laughter bubbled up like the frothy foam on my cappuccino, effortlessly dissolving the remnants of awkward tension left behind by Ethan. Each word exchanged felt like a brushstroke on the canvas of our burgeoning friendship, vibrant and full of promise.

"Okay, let's make a pact," I declared, a mischievous glint in my eye. "From now on, every Friday we meet here. You can play your sax, and I'll bring my sketches. We'll create our own little corner of the universe."

"Fridays, huh?" Felix mused, a playful smile curling his lips. "What if I have a last-minute gig or something? You could be stuck here twiddling your thumbs while I'm off dazzling crowds with my... ghostly charm."

"Then I'll just paint a portrait of you as a ghostly saxophonist, capturing your essence for all eternity." I couldn't help but giggle at the mental image of him floating around in a translucent cape, saxophone in hand, lamenting his unrecognized genius.

"Now that's a masterpiece waiting to happen," he laughed, the sound resonating through the air like the gentle notes of a saxophone. "But I'd prefer to stay corporeal for our sessions. It would be a shame to miss out on your cinnamon rolls."

"Noted," I replied, my smile widening. "But don't think I'm letting you off the hook that easily. You owe me a private concert first."

His eyes sparkled with mischief. "I suppose I can manage that. Just promise to keep the sugar coming. I'm a sucker for anything sweet—music and pastries included."

"Deal," I grinned, relishing the ease with which our conversation flowed. Each moment felt charged with unspoken understanding, an invisible thread weaving us together, drawing us closer.

We continued to share pieces of our lives, exchanging stories like trading cards, each tale revealing another layer of who we were beneath the surface. Felix spoke about his dreams of playing at larger venues, his fingers dancing through the air as he mimicked the notes he longed to produce. I listened, entranced, as he painted a vivid picture of smoky jazz clubs and dimly lit stages, where music enveloped the audience like a warm embrace.

"Sounds magical," I said, picturing the scene he described. "But you should know, the bigger the stage, the more likely someone might trip over a mic cord and fall flat on their face."

He chuckled, his laughter rich and melodic. "I'd rather not be that person. I'd much prefer to charm my audience into dancing than leave them gasping in horror."

"Good plan. Just make sure to keep your saxophone under control while you're at it. Wouldn't want it to become an instrument of destruction."

The playful banter continued until the café began to fill up with the lunchtime rush. Voices mingled into a cacophony of laughter and conversation, a soundtrack to our cozy bubble. I savored the moment, basking in the glow of connection as I watched Felix animate with passion, his hands moving as though conducting an unseen orchestra.

Suddenly, my phone buzzed on the table, its vibrations breaking the spell. I glanced down to see a message from Mia: "Emergency! Come outside!"

My stomach knotted with uncertainty. "I have to go," I said reluctantly, glancing back at Felix. "Something's up with Mia."

"Is everything okay?" he asked, concern etching lines across his brow.

"I'm not sure. I'll be right back." I rose quickly, the café's warmth slipping away as I stepped outside into the bustling street.

Mia was standing by her car, her expression a mix of urgency and excitement. "You won't believe what I just heard!"

"What is it?" I asked, my heart racing as I felt a strange mix of anticipation and dread.

"Ethan's planning a party tonight at his place," she blurted out, her eyes wide with intrigue. "It's supposed to be epic. He's inviting everyone from school, and I'm pretty sure he's trying to win you back. He keeps talking about you to anyone who will listen."

"Great," I muttered, the knot in my stomach tightening. "Just what I need. A room full of people I don't want to see, fawning over him."

Mia grabbed my arm, her grip firm. "Lila, you have to go. It could be the perfect chance to show him you've moved on, to remind him of what he lost."

I hesitated, torn between the urge to flee and the prospect of standing my ground. "I'm not sure I want to do that, especially if it means facing him again."

"But think of it this way—if Felix is your new saxophonist, wouldn't it be even sweeter to show Ethan you're thriving?"

Her words sparked something within me. Maybe I did want to prove that I could stand tall and shine in my own light. "You really think I should go?"

"Absolutely. Just imagine the look on his face when he sees you living your best life."

After a moment of contemplation, I nodded, determination hardening within me. "Alright, let's do this. But I'm not going alone."

"Great! We can pick up some snacks, grab your favorite dress, and show up in style!"

The adrenaline of planning swept over me, and a flicker of excitement mingled with my nerves. I raced back inside the café, eager to share my decision with Felix. I spotted him at our table, still lost in thought, the notebook lying open, filled with scribbles that had become a part of our story.

"Felix!" I called out, my voice cutting through the café's buzz. He looked up, a curious expression crossing his face.

"Everything okay?" he asked, standing as I approached.

"Mia just told me Ethan's throwing a party tonight. I think I'm going."

His brow furrowed slightly. "Are you sure that's a good idea?"

"Honestly, I don't know. But I feel like I need to show him that I'm moving on."

Felix's expression shifted to one of contemplation. "I don't think you should go alone."

"I wasn't planning on it," I assured him, a smile breaking through my anxiety. "Mia will be there, and you're invited, too. What do you say? Want to crash a party and keep me company?"

A glimmer of surprise flitted across his face, but it was quickly replaced with a grin. "Now that sounds like a challenge. Count me in."

"Perfect! Just promise me you won't play a sad sax solo in the corner if things get awkward."

He laughed, the sound light and infectious. "No promises, but I'll do my best to keep the mood lively."

The two of us exchanged glances, a flicker of excitement igniting between us. This could be our moment—an opportunity to stand side by side against the chaos of our pasts. But as I prepared to leave the café, the air shifted, a sense of foreboding settling around us.

Just then, my phone buzzed again, a message lighting up the screen. I glanced down, my heart dropping as I read the words: "You're going to want to see this. Ethan has a surprise for you tonight."

"Lila, what is it?" Felix asked, noticing the change in my demeanor.

I looked up, a mixture of dread and intrigue swirling in my chest. "I think tonight might be more than I bargained for."

And with that, I knew that whatever happened at the party, it was going to unravel far more than I could have ever anticipated.

Chapter 3: Unexpected Sparks

The moment I stepped into the dimly lit venue, the air wrapped around me like a cozy blanket, laced with the rich aroma of freshly brewed coffee and the faint, lingering essence of cigars. A low murmur of voices fluttered around like the jazz notes that would soon fill the space. Shadows mingled with golden light spilling from the vintage lamps, casting a warm glow that seemed to invite secrets to unfold. I took a deep breath, my heart thrumming in rhythm with the low hum of anticipation vibrating through the crowd.

A mix of patrons graced the venue, from wise old souls hunched over their drinks, savoring every word of the hushed conversations, to the wide-eyed dreamers scattered at the bar, their laughter light and carefree. Each face told a story, and the energy in the room felt like a collective heartbeat, thrumming with life and possibility. I felt slightly out of place yet curiously intrigued, like a wallflower at a grand ball, waiting for my moment to dance.

Tonight was about Felix—his invitation echoing in my mind like the promise of a secret. He had mentioned this jazz night with a sparkle in his eye, the kind that suggested this was more than just a gig for him; it was his sanctuary. As I slipped through the crowd, I caught glimpses of his friends, their playful banter a comforting backdrop to my nerves. It wasn't until I found a spot close to the stage that I realized I was actually going to hear him play live. I glanced around, trying to blend into the fabric of the evening, but there was an undeniable electric current between us, igniting the air whenever his gaze flickered my way.

When he stepped onto the stage, the world around me faded, leaving just him in that soft spotlight, as though the universe had conspired to paint this moment just for me. He wore a casual shirt, sleeves rolled up, a hint of rebellion in his style that perfectly matched his carefree spirit. His hair tousled as if he had just woken up from a dream, the way it caught the light drew a smile from my lips. But it was his eyes—those deep, soulful pools that seemed to capture the essence of the evening—that pulled me in like a moth to a flame.

The first notes floated through the air, wrapping around me like a warm embrace, and I felt myself leaning closer, caught in the sway of his melody. Each chord he struck resonated with unspoken emotions, layers of passion intertwined with hints of melancholy. His fingers danced over the keys, creating a rhythm that was intoxicating, mesmerizing. The music spilled forth, swirling around the room, coaxing smiles and tapping feet. I closed my eyes for a moment, allowing the sound to wash over me like a gentle tide, and when I opened them again, his gaze met mine, a spark igniting between us that felt as tangible as the notes swirling in the air.

I couldn't help but smile back, a grin so wide it felt like it could rival the moon hanging outside the window. He grinned, too, that boyish charm radiating through the dim light, and for a moment, I was convinced that the room had vanished, and it was just us, lost in this symphony of unspoken words and shared secrets. As the music swelled, I found myself swaying in my seat, the rhythm wrapping around me like a favorite song from my childhood. I was lost, enchanted, drowning in a sea of emotions I had never quite felt before.

But as the night wore on, the harmony of the music was interrupted by a sudden clang—a glass shattering somewhere in the back. The spell broke, and the crowd murmured with surprise, a few heads turning to see the source of the disruption. Felix's eyes flickered momentarily to the commotion, a slight frown tugging at the corners of his mouth before he deftly shifted his focus back to the keys. I admired his poise, how he seemed unfazed by the distraction, channeling the chaos into a deeper, more poignant piece that echoed the very heart of life's unpredictability.

The crowd settled back into the rhythm, and I found myself laughing softly, half in disbelief, half in admiration. It felt like an unexpected twist in a story I was eager to unravel, the kind of twist that made you lean forward, heart racing, wondering what might happen next. I noticed a couple at a nearby table, whispering animatedly, their laughter rich and infectious. It reminded me of Felix and me, two souls drawn together amidst the clamor, yet distinctly apart. As he played, I realized how much I wanted to step closer to him, to break down the invisible wall that separated us, to be more than just an audience member lost in his music.

After his set, the applause erupted like confetti, spilling over into a warm, celebratory cheer. Felix stood, taking a bow, his cheeks flushed with the thrill of performance. As he stepped off the stage, I felt the adrenaline coursing through my veins, my heart a chaotic mix of excitement and a hint of anxiety. What would I say to him? Would I manage to bridge the distance that felt both tantalizingly close and insurmountably far? Just as he began to approach, a swirl of people surrounded him, eager to praise his performance and share their admiration. I felt a twinge of disappointment as I watched him smile and laugh with them, his attention momentarily diverted.

I shifted in my seat, wrestling with the urge to join the throng of fans or retreat into the comforting shadows of anonymity. It was then that I caught his gaze again, and in that instant, everything around us faded into a blur. Time stood still, and the world shrank to just the two of us. I felt an unmistakable pull, a silent invitation wrapped in the warmth of his smile. This was my moment. With a deep breath, I stood, weaving through the crowd, a determined glint in my eye as I made my way toward him. The atmosphere buzzed with uncharted possibilities, and the evening had only just begun.

The crowd thinned out around Felix, and as I approached, I felt a delightful mix of excitement and uncertainty knotting in my stomach. He was in the midst of animated conversation with a couple, their laughter bouncing off the walls like confetti. I waited, pretending to be interested in a nearby painting—a vibrant depiction of a jazz band that seemed to pulse with life. The artist had captured not just the figures but the very essence of music, a swirl of colors and emotions that reflected how I felt at that moment, caught between hesitation and longing.

When the couple finally drifted away, leaving Felix alone, he turned to me, his expression shifting instantly from jovial to genuinely delighted. "You made it!" he said, his voice a mix of surprise and warmth. The way his smile lit up his face felt like a personal spotlight, making me blush. "Didn't think I'd see you here," he added, leaning against the edge of the bar, casually resting one elbow on the polished wood, his posture relaxed yet inviting.

"I couldn't resist," I replied, my heart racing as I stepped closer. "Your performance was mesmerizing. I felt like I was in a different world." I hoped my enthusiasm masked the slight tremor in my voice.

"Ah, the magic of jazz," he said, his eyes sparkling with mischief. "It's like catching fireflies in a jar—hard to describe, but once you've seen it, you're hooked." He leaned in slightly, and the warm scent of his cologne enveloped me, rich and woodsy, reminding me of autumn evenings spent cozying up with a good book.

We shared a laugh, the sound blending with the distant clinking of glasses and the soft murmur of conversations surrounding us. It felt like we were in our own little bubble, the chaotic world outside dimming, the only spotlight now on us. "So, are you going to tell me why you really came?" he asked, raising an eyebrow playfully, his tone teasing yet inquisitive.

"Maybe I just wanted an excuse to see you," I shot back, surprised by my own boldness. I instantly regretted it, my cheeks heating up, but Felix simply chuckled, a sound that vibrated through me like the bass of his music.

"I like that excuse. But what's next? A serenade?" He leaned in, pretending to be deep in thought. "I could use some fresh material, you know."

I couldn't help but laugh, the tension easing as we fell into a playful rhythm. "I'm afraid the only song I know is 'Awkward Silence,'" I retorted, trying to keep my tone light even as I felt a flutter in my stomach at his interest.

"Ah, my favorite genre!" he exclaimed dramatically, placing a hand on his heart as if I had delivered the most heartfelt confession. "I'm an expert in that particular composition."

As our banter continued, I realized how naturally our conversation flowed. Each quip felt like a note in a duet, building a connection that was both thrilling and terrifying. Just as I began to relax, a tall figure with an impressive mane of hair approached us, a wide grin plastered across his face. He clapped Felix on the back. "Great set, man! Seriously, you brought the house down," he exclaimed, his enthusiasm infectious.

Felix beamed, the light in his eyes even brighter now. "Thanks, Leo! Glad you could make it. I was just catching up with..." He paused, turning toward me, the warmth of his gaze sending a thrill through me. "This is—"

"Callie," I filled in, my smile faltering slightly at being interrupted.

"Callie! Right. Felix has told me all about you. You should totally join us for the next jam session," Leo said, his energy enveloping the conversation like a warm hug.

I blinked, caught off guard by the invitation. "I'm not really a musician," I said, half-laughing. "I'm more of an enthusiastic spectator."

"Spectator, schmespectator," Leo waved a hand dismissively, his enthusiasm unwavering. "You don't need to play an instrument to enjoy the music. Plus, you can give us feedback. I hear you're a critic now."

"Who told you that?" I asked, raising an eyebrow, suddenly self-conscious.

Felix chuckled. "Just a little birdie." His eyes twinkled, and I wondered if he had purposefully set Leo up to throw me off my guard.

"Very funny," I replied, feigning indignation. "I'll stick to my role as a humble admirer, thank you very much."

"Come on, Callie," Felix said, his voice dropping to a softer, more earnest tone. "You should definitely give it a shot. The more, the merrier."

Just then, the barista, a bubbly woman with a quick smile, interrupted us as she carried a tray of drinks toward the stage. "Felix, are you ready for round two? The crowd wants more!"

"Looks like my time's up," he said, a hint of regret in his voice as he glanced at the stage. "I have to get back. Will you be here when I'm done?"

"I wouldn't miss it," I promised, excitement bubbling inside me, my earlier nerves transforming into something sweetly exhilarating.

"Perfect," he said, flashing that charming smile again. "Save a spot for me, won't you?"

As he strode back to the stage, I found myself leaning against the bar, contemplating the whirlwind of emotions swirling within me. There was something uniquely intoxicating about Felix—his passion, his easy confidence, and that spark of connection we seemed to share. But beneath the excitement lay a thread of anxiety. What did this all mean? Was I merely infatuated, or was there a deeper connection waiting to be explored?

I tried to shake off the thoughts, focusing instead on the music as it filled the venue again, each note weaving its way through the air like a delicate thread binding us together. Felix lost himself in the melody, fingers dancing effortlessly over the keys, and I felt like a voyeur in a beautiful moment, watching him transform into something more than just a friend.

The evening wore on, and as the night deepened, so did the warmth in my chest. I realized that regardless of the twists and turns ahead, I wanted to see where this spark would lead us. The unpredictability was both terrifying and thrilling, a dance of emotions that felt impossibly right. And as I watched him play, a silent promise formed within me—a promise to embrace whatever came next, with him.

I stood there, a ghost in the thrumming crowd, my heart in my throat as Felix poured his soul into the piano, each note a whispered confession that sent ripples of energy through the air. The audience hung on every sound, swaying like leaves in a warm breeze, yet my focus remained solely on him. There was a magnetic pull between us that felt undeniable, like a thread of energy linking our hearts and minds, binding me to this moment.

As the final notes of the piece shimmered and faded, the crowd erupted into applause, and Felix bowed, his smile radiant under the warm lights. I clapped enthusiastically, feeling a surge of pride for him. The band joined in, laughter and chatter mixing with the lingering jazz in the air, creating a tapestry of life that felt rich and inviting.

He spotted me as he stepped off stage, weaving through the crowd like a skilled dancer navigating a crowded ballroom. My heart raced, anticipation bubbling within me. I was utterly captivated by the way he moved, with a grace that seemed both effortless and deliberate. When he reached me, the world around us faded again, leaving just the two of us wrapped in a shared cocoon of warmth and possibility.

"Did you enjoy the show?" he asked, genuine curiosity dancing in his eyes, the glimmer of mischief still evident.

"It was amazing! You have a way of making every note feel like it's meant just for the person listening." I gestured vaguely, trying to encapsulate the emotions swirling in my chest. "It's like you're speaking directly to me. I felt every beat."

"Wow, I didn't realize I had a fan club!" He chuckled, leaning closer, our conversation blending seamlessly with the low hum of voices surrounding us. "If I had known, I might have tried harder to impress you."

I laughed, feeling a warmth spread through me at his playful confidence. "You definitely don't need to try harder. Just being you is impressive enough."

His expression shifted, the teasing glint in his eyes softening into something deeper. "You're not so bad yourself, you know. The way you lit up when I played—makes me want to keep playing just for you."

For a moment, I held his gaze, feeling something shift in the air between us, a silent promise lingering like the last notes of a beautiful song. Just then, Leo reappeared, the life of the party and bursting with energy, his exuberance a stark contrast to the tender moment we were sharing.

"Felix! Callie! Come on, let's celebrate!" he said, practically bouncing on his feet. "Drinks are on me!"

Felix glanced at me, a hint of disappointment flickering across his features before he turned back to Leo, a grin breaking through. "Alright, let's do it!"

I found myself caught between wanting to bask in this newfound connection and the pull of Leo's infectious enthusiasm. "Sure, why not?" I said, trying to match their energy, though my heart was still racing from the intimacy of our moment.

As we made our way to the bar, I listened to Leo's animated recounting of Felix's latest antics, his laughter bubbling over and spilling into the atmosphere like champagne. I found myself laughing along, even as my mind wandered back to the unspoken tension lingering between Felix and me. The night unfolded like a well-crafted narrative, unexpected twists keeping me on my toes as we celebrated with drinks that sparkled under the low lights.

"Cheers to a fantastic night!" Leo exclaimed, raising his glass, and we all clinked our drinks together. "And to Felix, for reminding us all why we love jazz!"

Felix grinned, his charm lighting up the room as he took a sip of his drink. I caught his eye again, and in that moment, everything else blurred into insignificance.

"Hey, Callie," Leo said, nudging me lightly. "What about you? You into music, or are you one of those 'I prefer the silence' types?"

"Definitely not silence!" I replied, feeling the warmth of Felix's gaze on me. "Music is life! It's the rhythm of the heart, the echo of our emotions."

"Wow, someone's poetic tonight!" Leo laughed, nudging me again, his tone light. "I like it. You should join the band—give us some fresh lyrics or something."

"Oh, I think I'd scare everyone away," I said, feigning horror. "My idea of lyrics usually involves what I had for breakfast."

Felix chuckled, shaking his head. "You'd be surprised. Breakfast is a great muse." He winked, and I could feel my cheeks flush as I imagined crafting melodies about pancakes and coffee.

As the evening wore on, the energy in the venue shifted slightly. The crowd thinned out, leaving behind a more intimate atmosphere, and with it came a palpable tension that settled between Felix and me. Leo, seemingly oblivious, chatted animatedly with a few friends across the bar, leaving us to steal glances at each other, each look more charged than the last.

"So," Felix said, leaning against the bar, his body angled towards me, as if we were sharing a secret. "What are your thoughts on all this?" He gestured to the remaining patrons, the band beginning to pack up, the energy shifting like the final notes of a beautiful song.

I took a sip of my drink, considering my words carefully. "I love how music brings people together, you know? It's like a universal language that can express things words often can't."

He nodded, his eyes searching mine. "Exactly. It's the unspoken connection. You and I, we have that, don't you think?"

My breath caught in my throat. "I—"

Before I could finish, a sudden loud crash echoed from the back of the room, shattering the moment. Everyone turned, startled, as the commotion erupted into a flurry of movement. A tall figure had stumbled, knocking over a stack of chairs, sending them clattering to the floor.

Felix and I exchanged a glance, concern knitting our brows. "You okay?" he called out, instinctively moving toward the noise.

As we reached the chaotic scene, I spotted a woman, her face flushed with embarrassment as she tried to collect herself. "I'm fine! Just a little clumsy," she laughed nervously, her eyes darting between the fallen chairs and the people now staring.

"Need a hand?" I offered, stepping forward to help her gather her things.

"Thanks, I'm just a bit tipsy!" She giggled, brushing her hair behind her ear as she grabbed a wayward chair.

As we helped her, I could feel Felix's presence beside me, a steady anchor amidst the unexpected chaos. The tension we had built moments before now felt like a distant memory, overshadowed by the energy of the crowd responding to the woman's antics.

"See?" Felix leaned closer, his breath warm against my ear, a teasing lilt in his voice. "This is why we need to stay on our toes. You never know when someone's going to turn your night upside down."

I laughed softly, the tension of the earlier moment dissipating, though a part of me longed to return to it. But as we helped the woman to her feet, I felt a tug in my heart, a mix of excitement and frustration.

"Thanks, you guys!" she exclaimed, her smile brightening the mood. "I'm sorry for interrupting your evening! This place is just so lively, I couldn't help myself!"

"Just part of the charm," I replied, glancing at Felix, whose eyes sparkled with amusement.

"Are you going to be alright?" he asked the woman, who nodded enthusiastically, her spirit unfazed.

"Absolutely! I think I'll stick to dancing from now on!" she declared, her laughter infectious.

Just as we started to step away, a sudden commotion erupted from the entrance. The door swung open, revealing a gust of wind that seemed to carry a sense of urgency with it. A figure stood silhouetted in the doorway, a storm of energy that instantly drew every eye in the room.

"Felix!" the stranger called, voice filled with an intensity that sliced through the jovial atmosphere like a knife. "We need to talk. Now."

I felt my heart plummet as the stranger's gaze locked onto Felix, and suddenly, the warmth of our connection felt overshadowed by an impending storm I couldn't yet see, the undercurrents of uncertainty swirling around us like a rising tide. The vibrant world I had been lost in began to flicker, as if the very fabric of the night was being pulled taut, ready to snap. And in that moment, with the stranger's words hanging in the air, I realized that this was only the beginning.

Chapter 4: Shattered Facades

The first chill of autumn swept through the city like a whispered secret, curling around the corners of streets and into the crevices of everyday life. I stood by the window of my tiny apartment, cradling a steaming mug of chamomile tea, its delicate floral scent mingling with the faint aroma of burnt toast that stubbornly lingered from breakfast. As I watched the leaves begin their fiery descent from the trees, a kaleidoscope of reds and golds, I felt the weight of anticipation pressing against my chest. I was, at that moment, blissfully aware of how Felix had become a thread in the fabric of my life, weaving his way into my thoughts, my dreams, and even the muted sound of my laughter.

Late-night conversations with him had become a ritual, each exchange a stepping stone across the vast chasm of our pasts. Under the glow of soft fairy lights, we'd sit on the ragged couch that had seen better days, our words dancing between us like fireflies. He shared stories of his father—a once-celebrated musician whose brilliance had been dimmed by addiction. The way he spoke of him was tinged with a raw honesty, revealing not only the depth of his sorrow but also the remnants of love that clung stubbornly to the edges of his memories. I could see the hurt etched into his features, shadows that had settled in the creases of his smile.

"Sometimes," Felix said one evening, his fingers brushing the rim of his glass, "I wonder if my dad could've been something more if he hadn't gotten lost along the way. Music was his lifeline, and then it became his anchor, dragging him down." His voice had carried the weight of unspoken words, a heavy lament that hung in the air between us. I found myself leaning closer, drawn to the vulnerability behind his eyes, those windows that had witnessed far too much pain for someone so young. "I wanted to be proud of him, you know? But it's hard to be proud of someone who isn't proud of themselves."

The silence that followed felt suffocating, thick with unshared burdens. My heart ached for him, yet there was an unrelenting wall that stood between us, invisible but palpable. It was the fortress I had built to protect myself from the jagged edges of my own grief, one I was terrified to dismantle. My mother's death was a specter that hovered in the corners of my mind, a constant reminder of fragility, and I had learned to keep that part of myself tucked away, buried beneath layers of distraction and laughter.

But the days rolled on, and as we shared laughter and sipped cheap wine on those sacred nights, the wall felt both comforting and stifling. It wasn't long before the universe decided to toss a handful of chaos into our fragile connection. It happened at a local bar, a vibrant place buzzing with the energy of a live band, where the music poured out like liquid joy. We had been laughing over drinks, the dim lighting casting a warm glow around us, when I noticed a girl across the room. Her laughter was bright and infectious, and she seemed to float effortlessly through the crowd, her confidence like a magnet pulling everyone in.

It was a momentary flicker of jealousy that ignited a fire in my chest, a feeling I quickly tried to squash. Yet, as Felix's gaze lingered on her, something within me snapped. I didn't want to share him, not even for a second, and suddenly the world felt a shade darker. "Is she someone you know?" I asked, trying to keep my tone light but failing miserably, the bitterness curling at the edges of my words.

He turned to me, surprise dancing in his eyes. "No, just someone who looks like she's having a good time."

I couldn't tell if his sincerity or the simple fact that he was looking at her stung more. "Good for her, I guess," I said, the sarcasm slipping out before I could reel it back. "Maybe you should go say hello."

He raised an eyebrow, the corner of his mouth twitching up in a half-smile. "You're not serious, are you?"

"Why wouldn't I be? If you think she's that interesting, go for it. Who am I to stop you?" I was aware that my words dripped with irritation, a green-eyed monster gnawing at my insides.

His expression shifted, confusion replacing the lightheartedness of our previous conversation. "Cora, is this about her or—?"

"About what?" I shot back, my frustration bubbling over. "About feeling like I'm not enough? Because I thought we were building something real here."

His jaw tightened, a fleeting flicker of hurt crossing his face. "You're more than enough. But right now, it sounds like you're not even sure about that."

I looked away, heat rising to my cheeks, the weight of his words hitting me like a punch. The walls I had so carefully constructed around my heart began to tremble, but the thought of letting them fall was paralyzing. I hated the vulnerability it exposed in me, the fear that I would shatter into a million pieces if I dared to show him the truth. With that, I felt him retreating, the connection between us fraying like a well-worn thread.

As the laughter and music swirled around us, I felt a gnawing isolation settle in. The vibrant atmosphere of the bar transformed into a backdrop of muted colors, my heart a dull thud in my chest. I had allowed jealousy to seep in and fracture the moment, and now, like a ghost, it hung in the air, palpable and heavy. I had been afraid of losing him, and in my fear, I had nearly pushed him away.

That night, as I returned home, I couldn't shake the feeling that I was losing something precious—something I had never known I wanted until it was almost too late.

The days dragged by like molasses, thick and slow, as I found myself lost in a haze of uncertainty. My mornings had turned into a blend of lukewarm coffee and unremarkable routines, each moment steeped in the echo of that night at the bar. I tried to shake off the lingering unease, but it clung to me like a stubborn shadow, refusing to be ignored.

Felix, for his part, was a ghost of his usual self, his laughter muffled, his charm dulled. It felt as if I had not only pushed him away but had also extinguished the flicker of light he had brought into my world. He was a puzzle I could no longer solve, his pieces scattered across the chasm we had unwittingly created. Each text I sent felt like tossing a message into the void, and I dreaded the silence that often followed. I spent hours crafting the perfect words, only to erase them out of fear that they would sound desperate or too revealing.

One evening, I resolved to reclaim my narrative. Armed with a sense of determination, I decided to invite him to the community garden I had discovered nestled in a hidden corner of the city—a little slice of serenity where plants grew wild and unruly, much like the thoughts racing through my mind. The garden had become my refuge, a place where the scent of earth mixed with the sweetness of blooming flowers, where I could pretend that everything was just as it should be.

I arrived early, the sun hanging low in the sky, casting a warm golden hue over everything. The path to the garden was lined with hedges bursting with vibrant colors, and I could hear the soft rustle of leaves as the breeze whispered secrets. I picked a bench that overlooked a patch of daisies, their bright heads bobbing as if nodding in approval of my choice. With each passing moment, I felt a mix of anticipation and anxiety bubbling in my chest. Would this be the moment we'd bridge the distance? Or had I already lost him for good?

Felix arrived just as the sun dipped below the horizon, painting the sky with strokes of pink and orange, and my breath caught at the sight of him. He looked as good as ever, his hair tousled in that effortlessly charming way, but his eyes, usually so expressive, seemed shrouded in shadows. He approached cautiously, as if unsure of the welcome he would receive, and I felt a pang of guilt for the barriers I had erected between us.

"Hey," he said, his voice tentative, as he settled beside me on the bench. "This is nice. I didn't know this place existed."

"Just found it," I replied, my heart racing. "It's like a secret garden. I thought it might be a good spot for us to... talk."

He nodded, his gaze drifting toward the flowers, and for a moment, silence wrapped around us, heavy and filled with unspoken words. I could feel the tension thickening the air, each breath I took resonating with the weight of everything we hadn't said.

"So," I ventured, breaking the stillness, "I thought maybe we could start fresh? Clear the air?"

He turned to me, a flicker of hope sparking in his eyes, but it was quickly extinguished. "Cora, I'm not sure what there is to clear. You said what you meant that night."

A rush of frustration washed over me, hotter than I expected. "But I was jealous, Felix! I didn't mean it. You have every right to look at anyone you want. I just... I panicked."

He crossed his arms, his expression a mix of hurt and contemplation. "It felt like you were trying to push me away."

"Maybe I was," I admitted, feeling the truth tumble from my lips. "I've been scared of losing you, of letting you see that I'm not okay. My mom—she... she died a few years ago, and I never really dealt with it. I thought I could keep it locked away, but it's hard when you're around."

Felix's posture softened as he processed my confession. "Why didn't you tell me? I would have understood."

"Because," I breathed, the words heavy with emotion, "it's easier to smile and pretend everything's fine. I thought if I opened up, it would ruin everything we've built."

He leaned closer, his voice dropping to a whisper. "Cora, we're all a little shattered. You don't have to carry that alone." His gaze bore into mine, and I felt the walls crumbling, piece by piece.

Just as I opened my mouth to respond, an unceremonious squawk interrupted our moment. A pigeon had landed on the nearby fence, puffing out its chest as if it were the king of the world. We both burst into laughter, the tension dissipating like mist under the sun.

"Is that the best you could do?" I teased, gesturing toward the feathery interloper. "I thought you were going to impress me with something profound."

Felix chuckled, his smile brightening the dimming light around us. "I mean, it has its own unique charm. Who wouldn't be mesmerized?"

The laughter hung in the air, warm and inviting, and I felt my heart ease a little. Yet, I knew we still had a mountain to climb. The space between us was narrowing, but it wasn't gone. As we continued to talk, the conversation ebbed and flowed, dancing between our vulnerabilities and the laughter that felt like an old, comfortable blanket.

Then came a shift—an unanticipated turn. Just as I felt a connection re-emerging, my phone buzzed insistently in my pocket. I glanced at the screen, my stomach dropping as I saw my father's name flash. The last thing I wanted was to disrupt this fragile moment, but the urgency in his calls was unmistakable.

"Sorry," I murmured, pulling the device from my pocket. "I really need to take this."

Felix's expression clouded slightly as I answered the call, stepping a few feet away to give us both some space. "Hey, Dad," I said, forcing cheer into my tone.

"Cora! I need you to come home. We need to talk about Mom's things. It's getting overwhelming here." His voice was tight, laced with a stress I couldn't ignore.

"I'll be there soon," I promised, my heart sinking. I could feel the shadows creeping back in, threatening to swallow the light we had just found.

Hanging up, I turned to see Felix watching me, concern etched across his features. "Everything okay?"

I shrugged, forcing a smile that didn't quite reach my eyes. "Just family stuff. You know how it is."

He nodded, but the uncertainty lingered between us like smoke. "Want me to come with you?"

"No, it's… it's something I need to do alone," I replied, the weight of my words settling heavily in the air.

As I prepared to leave, I felt the distance between us stretching once more, the connection we'd started to rebuild beginning to fray at the edges. I hated the thought of returning to the shadows of grief, of stepping back into a reality that felt so much heavier than the moment we had just shared.

"I'll text you," I said, and with that promise, I left the garden, feeling the pull of the past closing in around me. Felix remained behind, a flickering light against the encroaching darkness, and I couldn't shake the fear that this was just another step toward losing him.

The late afternoon sun spilled golden light across the streets as I made my way to my father's house, a place that once felt like home but now loomed over me like an unwelcome specter. I could feel the familiar tangle of anxiety tightening around my chest, each step a reminder of the unresolved echoes of grief that followed me. The air was thick with the scent of impending rain, and dark clouds loomed in the distance, mirroring the tumult in my heart.

When I reached the old brick house, I hesitated at the door, my hand hovering over the knob. It was still adorned with the faded wreath my mother had insisted on every autumn, the colors dulled by time but somehow comforting. I inhaled deeply, steeling myself for the weight of memories that awaited me on the other side.

As I stepped inside, the familiar creak of the floorboards greeted me, a sound that felt like a long-lost friend. My father stood in the kitchen, the light above casting a halo around his graying hair, making him look older than I remembered. He was hunched over a pile of boxes, sorting through what remained of my mother's life, and my heart ached at the sight.

"Hey, Dad," I said softly, trying to inject some warmth into the chilly air between us.

He looked up, his eyes reflecting a mixture of weariness and relief. "Cora. Glad you're here."

We embraced briefly, and I felt the tremor in his grip, a silent acknowledgment of the shared loss that had become a silent specter between us. I wished I could say something comforting, but the words felt trapped, swirling around in my mind without finding an exit.

"I started going through her things," he said, gesturing to the clutter around him. "It's... harder than I thought it would be."

"Do you need help?" I offered, my voice barely above a whisper.

He shook his head, a resigned smile playing at his lips. "I've got this. Just takes time."

I wandered over to a box labeled "Books," the scrawl unmistakable. My mother had always been an avid reader, her shelves overflowing with volumes that seemed to whisper secrets of worlds long past. I gently opened the box and felt a rush of nostalgia wash over me as the smell of aged paper filled my senses. Each title was a chapter of her life, a fragment of the woman I adored, and the weight of loss settled heavily in my chest.

As I sifted through the titles, a small, worn notebook caught my eye. I pulled it from the pile and flipped it open. My heart sank as I recognized her handwriting, the neat loops and curls that felt like home. It was filled with thoughts and reflections, fragments of her life, her hopes and dreams laid bare. I felt as if I were invading a sacred space, yet I couldn't tear myself away.

"Cora," my father's voice broke through my reverie, and I turned to see him watching me with an expression that was equal parts sadness and pride. "There's something we need to talk about."

I felt a shiver run down my spine. "What is it?"

He hesitated, glancing at the notebook in my hands. "I've been thinking about what your mom would want. I can't keep holding onto everything. It's like holding onto her—some things need to be let go."

"Let go?" The words tumbled from my mouth before I could stop them. "You can't just throw away her memories like they don't matter!"

"I'm not saying that," he replied, frustration edging into his tone. "I just think we need to decide what to keep and what to let go of. It's too much."

I felt the familiar sting of tears threatening to spill, but I refused to let them fall. "What if I don't want to let go of anything? What if I need to hold onto every last piece?"

"Cora, we're both grieving in different ways. Holding onto everything won't bring her back," he said gently, his voice a soothing balm against my mounting panic.

His words sank in, and I found myself torn between the desire to preserve my mother's memory and the understanding that clinging too tightly could suffocate what remained of our connection to her. The air felt thick with unresolved feelings, and I took a step back, needing space to breathe.

"I'll help you sort through things," I said finally, my voice steadying. "But can we take our time?"

"Of course," he replied, relief washing over his features.

We settled into a rhythm of silence, the occasional sound of rustling paper filling the room as we began to sort through the remnants of my mother's life. Each item felt like a puzzle piece, some small part of a bigger picture, and as we delved deeper into the boxes, I felt a strange sense of peace wash over me, mingling with the sorrow.

Suddenly, my phone buzzed, shattering the quiet like a thunderclap. I fished it out of my pocket and saw a text from Felix: Can we talk?

The urgency in his message sent a thrill of anxiety through me, and I glanced at my father, who was absorbed in a particularly old cookbook, a hint of nostalgia playing across his face. "I need to step outside for a moment," I said, my voice clipped. "I'll be right back."

"Sure, take your time," he replied, barely looking up.

I slipped outside into the crisp evening air, the weight of the house pressing in behind me. I read Felix's message again, my heart pounding. What did he want? Had I pushed him too far away to pull him back again?

I replied quickly, my fingers trembling as I typed: Yes, please. Where?

The response came almost instantly: Meet me at the coffee shop. I need to see you.

A rush of adrenaline surged through me as I hurried to the café, a familiar haunt where we had shared so many laughs over lattes and pastries. The bell above the door jingled softly as I stepped inside, scanning the room for him. He sat at a corner table, his head buried in his hands, a picture of worry that sent a fresh wave of concern rippling through me.

"Felix?" I approached slowly, the warmth of the café a stark contrast to the coolness outside. "What's wrong?"

He looked up, his expression a mix of frustration and vulnerability. "I didn't want to overwhelm you, but... I've been thinking about everything. About us."

My heart raced at the intensity of his gaze, the air between us crackling with unspoken words. "And?"

"I can't keep pretending like I'm okay with how things are," he said, his voice steady but strained. "I feel this connection with you, but there's so much we haven't shared. I need to know if you're willing to open up."

I felt the weight of his words settle over me, thick and suffocating. The vulnerability in his request mirrored my own fears, and the barrier I had built around my heart felt increasingly fragile. "I want to, but..."

"But?" he prompted, leaning closer.

The moment felt electric, and I struggled with my thoughts, the walls of my heart threatening to crumble. Just as I opened my mouth to speak, the door swung open with a flourish, and a commotion erupted from the entrance. A group of people stumbled in, laughter echoing off the walls, and I turned to see what was happening.

That's when I saw her—one of the girls from the bar, the one who had sent that sharp twist of jealousy through me just days earlier. She was standing there, vibrant and brimming with confidence, her eyes scanning the room until they landed on Felix. The recognition in her gaze ignited a sense of dread that washed over me in a wave.

I felt my breath hitch, the moment stretching taut like a string ready to snap. "Felix, wait..."

But he was already standing, his expression shifting as he caught sight of her, and in that instant, I knew something had shifted irreparably.

"Cora, I—" he began, but I didn't wait to hear the rest. The ground beneath me felt unsteady as I stepped back, my heart racing with a sense of impending chaos.

The door behind me swung closed, the sound echoing in my ears, and I stood frozen, caught between the past and an uncertain future, the weight of my fears crashing down like a storm.

Chapter 5: Colliding Worlds

The streets of downtown Charleston were alive, pulsing with an energy that felt almost electric. The annual jazz festival had transformed the city into a vibrant tapestry of color and sound. Vendors lined the sidewalks, their carts brimming with tantalizing treats that mingled with the sultry notes of saxophones and trumpets wafting through the air. The aromas of garlic shrimp and fried dough wove a seductive spell, beckoning me closer. As I wandered through the throngs of people, the cacophony of laughter and chatter surrounded me, a symphony that felt like both a balm and a torment to my restless spirit.

Mia, ever the spark plug of my emotional engine, bounced beside me, her enthusiasm a stark contrast to my anxious demeanor. Her fiery red hair caught the sunlight, glinting like a beacon of hope. "You're doing this," she insisted, her voice cutting through my doubts like a knife. "You can't just stand on the sidelines anymore. You have to let him know how you feel." I nodded, the weight of her words settling in my chest, heavy but strangely comforting.

"Easier said than done, Mia. What if he doesn't feel the same?" I fretted, glancing down at the hem of my sundress, now scuffed and dusty from the bustling street. "What if he thinks I'm just a nuisance? Or worse, a reminder of…everything?" The air around us was thick with summer heat, but my internal temperature soared with the anxiety of potential rejection.

"Or," she countered, a glimmer of mischief in her eyes, "he might be just as scared as you are. You never know until you take the plunge." With a dramatic flourish, she threw her arms open wide as if to embrace the very idea of bravery. I couldn't help but laugh, the tension in my shoulders easing slightly.

"Okay, okay. You win," I conceded, a smile breaking through my nerves. "But if I do this, you're coming with me."

"Deal!" she chirped, and together we wove our way through the crowd, each step stirring the butterflies in my stomach into a wild frenzy.

As we approached the festival grounds, I could hear the familiar voice of Felix echoing through the air, a warm timbre that had haunted my thoughts for weeks. He was on stage, immersed in his music, the glimmering saxophone a natural extension of his being. My heart raced at the sight of him, that playful smile transforming into pure passion as he played. The moment felt surreal, as though I were witnessing a private performance meant only for me, despite the crowd around us.

Mia nudged me forward, her encouragement propelling me toward the backstage area, where the chaos of performers mingled with the electric anticipation of the audience. I was a bundle of nerves, each heartbeat reminding me of my hesitations and fears. The backstage buzzed with activity, musicians tuning instruments and sound engineers adjusting microphones, creating a sense of urgency that both exhilarated and terrified me.

Then, amidst the chaos, I saw him. Felix stood near the edge of the stage, his expression a mix of concentration and joy. When his gaze met mine, the world around us blurred into insignificance. He looked as if he had seen a ghost, the surprise etched on his face quickly giving way to confusion. My heart sank as I noticed the flicker of hurt in his eyes, a painful reminder of the distance that had grown between us.

"Hey," I managed to say, my voice barely above a whisper, yet somehow loud enough to cut through the din. He approached, the space between us crackling with unspoken words and unresolved tension.

"What are you doing here?" Felix asked, his tone laced with caution, as if he were bracing for an impact he couldn't quite predict.

"I... I wanted to talk," I stammered, my palms clammy as I gripped the strap of my bag. "About us."

His brow furrowed, and I could see the wheels turning in his mind, processing my unexpected arrival. "I didn't think you wanted to. After everything that happened..."

I took a deep breath, gathering my scattered thoughts. "I was scared, Felix. Scared of being vulnerable, scared of what you might think of me. I pushed you away because I didn't know how to handle...whatever this is between us."

He studied me, his blue eyes searching my face for sincerity. "You think I wanted to be pushed away? I thought we had something real, and then you just... disappeared." The pain in his voice hit me like a wave, drowning out the noise of the festival around us.

"Believe me, I didn't want to disappear," I replied, my voice steadying. "I was just overwhelmed. But standing here now, I realize how much I've missed you."

A moment hung between us, thick with unspoken truths and fears. Felix's expression softened, and the lines of tension on his forehead relaxed. "I missed you too, you know," he confessed, and my heart fluttered at his admission.

As we stood there, surrounded by the frenetic energy of the festival, something shifted. It was as if the world had narrowed to just the two of us, our pasts colliding in a beautiful mess of confessions and revelations. The shadows of our fears began to fade, replaced by the warmth of shared vulnerability. I felt a sense of clarity settling over us, as if we were finally peeling back the layers that had kept us apart.

"Can we start over?" I asked, my voice a thread of hope weaving through the chaos around us. "Can we see where this leads?"

Felix's smile broke through the remnants of our hesitation, a light illuminating the space between us. "I'd like that. More than you know."

In that moment, with the music spilling into the air and the scents of street food wafting around us, I felt a new beginning unfurling like the petals of a flower, vibrant and alive. Our worlds had collided, but rather than chaos, it was a promise of something beautiful on the horizon.

The moment Felix smiled at me, a weight lifted, though I knew it was only the beginning. We stood there, surrounded by the vibrant chaos of the jazz festival, and for the first time in what felt like an eternity, I could hear the music with clarity. It was as if the sound wrapped around us, weaving a tapestry of old rhythms and new possibilities. I glanced around, taking in the colorful banners fluttering in the light breeze and the kaleidoscope of faces filled with laughter and joy. I could feel a spark igniting, one that I hoped wouldn't fizzle out.

"Alright, let's not get too sappy here," Felix said, his grin widening as he shifted his saxophone strap. "We have a festival to enjoy, and I'm pretty sure my bandmates are going to think I've been possessed by the ghost of romance if I stand here too long." He shot me a teasing wink that sent my heart into an impromptu tango.

"Possessed by the ghost of romance?" I quipped back, crossing my arms. "Is that what you call it now? You know, it's a bold choice for a guy about to perform in front of a crowd."

He chuckled, the sound rich and warm, and it felt like an invitation to step deeper into this moment. "Well, it could also be the street food smell making me dizzy. I'm not sure which one it is yet."

We both laughed, the tension between us melting away like butter on a hot biscuit. I could feel a rhythm building—not just in the music around us, but between us, as if we were in sync again. The noise of the crowd faded into a comforting background hum as he gestured for me to follow him deeper into the backstage area.

OUR MELODY

"Let's get some air before I dive into the madness," he said, leading me past musicians warming up and techies adjusting equipment. "This is the chaotic heart of the festival, but I promise you it's just as beautiful as the main stage."

Stepping outside, we found a quieter corner behind the stage, where a tangle of trees offered a momentary refuge from the festival's energy. The air was cooler here, a gentle breeze rustling the leaves overhead. I leaned against the wooden railing, watching him as he leaned casually, his saxophone resting beside him, the sunlight catching the edges of his messy hair.

"Can I admit something?" he said, his tone suddenly serious. "I was worried you wouldn't show up. That you'd decided it was better to walk away."

"Trust me," I replied, my heart fluttering with the weight of his admission. "I considered it. But then I thought about how I'd feel if I didn't try. And the thought of you up here, playing your heart out while I was sitting at home with a tub of ice cream, just didn't sit right."

"Very relatable," he said, his smile returning. "Ice cream therapy has its merits, but I'm glad you took the plunge. This," he gestured back toward the festival, "is so much better with you here. I never knew you could pull off the 'surprise reunion' look so well."

I rolled my eyes playfully, trying to hide the blush creeping up my cheeks. "You know, I've had some practice. Surprising people seems to be my new hobby. Maybe I should consider it a career path."

"You should! Just imagine it: 'Surprise Specialist.' You could surprise people at their weddings, birthdays, and awkward family gatherings. I can see the business card now."

"Noted. Though I might have to hire you as my hype man. You're doing a great job."

He laughed, and I couldn't help but feel that this was the beginning of something new, something beyond the uncertainty that had shadowed our past. But just as that thought blossomed, I noticed a figure approach from the corner of my eye, a woman with dark hair cascading down her back like a waterfall. She wore a fitted dress that accentuated her curves and strolled toward us with an air of confidence. Felix's face shifted slightly, a flicker of tension returning.

"Felix!" she called out, her voice ringing with a familiar lilt. My stomach twisted. "There you are! I was looking everywhere for you."

"Lila," he said, his tone neutral.

The energy between us seemed to dissipate, replaced by something thick and uncomfortable. I watched as she approached, her eyes darting between us, her expression revealing the quiet recognition of the situation.

"Are you all set for your performance? You know the crowd is eager," Lila continued, oblivious or perhaps dismissive of the tension in the air.

"Yeah, just getting some last-minute air before I hit the stage," Felix replied, his tone lacking the warmth it held just moments ago.

"I was worried you wouldn't be ready in time," she said, an edge of playfulness in her voice. "You know how these festivals can get. You need to focus."

"Right," he said, turning slightly away from her. "I've got it under control."

The moment stretched, heavy with unspoken words. I sensed a history here, something that held Felix captive despite his attempts to shake it off. My pulse quickened, not with jealousy but with a determination to reclaim this moment.

"I should probably let you get back to your... fans," I interjected, injecting a forced lightness into the air. "I'll just—uh, I'll go grab some food or something."

"Wait—" Felix started, but Lila cut him off, her laughter ringing like a bell.

"Let her go, Felix! You're about to go on stage, and she's right—food is vital."

I forced a smile, though the knot in my stomach tightened. "Yeah, I'm sure I can find something edible among the endless sea of food trucks."

"Okay, but don't disappear for too long," he said, his eyes searching mine. There was an unspoken plea, a tether that wanted to keep me anchored to him even amid this sudden distraction.

"I won't," I promised, feeling the weight of both his gaze and Lila's scrutiny. As I turned to walk away, I heard the murmur of their voices, the casual way they fell into conversation like two old friends. It stung more than I expected, igniting a flare of insecurity that left me feeling raw.

The crowd enveloped me as I stepped back into the festival, the vibrant colors and sounds rushing back in like a tide. I wandered through the stalls, trying to shake off the discomfort clinging to me. The food vendors beckoned, each one promising a taste adventure, but my mind was tangled in a web of uncertainties. Did I truly have a chance with Felix, or was I just another temporary distraction before he fell back into the rhythm of his past?

"Hey! You look like you need a drink!" Mia's voice broke through my thoughts as she appeared beside me, a paper cup in hand. "I got you a lemonade. Extra sweet, just like you."

I chuckled, grateful for her presence. "Thanks, I needed that. But it's not just the heat; it's the Felix situation. You know, Lila just showed up. It's like a bad rom-com."

Mia raised an eyebrow, her expression shifting from playful to serious. "What did she want? Are they—?"

"Just catching up, I think. But it felt…complicated. I can't help but wonder if I'm in over my head."

"You're not. You just need to remind him how incredible you are, and trust me, he'll see it."

Her words were a balm, and as we moved through the festival, the sound of jazz wrapping around us, I felt a flicker of hope reignite. I wasn't just a part of Felix's story; I was ready to write my own alongside him, even if that meant confronting the ghosts of his past.

As the band prepared to take the stage, I felt a rush of anticipation. I wasn't done yet. I had to step into the spotlight myself, even if it meant confronting my fears all over again.

The festival pulsed with life as I weaved my way through the crowd, the vibrant sounds of jazz echoing against the brick buildings like a heartbeat. The lemonade Mia had handed me sloshed in its cup, a fizzy reminder of the sweetness I craved but couldn't quite grasp. My mind replayed the earlier moments with Felix, the flicker of hurt in his eyes still fresh in my memory. But I was determined not to let the unexpected appearance of Lila derail everything I had hoped to rebuild with him.

As I scanned the festival, the vibrant colors of the tents and the bright lights reflecting off faces filled with laughter and joy drew me in. Couples swayed to the music, their silhouettes dancing against the backdrop of the setting sun. I felt like an outsider in my own story, an observer peeking through the window of something I desperately wanted to be a part of.

"Hey, you!" A voice cut through the music, and I turned to see Mia bounding toward me, her face alight with excitement. "You ready to party? I have a plan to distract you from that annoying little ghost hovering over your shoulder."

"What ghost?" I asked, raising an eyebrow.

"Lila, of course! I mean, honestly, does she have to be so... Lila?" She wrinkled her nose, and I couldn't help but laugh.

"Right? It's like she's auditioning for a role in 'The Drama of Felix,'" I replied, shaking my head.

"Let's shake it off!" she declared, grabbing my hand and leading me toward the main stage, where a band was setting up for the next set. "Dance it out, channel your inner Beyoncé, and remind yourself that you're here for a reason. To eat, dance, and make Felix realize he's missing out!"

With a determined nod, I followed her to the front of the stage, the pulsating beat washing over us like a wave. The band kicked off their set, and I couldn't help but let the music move me, each note slicing through my anxiety. Mia twirled around me, her joy infectious, and for a few moments, I allowed myself to get lost in the rhythm, the sway of my hips guiding me to a place where Lila's shadow could not reach.

As the night unfolded, the world around me became a kaleidoscope of colors and sounds. Laughter filled the air, mingling with the sweet smell of roasted corn and spicy fried dough, and for the first time since I arrived, I felt a flicker of confidence rising within me. Maybe I didn't have to be defined by my fears or by the ghosts of the past. I was here now, present and alive in this beautiful moment.

"Look who's finally got their groove back!" Mia teased, nudging me as I caught my breath. "What happened to the girl who was ready to hide behind the nearest food truck?"

"Guess I found her dance partner," I replied, throwing my arms in the air as the music crescendoed.

But just as I began to embrace the energy surrounding me, I caught sight of Felix again. He stood at the edge of the crowd, saxophone slung casually over his shoulder, his eyes scanning the audience. When they landed on me, a smile broke across his face, lighting up the shadows that had lingered between us. He looked different—more alive, more in his element—and it made my heart skip a beat.

"Let's go talk to him!" Mia exclaimed, tugging my arm toward the side of the stage. "You can't just stare at him like a deer in headlights! Show him you're ready to claim your space."

"I'm not staring," I protested weakly, but the blush creeping up my cheeks betrayed me.

"Sure, keep telling yourself that," she replied with a laugh as we made our way toward Felix.

As we reached him, the band finished their set, and the crowd erupted into cheers. Felix turned to me, his expression brightening even further as he caught sight of me approaching.

"Hey!" he exclaimed, stepping closer. "I was wondering where you went. Did you enjoy the performance?"

"It was amazing! I mean, you were incredible. Seriously, I didn't realize you could blow a sax like that."

He chuckled, his eyes dancing with warmth. "You flatter me, but you should have heard the guy last year—he was a wizard. But I appreciate the compliment."

Mia excused herself with a wink, leaving us in our own little bubble of warmth amidst the fading festival lights.

"I'm glad you're here," he said, his voice dropping slightly as the crowd around us ebbed and flowed. "It means a lot."

"Me too," I replied, my heart racing at the weight of those words. "I—"

Before I could gather my thoughts, the lights dimmed as the next band took the stage. The spotlight illuminated Felix, casting him in a warm glow. I felt a surge of admiration for him, standing there with confidence, ready to perform again.

"I should probably—" he started, glancing at the stage.

"No, go! I want to hear you play," I encouraged, a mix of eagerness and fear igniting within me. "Just promise me you'll come back afterward?"

"Absolutely," he promised, his gaze lingering on mine a moment longer than necessary before he stepped onto the stage, the music enveloping him like a second skin. I watched him lose himself in the rhythm, each note resonating with the very core of my being.

As the performance unfolded, I lost myself in the melodies, the way Felix poured his heart into each note, weaving his emotions into the music. The crowd swayed, entranced, but all I could see was him—his passion and energy intoxicating, sending warmth coursing through my veins.

Yet as the night continued, an unsettling feeling crept in, like a distant storm cloud threatening to rain on my parade. Lila was still in the corner of my eye, laughing and chatting with others, her presence a stark reminder of the reality I didn't want to face.

Just as I was about to push the thought away, I felt a tap on my shoulder. I turned to find a familiar face—Ben, an old college friend, his eyes wide with surprise.

"Wow, look at you! Out here in the wild, huh? Last I heard, you were buried under work," he joked, but his grin faded slightly when he noticed my distraction. "Everything alright?"

"Yeah, just enjoying the music. You know how it is." I forced a smile, but my mind raced back to Felix, hoping he'd look over, hoping I wouldn't be swept away in a wave of old memories and insecurities.

"Right, of course. I actually came to find you! We should grab a drink, catch up. What do you say?"

As Ben spoke, I couldn't shake the feeling that the moment had shifted, the warmth of the evening turning just slightly colder.

"Sure," I replied, but my eyes remained fixed on Felix, who was now deeply engrossed in a duet, his focus entirely on the music.

"Good. Let's get away from the crowd for a minute. I have something to tell you," Ben said, leaning closer as he gestured toward the bar.

"Wait, hold on," I said, uncertainty creeping into my voice. "I—"

But before I could finish, I heard a voice cutting through the music. "Felix! Can I talk to you?" It was Lila, stepping forward with that same confident sway, her voice sharp as glass.

My heart sank, and I felt the ground shift beneath me. What was she doing? Wasn't she supposed to be with someone else? I glanced back at Felix, who had turned at the sound of her voice, his expression shifting from joy to something more complicated, as if caught in the middle of a tangled web.

"Just give me a minute!" he called back, but Lila was relentless, closing the distance between them with a determined stride.

"Felix, come on! We need to talk about us."

I felt the world tilt, my heart racing in a mix of dread and confusion. Ben was still speaking beside me, but his words faded into a blur as I focused on the scene unfolding in front of me.

"I didn't sign up for this," I murmured, clenching my fists.

"Hey, are you okay?" Ben asked, his brow furrowing in concern as he followed my gaze.

"Not really," I admitted, my stomach twisting painfully. "I think I need to go."

Before I could even process my own words, I turned on my heel, ready to confront whatever storm awaited me. But as I stepped away, I could feel the weight of Felix's gaze on me, heavy with unspoken questions. The night, once filled with promise, now felt like a fragile bubble on the verge of bursting.

"Wait!" Felix's voice broke through the chaos, but my feet carried me away, uncertainty swirling around me like a storm. I had to make a choice—face this head-on or let it slip away. And with every step, I could hear the tension brewing behind me, ready to explode in a way I never expected.

In that moment, I realized I was standing at the edge of something profound, something that could change everything. But as I glanced back, the sight that met my eyes sent a jolt of fear racing through me.

Chapter 6: Unlikely Collaborators

A swirl of vibrant colors greeted me as I entered the school's art studio, each canvas a bold proclamation of creativity, shouting for attention like eager children vying for their parents' love. I took a deep breath, inhaling the mixed scents of turpentine and fresh paint, grounding myself in the chaotic beauty that enveloped me. This was my sanctuary, my cocoon, where I transformed blank surfaces into vivid expressions of who I was. But today, the atmosphere felt different, charged with an energy that made the hairs on the back of my neck stand on end.

Felix was already there, his unruly curls illuminated by the sunlight streaming through the tall windows. He stood before an easel, his back to me, focused and serious, as if the weight of the world rested on his slender shoulders. I hesitated for a moment, the tension between us palpable—a taut string just waiting for a slight breeze to snap it. Despite the quarreling and emotional upheaval, our creative spirits pulled us together, and I felt the weight of anticipation settle heavily in the pit of my stomach.

"Good morning, maestro," I said, injecting a playful tone into the greeting, hoping to crack the ice that had formed between us. Felix turned, a faint smile playing on his lips, but it was shadowed by something else, an unshed emotion lurking just beneath the surface.

"Don't call me that. You know I hate it," he replied, the mock annoyance in his voice barely masking a flicker of warmth in his hazel eyes. His tone danced on the line between exasperation and affection, making me question if he truly meant it or was just trying to keep up his walls.

"Then what should I call you? The Great and Powerful Felix? Or maybe just Sir?" I quipped, crossing my arms and leaning against the doorframe, fully aware of the warring emotions beneath the surface.

"Don't flatter yourself," he shot back, though there was a glimmer of amusement there, like sunlight breaking through the clouds after a storm. "I've already had enough of your theatrics for one day."

As I stepped further into the room, I could feel the creative energy swirling around us like a tangible force, electrifying the air and crackling between us. It was both exhilarating and terrifying. We were about to plunge headfirst into a collaboration that could either ignite a spark or burn us both to cinders. I turned my focus to the space around us, the chaotic harmony of brushes, paints, and scattered sketches that told stories I was eager to mold into a new narrative.

"Okay, so what's our vision?" I asked, my fingers brushing the edge of a canvas, eager to dive into the depths of color and form. "I was thinking something vibrant, maybe exploring the juxtaposition of light and shadow. You know, the whole 'darkness exists to highlight the light' kind of thing."

Felix's brows furrowed as he considered my words, his fingers drumming thoughtfully against the side of the easel. "And you think that's going to resonate with an audience? I mean, everyone is doing light versus dark. It's a bit cliché, don't you think?"

I bit my lip to suppress a smile, amused by his unwavering confidence. "What's your brilliant idea, then?"

"Something unexpected," he replied, a mischievous glint flickering in his eyes. "What if we painted it as a scene from a dream? Something surreal that pulls the audience into a world they've never known, using music to deepen the immersion?"

"A dream?" I echoed, intrigued. "You mean like a surrealist nightmare with colors that don't exist in nature? I could get behind that."

"Exactly," he grinned, his enthusiasm sparking an undeniable connection between us. "But it needs depth. It needs emotion. It's not just about the visuals—it's about how they feel."

Our gazes locked, and in that moment, I could almost see the gears turning in his mind, the creative sparks igniting. The air thickened with possibility, each of us tossing ideas into the mix like confetti, fueling each other's passion. As we bounced concepts back and forth, I found myself fascinated not just by the art we were crafting but by the man standing before me, layers unfolding like petals of a flower.

"Okay," I said, stepping closer, emboldened. "Let's set the mood then. We'll create a soundtrack to accompany the visuals, something haunting yet beautiful that invites the viewer to linger."

Felix nodded, the fire in his eyes igniting as he grabbed his notebook, scribbling down notes faster than I could follow. I couldn't help but feel a warmth bloom in my chest as I watched him work, his brows furrowed in concentration, completely absorbed in the moment. There was something intoxicating about seeing him in this light, where the doubts and frustrations melted away, revealing the genius beneath.

"But if we're doing this," he continued, glancing up, "we have to push each other. No holding back, no safe zones. We have to dig deep and find what truly matters."

"Deal," I said, my heart racing at the thought of diving into those depths with him. "Let's unearth those treasures."

As we settled into our roles, painting and composing, I felt the walls we had built between us begin to crumble. The collaboration became more than just a project; it felt like a revelation, a shared exploration of creativity and vulnerability. Laughter broke through the tension, punctuating our discussions with an unexpected lightness that echoed through the studio, a symphony of voices in harmony.

And in those moments, even as shadows of doubt flickered around the edges, I couldn't shake the feeling that we were destined for more than just this project. We were uncovering something profound, and perhaps, just perhaps, the raw connection forming between us was the very treasure we sought.

The days unfolded in a kaleidoscope of colors and sounds, our studio becoming a sanctuary where creativity thrived, tempered by the lingering tension that hinted at something deeper between us. Each morning began with a ritual—a flurry of brushes and a raucous playlist that echoed through the walls, punctuated by our spirited banter. The air crackled with ideas as we flung ourselves into the project, only to pause when the weight of unspoken words threatened to suffocate the joyous atmosphere we'd cultivated.

One day, as I dabbed a bold cerulean on the canvas, Felix leaned back, arms crossed, studying my work with a critical eye. "It's too safe," he declared, a teasing lilt to his voice. "You know, it almost looks like you're trying to impress someone."

I turned to him, feigning shock. "What a preposterous notion! I'm merely trying to convey a sense of unease and beauty. Besides, who would I be trying to impress? You?" I raised an eyebrow, a playful smirk tugging at the corners of my lips.

"Ha! As if I'd be impressed by mere color choices," he shot back, leaning forward with an exaggerated air of seriousness. "You need to dig deeper, paint the fear of existential dread. You know, really get into the psyche."

"Existential dread?" I scoffed, laughter bubbling up. "Do you have a degree in pretentiousness, or is this just a side gig?"

"Both, actually," he replied, deadpan. "It pays well, and I get to critique your artistic genius at the same time."

As the laughter faded, I studied him, the way his eyes sparkled with a mix of mischief and vulnerability. There was a certain brilliance in his wit that drew me in, like moths to a flame, lighting up the shadows in my heart. It was hard to reconcile the sharp-tongued guy with the quiet moments when I caught glimpses of his hidden struggles, the burdens he carried like invisible weights.

"Alright, Mr. Existential Dread," I said, taking a step closer to him. "What would you do differently? Paint me a picture with your words."

His brow furrowed, but a spark ignited in his gaze. "I'd strip away the comfort. I'd drown the canvas in chaos and sorrow, toss in a few jagged edges to keep everyone on their toes."

"Wow," I said, genuinely impressed. "I never knew you had it in you. Maybe there's more to you than just that smooth exterior."

"Oh, there's plenty more," he retorted, a hint of playfulness threading through his tone. "But don't go falling for me just yet; I'm a mess of layers, and I don't have a manual for the emotionally challenged."

"Too late. I'm already in over my head," I shot back, the words tumbling out before I could stop myself. His gaze caught mine, a moment suspended in time, and I felt a flutter of something unfamiliar begin to take root—a mixture of hope and trepidation.

We resumed our work, the atmosphere shifting subtly, the playful banter morphing into a more profound exchange. I poured my heart into the canvas, each stroke a reflection of my turmoil and desires. Felix strummed his guitar, fingers dancing over the strings, coaxing notes that filled the space with warmth and melancholy. We were two halves of a whole, our creations intertwined, each note and color a conversation of unspoken truths.

But amidst the creativity, shadows crept in. The day of the showcase loomed, and the pressure to create something extraordinary weighed heavily on my shoulders. I could feel the anxiety creeping in, gnawing at the edges of my confidence, and as I painted, I caught myself second-guessing every decision. I needed to tap into my vulnerability, but the fear of exposing too much clawed at me.

"Hey," Felix said one afternoon, catching my gaze as I stared at the canvas, frustration brewing like a storm inside. "What's eating at you?"

I hesitated, the words caught in my throat. "It's just... I want this to be perfect. I want it to mean something, you know? But every time I try, I feel like I'm just... missing the mark."

"Perfection is a myth," he replied, setting his guitar aside. "Art is about the journey, the messiness, the pain. Embrace it. You're not alone in this."

His words hung in the air, a lifeline thrown into the turbulent sea of my thoughts. I felt a pang of recognition—his struggles mirrored my own. "What about you?" I asked softly. "What do you want from this?"

He took a breath, the moment stretched between us like an elastic band ready to snap. "I want to feel something again," he admitted, vulnerability spilling into his voice. "Music used to be my escape, but lately, it feels like I'm just going through the motions."

There was a heaviness in the air, an unguarded honesty that shifted the dynamics between us. I stepped closer, the distance narrowing as I reached for his hand, our fingers brushing against each other. "Then let's find that feeling together. Let's be a little reckless with this project. Let's make it raw and real, just like us."

He looked at me, surprise flitting across his features, and for a moment, it was as if the world outside melted away. "You really think we can do that?"

"Absolutely," I replied, emboldened by the spark of connection igniting between us. "But we have to trust each other completely. No holding back. No masks."

"Deal," he said, a tentative smile breaking through the weight of the moment. "But if we're doing this, we're going full chaos. I hope you're ready for that."

"Bring it on," I challenged, feeling the thrill of anticipation wash over me.

As we dove back into our work, the atmosphere transformed. The music flowed through the room, vibrant and wild, echoing the depths of our fears and hopes. Each brushstroke became an expression of freedom, each note a reflection of the tangled emotions we navigated together. We were no longer just collaborators; we were two artists, two souls, unearthing the raw essence of ourselves and our craft, inching closer to the heart of what it meant to truly create.

As the days slipped away, the studio transformed into a vibrant playground, the air thick with the scent of paint and the sounds of Felix's guitar weaving through our chaotic creativity. I became a creature of habit, losing track of time as we delved into the emotional heart of our collaboration. Each session peeled back layers, exposing the raw edges of our lives, the laughter punctuated by moments of quiet reflection that felt almost sacred.

"Tell me something no one knows about you," I suggested one afternoon, the sunlight slanting through the windows and casting a golden glow over our work. I was painting a swirling vortex of color, allowing my emotions to spill onto the canvas. There was something intoxicating about blending my thoughts with the bold strokes, the art becoming a mirror reflecting my innermost fears.

Felix looked up from his guitar, a thoughtful expression crossing his face. "Hmm, how about the fact that I'm terrified of being on stage?" His admission hung between us, unexpected and raw. "I can compose all day, but performing? It's like standing in front of a firing squad."

"You? Terrified?" I laughed, half in disbelief. "That's rich coming from the guy who plays the guitar like he was born with it. Are you sure you're not just playing it up for sympathy?"

"Ha! I wish I were that clever," he replied, his tone light but laced with sincerity. "It's the idea of exposing my heart to an audience that scares me. I mean, what if they hate it? What if they hate me?"

The vulnerability in his voice struck a chord deep within me. "But isn't that the beauty of it? The risk of sharing who you are? It's where the magic happens."

Felix met my gaze, something flickering in his eyes. "Maybe you're right. But it's easier to hide behind my music than to put myself out there."

"Then we'll put ourselves out there together," I suggested, buoyed by an unexpected surge of determination. "Our art is a reflection of us. If we can share this, then maybe the fear won't feel so daunting. We'll take the plunge."

He grinned, the previous weight in his eyes lifting slightly. "Alright, partner. Let's dive headfirst into the chaos, shall we?"

The following days were a whirlwind of inspiration and laughter. We flung paint like confetti, our canvases morphing into a vivid tapestry of dreams and nightmares. Felix composed piece after piece, his melodies swirling around us like a warm embrace. The music became our language, a dialogue woven through every brushstroke and note, revealing the uncharted territories of our souls.

One evening, as the sun dipped below the horizon, casting a warm, orange glow over the studio, Felix suggested we host a small gathering of friends to preview our project. "You know, to get some feedback before the showcase," he said, nervously tapping his foot.

"Feedback?" I echoed, a mixture of excitement and trepidation bubbling up inside me. "You want us to perform this? Like, for an audience?"

"Why not?" he countered, a determined glint in his eyes. "We've put our hearts into this. We should share it. Plus, it'll be a great way to break the ice."

The thought sent a thrill of anxiety racing through me, but there was a spark of exhilaration too. "Alright, but only if we invite people who won't be too harsh. I don't think I can handle the judgment of the entire school just yet."

"Deal," he laughed, and the tension that had brewed between us began to dissipate, replaced by a bubbling excitement that pulled us closer.

We spent the next few days preparing, inviting a small circle of friends who had been instrumental in our artistic journey. As the day approached, nerves fluttered in my stomach, a whirlwind of anticipation and fear.

When the night finally arrived, the studio buzzed with energy. Our friends gathered, their laughter mingling with the sounds of Felix's guitar, creating a soundtrack of camaraderie. I stood at the edge of the room, watching the people I cared about share in our creation, their faces illuminated by the soft glow of string lights hanging overhead.

"Are you ready?" Felix asked, his voice low as he joined me. I could see the tension in his shoulders, a mirror to my own anxiety.

"As ready as I'll ever be," I replied, forcing a smile. "Just promise me we won't trip over our own feet."

"Only if you promise to not set the place on fire with your brushwork," he teased, and I couldn't help but laugh, the weight of the moment lifting just slightly.

When we finally stepped into the center of the room, the world outside fell away, leaving only our small audience and the creative energy pulsating between us. Felix's fingers danced over the guitar strings, a haunting melody wrapping around us like a gentle embrace. I took a deep breath, letting the rhythm guide me as I painted on the canvas, each stroke a reflection of my heartbeat, my hopes, and my fears.

The room fell silent, the weight of our emotions hanging in the air like a delicate tapestry. It was exhilarating and terrifying, a reminder of everything we had shared and everything still left unspoken. The music flowed through me, and I lost myself in the act of creation, letting the art breathe life into my soul.

But as the final note echoed in the room, the applause erupted, a wave of warmth washing over us. We exchanged glances, the connection between us now charged with something more profound than before—a shared vulnerability, a promise of what could be.

Yet, just as the applause began to fade, a sharp sound shattered the moment—a loud crash from outside the studio. The door burst open, revealing a group of students from a rival art club, their faces twisted in mockery.

"Look who decided to throw a little party!" one of them sneered, a cruel smile playing on their lips. "Hope you didn't think you could actually get away with this."

Felix's grip on his guitar tightened, the tension snapping like a taut string. "What do you want?" he called, his voice steady but the underlying fury simmering just below the surface.

"Oh, we just thought we'd come and see what all the fuss was about," the leader of the group retorted, stepping forward, eyes gleaming with malice. "You two really think you can play with the big kids?"

A ripple of unease swept through the room as my heart raced. This was more than just an invasion; it felt like a threat, an attempt to undermine everything we had worked for. I exchanged a glance with Felix, and in that moment, I knew we had to stand our ground.

"Get out," I said, surprising myself with the strength in my voice. "This is our space, and we're not going to let you ruin it."

"Cute," the rival replied, but there was a flicker of uncertainty in their eyes. "Let's see if you can actually back that up."

Felix stepped closer to me, his expression fierce. "You want a show? Fine. Let's give them one they won't forget."

With the tension hanging thick in the air, I felt the adrenaline coursing through me. This was it—the moment where everything could change. We were about to turn the tables, but as I prepared to respond, a sinking feeling settled in my gut. This wasn't just about art anymore; it was a battle for our identity, our voices, and everything we had built together.

With the eyes of our friends and our rivals upon us, I took a deep breath, ready to unleash the storm brewing within, but before I could speak, the power in the studio flickered, the lights dimming ominously. An unexpected darkness loomed around us, and just as I opened my mouth to shout, the world went black.

Chapter 7: A Symphony of Secrets

The auditorium hums with a vibrant energy, a living organism thrumming with anticipation as the evening sun dips below the horizon, casting golden light through the tall windows. Hushed conversations blend with the sharp notes of tuning instruments, and the scent of freshly polished wood and a hint of paint from the recently hung art fill the air. I stand backstage, fingers nervously twiddling with the hem of my dress, a blend of deep emerald silk and lace that I chose with careful deliberation. It sways around my knees, its soft fabric a comforting presence amidst the chaos of my swirling thoughts. The venue is filled with familiar faces, their eager eyes bright with the promise of creativity that tonight's showcase holds.

Next to me, Felix leans against the wall, his presence a steady anchor in the storm of my nerves. He's wearing a crisp white shirt, sleeves rolled up to reveal the lean muscle of his forearms, the fabric contrasting sharply with the dark jeans he insists are more comfortable. I catch him stealing glances at the crowd, his dark curls falling into his eyes as he bites his lip in concentration. I want to tell him that he looks breathtakingly handsome, but the words die on my tongue, drowned in a tide of my own anxiety.

"Hey," he says, breaking the tension. His voice is low, a warm rumble that sends an electric thrill down my spine. "You ready for this?"

I nod, but my heart is racing, drumming in my chest like a frantic percussionist trying to outplay the rest of the orchestra. "As ready as I'll ever be," I reply, forcing a smile that I hope looks more confident than it feels. "What about you?"

He shrugs, the corner of his mouth lifting in a lopsided grin that could light up the darkest room. "Just another day at the office, right? Only this time, I'm not juggling flaming torches."

I laugh, the sound surprisingly buoyant, cutting through the nervous energy that swirls around us. We share a moment of quiet before the world rushes back in—a symphony of laughter, footsteps, and the occasional burst of applause from the audience eager for the evening to begin.

With a gentle nudge, Felix leads me toward the stage entrance. The lights are bright, illuminating the polished wood of the stage, making it feel both inviting and intimidating. As we step into the spotlight, my breath catches. The audience stretches out before us, a sea of expectant faces, each one a witness to our creation. I can almost feel their collective heartbeat, pulsing in time with my own.

We launch into our piece, a medley that intertwines music with visual storytelling, creating a tapestry of sound and light. My heart swells as Felix's fingers dance over the keys, each note ringing out like a promise, while I weave together images on the screen behind us. The energy shifts, and I find myself lost in the rhythm of our collaboration, the world outside fading into a beautiful blur. It's not just a performance; it's a glimpse into our intertwined lives, a manifestation of our dreams and struggles, a testament to everything we've shared.

As the final note lingers in the air, the auditorium erupts into applause, a wave of sound that washes over us. I glance at Felix, and his eyes shine with a mix of joy and disbelief, the joy radiating from his every pore. For that brief moment, everything feels right; we've created something magical together, something that transcends the ordinary.

But as we step off the stage, the applause still ringing in our ears, the mood shifts abruptly. Standing at the edge of the auditorium, arms crossed and face a mask of displeasure, is Felix's father. The crowd seems to part for him, his presence casting a long shadow over the post-performance excitement. The joy I felt moments ago evaporates like mist in the morning sun, replaced by a cold knot of dread in my stomach.

Felix's expression shifts instantly, the light in his eyes dimming as he approaches his father. "Dad," he begins, his voice cautious, the playful lilt replaced by a weighty seriousness. I can't hear the words they exchange, but the tension is palpable, crackling in the air like static before a storm. I feel like an intruder in their private world, an unwanted witness to a confrontation I can't defuse.

"Do you really think this is what you should be doing?" His father's voice cuts through the air, sharp and unyielding. "You've wasted enough time on this nonsense. It's time to focus on what really matters."

I see Felix's jaw tighten, the muscles in his face hardening. "This is what matters to me," he replies, his voice low but steady, betraying none of the turmoil I know is churning within him.

The words hang between them, a fragile thread of defiance woven through an ocean of disappointment. I want to reach out, to pull Felix back into the warmth of our shared moment, but I feel paralyzed, caught between wanting to shield him and the understanding that this is a battle he must face alone.

"Your art won't pay the bills, Felix," his father shoots back, the harshness of his words cutting deep, a jagged edge that finds its mark. I watch helplessly as the boy I care about begins to unravel, the cracks in his facade widening, exposing vulnerabilities he has fought so hard to conceal.

"You don't understand," Felix says, voice strained, the hurt evident in every syllable. "This isn't just a hobby for me; it's my passion. It's who I am."

The silence that follows is deafening, the air thick with unspoken words and shattered dreams. Felix's father stands firm, arms crossed, the embodiment of authority, while Felix appears small, shoulders slumped under the weight of his father's expectations. I want to scream, to tell Felix that he's brave and talented, that he should follow his dreams, but I remain frozen, paralyzed by the intensity of their confrontation.

In that moment, I realize how easy it is for dreams to get crushed under the weight of reality, how quickly the warmth of creativity can be doused by the cold water of disapproval. The vibrant world we had just created together feels like a distant memory, a bittersweet echo overshadowed by the starkness of the moment.

The tension in the air is electric, crackling like a live wire, and I feel it in every fiber of my being as I stand by, an unwilling spectator to this familial showdown. Felix's father's words hang heavy, a storm cloud hovering over us, and I can see the fight draining from Felix's shoulders, his usually bright spirit dulled under the weight of disapproval. The audience's applause fades into a distant murmur, their joy a stark contrast to the turmoil unfolding before me.

"Why can't you just see that this is important to me?" Felix's voice quivers, a mixture of frustration and hurt, but his father remains unmoved, his expression set in a grim line that suggests he's heard this song before but is unwilling to let it play on repeat.

"Important?" His father scoffs, shaking his head. "You think this is important? You think running around playing artist is going to secure your future?"

I feel my heart sink for him, my breath catching in my throat as I search for words to bridge the chasm that's opened between them. There's a storm brewing behind Felix's eyes, a mixture of rebellion and resignation that I can only hope doesn't spill over. It's one thing to fight for your dreams; it's another when the very foundation of those dreams is challenged by the person who should be your biggest supporter.

"Dad, it's not just playing artist," Felix replies, voice steady despite the turmoil swirling within. "This is my life. You can't just decide it's not worthy because it doesn't fit your idea of success."

The words hang there, heavy with unfulfilled expectations and dashed hopes. I want to step in, to tell Felix's father that he's wrong, that creativity isn't a frivolous pursuit but rather the lifeblood of innovation and joy. But I stay silent, acutely aware that my voice in this matter could just complicate things further.

As if sensing my presence, Felix glances at me, his eyes a mixture of gratitude and desperation. I offer him a small, encouraging smile, hoping to remind him that he's not alone. The warmth between us flickers, an unspoken bond that offers some solace amidst the storm. Yet, in that fleeting moment, I see the flicker of doubt in his eyes, a crack that threatens to break wide open.

"Don't look at her," his father snaps, as if my mere presence is a contagion threatening to infect his son's already wavering resolve. "She doesn't understand what it's like to make real choices, to prepare for the future."

My heart clenches, his words sharp and unyielding, but before I can formulate a response, Felix steps forward, the fire in him reigniting. "You have no idea who she is," he says, voice rising slightly, a challenge laced in each syllable. "She's not just a girl playing with colors and notes. She's talented, and she believes in me. Maybe if you took the time to see who I really am, you wouldn't be so quick to judge."

The silence that follows is like a thick fog, swallowing the vibrant energy of the auditorium and replacing it with an unsettling chill. Felix's father looks taken aback, as if struck by a sudden realization. For a heartbeat, it feels as if the world has paused, hanging in the balance between understanding and rejection. But the moment shatters as his father's brow furrows deeper, the disappointment swirling back to the surface.

"You're a fool to think this will lead you anywhere," he declares, his voice cold and firm, cutting through the air like a knife. "Art doesn't pay the bills, Felix. It's a dream, and dreams don't put food on the table."

With those words, he turns sharply, the heel of his shoe echoing against the polished floor as he strides away, leaving behind an oppressive silence that feels heavier than any applause. I watch as Felix's shoulders slump, the flicker of defiance extinguished, leaving behind the hollow shell of a boy battling his father's shadow.

"Felix..." I start, wanting to bridge the distance that now feels like a chasm between us, but he shakes his head, eyes dark and stormy.

"I need a minute," he murmurs, his voice barely above a whisper. And just like that, he walks away, leaving me standing in the aftermath of a confrontation I can't fix, a sense of helplessness washing over me like a tide of cold water.

The vibrant world of our showcase seems to fade into the background, replaced by the echo of harsh words and the remnants of dreams deferred. I take a step back, my heart heavy, wanting to reach out to him but unsure how to breach the barrier his father's words have erected between us.

The auditorium begins to empty, laughter and chatter rising as people spill out into the night, the energy shifting from that of creation to celebration. I stand on the sidelines, watching the joyous faces, their smiles a stark reminder of the joy we had just shared, now tainted by the reality of Felix's struggles.

With a sigh, I step outside into the cool evening air, hoping to find him. The stars twinkle overhead like tiny beacons of hope, and the faint glow of streetlights casts a warm hue over the pavement. As I wander, I try to shake off the weight of the encounter, my mind racing with thoughts and questions.

Finding a quiet corner of the courtyard, I lean against a rough stone wall, listening to the gentle rustle of leaves in the night breeze. It's serene here, a stark contrast to the chaos of emotions swirling inside me. I close my eyes for a moment, trying to gather my thoughts.

The soft crunch of gravel draws my attention, and I turn to see Felix approaching, his expression a storm of conflict and hurt. "I'm sorry," he says, his voice low, but I can see the vulnerability behind it, the cracks in his facade widening.

"Don't be," I reply quickly, stepping closer, wanting to wrap him in the warmth of understanding. "You're not the one who should be apologizing. You fought for what you believe in. That takes courage."

He laughs softly, but it's a bitter sound, devoid of humor. "Courage? I feel like a failure."

"Then you're doing it wrong," I say, trying to inject some lightness into the heavy air between us. "If courage meant never feeling like a failure, then half the artists I know would be out of work. Trust me, this is just part of the process."

His brow lifts slightly, a glimmer of that familiar spark returning. "So, what, I'm supposed to embrace my failures like a long-lost friend?"

"Exactly!" I grin, eager to pull him from the depths of despair. "Just think of it as an unexpected plot twist in your own personal novel. You know, the one where the hero discovers their true strength through adversity. Plus, every good story needs some conflict, right? It makes the resolution that much sweeter."

Felix regards me for a moment, a mix of confusion and curiosity on his face, as if he's trying to decipher my words while finding a thread of hope woven through them. "You really think it can get better?"

"I know it can," I insist, stepping closer, feeling the warmth of his presence fill the space around us. "You're talented, Felix. You have a gift. Don't let anyone take that away from you, especially not someone who doesn't see the beauty of what you create."

He looks down, the weight of his father's words still pressing on his shoulders, but I can see the flicker of determination reigniting in his eyes. "Thanks," he murmurs, a hint of gratitude threading through his voice. "I just... I don't want to disappoint you or myself."

"Then don't," I say firmly, my own heart swelling with conviction. "Follow your passion, no matter how many people try to pull you down. It's your life to live, after all. And if it makes you happy, then isn't that what really matters?"

For a moment, we stand there, the cool breeze wrapping around us like a protective shroud. In that shared silence, I feel the bonds between us strengthening, the delicate threads of understanding weaving together into something beautiful. The echoes of the showcase linger in the background, a reminder of what we had achieved, and I can almost hear the faint applause in my mind, a symphony of hope that promises brighter days ahead.

The night air is crisp, a gentle reminder that change is inevitable, and it carries with it a hint of the impending autumn. The moon hangs high in the sky, casting a silvery glow that dances across the courtyard as Felix and I linger near the edge of the art showcase, wrapped in a cocoon of our own making. His earlier storm has subsided, but the remnants of the confrontation still linger, shadows etched on his face.

"I'm serious about what I said," I venture, breaking the silence that stretches between us. "You have a gift, Felix. Don't let anyone tell you otherwise."

He shifts his weight, hands tucked deep into his pockets, a habit I've come to recognize as his way of guarding against the world. "It's hard to believe that when you hear those words from your own father," he replies, his voice thick with frustration.

"Fathers can be... well, difficult," I say, choosing my words with care. "Sometimes they forget that their expectations can suffocate the dreams they're supposed to nurture."

His gaze softens, and for a brief moment, I catch a glimpse of the boy I've grown fond of, the one who crafts magic with his music and brings colors to life on the canvas. "You make it sound so simple," he murmurs, a ghost of a smile ghosting across his lips. "Like I just have to toss my worries into the wind and let them fly away."

"Well, maybe you should try tossing some of that worry around," I tease, nudging him playfully. "Just picture it: you, a carefree artist, soaring above it all like a kite. I can almost see you drifting on the breeze, laughing at the ground below."

He chuckles, a low, warm sound that fills the air between us, and the tension eases just a bit. "Sounds nice in theory. In practice, I might just end up tangled in a tree."

"I could see that," I say, laughter bubbling up, buoyed by the ease of our conversation. "But I would totally be there to rescue you, superhero style. With a snack, of course. Can't save a falling artist on an empty stomach."

The corners of his mouth lift further, a glimmer of light sparking in his dark eyes. "Are you suggesting I'm a delicate flower in need of nourishment?"

"Hey, every great artist needs to refuel!" I reply with mock indignation. "What kind of sidekick would I be if I didn't keep you well-fed?"

His laughter breaks through the cloud of heaviness, and for a moment, we share an understanding that transcends the struggles around us.

But just as the warmth of our exchange begins to thaw the chill in the air, a familiar voice interrupts, cutting through our moment like a knife. "Felix, there you are!"

The voice belongs to Mara, his childhood friend, and fellow art enthusiast, who has a knack for showing up at the most inopportune moments. She strides toward us, her heels clicking on the pavement like an unwanted metronome. The excitement that radiates from her is palpable, but I can't help but feel the encroaching tension that returns, wrapping around Felix's shoulders like a heavy cloak.

"Did you see that? You were incredible out there!" She beams, wrapping her arms around him in an exuberant hug that seems to draw him back into the light. "The way you played that piece—it was like the entire audience was holding their breath!"

"Thanks, Mara," he replies, the warmth of her enthusiasm pulling him back from the edge of despair. "It was… something."

"Something amazing!" she insists, stepping back to look at him, her green eyes sparkling with pride. "I mean, honestly, you could practically hear the heartbeat of the room. Everyone was completely entranced!"

I watch as she talks, a slight edge of envy creeping in. It's not just her unyielding energy; it's the way she draws Felix into her orbit, effortlessly illuminating the darkness that threatens to swallow him whole. A pang of irritation flickers in my chest, but I stifle it, reminding myself that it's not a competition.

"And the visuals!" she continues, her voice rising with excitement. "Did you see how the images you created danced with the music? It was like they were alive! You guys are a dream team!"

Felix smiles, genuine appreciation flickering across his features as he basks in her praise. "It was definitely a team effort," he says, glancing at me with a hint of gratitude.

Mara's gaze shifts to me, and I can almost see the gears turning in her mind. "Oh! And we've got to celebrate! You both deserve a night out! There's this new café that opened downtown, and I hear they have the best hot chocolate! Let's go!"

The idea hangs in the air, a tempting invitation that pulls at my sense of belonging. I want to say yes, to dive into a world where laughter and warmth abound, but I can also feel the invisible wall that separates Felix and me from everyone else. He's still grappling with his father's words, and I don't want to distract him from what he needs to process.

Felix hesitates, his brow furrowing slightly. "I... I'm not sure I'm ready for a celebration just yet."

Mara's enthusiasm dims, but only slightly. "What? You can't let one cranky parent ruin your night! Besides, you've earned this. We all have!"

"I just need a moment," Felix says, his tone softer, the light dimming in his eyes as he speaks.

I feel my heart clench at the underlying pain in his voice, the echoes of his father's words still haunting him like a relentless specter. "Maybe we should just take it easy," I interject gently. "How about a quiet night instead? Just us?"

Felix meets my gaze, gratitude flickering behind the shadows. "That sounds... nice."

Mara's smile falters but she quickly masks it with a cheerful nod. "Fine, I guess a quiet night can be nice too. But you two better promise me a rain check on that hot chocolate."

"Absolutely," I say, my voice firm, wanting to reassure her that our friendship is still valued, even if it doesn't include a loud celebration tonight.

As she walks away, still buzzing with energy, I turn to Felix, who is looking at me with a mixture of relief and something deeper—an unspoken connection that binds us together in this moment.

"Thank you," he says quietly, stepping closer, his presence enveloping me in a cocoon of warmth. "I just... I don't know how to process everything right now."

"I get it," I reply, our eyes locking, the world around us fading away. "You don't have to do it alone."

Just then, my phone buzzes in my pocket, shattering the fragile intimacy of our moment. I pull it out, glancing at the screen to see a text from my mom, the words barely registering as my heart begins to race.

"Hey, I need to talk to you. Urgent."

I look up at Felix, the weight of my mother's message pressing down on me like a lead weight. "I—"

Before I can finish, a commotion breaks out across the courtyard. A group of students, their laughter ringing out like bells, bursts into the scene, and in their midst is a familiar face—one I never expected to see here tonight.

"Did you see that?" Felix exclaims, his attention diverted as the group draws nearer. "What are they doing here?"

I follow his gaze, and my heart drops as I recognize the figure standing at the center: it's Ryan, Felix's former best friend, the one who left their friendship in shambles. He strides toward us, an air of confidence about him that feels almost suffocating, and with him, the unsteady ground beneath our feet shifts dramatically.

"Felix! Just the guy I wanted to see," Ryan calls out, a cocky grin plastered across his face. The laughter from the group fades as they notice the tension brewing between us, the air thick with unspoken animosity.

I glance at Felix, whose expression morphs into one of apprehension, uncertainty clouding his features. "What do you want, Ryan?" he asks, his voice sharp, like glass being scraped against stone.

Ryan's smile widens, a mix of amusement and malice. "Oh, just wanted to catch up with an old friend. Heard you had a little showcase tonight. Impressive, really. Too bad your dad didn't think so."

A chill sweeps through me, and I can see the walls that Felix has painstakingly built around himself begin to crumble as Ryan's words pierce through the fragile calm we've created.

"Leave it alone," I say, stepping forward, the protective instinct surging within me. "This isn't the time."

Ryan's eyes flicker with surprise, clearly not expecting anyone to stand up to him. "Who's this? Your new sidekick?" He laughs, a hollow sound that makes my skin crawl.

"Back off," Felix warns, his voice trembling with barely contained rage. The shadows of the past threaten to swallow him whole, and I can see him teetering on the edge, fighting to stay afloat.

And just when I think we might be able to shake off the tension, Ryan steps closer, a menacing glint in his eyes. "Why don't you face the truth, Felix? You're just an artist with a shattered dream, living in a fantasy. It's time you

Chapter 8: The Reckoning

The gallery buzzed with a cacophony of voices, laughter, and the occasional clink of glasses. Vibrant art pieces adorned the walls, each telling a story more elaborate than the last. I stepped back, letting the spectacle wash over me, an oasis of color amidst the sharp outlines of anxiety etching into Felix's shoulders. He stood across the room, a human sculpture carved from worry, his gaze fixed on the crowd but distant as if he were observing a scene in a glass case rather than participating in it. The sharp lines of his jaw tightened, the shadows under his eyes deepening like dark clouds gathering before a storm.

My heart ached for him. I couldn't stand watching him suffer, torn between the dazzling display of creativity and the heavy chains of expectation his father had forged. I made my way through the throngs of art enthusiasts, the smell of wine mingling with the subtle undertone of oil paint, feeling the weight of anticipation in the air. As I approached him, I noticed his fingers gripping the edge of the bar like a lifeline, knuckles pale against the mahogany surface.

"Felix," I said softly, trying to peel away the layers of his isolation. "You did amazing tonight. The way your pieces spoke—it was like they were breathing."

He barely turned, his eyes glazing over with an unreadable expression. "Thanks, but it's not enough." His voice was a low rumble, almost lost in the chatter around us. It felt as if I were trying to catch smoke with my bare hands—fleeting, intangible, impossible to hold.

I reached out, placing my hand over his. "It is enough. You're enough." The warmth of my palm contrasted with his coldness, and I felt a slight tremor as he inhaled sharply, a mix of emotions swirling behind those deep-set eyes.

His gaze flicked to me, and for a fleeting moment, the veneer of strength cracked. "You don't know what it's like, Ellie. To constantly be compared to someone who seems to excel at everything. My father... he's impossible to please." His voice faltered, revealing the raw edges of his vulnerability.

"I'm not comparing you to him. You're your own person, and your art is so much more than a reflection of him. It's real. It's you." I searched his eyes, willing him to understand the depth of my conviction.

"You think I want to be my father? To become a shell of a man, wrapped in accolades but empty inside?" His words were sharp, a bitter slice that sent shivers racing down my spine. "I'm terrified of that. I can't bear the thought of becoming him."

The honesty in his confession struck me like a physical blow, and the air around us thickened. I squeezed his hand tighter, grounding us both in that moment. "You won't. You're fighting to be someone else, Felix. And that's what makes you brave. You're not a carbon copy."

But as the words left my lips, a sudden commotion erupted across the room. Shattered glass shattered the delicate atmosphere, and gasps punctuated the air. I turned instinctively, the warmth of our shared moment evaporating as reality intruded.

A figure stumbled into view, a cascade of crimson painting the white walls as he fell to the floor. The sight of him sent a chill spiraling through my core. The crowd erupted into chaos, people rushing to help, but I couldn't move. My heart thundered in my chest, and the laughter faded into a haunting silence that echoed louder than the shattering glass.

"Ellie!" Felix's voice broke through my stupor, his hand slipping from mine as he sprinted toward the scene. "Call for help!" He was gone, swallowed by the sea of panicked bodies. I stood frozen, rooted to the spot, the surreal horror of the moment pressing down on me like a heavy fog.

Panic clawed at my throat as I fumbled for my phone, my fingers shaking so violently that I struggled to dial. The emergency services felt like an eternity away, each ring stretching into a thin thread of desperation. I could barely focus, thoughts spiraling, the gravity of the situation crushing the air from my lungs.

Just then, a warm hand clasped my shoulder, jolting me back to the present. "What happened?" a voice demanded, fierce and steady. I turned to find Sophia, her expression taut with concern.

"There's a man... he's hurt." My voice trembled, unsteady like a tightrope walker in a windstorm. "We need to—"

She was already moving, her instincts sharp as a hawk's. "Get everyone back! We can't let anyone near him until help arrives!"

As she surged forward, I felt a flicker of hope. Sophia's presence radiated strength, a beacon amidst the encroaching darkness. The crowd began to obey her, a wave of humanity retreating in a disorganized shuffle. I followed, adrenaline surging, my heart racing to match the urgency of the moment.

The world felt surreal as we formed a barrier around the fallen figure, the edges of reality blurring. The mingled scents of paint, sweat, and fear hung heavily in the air, each inhalation a reminder of the fragility of life. Felix's voice pierced through the cacophony, an anchor in the storm of chaos, demanding answers, reassurance, and clarity as he hovered near the man.

In that moment, amidst the flurry of uncertainty, I realized that no matter how heavy the weight of our pasts, the connections we forged had the power to transcend even the darkest of shadows. My heart raced for him, knowing that whatever lay ahead, our journey together was just beginning.

The swirling chaos around us gradually gave way to a tense silence, the initial shock settling like dust in the aftermath of an explosion. I stood by Felix, who crouched over the fallen man, his face drawn tight with concentration, worry etched into every feature.

The world faded into the background, all other sounds muffled as if we were encased in glass. The scent of paint and fear clung to the air, creating an atmosphere that felt both surreal and painfully real.

I had never seen Felix like this, stripped of bravado, his usual charm swallowed by a sense of urgency. "He needs help," he muttered, his fingers trembling as they brushed against the man's neck, searching for a pulse. "Please, God, just be okay."

"Help is on the way," I assured him, though my voice wavered, a thin thread of hope that could snap at any moment. I felt the heat of panic rising in my chest, a pressure building like a wave ready to crash over me. I could hardly bear to watch as Felix fought against the encroaching shadows of despair. "Stay focused. You're doing great."

The moments stretched and twisted, each second a cruel reminder of the fragility of life. The crowd had formed a semicircle, faces painted with a mix of curiosity and horror, their murmurs a distant hum. I could see Sophia darting through the crowd, directing people away with her commanding presence. Her sharp voice cut through the haze, gathering momentum like a ship ready to set sail in a storm. "Make space! Stand back!"

Felix's focus remained unwavering, yet I could see the doubt creeping in, shadows flitting across his features as the minutes dragged on. "What if...?" He trailed off, the unspoken fear hanging in the air between us, heavy and suffocating. "What if it's too late?"

"Don't say that," I insisted, my heart thundering in my chest. "You can't think like that. Just keep talking to him." My words felt feeble, yet I clung to them like a lifeline, hoping to pull us both back from the edge.

"Hey, buddy," Felix called out, his voice steady despite the tremor beneath it. "Can you hear me? Just hold on. Help is coming."

As he spoke, the man's eyes fluttered open, glassy and unfocused. A flicker of recognition crossed his face before his gaze settled on

Felix, and I could see the confusion swirl like a tempest. "Who...?" The word was barely a whisper, yet it shattered the tension in the air.

"Stay with me," Felix urged, his tone a mix of desperation and determination. "You're safe. You're going to be okay."

Then came the sirens, cutting through the thick veil of silence like a knife. Relief surged within me, a breath of fresh air in the thickening fog. The emergency responders arrived, a flurry of movement, their presence transforming chaos into action. Felix stepped back, letting the professionals take over.

I watched him, worry gnawing at my insides as I noticed the way his shoulders slumped slightly, as if the weight of the moment had finally broken through his carefully constructed armor. I approached him slowly, the noise of the crowd fading into the background. "You did everything you could," I murmured, reaching for his arm.

But he was distant again, a wall rising between us. "What if I hadn't been fast enough? What if I hadn't tried?" The questions poured from him like a deluge, heavy and suffocating.

"You can't carry that burden," I insisted, my voice firm but gentle. "You're not responsible for every life you encounter. You saved him. That counts for something."

His eyes met mine, and for a brief moment, I could see the cracks in his facade. "You don't understand. I'm terrified of failing, of becoming what my father is—a ghost who's forgotten how to feel, how to connect."

"Then let's not let fear define you," I said softly, feeling the heat of my own emotions rise. "You're more than your father's shadow, Felix. You're a brilliant artist with a heart that beats fiercely. That's what makes you who you are."

He shook his head, a bitter smile curling his lips. "And what if that heart breaks? What if I can't handle it?"

"Then we'll pick up the pieces together," I promised, squeezing his hand gently. "You're not alone in this. Not anymore."

Just as the paramedics began to transport the injured man, the tension between us shifted. An unexpected voice sliced through the moment, smooth and sharp like glass, snapping our attention back to reality. "Well, well, well. Look who's in a bind."

I turned to see Felix's father, his presence darkening the atmosphere. He surveyed the scene with a hawkish gaze, taking in the chaos, the paramedics, and finally, his son. There was no warmth in his eyes, only a cold calculation that sent a shiver racing down my spine.

"Dad, this isn't the time," Felix snapped, his voice strained.

"Oh, I think it's the perfect time," his father replied, a sly smile twisting his lips. "Just look at you—playing hero again. How quaint. Are you really trying to impress me, Felix?"

The contempt dripped from his words, each syllable a deliberate thrust. I felt the tension spiral into something more dangerous, a tempest brewing beneath the surface. Felix's jaw tightened, and I could sense the anger radiating from him, a flame ready to ignite.

"This isn't about you," Felix shot back, his voice fierce. "Stop making everything about your twisted expectations. I'm done trying to be the son you want me to be."

His father's smile faltered, just for a moment, revealing the anger simmering beneath. "Is that so? Because it looks to me like you're still lost in the shadow of my achievements, desperate for validation. Pathetic."

The air crackled with hostility, and I felt my heart race as Felix squared his shoulders, determination burning in his gaze. "You don't get to define my worth anymore."

As their confrontation escalated, I sensed the delicate balance of emotions shifting, the turmoil of anger and fear churning within me. I stood on the sidelines, witnessing the raw, unfiltered exchange between father and son, caught in a storm where the winds howled and the ground trembled beneath my feet.

In that moment, I knew that the fight for Felix's heart was only just beginning. Whatever lay ahead would require us both to confront the shadows of our pasts and carve out a future defined not by fear but by the strength of our connection.

The moment hung in the air like a loaded gun, tension thick enough to cut through with a knife. Felix's father glowered, his expression a cocktail of disappointment and derision. "Pathetic?" The word lingered in the air like a foul odor. "You're the one throwing a tantrum in front of a crowd, Felix. Do you think this is going to earn you any respect?"

Felix's hands curled into fists at his sides, and I could see the muscles in his jaw twitching, a warning sign that the storm inside him was about to break. "Respect?" he spat back, his voice low and trembling with suppressed fury. "You think respect comes from tearing people down? I'm not you, Dad. I won't hide behind your shadow anymore."

The air crackled with animosity, and I could feel the weight of every gaze in the room turning toward them, a captivated audience in the theater of their familial discord. I shifted uncomfortably, feeling the prickling heat of embarrassment wash over me. This wasn't the place for a family confrontation, yet here we were, the spectacle unfolding in front of an audience who relished the drama.

"Is that what you think? That I'm some shadowy figure lurking in the corners of your life?" His father stepped closer, his voice laced with mock concern, and I could see the flicker of anger in Felix's eyes intensifying. "You're just running away, Felix. Running away from the very talents you've been given. You think a little art show makes you special?"

"Maybe it's not about being special," I chimed in, desperation creeping into my voice. I took a step forward, hoping to diffuse the mounting tension. "Maybe it's about finding your voice and living it, regardless of what anyone else thinks."

His father turned his steely gaze toward me, sizing me up as if I were a puzzle he couldn't quite piece together. "And who might you be to lecture my son about worth? Do you think art will keep him fed?" His contempt dripped like poison, and I felt my pulse quicken.

"Better than a cold shoulder and a bank account filled with hollow accolades," I shot back, my frustration bubbling over. Felix shot me a grateful glance, a brief flicker of warmth in the otherwise bleak situation.

Felix's father opened his mouth, but before he could deliver another barb, the paramedics, now finished with their work on the injured man, swept through the throng. "We need to clear this area," one of them called out, his voice firm yet professional.

The atmosphere shifted, a collective exhale echoing through the crowd. Relief washed over me, though it was short-lived as Felix's father continued his verbal assault, unrelenting. "You think you can stand up to me? To this?" He gestured to the crowd, his disdain palpable. "You've always needed my approval. Just look at yourself—pathetic."

Something inside me snapped, a long-simmering anger igniting like a match against kindling. "You're the one who's pathetic," I said, my voice rising above the fray, "hiding behind your own failures and trying to drag your son into your darkness. This isn't about him anymore; it's about you trying to feel powerful."

The crowd seemed to collectively gasp, the shock hanging in the air as Felix's father's face flushed a deep crimson. I felt Felix's presence beside me, an anchor amidst the storm.

"Ellie—" he began, but I shook my head, the fire of my words propelling me forward. "No, Felix. This is your moment too. You don't need to live under his shadow."

His father sneered, but there was a flicker of uncertainty in his gaze. "How quaint. A little speech from someone who thinks they can save the day. The truth is, Felix will always be my son, whether he likes it or not."

"Being your son doesn't have to mean living in your shadow," I insisted, feeling the swell of emotion tighten my throat. "Felix is his own person, and he deserves to live authentically. You can't take that from him."

For a moment, silence enveloped us, the weight of my words hanging thickly in the air. Then, as if a dam had burst, Felix's father turned on his heel, the disappointment radiating from him like a dark cloud. "This isn't over, Felix. You'll regret this."

He strode away, leaving behind an unsettled crowd and a churning sea of emotions. I watched him go, feeling the remnants of his presence lingering like a storm cloud overhead.

Felix turned to me, his eyes wide, reflecting the tumult within him. "I can't believe you did that," he said, incredulity mixing with something deeper—admiration, perhaps? "You stood up to him. No one does that."

"I couldn't just stand by and watch," I replied, my heart racing. "You deserve to be heard, Felix. Not just as his son but as yourself. We all deserve that."

He took a deep breath, letting it out slowly, the tension in his shoulders easing slightly. "I don't even know what to say."

"Then don't say anything," I suggested, my voice softening. "Just breathe. Let it sink in."

But even as I spoke, a sense of unease settled over me. The confrontation had done more than rattle the atmosphere; it had stirred the waters of Felix's past, and I couldn't shake the feeling that this was just the beginning of a storm.

As we stood there, the crowd slowly dissipating, Felix's face turned grave. "You know he won't stop, right? He'll find a way to get to me."

"Let him try," I replied fiercely, my heart pounding with determination. "You have me, Felix. We'll figure this out together."

Suddenly, my phone buzzed in my pocket, pulling me from the moment. I fished it out, glancing at the screen, my heart skipping a beat as I read the message. It was from my sister, urgent and short: Get out. It's not safe.

"Ellie?" Felix's voice cut through my panic.

"What? What's wrong?" I could feel a sense of dread pooling in my stomach, a gnawing instinct that warned me this wasn't just a casual message.

"Ellie!" His voice was sharp, pulling me back to him. "What's going on?"

"I don't know," I said, my hands trembling slightly. "It's just... my sister. She's worried about something. I need to—"

Before I could finish, a commotion erupted behind us, the sound of raised voices and hurried footsteps drawing my attention. I turned just in time to see Felix's father re-enter the gallery, a glint of something dangerous in his eyes.

"Dad!" Felix shouted, alarm rising in his voice.

But before he could reach for me, before I could react, his father's gaze locked onto mine, a predatory smile spreading across his lips. "You've really stirred the pot this time, haven't you?"

And in that instant, I knew we were in deeper than we ever intended. The air shifted, the tension snapping like a taut wire, and I could feel the ground beneath us trembling with the weight of uncertainty. What had I stepped into? What had we awakened?

"Get behind me," Felix commanded, his voice low and urgent, a protective instinct igniting within him.

As I moved closer, the reality of our situation dawned on me. This wasn't just about art, or fathers and sons. It was about survival, and the depths people would sink to protect their own secrets. And as Felix's father took a step forward, I could sense the darkness closing in around us, a maelstrom of unresolved pasts and volatile futures, leaving me breathless with anticipation and dread.

Chapter 9: Shattered Hearts

Grief has a way of distorting reality, wrapping the world in a shroud that both dulls and amplifies sensations, like being underwater, where every sound is muffled yet echoing with an urgency that pierces the stillness. The day we learned of Mrs. Marshall's accident began like any other. The morning sunlight spilled through the classroom windows, casting cheerful patterns on the walls, blindingly bright against the backdrop of our shared sorrow. Laughter bubbled up in the hallways like soda fizz, unaware that just beyond the threshold, a shadow loomed over us, dark and suffocating.

As the news rippled through our small town, whispers filled the air, heavy with disbelief. Mrs. Marshall had been more than a teacher; she was the kind of person who lit up the room with her laughter, whose passion for literature made even the most reluctant readers lean forward in their seats. She had a way of turning Shakespearean tragedies into discussions about life and love, drawing out the emotions that simmered beneath the surface. I remember the way her eyes sparkled when she spoke of hope, her words weaving a tapestry of dreams that felt just within reach. She had once told me that pain was an inevitable part of growing, a stepping stone to something greater, but now, standing in that classroom, I felt the weight of her absence crush me.

Felix and I had been inseparable, bonded over late-night study sessions and shared secrets. We had been each other's anchors during turbulent times, yet as the reality of our loss settled in, a rift began to unfurl between us. I caught glimpses of him in the hall, his eyes darkened with an anger I couldn't quite fathom. The way he clenched his fists at his sides, his jaw set like granite, made me ache to reach out. I wanted to shake him, to demand he talk to me, but I knew the futility of such gestures. Anger had become his shield, and

I, the would-be interloper, didn't know how to breach the fortress he had built around his heart.

The memorial service was a muted affair, the school auditorium draped in somber colors, the air thick with sorrow. Students, teachers, and parents gathered, united in their grief yet isolated in their pain. As I stood at the back, clutching my program like a lifeline, I scanned the faces around me. I saw tears, raw and glistening, and heard the occasional sob pierce through the silence, each sound echoing the weight of our collective loss. The principal spoke softly, his voice trembling as he recounted stories of Mrs. Marshall's kindness and wisdom. Each anecdote was a reminder of what we had lost, a stark contrast to the joy that had once filled our days.

I searched for Felix, hoping to catch his eye, to remind him that he wasn't alone in this dark labyrinth of despair. But he remained a ghost, fading in and out of view, his presence overshadowed by the grief that enveloped him. It was as if he were standing on one side of a glass wall, while I was on the other, desperate to connect, to show him that we could navigate this storm together. But he only turned his back, retreating deeper into himself, and the fissure between us widened, a chasm filled with unspoken words and unacknowledged feelings.

After the service, I wandered outside, the sun blazing down as if mocking our sorrow. The world moved on, completely indifferent to the tragedy that had unfolded. I felt a swell of anger rise within me—why did it feel like life was continuing without us, like we were caught in a perpetual moment of mourning? I needed to scream, to break the silence that threatened to engulf me, but instead, I sank onto a bench, the wood rough beneath my palms, and let my thoughts swirl like autumn leaves caught in a windstorm.

A soft voice broke through my reverie. "You okay?" It was Anna, a girl from my English class, her brows furrowed with concern. She had always been kind, a bright light in the shadowy corners of our school.

"Just... trying to process," I admitted, my voice barely above a whisper.

"Yeah, me too," she replied, settling down beside me. "It feels like we're all walking around in a fog. No one knows what to say."

"I just wish Felix would talk to me," I confessed, the words tumbling out like a dam bursting. "He's so angry. It's like he blames the world for what happened."

Anna nodded, her gaze distant. "He's hurting. Sometimes people think pushing others away is easier than letting them in."

Her words struck a chord deep within me. It was true; Felix had always been the one to bottle up his feelings, a fierce protector of his heart. And now, as I stood on the precipice of understanding, I realized that I had to break through his walls, to reach him before he sank too deep into his anger.

As we talked, the sun dipped lower in the sky, painting the horizon in hues of gold and crimson. The beauty of the world outside seemed a cruel contrast to our shared grief. I could feel my resolve strengthening, the desire to be the beacon of hope for Felix blossoming within me. But as I looked down at the small scar on my wrist—a remnant of my own battles—I knew that healing was a two-way street. It demanded vulnerability, a willingness to face the darkness together.

"Maybe," I said slowly, "maybe love can heal us. Even when the world feels so heavy."

Anna gave me a soft smile, a flicker of hope igniting in her eyes. "Sometimes it just takes a little spark to light the way."

And with those words, I felt a glimmer of determination blossom within me. I would reach for Felix, and somehow, we would find our way back to each other, through the murk of grief and into the light of understanding.

The air in the days that followed hung heavy, thick with unspoken grief and the lingering scent of Mrs. Marshall's favorite vanilla candles that had permeated her classroom. It clung to us like a second skin, a reminder of what was lost. I found myself wandering the school halls, each corner steeped in memories of her laughter, the gentle way she had encouraged us to dream, to challenge ourselves. With every turn, I felt like a ghost haunting a place once filled with light and laughter. But in the midst of this darkness, my mind kept drifting back to Felix. His absence felt like an ache, a missing puzzle piece that rendered everything incomplete.

He had stopped coming to our usual hangout spots—the little coffee shop downtown where we used to laugh over steaming mugs and slices of cake, and the park bench that bore witness to countless conversations under the sprawling oak trees. Instead, I saw him lurking in the shadows, his face a mask of anguish that made my heart sink. The boys in our class exchanged worried glances, each one reflecting their concern for him, but no one dared to approach him. It was as if we were all waiting for a cue, some sign that he was ready to let us in on his pain.

One afternoon, determined not to let the distance between us grow any larger, I ventured to the spot where I last saw him—an old dilapidated shed behind the football field. It was a place we had claimed as our own, a hideaway filled with memories of laughter and secrets shared in hushed tones. As I approached, the scent of damp wood and the rustle of leaves stirred memories of simpler times, times when the world seemed full of promise rather than heartache. I pushed the door open, the creak echoing eerily in the quiet.

There he was, perched on a pile of forgotten equipment, a portrait of despair. Felix's usually vibrant blue eyes were clouded, staring out at the overgrown grass as if it held the answers to his turmoil. His shoulders were hunched, the weight of the world pressing down on him, and I felt a surge of urgency rise within me. I needed to reach him, to remind him that he didn't have to carry this burden alone.

"Felix?" My voice was soft, barely above a whisper, but it pierced the stillness.

He turned, surprise flickering across his face before it hardened again, the walls he had constructed rising even higher. "What do you want?" he snapped, the bite in his tone making my heart race.

"I just... I wanted to check on you." My own frustration simmered beneath the surface. "You've been disappearing. I'm worried."

"Worried? Or just bored?" His retort was sharp, each word a blade aimed at my heart. "You want to be the hero, don't you? Fix everything with your endless optimism."

"I'm not trying to fix anything, Felix. I just want to help." The desperation crept into my voice, and I took a step closer, my hands held up in a gesture of peace. "We're in this together. You don't have to push me away."

He sighed, the sound heavy with a mix of anger and grief. "You don't get it. You don't know what it's like to lose someone like that. To feel like you should have done something, anything, to prevent it."

"I lost someone too," I replied, my voice trembling. "Mrs. Marshall was my teacher, my mentor. She believed in me when I didn't believe in myself. I'm hurting too, Felix."

For a moment, the air crackled between us, charged with the weight of our shared grief. I could see the fight draining from him, the hardness in his eyes softening as my words settled. But just as I thought I had reached him, he recoiled, pulling away like a wounded animal.

"Hurting doesn't make it any easier," he said, his voice a low growl. "I don't want your pity."

"I'm not here to pity you!" I shot back, my frustration boiling over. "I just want to remind you that it's okay to feel angry, to feel lost. But shutting everyone out won't bring her back. We need each other now more than ever."

He faltered, his expression wavering as if he were standing on the edge of a cliff, teetering between despair and the possibility of healing. But the walls he had built were thick and strong, fortified by his determination not to show weakness. I held my breath, hoping he would step forward, that he would let me in.

"Fine," he finally muttered, his voice barely above a whisper. "But don't expect me to just—"

"I don't expect anything," I interjected, stepping closer, my heart pounding in my chest. "I'm not going anywhere."

His gaze flickered to the ground, and I could see the internal struggle etched across his features. "You don't understand how hard this is."

"Then tell me!" I urged, my voice rising with passion. "Let me in. Let me share this with you. We can find a way to remember her together, to honor everything she meant to us."

The silence stretched between us, thick and palpable. And in that moment, it felt like time had stopped, the world outside fading into oblivion. I could see the conflict within him—a desire to reach out, to connect, battling against his instinct to retreat. Finally, he let out a long, shuddering breath, his shoulders relaxing just a fraction.

"Okay," he said, the word tumbling out as if he had been holding it back for an eternity. "But it's not going to be easy."

"Nothing worth fighting for ever is," I replied, a flicker of hope igniting in my chest. "But we'll do it together."

As we sat on that old pile of forgotten dreams, the sun dipped lower in the sky, casting a golden glow over us. I could feel the warmth of his presence beside me, the walls beginning to crack, allowing a sliver of light to seep through. Perhaps, just perhaps, we could navigate this darkness together. The journey ahead would be filled with uncertainty, but with every word spoken, every shared memory, I felt the chains of grief begin to loosen, our hearts slowly stitching back together in a way that felt both fragile and fiercely resilient.

The days that followed were a cacophony of memories, laughter trapped in frames, and the specter of Mrs. Marshall's smile lurking around every corner. The sunlight pouring into the classroom felt almost sacrilegious now, its warmth a stark contrast to the chill in my bones. Felix and I had forged a tentative truce, a shared understanding that had begun to peel back the layers of our grief. Yet as we trudged through this emotional quagmire, I sensed the ground shifting beneath us. With every shared memory, every hushed conversation, a new tension bubbled to the surface, the kind that felt like it might explode at any moment.

One afternoon, as the sky turned a muted gray, mirroring the heaviness in our hearts, Felix suggested we gather our thoughts and memories of Mrs. Marshall. He wanted to compile them into something tangible, something that could honor her legacy. "Let's create a book," he said, his voice steady but his eyes betraying a flicker of vulnerability. "Something that reflects how she touched our lives."

"Like a yearbook but less... cheesy?" I offered, my heart racing at the idea of crafting something meaningful together.

He smirked, the ghost of his former self flashing across his face. "Exactly. More 'homage' and less 'senior portrait.' We can include contributions from other students. It could help—make us feel connected."

My heart warmed at the thought of channeling our grief into something constructive. "I love it. We can set up a drop box for submissions. I'll reach out to everyone."

Over the next few days, we poured ourselves into the project. Each lunch break became a strategy session, punctuated by playful banter and occasional silence as we dug deep into our memories. We swapped stories about Mrs. Marshall, each anecdote serving as both balm and dagger to our wounded hearts. The way she danced around the classroom when she got excited about a literary debate, or how she made us feel seen, even on our worst days. With every word we shared, I could feel the distance between us closing, a bridge formed through shared sorrow and purpose.

Yet as our collaboration flourished, I couldn't shake the sense that something unspoken lingered in the air. Felix was more present than ever, yet shadows flickered in his eyes—moments where grief would overtake him, and I could see him retreating behind that familiar wall. I often wondered if I was strong enough to pull him from the depths of despair without drowning myself in the process.

One afternoon, as we sat in the old shed, surrounded by crumpled papers and the remnants of our brainstorming, Felix leaned back against the wall, his expression distant. "What if this doesn't change anything?" he murmured, staring up at the peeling paint. "What if we just end up like everyone else—mourners who forget?"

"Maybe it's not about changing anything," I replied, searching for the right words. "Maybe it's about remembering. It's about honoring her in a way that keeps her alive in our hearts. And if we can help others through their grief... well, that's a legacy worth fighting for."

He turned his head to meet my gaze, a hint of something softer flickering in his eyes. "I guess you're right. But what if it's not enough?"

My heart clenched at his uncertainty, and I reached for his hand, intertwining my fingers with his, hoping to convey the strength I felt bubbling inside me. "We'll make it enough. Together. We're not alone in this."

But just as I felt a connection reigniting, the door creaked open, and there stood Anna, a look of urgency etched on her face. "You two need to see this. It's important."

Felix and I exchanged puzzled glances as we followed Anna outside, our hearts racing with curiosity. The wind whipped through the trees, the scent of impending rain hanging heavy in the air. Anna led us toward the main building, her footsteps quickening as she whispered, "I overheard something that you both need to know."

We rounded the corner and found a small group of students huddled around a cell phone, their expressions a mix of shock and disbelief. The screen flickered with images of a local news report, the anchor's voice barely audible over the murmurs. "...investigation ongoing into the tragic accident that claimed the life of beloved teacher Caroline Marshall..."

"What is this?" I breathed, straining to see the screen.

Anna pulled me closer, her voice urgent. "There are rumors... some people think it wasn't an accident."

A chill swept through me, the warmth of the sun retreating as if it could sense the tension brewing. Felix's grip tightened around my hand as we exchanged uneasy glances. "What do you mean?" he asked, his voice low and guarded.

"Someone saw a car following her that night," Anna explained, her eyes darting nervously. "They think it might have been intentional."

My heart raced, a mixture of disbelief and anger bubbling to the surface. "That's insane! Why would anyone want to hurt Mrs. Marshall?"

"I don't know," Anna admitted, her voice trembling. "But you know how small towns can be. Rumors spread like wildfire."

Felix stepped forward, determination etched into his features. "We need to find out the truth. If there's even a chance this was deliberate... we can't just sit back and let it go."

"Are you serious?" Anna's voice cracked. "What if it puts you in danger?"

"Better to know than live in ignorance," he replied, his gaze steady and unwavering. "We owe it to her. We owe it to ourselves."

As I stood between them, torn between fear and a fierce sense of duty, I realized this was more than just a quest for answers; it was a fight to reclaim our agency in a world that had turned upside down. The darkness that had threatened to consume us now took on a new shape—an adversary that required us to confront not only our grief but the potential betrayal that lay beneath the surface.

With every step toward the truth, I felt the weight of uncertainty pressing down, but also a flicker of hope igniting within me. Together, we would uncover the secrets hidden beneath the layers of loss, risking everything to honor Mrs. Marshall's memory. And as we plunged into the unknown, the chill in the air deepened, leaving us to wonder just how far we were willing to go and what we might uncover in the shadows.

As the first drops of rain began to fall, I felt the world shift again, the storm brewing not just overhead but within us. In that moment, I knew we were standing on the brink of something far greater than grief, a reckoning that could unravel everything we thought we understood. The question loomed large: Were we ready to confront the ghosts of our past, and what would we find when we did?

Chapter 10: Whispers of Grief

The funeral unfolds like a muted symphony, each note heavy with the weight of our collective grief. The crowd gathers beneath a sky the color of ash, the trees standing as solemn witnesses to the heartache that ripples through the air. I stand beside Felix, our shoulders almost touching but our hands stubbornly refusing to meet. There's a comfort in this closeness, an unspoken understanding that flows between us like the gentle pull of an undertow. I glance sideways, stealing a look at him; his eyes, usually bright and mischievous, are now clouded, darkened by the sorrow of loss. It's as if someone has snuffed out his inner light, leaving only a hollow ache behind.

Around us, the school community has gathered, a tapestry of familiar faces stitched together by shared experiences and memories of our beloved teacher, Mrs. Hawthorne. Each person clutches a white lily, a symbol of purity and renewal, though the flowers only seem to deepen the pallor of the day. The soft rustle of leaves whispers secrets of the past, while the air hangs heavy with the fragrance of blooming jasmine, a bittersweet reminder of the beauty that can still exist amidst the pain. The warmth of the sun, usually so inviting, feels cold and distant today, a mere spectator to our mourning.

As the first speaker steps up to the podium, a hush descends over the crowd. I can see the tremor in his hands, the way he clutches the edges of the podium as if it were a lifeline. His voice wavers at first, but as he begins to recount his memories of Mrs. Hawthorne, it gains strength. He shares stories of her laughter, her unyielding belief in us, her ability to see the potential in each of her students. I feel tears prick at the corners of my eyes, a visceral reminder of how fragile life truly is, and the realization that even the most vibrant spirits can be extinguished.

When Felix finally speaks, his voice is a soft murmur, almost drowned out by the gentle breeze that stirs the leaves. "She taught me that kindness is a strength," he says, and I can hear the rawness in his tone, the quiver that betrays his composed facade. "She showed us that our stories mattered." I want to reach for him, to squeeze his hand and remind him that he's not alone in this, but instead, I remain rooted to the spot, fighting my own rising tide of emotion. The weight of his grief presses against me, a palpable force that threatens to swallow us whole.

The speeches continue, each one a tribute, a slice of remembrance that slices deeper than the last. With every story shared, I catch glimpses of the woman who shaped so many lives—her infectious laughter, her fierce loyalty, and the way she could turn a mundane lesson into an adventure. I can almost see her in the crowd, nodding approvingly as we honor her memory. But this isn't just about remembering; it's about the aching void she has left behind. I can feel it in the collective sighs, the way shoulders sag with the weight of loss, the way laughter feels out of place today.

As the sun begins to dip lower in the sky, casting elongated shadows that dance mournfully across the ground, I turn to Felix. "You okay?" My voice is barely a whisper, and I hope he can hear the sincerity beneath my words. He nods slowly, his expression a mixture of gratitude and despair. "It's just... hard to think she's really gone, you know?"

I nod, unable to find the right words. It feels like an insurmountable chasm has opened between us and our past, one that will take time—and perhaps courage—to bridge. "I get it," I say finally. "It feels like a part of us is missing."

He meets my gaze, and for a moment, the world around us fades into the background. I can see the flicker of understanding in his eyes, the way we're both searching for something—answers, solace, hope. The crowd disperses as the final speech concludes, leaving behind a lingering echo of sorrow. People drift away, some offering hugs, others sharing quiet words of comfort, but we remain, two figures ensnared in a moment that feels suspended in time.

In the silence that follows, I can hear the distant sound of laughter from a group of children playing in the park nearby. It's a stark contrast to the weight we carry, yet I find it oddly comforting, a reminder that life goes on despite the heartache. Felix takes a deep breath, and I can see the tension in his shoulders ease, if only slightly.

"I wish I could just... talk to her one more time," he says, his voice breaking. There's a vulnerability in his admission, a raw honesty that makes my heart ache for him. I can feel the tears pooling in my own eyes, the desire to mend his broken spirit swirling within me.

"We could," I say suddenly, the words spilling out before I can second-guess myself. "We could visit her favorite spot—where she always took us for field trips. Maybe... maybe we can feel her there."

Felix's eyes brighten slightly, the glimmer of hope cutting through the cloud of grief that clings to him. "You mean the old oak tree by the river?"

"Yeah," I reply, feeling a surge of determination. "It's where she taught us to appreciate the little things—like how to find joy in the simplest moments."

His smile is small but genuine, and for the first time today, I feel a flicker of warmth between us. I know this journey won't be easy, but together, we might just find a way to carry her memory forward, to honor the light she brought into our lives even as we navigate this profound loss.

The oak tree stands as a silent guardian, its ancient branches stretching wide like open arms, welcoming us into its shaded embrace. I can almost hear Mrs. Hawthorne's laughter mingling with the rustle of the leaves, a sweet melody that reminds me of sunny afternoons spent beneath this very tree. I glance at Felix, who lingers a few steps behind, his hands shoved deep into the pockets of his well-worn jeans. He looks like he's trying to shrink away from the world, the way his shoulders hunch slightly and his gaze stays glued to the ground. I can feel the heaviness in the air, thick enough to suffocate, yet I know we need to be here.

"Want to race to the trunk?" I challenge, my voice breaking the stillness like a pebble tossed into a pond. It's a desperate attempt to draw him out, to coax a hint of that infectious grin from him, but he merely raises an eyebrow, his expression an uneasy mix of skepticism and intrigue.

"Isn't that a bit childish?" he replies, a smirk tugging at the corners of his lips. There's the Felix I know, the one who can banter with me as easily as breathing.

"Childish? Maybe. But we're here to remember her, right? And she always said a little laughter goes a long way." I start jogging toward the massive trunk, the sun filtering through the leaves, casting dappled shadows on the ground. It feels like the right thing to do, to bring a sliver of joy back into this day.

With an exasperated chuckle, Felix takes off after me. I can hear him gaining ground, his feet pounding against the earth, a rhythm that matches the wild thump of my heart. Just as I reach the trunk, I turn and spin around, arms flung wide in triumph. "Ha! I win!"

"Barely," he retorts, panting slightly as he leans against the trunk for support. There's a spark in his eyes now, a flicker of life that makes me want to cheer like a child on a playground. "If we're keeping score, you should know I let you win."

"Right, right," I tease, rolling my eyes. "Because nothing screams victory like letting the other person win on the day they're grieving." He smirks, and for a moment, it feels like we've stepped out of the shadow of sorrow, just a bit.

"Okay, so maybe you did earn it. You're the competitive type," he admits, pushing off the tree to stand straighter, the shadows of grief beginning to lighten. "But what's the plan now, oh great strategist?"

I take a deep breath, the familiar scent of earth and bark wrapping around me like a warm blanket. "Let's sit for a bit and share our favorite memories. Maybe it'll remind us why we loved her so much." I find a spot on the grass, the blades tickling my ankles as I settle in. Felix follows suit, sitting cross-legged beside me.

"Alright, I'll go first," I say, letting the memories wash over me. "Remember that time she brought in those terrible homemade cookies for our class party? I swear, they were more like edible hockey pucks than actual treats."

Felix laughs, and the sound is like a balm to my soul. "And we all pretended to love them, even though they were so hard we could've used them for self-defense. I think I chipped a tooth."

"And then she made a big deal about how she spent all night baking," I add, chuckling. "She was so proud, and we all just smiled and nodded like it was the best thing we'd ever tasted."

Our laughter melds with the gentle rustling of leaves, and for a moment, I can feel the heaviness in my heart start to lift. "Your turn," I say, nudging him playfully.

Felix's expression shifts, the humor fading slightly. "Okay, I'll try. There was that day in class when she wore that awful sun hat, you know, the one with the giant daisies? She thought it was the latest trend, but we all couldn't stop laughing."

I nod vigorously. "And she wore it with such confidence, like she was ready to walk the runway. I remember thinking that if she could rock that hat, then we could face anything."

"Exactly! And she just laughed with us, like she was in on the joke." His eyes shine with fondness. "It's funny how she could make us feel so comfortable being ourselves, even when we were being ridiculous."

"Ridiculous is an understatement," I reply, my tone light. "She was a master at making us feel special, no matter how silly we got.

I still remember the way her eyes sparkled when she talked about literature. It was like she was inviting us into a whole new world."

Felix nods, a soft smile on his lips as we both become immersed in our shared memories. "She really was a wizard at that. I often think back to those lessons, how she would take us on imaginary journeys through the pages of those books. It felt like we were living the stories instead of just reading them."

"And now we're left with a whole library of memories," I say, my heart swelling with both joy and sorrow. "But it feels like a weight, too, doesn't it? Like we have to carry those stories and do something with them."

Felix meets my gaze, and the air between us thickens with understanding. "You're right. It's almost like a responsibility. We need to honor her legacy, keep her spirit alive."

Suddenly, a playful breeze whirls around us, carrying the scent of fresh earth and fading blooms. I smile, an idea sparking in my mind. "What if we started a club? A book club or something? We could read her favorite books, share them with others, and maybe invite new students to join. It could be a way to remember her and keep her spirit alive."

"Now that's an idea," Felix replies, the gleam in his eyes igniting with enthusiasm. "We could even host events, like writing workshops or storytelling sessions. It could be a safe space, just like she created for us."

"I love it!" I exclaim, excitement bubbling inside me. "We could call it 'Hawthorne's Haven' or something cheesy like that. It sounds so inviting and warm, just like she was."

"Cheesy can be good," he counters, a smirk dancing on his lips. "And I'm all in. We'll make sure her memory lives on in every book we read and every story we share."

With that simple vow, a flicker of hope ignites within me, mingling with the grief that still lingers. We might be navigating a world marked by loss, but together, we can transform that pain into something beautiful, something that honors the woman who believed in us. In this shared venture, I see a future where joy and sorrow coexist, and where every laugh can pierce through the shadows, reminding us that even in grief, there can be light.

The idea of starting a book club blooms between us like the flowers we laid at Mrs. Hawthorne's grave, vibrant and full of promise. We sit in the soft shadows beneath the oak, the weight of our grief slowly morphing into a mission, an endeavor that feels both daunting and exhilarating. Felix leans back against the rough bark of the tree, his expression thoughtful, as if he's weighing the potential of our idea.

"What if we don't get enough people to join?" he muses, biting his lip. "What if we end up sitting here reading to ourselves, just you and me?"

"Then we'll have a two-person book club," I reply with a grin. "We can call it 'The Dynamic Duo of Literary Shenanigans.' Just think of the snacks we could devour while dissecting our favorite characters."

"Now you're talking," he chuckles, his voice lightening. "I'm all in for the snacks. Just promise me no more of those hockey puck cookies."

I laugh, picturing Mrs. Hawthorne's face, full of pride as she watched us struggle to chew through her latest baking fiasco. "Deal! No more questionable baking experiments. But I can't make any promises about the weird drinks. You know how she loved to experiment with those, too."

The conversation flows easily, like the gentle breeze that sways the branches above us. We begin sketching out our plans for the book club, tossing ideas back and forth like a game of catch. What if we included a community service aspect? Perhaps we could raise funds to purchase books for the school library or host storytelling nights for younger kids.

As the sun dips lower in the sky, the golden light transforms the world around us, illuminating the path forward. "We could even create a scholarship in her name," Felix suggests, his voice rising with enthusiasm. "Something to support students pursuing literature or education."

"That's a brilliant idea," I respond, my heart swelling with pride for him. "It could help others feel the same way she made us feel."

Just as I'm about to suggest we pick a date for our first meeting, my phone buzzes, cutting through the moment like a sudden clap of thunder. I pull it from my pocket, glancing at the screen. It's a text from a number I don't recognize.

"Who is it?" Felix asks, his brow furrowing as he leans closer.

"It's… I don't know," I reply, the text blinking at me, cryptic and unsettling. "It just says, 'We need to talk. About Mrs. Hawthorne.'"

"Sounds ominous," he replies, the playfulness in his voice dissipating like smoke in the wind. "What do you think it means?"

"I have no idea," I admit, my pulse quickening. "Maybe it's someone who knew her better than we did? Or…" I trail off, the words slipping away as uncertainty settles over me.

"Or what?" Felix presses, leaning in closer, his eyes wide with curiosity.

"Or maybe it's someone who knows something we don't," I finish, a chill running down my spine. The warmth of the afternoon feels suddenly distant, the shadows of the trees lengthening like fingers reaching toward us.

Felix's expression shifts, concern etching lines into his brow. "Do you think it's about her death?"

I shake my head, trying to dispel the uneasy feeling that knots in my stomach. "I don't know, but we can't ignore it. We should meet whoever it is."

Felix nods slowly, and I can see the gears turning in his mind. "Where do you want to meet them?"

"Let's suggest the café down the street," I say, my heart racing. "It's public, and there will be people around. I'd rather not have this conversation alone."

"Agreed. Safety first," he replies, his tone serious now. "And we can always make a hasty exit if things get weird."

"Like you know how to be subtle?" I tease lightly, trying to ease the tension that crackles between us. "I've seen you run from a harmless spider."

"Hey, those things are terrifying!" He grins, but the laughter doesn't quite reach his eyes.

We spend the next few minutes drafting a response, my fingers trembling as I type, a mix of excitement and dread swirling within me. Finally, we hit send, the message flying off into the digital void, leaving us in a heavy silence.

"What if they don't respond?" Felix asks, his voice low. "What if this is all just a prank?"

"Then we'll chalk it up to bad luck and go back to our plans for 'Hawthorne's Haven,'" I say, forcing a smile. "No harm done."

But as I speak the words, a gnawing anxiety settles in my gut. What if it isn't a prank? What if someone truly had information about Mrs. Hawthorne? The possibilities twist around my mind, dark and dangerous.

Moments stretch into an eternity as we wait, the shadows growing longer, the light fading into a muted twilight. Just as I start to feel the weight of uncertainty settle in my chest, my phone buzzes again.

"Speak of the devil," I murmur, glancing down at the screen. It's a reply from the mysterious number. "Meet me at the oak tree tomorrow at noon. I'll tell you everything."

"What do you think?" Felix asks, his tone cautious.

"I think we're diving headfirst into something we might not be prepared for," I reply, the hairs on my arms prickling with unease. "But I can't ignore it, Felix. I need to know."

Felix shifts beside me, a sense of determination washing over his features. "We're in this together. Whatever it is, we'll figure it out."

The darkness creeps in as the sun sinks below the horizon, painting the sky with deep purples and blues, but a different kind of darkness looms ahead of us. I stare at the message, the weight of it heavy in the air, feeling a pull toward the unknown. "Tomorrow, then," I whisper, a mix of excitement and dread bubbling inside me.

As we rise to leave, the oak tree stands behind us, a silent witness to our decision. With each step away, the world around us feels charged with anticipation, like the calm before a storm. The gravity of what awaits us tomorrow presses down, a ticking clock counting down to an uncertain revelation. In that moment, I can't shake the feeling that something profound is about to unfold, a secret lying just beneath the surface, waiting for us to uncover it. And as I take one last glance back at the tree, a single question echoes in my mind: What truths lie hidden in the whispers of grief?

Chapter 11: Bridges Burned

The jazz club, once a sanctuary of laughter and warmth, now reverberates with a haunting emptiness. Shadows dance across the worn wooden floor, and the dim light flickers like the last ember of a dying flame. The rich scent of bourbon and bitters hangs in the air, but the usual melody of brass and bass has been replaced by the sorrowful echo of a lone saxophone. It was a place where Felix and I had woven dreams together, those dreams now unraveling like the frayed edges of an old tapestry. I glance at the stage, where a musician plays a sorrowful tune, his fingers gliding over the keys with a melancholy grace. The notes hang in the air, thick and heavy, like the unsaid words between Felix and me.

With every day that passes, Felix retreats further into himself, and I feel like I'm chasing after a ghost. Our once vibrant conversations have faded into the backdrop of his silence. I can't shake the feeling of helplessness that clings to me like the remnants of last night's perfume, sweet but suffocating. I pull out my phone yet again, my fingers hovering over the screen, hesitating before sending another message. I remind myself to be patient, to give him space. But my resolve crumbles as each unreturned text digs deeper, like a splinter embedded in my heart.

"Hey," I type, trying to sound casual despite the storm brewing inside me. "I miss you. The club feels different without your laughter." I press send, the message flying into the void, landing softly without a trace. Moments tick by, stretching into an agonizing silence. I take a sip of my drink, the sharp tang of gin hitting my tongue like a bitter reminder of what we once shared. The bartender glances my way, his eyes filled with unasked questions. I can only offer a weak smile, one that doesn't reach my eyes.

The silence drags on, heavy and oppressive, and frustration bubbles up within me, boiling over like a pot left too long on the stove. My hands tremble slightly as I fire off another message, one laced with all the unspoken fears and doubts that have been simmering beneath the surface. "Are we even still a thing? Do you even care about us anymore?" I hit send, immediately regretting the sharpness of my words but feeling a sense of relief wash over me. It's out there now, the question hanging in the air, a raw confession of my insecurities.

The seconds turn into minutes, and then an hour passes. I stare at my phone, willing it to buzz, to light up with some sign of life from Felix. But the screen remains dark, a stark reflection of the distance that has grown between us. I drown my frustration in another sip of gin, but it does little to quell the storm inside me. I glance around the club, noting the couples nestled in corners, their laughter ringing out like music, a cruel reminder of what I once had.

In the back of my mind, I hear the whispers of my friends—well-meaning but often misguided. "Give him time," they said. "He'll come around." But the truth is, I can't just sit back and wait. I feel like a moth drawn to a flame, desperate to connect but terrified of getting burned. I decide to head outside for some air, hoping that the cool breeze might temper the heat of my emotions.

Stepping into the night, I'm greeted by the crispness of autumn, the air sharp and invigorating. The moon hangs high, casting a silvery glow over the cobblestone streets, illuminating the path ahead but also highlighting the shadows lurking behind me. As I walk, I let my thoughts spiral. What if this is it? What if I've pushed him too far away, and there's no way back? I shake my head, trying to dispel the darkness that creeps into my mind.

Suddenly, I hear footsteps behind me. I turn, heart racing, hoping against hope that it's Felix. But it's just a couple strolling hand in hand, their laughter echoing through the night. I feel a pang of envy, a deep yearning for the closeness we once had. In that moment, I realize that I don't just miss Felix; I miss us—the electric connection, the way we lit up the room together.

I glance at my phone again, half-expecting a message, but there's still nothing. Anger and hurt swirl inside me, a tempest of emotions threatening to overflow. I reach a quiet corner of the street, away from the chaos of the club, and lean against the cool stone wall. My thoughts race, grappling with the reality that I might be losing him, the one person who truly understood me. I take a deep breath, willing myself to calm down.

Just then, my phone buzzes in my pocket. I pull it out, my heart racing as I see Felix's name light up the screen. I open the message eagerly, but my heart sinks as I read his words, simple and detached: "I need some time. I'll reach out when I can." I stare at the screen, feeling the sting of rejection and the weight of his distance crushing me. The night feels darker now, the moon obscured by clouds as I struggle to hold back the tears that threaten to spill.

As I look up at the sky, I can almost hear the echoes of our laughter, the sweet melodies we once shared. The world feels heavy, and I wonder if our bridges have been irrevocably burned, leaving only ashes in their wake.

The next morning dawns with a muted light filtering through the curtains, casting a soft glow on my cluttered apartment. I sit up in bed, the remnants of last night's anguish clinging to me like an unwelcome blanket. The realization that I've unleashed my frustrations on Felix hangs heavily in the air. My phone lies on the bedside table, still silent, a mocking reminder of the disconnect that has grown between us. I reach for it, fingers trembling slightly, half-hoping to find a message from him—anything that might bridge the widening gulf—but the screen remains blank.

With a resigned sigh, I swing my legs over the side of the bed, feeling the cool floor beneath my feet. The city outside is alive, the sounds of honking horns and distant chatter spilling through the window. I step into the kitchen and pour myself a cup of coffee, its warmth seeping into my hands, but even the rich aroma can't chase away the bitterness that lingers in my heart. The café down the street has always been our go-to, a little haven where we would lose track of time over steaming cups and shared pastries. Now, it feels like a battleground of memories, tainted by the weight of unspoken words.

I need to clear my head, to break free from this spiral of despair, so I decide to take a walk. The streets are buzzing with life as I meander through the city, the early autumn air crisp and invigorating. I watch as people bustle about, lost in their own worlds, and envy stirs within me. Each couple I pass holds hands, each burst of laughter feels like a reminder of what I'm missing. I turn a corner and find myself at the park where Felix and I once shared long, lazy afternoons, discussing everything and nothing.

Settling onto a bench, I pull out my phone again, scrolling through our old messages, each one a little time capsule of happiness and hope. But scrolling through the snapshots of our past only deepens the ache in my chest. Suddenly, a small, scruffy dog bounds over, its tail wagging furiously as it approaches me with the enthusiasm of a tornado. I can't help but laugh, the pure joy radiating from the little creature lifting my spirits, if only slightly.

"Hey there, buddy!" I crouch down, offering my hand, and the dog sniffs it enthusiastically before plopping down beside me. A woman jogs over, breathless but smiling. "Sorry about that! He's just a ball of energy," she says, her hair bouncing with each step.

"No need to apologize. I think he's just what I needed," I reply, scratching behind the dog's ears.

The woman sits on the opposite side of the bench, watching the dog as he rolls over, begging for belly rubs. "I know what you mean. Sometimes a little furball can make everything seem better."

I nod, grateful for the moment of camaraderie. "I could use a bit of sunshine today. My... well, my boyfriend has been a bit distant lately."

"Boyfriend?" she asks, tilting her head, her expression shifting to one of curiosity. "Is he always like this? Or is something bothering him?"

I hesitate, unsure how much to share with a stranger. "It's complicated. He's been going through something, and I'm not sure how to reach him."

"Men can be like that—especially when they're in their own heads," she says, rolling her eyes playfully. "Sometimes they need a little nudge. Or a good kick in the pants."

I chuckle, the tension in my shoulders easing slightly. "I think I might have given him the kick he needed last night."

"Oh no! What did you say?" she asks, leaning in, her eyes wide with interest.

I take a breath, feeling the need to unburden myself to someone. "I sent him a message that probably came off a little strong. I asked if he even cared about us anymore."

Her expression shifts to one of sympathy. "Yikes. That's rough. But you know, maybe it's what he needs to hear. Sometimes the truth hurts, but it can also wake someone up."

"You think so?" I ask, feeling a flicker of hope.

"Absolutely. Just remember, communication is key. And if he really cares, he'll appreciate your honesty."

We chat for a little longer, sharing our stories and laughing at the absurdities of life. As I listen to her, I feel a renewed sense of determination. Maybe I can't control how Felix responds, but I can control how I express my feelings.

As our conversation winds down, I thank her for the unexpected boost. "It's funny how a small encounter can change your perspective."

"Exactly! And don't forget to take care of yourself, too. It's easy to lose yourself in someone else's struggles."

With that, I stand up, feeling lighter, as if I've shed some of the weight I've been carrying. I head back home, the dog's joyful barks echoing in my mind, reminding me that even in tough times, there can be moments of brightness.

Once back, I pull out my laptop and start typing, pouring my feelings into a message to Felix. I don't want to accuse or blame; I want to share how I feel while inviting him back into the fold without pressure. I tell him I understand he's going through a lot and that I'm here, waiting for him to reach out when he's ready.

After hitting send, a wave of relief washes over me, but the uncertainty still gnaws at my insides. What if he doesn't reply? I lean back in my chair, eyes drifting to the window. The sun is setting, casting a warm golden hue over the city, illuminating the world in a soft glow.

Just then, my phone vibrates, and I lunge for it, heart pounding. Felix's name flashes on the screen, and my breath catches. I take a moment to steady myself, then open the message.

"Can we talk later? I think we need to."

I stare at the words, a mix of relief and apprehension swirling inside me. There's still hope, still a chance to rebuild what's been broken. The evening air feels charged with possibilities, and for the first time in days, I dare to believe that perhaps we can find our way back to each other.

The sun dipped low on the horizon, casting a warm, golden hue across the city, but it did little to ease the chill that had settled in my chest. The message from Felix lingered in my mind, a faint glimmer of hope amidst a storm of uncertainty. "Can we talk later? I think we need to." I kept replaying it, as if hoping to unravel the meaning behind those few words, but clarity remained elusive.

I paced my small apartment, the floor creaking beneath my feet, feeling as restless as a caged bird. My heart raced at the thought of our impending conversation, and I wondered what he might say. Was he ready to face the truth? Or would he retreat even further into himself? The quiet hum of the city outside seemed to mock my anxiety, a reminder that life continued, unfazed by my internal chaos.

As evening set in, I tried to distract myself with a movie, the familiar comfort of a romantic comedy serving as a flimsy bandage over my nerves. But even the most ridiculous plot twists failed to draw my attention. My mind kept drifting back to Felix, his absence heavy like a stone in my gut. I glanced at the clock, the minutes dragging on as I awaited his call. Each tick felt like a countdown, amplifying the tension that crackled in the air.

When my phone finally buzzed, I nearly dropped it in my haste to answer. "Felix?" I said, unable to keep the hope from my voice.

"Hey, it's me," he replied, his voice sounding far away, as if he were speaking from a different world.

I took a deep breath, grounding myself. "I'm glad you called. I… I've been worried about you."

"I know." He paused, and the silence stretched between us, thick and heavy. "I've been doing a lot of thinking."

"Good thinking or bad thinking?" I asked, trying to lighten the mood, but my heart raced, unsure how he would respond.

"Complicated thinking." His voice was laced with exhaustion, and I could picture him running a hand through his hair, a familiar gesture that always made my stomach flutter. "I've been trying to process everything that's happened. I feel like I'm in a fog."

"Then let's clear the air. Please, tell me what you're feeling," I urged, sensing that we were standing at the precipice of something significant.

He took a long breath before speaking again. "I've been hiding from everything, from you. It's easier to just dive into music than to deal with the mess in my head."

"That's understandable," I replied, my voice softer now. "But shutting me out only makes it harder for both of us. You don't have to go through this alone."

"I just don't know how to face it," he admitted, his vulnerability evident. "There are parts of my life that I've kept hidden, even from myself. I thought I could handle it, but... maybe I can't."

"What do you mean?" I asked, my pulse quickening as I tried to piece together the fragments of his turmoil.

"There are things about my past, things I've never told you. It feels like a weight I've carried for too long, and it's suffocating me."

"Felix, you can share anything with me. I promise I won't judge," I said, desperation creeping into my voice. "We're a team, remember?"

He chuckled softly, but it was tinged with sadness. "I remember. But sometimes, teams can't handle the truth. What if it changes everything between us?"

"Maybe it will," I admitted, "but isn't that better than living in this limbo? You deserve to be free of whatever's holding you back."

There was a long pause on the other end, and my heart sank, wondering if I had pushed too hard. "I don't want to hurt you, but... I think I owe it to you to be honest."

"Then please, just tell me."

I could almost hear him steeling himself, the rustle of fabric as he shifted. "When I was younger, I made some choices—bad choices. Choices that I thought I had moved on from, but they keep creeping back. I thought I could escape them through music and the new life I built, but it turns out they're always lurking, waiting to pull me back down."

"Felix, you're not that person anymore. We all make mistakes," I said, my heart aching for him. "It doesn't define who you are now."

"I wish I could believe that," he said, a tremor in his voice. "But what if I'm still that person underneath? What if I hurt you, too?"

My breath caught in my throat. "You won't. I trust you."

"Trust is fragile, isn't it?" he murmured. "What if I break it? What if I ruin everything we have?"

The weight of his words hung in the air, an unsteady balance on a tightrope stretched between us. "Then we'll figure it out together. I'd rather face the fallout than stay in this silence."

"Okay." His voice was barely above a whisper, a tremor of hope flickering amidst the darkness. "I think it's time I share the truth. But you have to promise me something."

"Anything."

"Promise me you won't turn away. No matter how difficult this is."

"I promise."

"Alright," he said, taking a deep breath. "It all started years ago when I was part of a band—a different band, before everything changed. We were reckless, chasing fame and fortune, but we were also doing things we shouldn't have. There was a night... a really bad night. We got involved with the wrong people, and it spiraled out of control. I was scared and angry and... I didn't handle it well."

My heart raced as I listened, the urgency of his words cutting through the static of uncertainty. "What happened?"

"There was an accident," he continued, his voice shaking. "Someone got hurt. And I was there. I didn't pull them back when I should have, and..."

His voice faltered, a crack in the facade he had built. "It changed everything. I was terrified, and I ran away. I thought I could escape the consequences by burying it deep down. I thought if I didn't talk about it, it wouldn't haunt me anymore."

"Felix, you can't keep carrying this alone," I urged, my heart aching for him. "You've already been through so much."

"But it's not just my burden to bear. It affects you, too," he insisted. "I don't want to drag you into my mess."

"I'm already in it, Felix. We're in this together."

"Maybe it's too late for us," he murmured, and my heart sank.

"Don't say that!" I exclaimed, fear flooding through me. "We can work through this. You're not the same person you were then. You've grown."

He fell silent, and the weight of his words loomed in the air. Just then, my phone buzzed again, the sound startling us both. I glanced down, my heart racing as I saw a message flash on the screen.

"Wait, I need to—"

But before I could read it, Felix's voice cut through the tension. "I need to tell you something else. Something I've never shared with anyone."

I froze, caught between his revelation and the mysterious message that lingered at the edge of my vision. "What is it?"

"Remember that night? The accident? It wasn't just an accident. I—"

The phone buzzed again, a relentless reminder of whatever news awaited me. My heart thudded wildly in my chest, torn between the past and the present, between Felix's haunting confession and the weight of the unknown.

"Felix, wait—"

But his voice was drowned out by the blaring sound of a siren echoing through the city, an ominous wail that wrapped around my thoughts, and then I looked down at my phone, reading the message that made everything feel like it was spiraling out of control.

"Are you still with him? We need to talk. Now."

In that instant, the world shifted, and I realized that I was standing at a crossroads, teetering on the edge of chaos, unsure which path to take.

Chapter 12: A Fragmented Melody

The music throbbed around me, a living entity pulsing with energy that felt both familiar and foreign. I pressed my back against the damp, cool brick wall of the club, watching as Felix poured himself into a performance that was no longer mine. The crowd swayed in a haze of blue light, entranced by his voice, a rich baritone that seemed to reverberate from deep within his soul. I had spent countless nights dreaming of this moment, but now, as I stood in the shadows, a storm brewed in my chest, turning anticipation into bitter resentment.

The room filled with the scent of cheap beer and the sharp tang of sweat, mingling in the air like a bitter cocktail. I could feel the beat of the bass in my bones, each thud echoing the tumult in my heart. His guitar, once a bridge between us, now felt like a barricade. Each note he struck, each lyric he belted out, cut deeper than I had anticipated. It was supposed to be our dream—our music, our shared passion—but there he was, under the spotlight, radiating charm and charisma, while I lurked in the dark like a specter of jealousy.

I clenched my fists at my sides, my nails digging into my palms as I fought against the wave of betrayal threatening to engulf me. How could he do this? How could he share his gift with strangers, without me by his side? I had always imagined us on that stage together, the crowd roaring in appreciation as we lost ourselves in a shared melody. But tonight, the music was a dagger aimed at my heart, each cheer from the audience a cruel reminder of the bond I felt slipping away.

Felix's eyes sparkled as he engaged with the crowd, and I felt a rush of heat to my cheeks. I wanted to scream out his name, to shatter the illusion that he was still mine, but the words stuck in my throat like an unyielding lump of despair. I glanced around the dimly lit room, noting how people laughed and danced, completely absorbed in the moment, while I felt like an interloper in my own life.

As the final chords reverberated through the air, the audience erupted into applause, and I turned on my heel, the sharp edges of my emotions threatening to overwhelm me. I navigated through the crowd, dodging the smiling faces and carefree laughter, until I found myself outside in the brisk night air. The cool breeze did little to soothe the fire in my veins, and I leaned against the rough brick of the building, gasping for breath.

Moments later, the door swung open, and Felix stepped out, his hair tousled, a wild grin plastered across his face. The sight of him ignited the anger I had been trying to suppress. "Hey!" he called, his voice laced with genuine surprise. "What are you doing here?"

"What am I doing here?" I shot back, crossing my arms tightly against my chest as if I could physically hold back the flood of emotions ready to spill over. "I came to support you, Felix. But I see that you don't need me anymore."

His expression shifted, confusion mingling with the remnants of his earlier elation. "What are you talking about? You know I want you with me."

"Really?" I challenged, stepping closer, the space between us charged with unspoken tension. "Because it certainly doesn't seem that way. You've been performing without me, like I'm just some footnote in your story."

He took a step back, running a hand through his hair in that frustrated way that always made my heart twist. "I had to. I thought you were busy with your own projects, and I didn't want to wait for you to catch up."

The air thickened between us, and I could hear the words forming in my mind, each one sharper than the last. "So you just decided to move on without me? To forget that we had a plan?"

Felix's face darkened, and for a moment, the playful artist I loved vanished, replaced by someone more serious and defiant. "You think I wanted to do this alone? I thought I was doing what's best for both of us. You've been so preoccupied with your own music. I didn't want to push you, but I also can't just sit around and wait forever."

"I was trying to find my voice," I said, the hurt spilling over as I crossed my arms tighter, the physical barrier mirroring the emotional distance I felt. "And you didn't even bother to tell me you were playing gigs without me."

"Because I didn't want to fight! Every time we talk about music, it ends up in an argument," he countered, his voice rising, frustration mingling with desperation. "I thought this was what you wanted! To focus on your own career. It feels like you're mad at me for being successful, but I'm just trying to carve out a place for us in this world."

"Us?" I echoed, incredulity washing over me. "You mean 'you,' right? Because it feels like you've left me behind in all of this. You're shining so bright, and I'm left in your shadow."

The silence that followed felt heavy and suffocating, filled with all the things we had never said but had always felt. I could see the wheels turning in his mind as he struggled to find the right words, but none seemed to surface. Finally, he took a deep breath, and the moment hung in the air, pregnant with unresolved feelings.

"I didn't mean to push you away," he said finally, softer now, the edge in his voice replaced by something more vulnerable. "I just thought… I thought you would be proud of me."

My heart ached at the admission, the tenderness cutting through the anger like sunlight through clouds. "I am proud, Felix," I confessed, my voice barely above a whisper. "But I can't help feeling like I've been left behind."

He stepped closer, the warmth radiating from his body igniting the embers of our connection. "Then let's fix this. We can make it work. I need you in my life, on that stage, making music together. I miss you."

The sincerity in his eyes pulled me closer, tempting me to take a step forward. But the weight of our argument still hung like a shroud, thickening the air between us. I wanted to believe him, to trust that we could bridge this chasm that had opened up between us. But as I stood there, torn between my anger and the warmth of his presence, I couldn't help but wonder if we could truly find our way back to each other.

The night air wrapped around us, thick and electrifying, while I wrestled with the warmth radiating from Felix, the familiar scent of his cologne mixing with the crispness of the evening. My heart danced between longing and frustration, a peculiar rhythm that felt foreign in this moment of confrontation. The way he looked at me, eyes glimmering with uncertainty and hope, almost made me forget the turmoil roiling inside. Almost.

"Look," he said, shifting closer, the tension between us palpable, like a taut string ready to snap. "I didn't mean to hurt you. I just—"

"Just what?" I interrupted, my voice sharper than I intended, echoing off the walls of the alley. "Just decided to go solo? Just thought I wouldn't care?" I could feel the raw edge of my words slicing through the fragile space we occupied.

"I thought you'd be busy," he said, frustration seeping into his tone. "You're always lost in your own projects. I didn't want to intrude on that. I thought it would be better for you if I tried to make a name for myself while you worked on your own stuff."

"And now?" I challenged, unable to rein in the torrent of emotion. "Is this really about us, or is it just about you and your career?"

Felix took a step back, hands raised in a gesture of surrender. "It's about both of us! I'm trying to create something that can support us—together! But you're acting like I've betrayed you. I need you to trust me."

His plea struck a chord, but the sound was discordant against the melody of betrayal still playing in my mind. "Trust? You're the one who kept me in the dark. Trust isn't something you can just demand, Felix. It's earned."

He rubbed the back of his neck, a telltale sign of his frustration. "What do you want from me, then? A grand declaration? A duet in front of the crowd? Because I'm not sure I can give you that right now."

I scoffed, incredulous. "Oh, so you do know how to charm an audience! Why not try it on me?" The sarcasm dripped from my words like honey gone sour, but a part of me was still waiting, aching for his answer.

Felix stepped forward, eyes bright with emotion, and my breath caught in my throat. "Because I don't want you to feel like you have to compete with me! That's not what this is about."

The sincerity in his voice washed over me, softening the sharp edges of my anger, but it wasn't enough. "What about our plans? Our dreams? You're acting like they don't matter anymore."

"They do matter! But you're acting like I'm the one who decided this." He looked at me, frustration flickering in his gaze, and for a moment, I wondered if I could see the hurt hiding behind his bravado. "You've been pulling away. I'm trying to bring us both along, but it feels like you're pushing me out."

"Because you're not giving me any choice!" I shot back, feeling the heat of the argument pulse between us like an electric charge. "You're out there playing your heart out, and I'm stuck wondering why I'm not enough for you to wait."

In that moment, I could see the shifting of emotions on his face—understanding, regret, and a flicker of something that looked an awful lot like fear. He took a deep breath, and the moment hung heavy in the air. "What if I'm scared, too?"

"Scared of what?" I asked, genuinely curious, the sharpness of the confrontation softening a bit.

"Scared that if I wait too long, I'll lose you for good," he admitted, his voice dropping to a whisper. "And I can't bear the thought of that."

A lump formed in my throat, the fight draining from my body as vulnerability took its place. "Felix..." I started, but the words faltered as emotions threatened to spill over. The air between us shifted, and I sensed the weight of our shared dreams hanging in the balance.

"Can we just... take a step back?" he suggested, the tension still crackling between us. "Maybe we can find a way to work together, to communicate without this constant pressure."

I nodded slowly, uncertainty dancing with a flicker of hope. "Maybe. But you have to promise me something."

"Anything."

"Stop assuming what I want. Just ask. I might surprise you."

"Deal," he said, a hint of a smile tugging at the corners of his mouth, the tension easing just a bit. "And I'll never play without you again. If you want to join me, I want us to be in it together."

We stood there, caught in a moment of fragile understanding. The music from inside the club still echoed in the air, a haunting melody that seemed to resonate with the turmoil of our exchange. As I took a deep breath, I could feel the tension melting away, replaced by a tentative hope.

But just as I began to feel a flicker of optimism, a shrill voice broke through the night, cutting through our fragile truce like a knife. "Felix! There you are!"

A woman emerged from the shadows, her presence striking and assertive, with a wild mane of curls and a confidence that crackled in the air. She wore a leather jacket that hugged her figure in all the right places, and the way she approached him made the hair on the back of my neck stand up. "I've been looking everywhere for you! The club wants you back for an encore. They love the new stuff!"

I could feel my heart plummet, irritation bubbling up once more as Felix turned to her, a flicker of surprise crossing his face. "Uh, yeah. Just a minute..." He glanced back at me, but I could see the tension creeping back into his posture.

"Who's this?" the woman asked, her tone flirtatious and teasing, making me want to claw my way out of my skin.

"Just a friend," Felix replied, but the way he said it stung more than I expected.

I forced a smile, the bitter taste of jealousy rising in my throat. "Just a friend, huh?" I echoed, sarcasm dancing on my tongue. "Nice to meet you."

The woman looked me up and down, a smirk playing on her lips. "Right. Well, I hope you don't mind if I borrow him for a moment. We have a show to finish."

I could feel the heat rising in my cheeks, the unmistakable sense of being sidelined creeping in. "Actually, I think we were having a moment," I said, attempting to keep my voice steady, but it came out sharper than I intended.

Felix shot me a look, an unreadable expression in his eyes, and I could see the struggle written all over his face. "It'll just be a second, I promise," he said, turning to the woman, a hint of discomfort evident in his tone.

"Sure, darling. But you're on stage in five," she said, her voice laced with a faux sweetness that made my skin crawl.

As she linked her arm through his, a possessive gesture that set my teeth on edge, I felt the weight of my insecurities slam into me like a freight train. There was something in the way she smiled at him, a confidence I had once admired in myself, now twisted into a bitter reminder of my vulnerability.

"Felix," I said, the word spilling out before I could hold it back. "Can I talk to you for a second?"

"Just wait," he said, caught between the two of us, and I felt a rush of indignation surge through me.

The night suddenly felt colder, the laughter from inside the club fading into a distant memory. I could feel the weight of my words pressing against my chest, the fleeting hope I had clung to slipping away. I turned to leave, feeling the weight of uncertainty pressing down on me, only to hear him call my name.

"Wait! Can we talk?"

I paused, torn between the desire to flee and the instinct to confront the truth hanging in the air. The woman's grip on his arm tightened, and I could see the tension etched on Felix's face.

"Fine," I replied, biting back the emotion threatening to spill over. "But I'm not waiting long."

With that, I turned, ready to take a step back into the night, leaving the fragments of our melody echoing in the silence.

The night air crackled with unspoken tension as I turned away from Felix, my heart pounding with a mix of frustration and vulnerability. I took a deep breath, desperately trying to collect my thoughts. The cool breeze brushed against my skin, bringing with it a moment of clarity as I felt the stares of the crowd shift away from us, the cheers from the club now just a distant echo in my ears.

"Wait!" Felix called again, his voice weaving through the darkness as he pulled away from the woman's grip. The urgency in his tone made me stop, turning back to face him, my heart racing as a mix of anger and curiosity washed over me.

"Look, I—" he began, but the woman interjected with a scoff, crossing her arms defiantly.

"Really? You're just going to stand here arguing with a random girl when you have a gig?" she asked, her voice dripping with sarcasm. "I thought you were serious about your music, Felix. You can't let anyone hold you back."

A lump formed in my throat as I recognized her for what she was: a distraction, a thorn in the side of everything we had built. "And you're just going to stand there and watch him forget his roots?" I shot back, my voice steady even as the turmoil inside me threatened to burst.

Felix glanced between us, frustration etched across his face. "This isn't helping," he said, taking a step toward me. "I don't want to lose you over something that can be worked out."

"Can it?" I shot back, the edge in my voice sharper than I intended. "You're the one who made this choice, and now you're trying to play the hero?"

The woman laughed, a sound both amused and condescending. "Oh, come on. You're just mad he's moving on without you. You're clearly not cut out for the spotlight."

"Excuse me?" I replied, my fists clenching at my sides. "Who do you think you are?"

Felix stepped between us, attempting to mediate. "Let's not do this here. Can we just go inside? Talk about it?"

"No!" I exclaimed, my heart racing as emotions surged. "I'm done playing games. You can have your spotlight, Felix. I just thought we were in this together."

I felt the sting of tears in my eyes, and I turned away, fighting against the overwhelming tide of vulnerability. The cool air felt electric against my skin, the emotions swirling around us becoming too intense to bear.

"Wait! Please!" he called, desperation lacing his voice. "I don't want you to walk away. I want to fix this."

"Fix it how?" I spat, not allowing the hint of uncertainty in his tone to sway my resolve. "By allowing this woman to distract you while I stand in the shadows? No, thank you."

"Felix, come on. We're on a tight schedule," the woman urged, impatience creeping into her voice.

He hesitated, caught between the two of us, and I could see the internal struggle written all over his face. "Just give me a second!" he barked at her, the frustration in his voice growing.

I took a step back, feeling the weight of my choices. "You know what? Maybe it's better if I just go. I can't be part of this mess. Not like this."

"Don't," he said, his voice almost pleading. "Don't walk away. We can talk about this. Just give me a moment to—"

"To what? Make excuses? Justify your actions?" I interrupted, my heart racing. "You think that will fix things? I feel like I'm fighting for something you don't even want anymore."

His eyes flared with determination, the intensity of his gaze anchoring me for a moment. "That's not true! I want us—"

But before he could finish, the woman stepped in, her tone patronizing. "This isn't high school drama, Felix. You have a career to think about."

With that, she grabbed his arm, her fingers curling possessively around his bicep, and I felt my stomach twist. I couldn't let her assert this kind of dominance over him, over us.

"Felix," I said, a raw urgency seeping into my voice. "Don't let her dictate your choices. Don't let her pull you away from what we had."

He shifted his weight, glancing between the two of us, clearly torn. "You don't understand. I can't just walk away from this opportunity. It's not just about us anymore. It's about my career."

The words hung in the air, thick with tension, and I felt a cold realization settle in my stomach. "So, what? I should just stand by and watch you chase your dreams without me? Be the girlfriend on the sidelines?"

His expression shifted, and I could see the flicker of regret cross his features. "No, that's not what I meant," he started, but I interrupted again, frustration bubbling over.

"It sure sounds like it! You're choosing her, Felix. She's clearly here to make sure you don't forget it."

The woman leaned closer, her smile a mix of triumph and amusement. "Maybe you should focus on what matters instead of clinging to some outdated idea of 'us.' He has a future to think about."

"Yeah, and it's not going to include you," I shot back, heat rising in my cheeks. "Felix deserves better than this—whatever this is."

"Better?" she laughed, a sharp, derisive sound. "You're right; he deserves better, and he can have it. The question is whether he wants to drag along someone who can't keep up."

I took a deep breath, fighting against the wave of emotions threatening to wash over me. "You're right about one thing: I won't drag myself into a mess like this."

Felix stepped forward, the resolve in his eyes hardening. "You don't get to make that choice for me. I'm still in this, regardless of what she says."

But before I could respond, he glanced at the woman, and I saw the glimmer of doubt flash across his features. The moment stretched like a rubber band, and I felt the air crackle with tension.

"I need to perform," he said, almost resigned, as if he were trying to convince himself. "I'll see you later, okay?"

I opened my mouth to protest, to scream that I wouldn't just wait around, but the words faltered as he turned his back, heading toward the entrance. My heart sank as the door swung shut behind him, leaving me alone with the woman who had just stepped into the gaping hole that had opened between us.

"You think he'll come back?" she asked, amusement dancing in her eyes.

I clenched my fists, a mix of rage and despair threatening to erupt. "You don't know him like I do."

"Oh, honey," she replied, her tone dripping with false sympathy. "I think he knows exactly what he wants."

The ache in my chest felt heavy, suffocating, as I stared at the door that had just closed behind him. My heart raced with a mix of anger and fear, knowing that whatever happened next could unravel everything we had built.

I turned, the night air stinging my cheeks, the world around me fading into a blur of lights and shadows. Just as I started to walk away, the door swung open again, and I froze in place, a rush of dread coursing through me.

Felix stood there, his silhouette framed against the light, a look of sheer panic on his face. "Wait! I—"

But before he could finish, the sound of shattering glass echoed through the alley, followed by a muffled scream. My heart dropped, and the world narrowed to the chaos unfolding before us, uncertainty clinging to the night like fog.

I felt Felix's presence at my side, and we exchanged a fleeting glance filled with unspoken questions and fears. As we rushed toward the noise, I couldn't shake the feeling that everything was about to change—forever.

Chapter 13: Rebuilding Harmony

The diner buzzed with the clatter of plates and the hum of soft jazz wafting through the air, wrapping around us like a comforting embrace. The scent of frying oil mixed with the sweet hint of vanilla from my milkshake, creating an aroma that felt like nostalgia, the kind that whispered memories of simpler times. I slid into the booth across from Mia, her youthful spirit contrasting sharply with the weariness that weighed heavy on my heart. Her vibrant eyes shone with a flicker of hope, a spark that reminded me of the warmth Felix used to radiate, before shadows crept into his world.

Mia's fingers toyed nervously with the edge of the checkered tablecloth, her gaze flitting to the door as if she were expecting Felix to walk in at any moment. "I just don't understand what happened," she said, her voice trembling slightly, as if the very act of speaking his name was an invocation. "He used to be so full of life, and now..." Her words trailed off, lost in the swirling thoughts that filled the small space between us.

I leaned forward, the weight of our shared concern hanging heavy in the air. "He's been dealing with so much. It's like he's trapped in a storm, and the more we reach out, the more he seems to retreat. I thought, maybe... we could bring a little light back into his life." I hesitated, gauging her reaction, but the flicker of curiosity in her eyes urged me on.

"Light?" Mia echoed, her brow furrowing. "What do you mean?"

"A jazz night," I declared, feeling a rush of adrenaline. "Just the three of us, like old times. We could pick a cozy spot, maybe even set up in the backyard if the weather's nice. We can play some records, bring some food, and just remind him of who he is. Who we all are together."

Mia's expression shifted, the corners of her lips tugging up into a tentative smile. "You really think he'd enjoy that? He hasn't been himself for so long."

"It's worth a shot," I replied, my heart pounding with a mix of excitement and fear. "He needs to see that he's not alone in this. And if we can bring a little music back into his world, maybe he'll start to remember what it feels like to be free."

The flickering neon lights outside cast playful shadows on our table, echoing the flickers of hope dancing in my chest. As we brainstormed our plans, the ideas flowed like the milkshake that slid down my throat, thick and sweet. Mia suggested pulling together a playlist of Felix's favorite jazz tracks—"Something he can lose himself in," she added, her enthusiasm contagious. I threw out the notion of adding some lights to the backyard, twinkling like stars against the evening sky, creating a haven where he could feel safe to let down his guard.

Mia's laughter punctuated our conversation, filling the space with a lightness that was sorely missed. I found myself caught up in her energy, each word shared between us building a bridge, reconnecting us to the brother who had become a distant memory. "And maybe," I suggested with a teasing lilt, "we could even bake something? I make a mean batch of cookies."

"Oh, God," Mia replied, shaking her head with mock seriousness. "As long as you don't set the kitchen on fire again, we might just stand a chance."

I chuckled, the tension that had been coiling in my chest beginning to unravel. "It was one time, and the smoke alarm was overly dramatic!"

The laughter hung between us, a fragile thread of connection that felt stronger than any silence that had preceded it. For the first time in days, I felt a sense of clarity wash over me. The ache of concern for Felix was still there, but it was now intertwined with a flicker of determination. We had a plan. And for the first time in ages, I felt like we were stepping back into the light.

As we finalized our ideas, I noticed the way Mia's shoulders began to straighten, the light returning to her eyes. It struck me how much Felix had anchored her, and how his pain had rippled through her own world. "I'm glad we're doing this," she said softly, a newfound resolve in her voice. "He needs us."

"Yes, he does," I replied, meeting her gaze with earnestness. "And I think we need him, too. It's like a part of us is missing without him."

The diner faded around us, the sounds of laughter and clinking glasses blending into a soothing backdrop as our shared mission took root. The world outside continued to spin on its axis, but in this moment, it felt like we had crafted our own little pocket of hope. Our ideas flowed like the syrup in our milkshakes, thick with potential and sweetened by the promise of rekindling something beautiful.

Mia and I exchanged excited glances, our hearts racing as we began to visualize the evening: Felix's laughter ringing out, music enveloping us like a warm embrace, and the three of us once again finding solace in each other's company. I couldn't shake the feeling that we were about to embark on something transformative—a chance to pull Felix back from the edge and remind him of the vibrant life waiting for him just beyond the shadows.

As I finished my fries, the crunching of each piece echoed in my mind like a drumbeat, urging me forward. With every shared dream and laughter, we wove a tapestry of resilience, threaded together by our love for Felix. Together, we would reclaim the joy that had slipped through our fingers, one note at a time, until the music of our hearts filled the air once more.

The day arrived, glowing with a promise of warmth and the scent of freshly baked cookies wafting through my kitchen. I had spent the morning in a frenzy of preparation, flour dust swirling in the air like tiny specters of doubt. Baking was my therapy, a way to pour my anxiety into something tangible, something that would fill the air with sweetness and hope. As I scooped the soft dough onto the baking sheet, I imagined the moment when Felix would step through the door, the confusion in his eyes melting into a smile as the aroma enveloped him.

Mia arrived just as I was sliding the cookies into the oven, her energy buzzing through the space like a live wire. She was the embodiment of youthful exuberance, her hair pulled back into a messy bun that seemed to defy gravity, and her oversized T-shirt emblazoned with a jazz legend only added to her charm. "What's the plan, oh fearless leader?" she asked, her voice brimming with mischief.

"First, we bake these beauties," I said, gesturing to the oven with a flourish. "Then we set up the backyard. I picked up some fairy lights that should twinkle just right as the sun sets. And we're going to need Felix's favorite records. You know, the ones that always made him dance like no one was watching."

Mia clapped her hands together, the sound bright and infectious. "You're right! We'll need a playlist that'll make him forget all his troubles. What about the one with that song he used to play on repeat? The one about finding solace in chaos?"

"'Autumn Leaves,'" I said, nodding in agreement. "Perfect choice. It was like a balm for his soul."

As we worked together, our laughter mingled with the rhythmic ticking of the clock, each tick echoing our shared excitement. There was something almost magical about how easily we fell into a comfortable rhythm, our movements synchronizing as we prepped the backyard for our surprise. Mia strung up the lights while I arranged the seating, a mismatched collection of chairs and cushions that would invite Felix to sink into comfort.

The sun dipped low in the sky, casting long shadows across the yard as I stepped back to admire our handiwork. The fairy lights twinkled like stars just waiting for the night to deepen, casting a soft glow over the makeshift stage we had created. The sight filled me with a swell of pride and an unexpected surge of hope. It felt like we were building a sanctuary for Felix, a place where he could feel embraced by love and laughter.

Mia flitted around, her excitement contagious. "Okay, what else do we need? Snacks? Drinks? A marching band?"

I chuckled, shaking my head. "I think we're set with cookies and milkshakes. Anything more and we might give Felix a sugar-induced existential crisis."

As we moved about the yard, Mia paused to gaze at the setting sun, the colors melting together in a glorious display. "You think he'll actually come?" she asked, her voice softening.

"Absolutely," I said, attempting to quell the gnawing doubt that threatened to surface. "We just have to believe he will."

Just then, a car rolled into the driveway, the crunch of gravel under tires pulling both our attention. A moment later, Felix stepped out, looking as if he had just emerged from a dream—disheveled hair and a hoodie that hung off him like an afterthought. His eyes, once bright with mischief, now carried a weight that made my heart ache.

"Surprise!" we shouted in unison, and I watched as confusion flickered across his face before it was quickly replaced by something softer, perhaps even a hint of joy.

"Mia? What's going on?" he asked, glancing from her to me, suspicion mingling with curiosity.

I stepped forward, heart racing. "We wanted to do something special for you. A jazz night, just like the old times."

The corner of his mouth twitched, a shadow of a smile that made my pulse quicken. "Jazz night?" he echoed, skepticism lacing his tone.

"Yep! With cookies and milkshakes," I added, trying to inject enthusiasm into my words. "We thought it might remind you of better days."

Felix's gaze softened as he surveyed the twinkling lights and our makeshift setup. The tension in his shoulders relaxed, if only slightly. "You guys really went all out, huh?"

Mia stepped closer, her hand reaching out to touch his arm gently. "We just wanted you to know that we're here. You're not alone, Felix. You never were."

For a heartbeat, silence enveloped us, heavy with unspoken feelings and the weight of all that had been left unsaid. Felix looked down, rubbing the back of his neck as if warding off the ghosts of his past. "I don't know if I can..." he began, his voice barely above a whisper.

"We're not asking for much," I interjected, desperate to fill the void. "Just a chance to reconnect. Let's just try to enjoy the music, yeah?"

He hesitated, casting a furtive glance back at the car as if contemplating making a run for it. But then he sighed, the sound almost a release. "Alright, let's see what you've got."

As we settled into the makeshift gathering, I felt a flicker of hope ignite within me. We poured milkshakes into tall glasses, the cold sweetness a comfort against the evening warmth. The cookies were still warm from the oven, and I handed one to Felix, who accepted it hesitantly, as if it might bite back.

Mia queued up the first record, the crackle of vinyl filling the air before the sultry tones of a saxophone wrapped around us. I watched Felix as the music began to weave its magic, a subtle change in his demeanor as he leaned back against the chair, a glimmer of something resembling relaxation settling in his eyes.

"Not bad," he said, a hint of mischief returning to his voice as he took a tentative bite of the cookie.

"Just wait until you try the milkshake," I teased, and for the first time in what felt like an eternity, we were laughing together.

With each passing moment, the atmosphere transformed from tense uncertainty to a warm cocoon of camaraderie. I could see Felix slowly peeling back the layers of despair, the weight of his troubles temporarily lifted by the simple joy of good company and familiar music. And as the saxophone crooned its sweet melody, I dared to believe that this night might just be the first step in rebuilding what had been lost.

The night enveloped us in a soft embrace as the first notes of music poured out of the speakers, weaving through the warm air like smoke from a fragrant candle. The flickering fairy lights cast a gentle glow over our little gathering, the atmosphere transforming from mere survival to something altogether different—a refuge, a sanctuary built on love and shared memories. Mia and I exchanged glances, her excitement mingling with the apprehension that had once clouded the evening.

Felix leaned back in his chair, a cookie crumbling in his hand as he tried to balance a mouthful with a smirk. "What's this secret ingredient in these cookies? A sprinkle of guilt and a dash of pity?"

"Why yes," I replied with a dramatic flair, feigning shock. "You caught me. It's my special recipe for coaxing grumpy jazz musicians out of their shells."

"More like coaxing them into sugar comas," he quipped, but I could see the faintest glimmer of playfulness in his eyes, a flicker of the man I once knew.

"Hey, you'd be amazed at what sugar can do. Besides, it's better than sitting alone in your room scrolling through... whatever dark hole you've been dwelling in," Mia chimed in, her laughter bubbling over like the soda in her glass. "Don't think I don't know about your late-night binges of existential dread on social media."

Felix chuckled, and the sound was like a balm for my own soul. "Alright, alright. You've got me there. But I might just become the world's first jazz-loving hermit."

As the music swelled around us, I felt a warmth blooming in my chest, a sense of belonging that I had longed for during those days of silence. I reached for my own cookie, watching as Felix's demeanor softened under the melodic embrace of the jazz tunes, the way he closed his eyes for a brief moment, savoring the moment like a sip of fine wine. The saxophone wailed and crooned, threading through the evening like a storyteller spinning tales of love and heartache.

But just as the atmosphere grew sweeter, the door swung open with an unexpected gust, a sudden rush of cool air breaking the cozy spell. I turned, heart racing as my stomach twisted in anticipation. It was Noah, a familiar face from Felix's past, the kind that could light up a room and extinguish it just as quickly. He had that reckless charm, an unpredictability that always seemed to draw Felix in, and I knew the mix of emotions that his presence could stir.

"Hey, man! What's up?" Noah called out, his voice boisterous and confident. His gaze swept across the backyard, landing on Felix with an intensity that felt both welcoming and dangerously intrusive.

Felix's expression flickered for a moment, indecision etched across his features. "Noah," he replied cautiously, sitting up straighter, as if the weight of their shared history was pressing down on him. "What are you doing here?"

Noah shrugged, stepping further into the light. "Just passing through. Thought I'd check on you. You've been MIA, and I figured you might need some… company." He gestured to the music, the fairy lights, and the makeshift setup we had created. "Looks like you've already got a party going."

Mia exchanged a worried glance with me, her earlier enthusiasm dimming. Felix's face had tightened, and I could see the walls going up, the protective barriers rising as he squared his shoulders against the past he was trying to escape.

"Not a party, just a little gathering," Felix said, his voice clipped. "We're fine."

Noah's eyes narrowed slightly, and for a moment, the air crackled with tension, like the moments before a storm. "You sure about that? You look like you could use a good time, man. It's all about seizing the moment, right?" His words dripped with a mixture of challenge and camaraderie, and I felt the pulse of unease thrumming through the air.

Mia and I shared a look, her brow furrowing as I sensed her worry shifting to concern for Felix. "Maybe you should just join us for a bit," I suggested, trying to keep the atmosphere light even as my heart raced. "We've got cookies, and the music's pretty great."

"Cookies?" Noah echoed, his expression shifting to playful intrigue. "Well, now you've got my attention. You know I'm a sucker for cookies."

Felix's eyes darted between us, and I could see him grappling with the unwelcome arrival of his friend, the familiar dance of old habits and new struggles playing out before us. "I don't think this is a good idea," he muttered, shaking his head slightly.

"Come on, Felix," Mia chimed in, her voice steadying. "Just a few minutes. We're here for you, and we just want you to be happy."

Noah stepped closer, an easy grin spreading across his face. "What's the worst that could happen? We eat cookies, listen to some jazz, and remember how to be friends again? I mean, we used to be good at that."

Felix looked away, his jaw tightening as if caught in a battle he didn't want to fight. The music swelled again, an almost pleading note that filled the gaps in the conversation, wrapping around us like an invisible thread. I sensed the cracks in his resolve, the way he shifted in his seat, unsure of whether to embrace the familiarity of Noah or to cling to the fragile peace we had worked so hard to create.

"I... I don't know," he said at last, his voice low, almost vulnerable. "Things have changed."

"Yeah, and they can change again," Noah replied, his tone earnest yet lightly teasing. "Besides, a little chaos might be exactly what you need. What's life without a little unpredictability?"

Just as Felix was about to respond, the sound of a crashing bottle echoed from the side of the house, the sharp shatter slicing through our fragile bubble. All heads turned, hearts pounding as we exchanged alarmed looks. My stomach dropped as I realized the commotion was coming from the old shed, a place filled with long-forgotten memories and shadows of our past.

"Uh, I'll check that out," I offered, the instinct to investigate overpowering the trepidation that was now coiling tightly in my chest.

"Wait," Felix said suddenly, his voice urgent. "Don't—"

But it was too late. Curiosity pulled me toward the source of the sound, the shadows flickering like ghosts around me as I approached the shed door. With every step, the air grew heavier, thick with the unspoken weight of what lay beyond. Just as I reached for the handle, a sense of foreboding washed over me, a feeling that whatever awaited on the other side might not be the lighthearted reunion we had envisioned.

As the door creaked open, darkness loomed within, and I could barely make out a shape shifting just inside the threshold. Before I could take a breath, a low voice emerged from the shadows, laced with familiarity and the edge of menace. "Well, well, look who we have here..."

And just like that, the night that had begun with hope teetered on the brink of chaos, leaving me suspended between the past and an uncertain future, the air thick with tension and the promise of what was yet to come.

Chapter 14: Under the Neon Lights

The air is thick with anticipation as I navigate through the throngs of people, their laughter a melodic backdrop against the rhythmic pulse of the band. The vibrant colors of the club swirl around me, a dizzying kaleidoscope of neon lights that dance in harmony with the music, casting playful shadows that tease at the corners of my vision. Each step I take feels heavier with expectation, yet lighter with the promise of change. My vintage dress clings to my curves, a bright hue of cerulean that stands out amidst a sea of black and gray. It sways gently with my movements, a reminder that I am here, present, and ready to embrace whatever tonight holds.

As I approach the bar, I catch a glimpse of my reflection in the mirrored wall—a flash of confidence beneath a curtain of self-doubt. My dark curls, wild and unrestrained, frame my face, highlighting the determination in my hazel eyes. They twinkle with a mix of excitement and apprehension, reflecting the flickering lights overhead. I take a moment to breathe, feeling the rhythm of the bass thumping in my chest, grounding me. This night is not just about celebration; it's about connection, about weaving together the frayed threads of my relationship with Felix.

Glancing toward the stage, my heart flutters at the sight of him. Felix is a tempest of energy, his fingers dancing across the guitar strings as if they are an extension of his soul. He leans into the mic, his voice a rich baritone that carries over the crowd, smooth and comforting like a warm embrace. But tonight, I can see the shadow of uncertainty in his eyes as they scan the audience. It's a look I know well—one that mirrors my own fear of vulnerability. I'm not just here to watch him play; I'm here to remind him of the connection we once shared, the magic that brought us together in the first place.

The first notes of our song reverberate through the room, and the crowd erupts in cheers. I can feel the collective energy surge, a wave that pulls me closer to him. I want to jump up on stage, to share this moment with him, but instead, I take a step back, allowing the space to fill with laughter and music. For now, I will be the audience, silently cheering him on as he pours his heart into the performance.

As the song unfolds, memories flood my mind—late-night talks beneath starlit skies, laughter echoing in dimly lit cafés, the thrill of our first kiss shared under a canopy of autumn leaves. Each note strikes a chord deep within me, resonating with the longing I've tried to bury since we drifted apart. My heart aches with nostalgia, a bittersweet reminder of what we had and what we might still salvage.

After the song ends, Felix takes a moment to address the audience. "I've got a special surprise tonight," he announces, his voice cutting through the lingering echoes of the last melody. I can feel the tension in the air shift, a ripple of curiosity spreading like wildfire. "Someone very important to me is here, and I want to dedicate this next song to her." The crowd erupts in applause, but my heart stutters at the sudden swell of his words. He doesn't know it's me, not yet. But when he looks back at me, recognition dawns, and my breath catches.

"Emily!" he calls, his voice piercing through the cacophony, beckoning me toward him. The world around me fades into a blur; all that exists is the intensity of his gaze. My feet move instinctively, carried by an invisible thread pulling me closer to the stage. As I climb up the steps, I can feel the warmth of the spotlight washing over me, illuminating my doubts and insecurities. It's as if time stands still, the clamor of the crowd fading into a hushed anticipation.

"What are you doing up here?" he asks, a playful smile breaking through the tension on his face. "You didn't think you could hide in the audience forever, did you?" His teasing words wrap around me like a favorite blanket, comforting yet unsettling.

I smirk, my heart racing. "I figured I'd let the real talent shine for a while." The crowd laughs, and I can't help but bask in the shared joy, the warmth of their acceptance fueling my confidence.

"Real talent?" He raises an eyebrow, the playful banter igniting a spark between us. "I think you just outshine me, Em."

As he launches into the next song, the melody envelops me, and I can't help but sway along. Each note reverberates through my chest, echoing the hope that tonight could be a turning point for us. I catch his eye again, and in that brief moment, the rest of the world fades into insignificance. We are two souls tethered by a shared history, a bond that refuses to unravel despite the distance that has grown between us.

The crowd sways and dances, and for a moment, I let myself forget the weight of our past. I'm swept up in the rhythm, the pulse of the music a reminder that life is meant to be lived fully, in vivid colors and bold strokes. I lean into the moment, allowing myself to be vulnerable, to believe that maybe, just maybe, this night could mend the cracks in our foundation.

When the final notes of the song linger in the air, the applause swells, filling the room with a palpable energy. Felix steps closer, his eyes searching mine, and I can see the questions swirling there—the uncertainty, the longing, the fear. It's the same cocktail of emotions swirling within me, but tonight, I refuse to let fear dictate my actions. I take a breath, grounding myself in this moment of honesty, of shared vulnerability.

"What now?" I ask, the words slipping out before I can overthink them. It's a question that hangs between us, electric and full of potential.

His question hangs in the air like the last note of a song, quivering with possibility. I swallow hard, feeling a rush of warmth at the intensity of his gaze, a magnet pulling me closer. "What now?" I repeat, the weight of the words heavy with anticipation. The truth is, I've been asking myself that for weeks, caught in a whirlwind of what-ifs and maybes. But standing here, just feet away from Felix, the future feels both exhilarating and terrifying.

He runs a hand through his tousled hair, a habit of his that has always made my heart skip. "I guess we could talk," he says, a hint of vulnerability threading through his playful tone. "Or we could grab a drink and pretend we're not both terrified right now."

"Why not both?" I quip, raising an eyebrow in challenge. "Talking and drinking? Sounds like a perfect recipe for disaster."

Felix chuckles, the sound rich and deep, and I feel my worries begin to fade. Maybe this was the intention behind the surprise, to strip away the layers of tension and fear that had built up between us like dust on a forgotten shelf. We could start fresh, or at least, as fresh as two people with a tangled past could manage.

The crowd begins to disperse, and I watch as familiar faces flood the space, friends and family buzzing with excitement. Mia bounces up to us, her eyes sparkling with mischief. "Did I miss the part where you two fell madly in love again?"

"Not yet, but we're working on it," I reply, unable to keep the smile off my face.

Felix raises an eyebrow, feigning offense. "I thought we had a plan, Emily. You know, the 'We'll just pretend we're still in love' plan?"

Mia claps her hands, reveling in the unfolding drama. "Oh, I need popcorn for this!"

"Don't you dare!" Felix warns, pointing a finger playfully at her. "If this is going to be a romantic comedy, I expect it to have some actual romance."

"Agreed," I add, leaning into the playful banter. "And some excellent comedic timing, preferably from you."

As the laughter dies down, I feel a shift in the air, a moment suspended in time where it's just us, tangled in a web of old memories and new hopes. I can't shake the feeling that we're on the brink of something important, a moment that could redefine everything.

"Come on, let's grab that drink," Felix suggests, his voice dropping to a more intimate register, drawing me closer as he gestures toward the bar.

We weave through the crowd, and I can feel the warmth of his presence beside me, a comforting reminder of who we used to be. The bar glows like a beacon, neon lights reflecting off the polished surface as we find our place in line. The bartender, a guy with an impressive collection of tattoos and an easy smile, nods in our direction. "What can I get you two?"

"Surprise us," Felix says, flashing that charming grin that has a way of turning the room in his favor.

I chuckle softly, rolling my eyes. "Really? You're going to let fate decide our drinks?"

"Why not?" He shrugs, leaning against the bar as if he owns the place. "Besides, if we're getting back together, we might as well embrace the unexpected."

There's something freeing about his nonchalance, a carefree attitude that reminds me of the best parts of us. "Alright, Mr. Spontaneous," I say, smirking. "But if I end up with a drink that tastes like it was brewed in a swamp, I'm holding you responsible."

"Fair enough," he replies, crossing his arms, his playful demeanor softening for a moment. "But if it's fantastic, I want credit for being a risk-taker."

As the bartender returns with two colorful cocktails, one a vibrant pink concoction and the other a deep blue, I can't help but laugh. "Okay, swamp or paradise? Let's find out."

I take a sip of the pink drink, the flavors bursting on my tongue like a summer sunset. "Oh, this is definitely not from a swamp," I declare, eyes widening with delight.

"Mine tastes like a vacation in a glass," Felix says, taking a hearty sip from his blue drink, a look of approval washing over his features. "Maybe we should ditch the conversation for some beach chairs and a piña colada instead."

"Just like old times?" I ask, my voice laced with nostalgia. The memories hit me like a wave, sweeping me back to lazy afternoons spent lounging in the sun, our laughter dancing on the breeze.

"Exactly." His expression shifts, the warmth of our laughter replaced by a momentary seriousness. "But I want more than just the old times, Em. I want us to move forward, whatever that looks like."

The sincerity in his voice sends a tremor of hope through me, a flicker of light in the shadowed corners of my heart. "I think I want that too," I admit, my voice barely above a whisper. "But what if we mess it up again?"

Felix leans closer, the world around us fading into a blur. "We will mess it up, but that's part of being human. It's how we deal with it that counts. We can't just let fear dictate our lives."

The truth of his words hangs between us, tangible and raw. I take a breath, letting it settle into my heart. "You're right. I can't keep hiding behind my fear. It's just... the thought of losing you again terrifies me."

His expression softens, and I can see the depth of his understanding. "I get that. But what if we tried to be honest with each other? Like really honest. No games, no pretending."

"Sounds like a tall order," I tease, but the underlying seriousness in his tone doesn't escape me.

"I'm willing to take the leap if you are," he says, his eyes glinting with determination. "Let's take it one step at a time."

I raise my glass, feeling the weight of his words settling in my chest. "To taking leaps," I say, our glasses clinking with a resonant cheer, a promise hanging in the air.

With that simple gesture, the tension between us begins to unravel. I can feel the warmth of hope spreading through me, igniting a small spark that has lain dormant for too long. As the night continues to unfold, I realize that this moment—the two of us, standing side by side beneath the neon lights—could be the turning point we both need.

The clink of our glasses signals an unspoken truce, a shared commitment to navigate the unpredictable waters of our relationship. The bar, once bustling with activity, slowly becomes a sanctuary, the warm glow of overhead lights casting soft shadows around us. I can feel the hum of conversation around us, but it fades into a comforting background melody as we lean closer, eager to unearth the layers beneath the surface.

"So," Felix starts, a teasing glint in his eyes, "what was it that brought you here tonight? A secret longing for my melodious voice or the siren call of free drinks?" He takes a dramatic sip from his vibrant blue cocktail, nearly spilling it down his shirt in an exaggerated gesture.

I laugh, shaking my head. "I must admit, the prospect of hearing you croon was certainly enticing. I'm just here for the cocktails and the spectacular chance to witness your inevitable embarrassment on stage."

He feigns a gasp, a hand clasped dramatically to his chest. "Oh, the betrayal! I thought we were embarking on a heartfelt reunion, and here you are, plotting my downfall."

"Reunion? I'm not ready for the 'R' word just yet. Let's stick to 'a fun night out with a side of nostalgia.'"

The playful banter continues, weaving a tapestry of comfort around us, and for a moment, I almost forget about the tension that had frayed our bond. There's a beauty in the vulnerability shared through laughter, a balm for old wounds.

But then, as the laughter begins to die down, a silence falls between us—a charged moment where words hang in the air like the last notes of a fading song. Felix's gaze softens, and I can see the flicker of emotions swirling in his eyes. "Emily," he says, his voice low and steady, "I've missed you more than I thought I could."

The sincerity of his confession lands like a weight in my chest, both thrilling and terrifying. "I've missed you too," I admit, my heart racing as if it's trying to leap from my chest. "But things have changed."

His brow furrows slightly, a shadow crossing his face. "I know. But maybe that's not a bad thing. Maybe it's a chance for us to be… something different."

"Different how?" I challenge, unsure whether I'm ready to peel back the layers of my guarded heart.

He pauses, as if weighing his words carefully. "More honest. More real. We both know what we had wasn't perfect. But I believe it can be better."

My stomach knots, and I want to believe him. I want to leap into that future he's offering, but the hesitation clings to me like a shadow. "Better doesn't come without risks, Felix. What if we just end up hurting each other again?"

"Isn't that the gamble we take with everything? Love, life, a night out at a bar with free drinks? There are no guarantees." His voice is earnest, cutting through the veil of uncertainty that shrouds us.

"Okay, Mr. Philosopher," I reply, trying to inject some levity into the heavy air. "But let's not forget that our past is riddled with broken promises and misunderstandings."

He leans closer, the playful banter replaced by a seriousness that makes my heart race. "But it's also filled with moments of joy, laughter, and—if I remember correctly—a lot of dancing in our living room."

I can't help but smile at the memory. "You mean your awkward flailing and my attempts to maintain some semblance of rhythm?"

"Precisely! That was our magic!"

Our eyes lock, and in that moment, the world around us fades. I can see the earnestness in his gaze, a flicker of hope igniting the remnants of my guarded heart. "Okay," I say, feeling a rush of courage. "Let's take a leap, but with a safety net this time."

His smile widens, and it feels like the sun breaking through after a long, stormy night. "I'll hold you to that."

The atmosphere shifts again, a palpable tension filling the space. We're standing at the precipice of something new, and I can feel the adrenaline coursing through my veins. I raise my drink, ready to toast to this new beginning, when the unmistakable sound of a commotion draws my attention.

Across the club, a figure stands out in stark contrast to the laughter and music—a woman, wild-eyed and frantic, waving her arms like a flailing bird. She's shouting something, and the energy in the room shifts from playful to concerned in an instant.

"Hey, everyone!" she cries, her voice cutting through the noise like a knife. "I need everyone's attention! It's an emergency!"

A hush falls over the crowd, a wave of confusion rippling through the patrons as we turn to see what's happening. Felix and I exchange worried glances, our previous lightheartedness evaporating like the last dregs of summer.

"What the hell is going on?" he mutters, his playful demeanor replaced by concern.

"I don't know, but it doesn't look good," I reply, my heart pounding.

The woman continues, her voice trembling with urgency. "There's been an accident outside! A car crashed into the club, and there are people trapped!"

Gasps ripple through the crowd, shock mingling with fear as the gravity of her words sinks in. I feel the world shift beneath me, a tide of dread washing over my exhilaration.

"Stay here," Felix says, his voice firm, a protective instinct sparking to life as he prepares to move toward the door.

"Wait!" I grab his arm, my pulse racing. "We need to help!"

His eyes flash with determination, but they're also tinged with worry. "No, Emily. We don't know what's happening out there. It could be dangerous."

But as the tension in the room builds and the sounds of chaos begin to filter through the walls, I feel a different kind of urgency—a call to action that overrides my fear. "We can't just stand here!"

With that, I pull him toward the exit, the crowd parting as we push through. The neon lights cast a surreal glow on the chaos unfolding outside, and my heart races at the thought of what we might find.

As we step through the doorway, the cool night air rushes in, and I can see the remnants of the accident—a crumpled car, glass scattered like confetti across the pavement, and the growing crowd of onlookers, their faces painted with shock and concern.

Felix grips my hand tightly, the connection between us solid and grounding as we make our way closer. "We need to get closer, see if anyone needs help," he urges, his voice low, but I can hear the tension beneath it.

Suddenly, the air crackles with more than just shock; a frantic yell cuts through the night. "Help! Someone's still inside!"

My breath catches, fear pooling in my stomach. With a shared look of determination, we push forward, ready to face whatever chaos lies ahead, unaware that the night is about to change everything.

Chapter 15: The First Step

The moment Felix stepped onto the dance floor, the air shimmered with possibility. The strobe lights twirled overhead, casting a kaleidoscope of colors that danced along with us, wrapping us in their vibrant embrace. Music pulsed through the room, a throbbing beat that seemed to sync with the rhythm of my heart, each thump echoing the anticipation bubbling within me. Around us, laughter and clinking glasses formed a symphony of celebration, but all of that faded into a gentle murmur as our eyes locked, each of us grounded in a world that was uniquely ours.

Felix's usual hesitance melted away like ice in the sun as he found his footing next to me. His movements were awkward at first, as though he were rediscovering a part of himself long buried beneath layers of doubt and reluctance. The way he stepped forward reminded me of a flower pushing through the frost in early spring, delicate but determined. I couldn't help but smile, a grin that felt almost too big for my face, but the joy was intoxicating, an elixir I wanted to share with him. With each sway and turn, I could see him shake off the shadows that had clung to him for far too long.

"See? Not so scary," I teased, leaning close enough that I could feel his breath mingle with mine, a soft whisper of warmth that sent a thrill down my spine. He chuckled, the sound rich and deep, sending butterflies fluttering wildly in my stomach. I took a step back, spinning him into the dance as the tempo picked up, laughter bubbling forth from our lips as we found our groove. I noticed how his shoulders relaxed, the tightness of his expression easing into something that resembled pure joy.

"You make it look easy," he replied, his eyes sparkling under the flickering lights. "I just hope I don't step on your toes."

"Trust me, I've survived worse," I shot back, spinning away from him, reveling in the playful banter. The scent of fresh citrus from the nearby bar mixed with the faint notes of his cologne, wrapping around me like an embrace. It felt good, this mingling of senses and sounds, a reminder of all the nights spent dancing away the weight of the world. I returned to him, our laughter weaving through the air like a secret shared between friends.

As the song shifted, something more intimate settled over us. The melody softened, the heavy bass giving way to a gentle rhythm, coaxing us into a closer proximity. It felt like an invitation, one that drew us together in a way that made my heart race. I glanced around, the faces of our friends blurring into a background of smiles and joy, but Felix was the only one I could see. He leaned in slightly, his forehead brushing against mine, and for a moment, time suspended.

"I never thought I'd be here," he confessed, his voice a quiet murmur that barely rose above the music. The vulnerability in his words cut through the celebratory chaos, and I felt a pang of understanding deep within me. "I thought I'd be sitting at home, avoiding this."

"Sometimes, the first step is the hardest," I replied, my heart swelling with empathy. "But look at you now." I gestured around us, the vibrant energy swirling like the colors of the lights above. "You're dancing, Felix. You're alive."

He chuckled softly, shaking his head as though trying to dispel his own disbelief. "I never pictured you as the type to coax someone out onto the floor."

"Maybe you just didn't know me well enough," I teased, nudging him lightly. "I can be quite persuasive when it comes to having fun."

"Persuasive, huh?" His tone was light, but I could see a flicker of something deeper in his gaze, a spark of curiosity mingling with the uncertainty. I wanted to reach in and reassure him that it was okay to step out of his comfort zone, that even if he stumbled, I would be right there to catch him.

The song shifted again, picking up tempo, and as we danced, I felt the energy of the crowd swell around us, lifting us higher with each beat. It was electric, a collective joy that surged through the air like a current. The energy became infectious, each sway and twirl igniting our spirits, fueling a shared liberation. In that moment, we weren't just moving; we were weaving our stories into the very fabric of this night, a tapestry of laughter, music, and the sweet thrill of stepping out into the unknown.

"You're really good at this," he said, a hint of admiration in his voice as he twirled me around, our bodies moving in tandem. "I could get used to it."

"Good, because I plan to make this a regular thing," I declared, the excitement bubbling inside me like soda fizz. "Dancing, laughing, living—these are the things we can't afford to miss."

His eyes widened slightly, surprise etched on his face. "Regular, huh? You mean I'll have to keep showing up?"

"Only if you want to. But I promise, you'll be glad you did." I grinned, feeling a warmth spread through me, an electric connection that felt new and exhilarating. This was just the beginning, and I wanted him to know that there were endless possibilities awaiting us beyond the dance floor.

The music shifted once more, plunging us into a slower, more intimate beat, wrapping us in an embrace that felt both comforting and daring. I moved closer, our bodies almost touching as we swayed gently to the rhythm. I could hear his heart beating, a steady thrum that matched my own, and the world around us faded into the background. In this moment, it was just us, two souls finding their way through the chaos, finally letting go of the burdens that had weighed us down for far too long.

As the last notes of the slow song faded into a lingering silence, I felt an exhilarating mix of exhilaration and vulnerability. The energy around us shifted, creating a palpable tension, as if the air had been charged with unspoken words and shared glances. I watched Felix, still catching his breath, his face flushed with a delightful mix of joy and disbelief. It was as though he had stepped off a precipice, and I could see the rush of liberation coursing through him. The intoxicating atmosphere clung to us like the sweet scent of cotton candy wafting through the air, promising a carnival of experiences waiting just beyond the horizon.

"I can't believe I did that," he said, a soft chuckle escaping his lips. His laughter, once laced with uncertainty, now rang with newfound confidence. "You might have unleashed a monster."

"Oh, don't worry," I teased, nudging him playfully with my shoulder. "I've dealt with worse monsters in my time." The corners of my mouth curled up as I imagined the chaos of my own past adventures—late-night escapades that usually ended in laughter, and occasionally in something resembling a disaster. "Besides, we'll just put a leash on you."

"Maybe a leash isn't the best idea," he quipped, his eyes sparkling with mischief. "I might just take off running."

"Good luck outrunning me," I replied with mock bravado, raising an eyebrow as I met his gaze. "I've got stamina." We both laughed, the tension easing between us, as we gravitated toward the edge of the dance floor where our friends had gathered in cheerful clusters, each group illuminated by the warm glow of fairy lights strung overhead.

I scanned the room, spotting Hannah at the bar, her vibrant red dress twirling as she gestured animatedly to a couple of friends. With her ever-present charm, she was the life of the party, and I couldn't help but admire her effortless ability to draw people in. "Look over there," I said, nodding toward Hannah, "you'd think she was a firework with how bright she lights up the room."

Felix's gaze followed mine, and he smiled, a genuine warmth radiating from him. "I guess that makes us the sparklers—shaky but with a bit of flair."

"Exactly! And a whole lot of fun," I said, playfully nudging him again. "But we can't get too comfortable. We're not done dancing yet."

"Oh, so there's more?" He raised an eyebrow, a teasing challenge in his tone.

"Absolutely! And I'm not taking no for an answer." I gestured dramatically toward the DJ booth, where the next track was already beginning to pulse through the speakers. A thumping bass filled the space, and before I could lose my momentum, I grabbed Felix's hand and pulled him back into the fray. The music wrapped around us like a familiar embrace, urging us to let go of our worries and dive deeper into the moment.

As we moved, I noticed a shift in Felix. His movements became more fluid, his laughter more infectious. He was no longer just keeping up with the beat; he was finding his rhythm, a melody that felt uniquely his own. I could see the weight of his burdens begin to lift, each step he took shaking off a little more of the doubt that had clung to him. The world around us began to fade again, leaving just the two of us in our own little universe, dancing as if nobody was watching.

"Okay, I have to admit," he shouted over the music, "this is way better than scrolling through memes on my couch."

"See? I knew you had it in you!" I beamed at him, unable to suppress the joy bubbling within me. "Who knew you were secretly a dance machine?"

"Only when coerced," he replied, a mock-serious expression overtaking his face. "I'm still not fully convinced this isn't a dream and that I'll wake up to find myself buried under a pile of laundry."

"Trust me, if this is a dream, I don't want to wake up either," I said, feeling the thrill of spontaneity swirl around us. "Just let it happen!"

And let it happen we did, lost in the chaos of colors and sounds, our laughter mingling with the music as if it were another layer to the symphony around us. But as the night continued, a lingering thought gnawed at the edges of my happiness, a soft whisper reminding me that while tonight was a celebration, it was also a first step into something deeper, something uncertain. I could see Felix starting to break down barriers, but the road ahead wouldn't be without its bumps.

The song shifted once more, and a surge of energy rippled through the crowd. The tempo quickened, inviting everyone to give in to the rhythm. I couldn't help but twirl Felix again, pulling him into the frenetic energy of the dance floor. "Look at us! Just two sparklers lighting up the night!"

"More like two fire hazards," he quipped, but I could see the laughter dancing in his eyes. The playful banter fueled our momentum as we twirled and spun, creating a whirlwind of movement that drew attention from onlookers.

Suddenly, the music came to an abrupt halt, plunging us into a moment of stunned silence, leaving us breathless and slightly disoriented. I glanced around, momentarily bewildered, before spotting a group of friends near the DJ booth, who were now shouting out song requests like a game show.

"Okay, I don't like where this is going," Felix said, eyeing the group warily. "They're going to pick the worst song, aren't they?"

"Probably," I said with a chuckle. "But that's the beauty of it! We'll make it work." I could already see the potential for hilarity; our improvised dance moves might turn into a comedy routine, and I was all in for that kind of fun.

Just then, the DJ leaned into the mic, announcing a sudden switch-up. "Alright, everyone! I hear a lot of requests for some retro magic! Get ready for the classics!"

The first notes of a familiar tune filled the air, and a collective cheer erupted from the crowd. Felix groaned, half-laughing, "I can't believe it's come to this."

"Oh, come on!" I said, beaming at him as I caught the rhythm of the music. "It's all about embracing the chaos. Now, follow my lead!"

With a wink, I broke into an exaggerated dance move, throwing my arms wide and swaying my hips with abandon. Felix stared at me for a split second, bewildered, before succumbing to laughter and joining in. The spectacle of us—two unlikely dance partners weaving through a whirlwind of nostalgia—was so ridiculous that it felt electric. With every awkward twirl and spontaneous shimmy, we were crafting a memory that would spark laughter for years to come.

The world around us faded back into the music, and in that moment, everything felt possible, as if the night were a blank canvas waiting for us to paint our wildest dreams. We danced without inhibitions, each move an expression of freedom and joy, an exhilarating escape from the mundane.

As the retro tune blared around us, I flung my arms wide, inviting Felix into a dance that could only be described as wonderfully chaotic. He mimicked me, albeit with a touch of hesitance that only made him more endearing. Our movements turned into an impromptu contest of ridiculousness, with exaggerated hip thrusts and goofy spins that sent us both into fits of laughter. I could hardly believe how quickly we had transformed the dance floor into our personal stage, the weight of the world lifting with each ridiculous move.

"You know," Felix said between breaths, a playful smirk dancing on his lips, "if we keep this up, we might just start a trend. The next viral dance challenge could be all ours."

"Oh, absolutely! I can already see it now: the 'Two Left Feet Shuffle.' The world will thank us," I shot back, pretending to strike a pose as I twirled again, sending my hair flying. I felt like a star in a low-budget musical, and honestly, I couldn't have been happier.

The chorus hit, and I couldn't help but go all out, adding a dramatic flair to my movements. "Come on, Felix! Feel the music!" I shouted, flailing my arms as if trying to summon some ancient spirit of dance. He rolled his eyes but couldn't help breaking into a full grin, his laughter echoing off the walls.

But just as we were reaching a delightful crescendo of silliness, a loud pop pierced through the music, followed by an eerie silence. The lights flickered, and I felt a sudden rush of uncertainty sweep over the crowd. A wave of murmurs spread, shifting from the laughter and cheers we'd been basking in to a palpable tension. Felix's face dropped as he glanced around, eyes wide with confusion.

"Is it me, or did the party just get interrupted by a horror movie soundtrack?" he quipped, but the levity of his words did little to lift the sudden weight in the air.

"Maybe it's the sequel to our dance challenge," I replied, trying to maintain some semblance of humor. I could feel my heart race, an unsettling instinct prickling at the back of my mind. Just when the night felt like it was reaching a fever pitch, a woman's voice crackled through the speakers.

"Sorry for the disruption, folks! We're experiencing some technical difficulties. Please remain calm as we fix this!"

A chorus of groans erupted from the crowd, and I could see Felix's shoulders tense, the carefree atmosphere evaporating like mist under the sun. "What kind of technical difficulties are we talking about?" he asked, scanning the room as if expecting something dramatic to unfold.

"Maybe it's just a blown fuse or a wayward disco ball," I suggested, trying to downplay the unease creeping in. The strobe lights flickered back to life, and for a brief moment, they illuminated the worried faces of our friends, who were now gathering close together, whispering amongst themselves.

"What if it's not a blown fuse? What if someone's taken the whole DJ booth hostage?" Felix replied, the lightness of his tone fading into something more serious. "You know, the real horror story."

I couldn't help but chuckle nervously at the absurdity of it all. "If that happens, I'll volunteer as tribute. I've always wanted to know what it's like to negotiate with a DJ."

"Good to know I'll have a skilled negotiator in my corner," he said, rolling his eyes with a mix of amusement and concern. "What do you think we should do?"

"Maybe we just hang tight until the music comes back. It's not the end of the world, right?" I offered, casting a glance at the crowd. While many seemed to be shifting nervously, others were busy checking their phones, a universal signal that the chaos of the outside world was inching closer, inching into our little bubble of joy.

And just as the laughter started to return, the lights dimmed, plunging us into an unsettling gloom. Whispers of unease spread through the room like wildfire. I caught a glimpse of Hannah, her eyes wide with confusion as she turned to me, and I could see that her usual confidence was wavering.

"Maybe we should find a way out," she said, her voice barely above a whisper, as if she feared the very walls were eavesdropping. "I don't like this. It feels... wrong."

"Just a temporary glitch," I reassured her, but the tremor in my own voice betrayed my growing apprehension.

Felix stepped closer, his expression suddenly serious. "What if it's something more? You know, maybe the DJ really is in trouble. It wouldn't be the first time someone tried to pull a stunt at a club."

"Stunt? Like what? A performance art piece gone wrong?" I shot back, trying to mask my anxiety with humor, but the uncertainty loomed larger.

Before he could respond, the lights flashed back on, revealing an unexpected scene. The DJ had stepped down from his booth, and a commotion erupted near the entrance. People turned their heads, and I could see a figure standing in the doorway, silhouetted against the blinding light. They were tall, draped in a long coat that billowed around them like smoke.

"Now that's not ominous at all," Felix murmured, tension radiating from his body.

I felt my heart skip a beat as the figure stepped forward, their face coming into view, but the lights flickered again, casting eerie shadows that distorted their features. I squinted, trying to get a better look, and that's when I caught the glint of something metallic in their hand.

"Stay here," I whispered, but even as the words left my mouth, I felt the magnetic pull of curiosity drawing me closer. I wanted to know what was happening, to peel back the layers of this unexpected twist.

"Don't be reckless," Felix warned, grabbing my wrist gently. "You don't know what they want."

But before I could respond, the mysterious figure spoke, their voice slicing through the tension like a knife. "Ladies and gentlemen, I hope you're ready for a change of pace. Tonight, the dance floor is not just for fun—it's a battleground."

The room held its breath, caught between fear and intrigue, and in that moment, the air crackled with uncertainty. I could feel my heart racing, the exhilaration of the night colliding with an unsettling thrill that left me breathless. The night was far from over, and whatever lay ahead was bound to turn our world upside down.

Chapter 16: Hidden Echoes

The bar hummed with an energy that vibrated beneath our feet, each beat of the music spilling into our conversation like the flickering candlelight on the table. The soft glow flickered across Felix's features, illuminating the shadows that danced in his eyes. I had always thought he possessed an easy smile, one that could light up even the dullest days. Yet now, as I watched him, it felt as if the weight of the world had descended upon those delicate shoulders.

His fingers tightened around mine, a lifeline in a sea of swirling emotions. "You don't know what it's like to have someone you look up to just... disappear," he said, his voice a low rumble laced with vulnerability. I wanted to reassure him, to tell him that I could imagine the pain, but the truth was I couldn't. Not really. My heart raced, caught between empathy and the wish to shield him from the storm of his past.

He leaned back against the booth, his gaze lost somewhere in the distance as if he could see the ghosts of memories that haunted him. "My dad was a hero to me once. An artist, a dreamer. I remember the way he used to paint in the garage, his fingers stained with bright colors that never quite washed off. But somewhere along the way, he traded those dreams for a bottle."

I could see it all in my mind's eye—the vivid swirls of paint, the scent of turpentine mingling with the warmth of sunlight streaming through the open garage door. It was the picture of a father I had never known, one whose vibrant spirit had dimmed into shadows. My chest tightened as I listened, each word a brushstroke painting a portrait of loss.

Felix swallowed hard, and for a moment, I feared he might retreat into that familiar fortress of silence. But instead, he pressed on. "He used to say that life was just a canvas, waiting for us to fill it with colors. But now... now he's just another dull shade, blending into the background of my life."

A pang of sorrow echoed through me. "He sounds like a complicated man," I replied, my voice soft yet firm. "Complicated doesn't mean he doesn't care. Maybe he just lost his way." I wanted him to see that there was still hope, still a path back to the vibrancy that life could offer.

Felix shook his head, a bitter smile curving his lips. "Hope? It feels like a cruel joke sometimes. You don't understand. He chose his addiction over me. Every birthday, every graduation, he'd promise he would be there, but he never showed up. It was always the bottle over me."

The pain in his eyes mirrored the sadness in my heart. It was a revelation I hadn't expected. "And yet here you are," I said, squeezing his hand gently. "You're not your father. You've become someone worthy of hope. You can break that cycle."

He met my gaze, a spark igniting in those troubled depths. "I want to believe that. But sometimes it feels like I'm fighting against ghosts. They whisper to me, reminding me of every failure, every moment he wasn't there."

"Those ghosts don't define you," I insisted. "You're not your father's mistakes. You're not the echoes of his choices. You're standing right here, alive, and you have a choice."

A silence enveloped us, heavy with unspoken thoughts. I could see the tension in his shoulders, the way his brow furrowed as he wrestled with his inner demons. The bar around us faded into a soft murmur, the laughter and chatter of patrons blending into a distant symphony. It was just him and me, trapped in our own little world.

He took a deep breath, his features softening. "Maybe you're right," he murmured, a flicker of hope igniting in his voice. "I've spent so long trying to escape what he did that I forgot I could create something new. But how do I do that?"

I leaned closer, my heart racing with the sudden warmth between us. "We do it together. We face these memories head-on. You can reclaim your life, your art. Let the canvas of your life be painted with your own colors."

Felix smiled then, a genuine smile that transformed his entire face. "You really believe that, don't you?"

"I do," I replied, my voice steady. "You have the power to fill that canvas however you want. Just like your father once did."

A chuckle escaped his lips, lightening the heaviness that had settled between us. "You make it sound so simple. I've been trying to unlearn everything he taught me."

"Unlearning can be just as powerful as learning," I said, my spirit buoyed by the connection that seemed to deepen with every shared thought. "Besides, you're not just carrying his legacy. You're forging your own path, a masterpiece waiting to happen."

Felix's eyes danced with unguarded emotion. "I can't imagine doing that without you," he said, his voice barely above a whisper.

My heart fluttered at his words, a gentle warmth radiating through me. "You won't have to."

With each passing moment, the bar became less of a backdrop and more of a sanctuary, a space where dreams could be woven into reality, and laughter could rise above the pain. In that little booth, we forged a pact—one that promised to take on the ghosts together, to paint over the faded echoes of yesterday with the vibrant strokes of hope for tomorrow. The music surged around us, a melody that harmonized with the rhythm of our budding connection, the spark of something beautiful beginning to take flight.

The bar around us pulsated with life, laughter, and the occasional clink of glass, but in our little bubble, the world outside faded to a mere whisper. Felix's laughter, warm and genuine, sent ripples of joy through my chest. "You know," he began, his tone teasing, "for someone who claims to be a hotshot at cheerleading people through their emotional crises, you've got a way of making it sound like I'm about to run off and paint the next Mona Lisa."

I grinned, feeling the lightness of the moment. "Well, if you do, I'll be your biggest fan. We could start a gallery called 'The Trials and Triumphs of Felix.'"

"Just what the world needs," he said, feigning a dramatic sigh. "Another gallery filled with half-finished canvases and existential dread. No one would want to buy a ticket."

"You underestimate the allure of existential dread," I shot back, unable to contain my laughter. "Besides, you'll have to throw in some snacks to lure them in. Wine and cheese can work wonders, especially if you promise a side of angst."

As the banter flowed effortlessly, I felt the tension begin to dissolve, replaced by a lightness that hung in the air like the sweet notes of a jazz saxophone. For the first time that evening, I could see glimpses of the artist he once was, the young boy who wielded paintbrushes like swords against the darkness. "You know, I haven't painted in years," Felix admitted, his expression turning thoughtful. "I used to think it was my way to escape, but now I see it was my way to create something beautiful out of the chaos."

"Why don't you start again?" I asked, leaning forward, intrigued. "I mean, it doesn't have to be a grand gesture. Just pick up a brush and let your thoughts flow. You don't have to paint the next great masterpiece; just let it be a reflection of where you are now."

Felix looked pensive, his fingers tapping a rhythm against the table. "It's hard to shake the feeling that I'm not good enough. That anything I create will just echo his failures."

"Are you kidding?" I rolled my eyes playfully. "You have a unique voice. It deserves to be heard, even if it's a little off-key. Besides, you'll never know until you try."

A shadow crossed his face, and I quickly changed the subject. "What if I join you? We could have a painting date! Just think of it—paint splatters everywhere, possibly even some creative catastrophes. But it would be ours."

He chuckled softly, a glimmer of excitement lighting his eyes. "You'd risk ruining your clothes for a chance at my splatter art? That's quite the leap of faith."

"I'm an artist in my own right," I declared, mockingly serious. "I've mastered the art of chaos on a canvas. Just wait until you see my finger painting."

Felix laughed, and it warmed me, igniting an infectious energy between us. "Okay, okay. A painting date it is. But only if you promise to wear an old t-shirt and accept the inevitable mess."

"Deal!" I said, thrusting my hand out dramatically as if sealing a sacred pact. "But fair warning: I'm known to get overly enthusiastic with my colors. There might be some accidental abstract work on the floor."

"I'll take my chances," he replied, shaking my hand with a grin.

Just then, the bartender, a burly man with a thick beard and tattoos weaving like vines up his arms, approached our table. "Everything good here?" he asked, wiping his hands on a rag that looked like it had seen better days.

"Absolutely," I replied, eager to include him in our playful atmosphere. "But we might need a round of paint and a side of inspiration."

The bartender raised an eyebrow, a smirk forming on his lips. "You two artists, huh? Last time I checked, paint didn't pair well with whiskey."

Felix leaned back in his seat, a mischievous spark in his eyes. "What if we told you we're painting the next great American classic? The kind that could redefine modern art?"

"Yeah, with a side of existential dread," I added, grinning.

"Right," the bartender said, crossing his arms and leaning in conspiratorially. "And what's the title of this masterpiece?"

"'The Wine and Whine Chronicles,'" Felix replied, barely containing his laughter. "It's about our struggles, you see. It's a reflection of life's messy nature, with maybe a dash of humor thrown in."

The bartender chuckled, shaking his head. "You kids are alright. I'll let you know if I see it at the Louvre."

"Better watch out," I said, adopting a faux serious expression. "You might be the next muse in our chaotic canvas."

Felix turned to me, eyes bright with mischief. "A tattooed bartender as our muse? Now that's a twist I didn't see coming."

Just then, the bar door swung open, letting in a gust of cool night air, and I caught sight of a figure stepping inside. My heart sank as I recognized the unmistakable silhouette of my ex, Jake, striding toward the bar with that familiar cocky swagger. "Well, isn't this a delightful reunion?" he said, his voice oozing with self-satisfaction as he approached.

Felix's hand tensed in mine, a flicker of uncertainty crossing his face. I squeezed his fingers gently, wanting to reassure him that this was just a blip in our evening. "What are you doing here?" I asked, trying to keep my tone steady, though the words tasted bitter on my tongue.

Jake flashed a grin that didn't quite reach his eyes, his gaze sweeping over Felix and then back to me. "Just grabbing a drink. Didn't expect to find you here, with... your new friend."

The implication hung heavy in the air, and I bristled. "What's it to you?" I shot back, a hint of defiance slipping into my tone.

He shrugged, nonchalant, but there was a glint of something more—maybe jealousy, or was it disdain? "Just making observations. Looks like you've moved on to the 'sensitive artist' type. How quaint."

"Better than being a self-absorbed jerk," Felix replied, his voice firm and steady.

I shot him a grateful glance, and the tension shifted, creating a bubble of solidarity between us. Felix's loyalty stoked a fire within me, propelling me to stand my ground. "You don't get to judge who I choose to spend my time with," I said, my heart pounding in my chest.

Jake raised an eyebrow, feigning innocence. "I'm not judging. Just observing the transformation. You've always had a penchant for the tragic."

"Goodbye, Jake," I said, cutting through the air like a knife, my voice unwavering.

"Feisty," he remarked, but the charm in his tone had dimmed, replaced by something more sour.

With a final, disdainful look, he turned on his heel and walked away, the door swinging shut behind him.

Felix exhaled a shaky breath, his expression shifting from uncertainty to admiration. "Wow, you handled that like a pro."

I let out a small laugh, feeling lighter. "Thanks. It's amazing what you can do when you're finally fed up with someone."

"Can't believe I'm saying this, but I think I like this new side of you."

"Glad to hear it," I said, my heart swelling with pride. "This side of me is here to stay."

As the evening progressed, laughter and playful banter became our armor against the lingering shadows of the past. The chaos outside faded into the background as Felix and I ventured deeper into our new pact—a promise to face life's messiness together, brush in hand and hearts wide open.

The energy in the bar surged, a lively tide that seemed to match the rhythm of my heart, which had begun to dance in tandem with Felix's laughter. It was as if the encounter with Jake had acted as a catalyst, stripping away the layers of unease that had initially settled over our evening. Now, sitting across from Felix, I felt a new clarity—an electric current of possibility zipping between us like fireflies igniting a summer night.

"What should we paint first?" Felix asked, leaning back, his eyes sparkling with mischief. "A self-portrait? I could capture your radiant beauty in all its chaotic glory."

"Oh, please, don't flatter me," I replied, waving a hand dramatically. "You might just make me blush, and we wouldn't want that. What about a still life? You know, fruit or flowers. Something boring to ease me into the artistic process."

"Boring? What's more exciting than painting the tragic tale of a wilted flower?" he shot back, grinning widely. "But I have a better idea. Let's paint something completely ridiculous—a rainbow unicorn galloping through a field of existential dread."

My laughter erupted, spilling into the air like champagne bubbles. "Now that sounds like a work of art that would sell for millions! I can see it now: 'The Sorrow of the Unicorn.'"

Felix took a sip of his drink, his gaze locked onto mine, eyes full of possibility. "Maybe we'll start a trend. Who knows? We could be the next art sensation."

"Or we could end up with paint in our hair and an unexpected visit from a therapist," I joked. "But hey, art is all about taking risks, right?"

As the laughter lingered between us, I felt the last remnants of the evening's earlier tension drift away, replaced by a burgeoning sense of camaraderie. We began to brainstorm ideas for our impending art session, the back-and-forth banter sparking creativity that felt both invigorating and liberating.

"I can't wait to see you in paint-stained clothes," Felix mused, shaking his head with a chuckle. "I bet you'll look like a modern-day Jackson Pollock."

"Hey, at least it'll be a fashion statement," I countered. "Why wear black when you can wear chaos?"

Suddenly, Felix's expression shifted as he glanced toward the entrance of the bar. My gaze followed his, and my heart sank. There stood Jake, again, but this time he wasn't alone. A woman with a confident stride and a magnetic presence followed closely behind him, her laughter cutting through the air like glass.

"Of course he'd bring reinforcements," I muttered under my breath, feeling a flare of annoyance mixed with something sharper—anxiety.

Felix noticed my reaction, his brow furrowing slightly. "Do you want to leave?"

"No," I said firmly, drawing strength from the promise we'd made earlier. "We're not going to let him ruin our night."

But as Jake and the woman approached, I could feel the familiar knot of tension tightening in my stomach. Jake's eyes landed on us, a smirk tugging at his lips, and the woman leaned in closer, her laughter ringing like a bell.

"Look who it is, the art duo," Jake said, his tone dripping with feigned innocence. "You must be having a great time. Is that a paintbrush I see, or is that just your latest attempt at grabbing attention?"

Felix's jaw tightened beside me, and I could feel the protective energy radiating off him. "We're just having a bit of fun. What brings you here, Jake? New dates to impress?"

Jake shot Felix a glance that was both dismissive and disdainful. "This is my friend Lila. She's an artist too," he said, gesturing to the woman beside him. "I thought I'd bring someone who could appreciate real talent."

Lila turned, her gaze lingering on Felix and me, a mix of curiosity and amusement dancing in her eyes. "Nice to meet you both," she said, her voice smooth and confident. "I've seen some of your work around. Heard you're quite the talent."

"Oh, I don't know about that," I replied, forcing a smile that felt tight on my lips. "We're just dabbling in existential unicorns."

"Sounds like a masterpiece in the making," she replied, her tone genuine. "Maybe I can join you sometime. I'd love to see how you translate your experiences onto the canvas."

Her sincerity caught me off guard, a welcome surprise amid the mockery. "That could be fun," I said, glancing at Felix, who seemed to relax slightly.

Jake, however, wasn't finished. "Just be careful. The last thing you want is to get tangled up in their little art project. It's bound to be a mess."

My heart raced with indignation, and before I could think better of it, I shot back, "At least we're creating something meaningful, unlike you, who seems to thrive on belittling others."

The atmosphere shifted as Lila's eyes widened slightly at my boldness. Felix's grip tightened around my hand, the tension sparking like static electricity. "Easy there," he said, his voice low, but I could see a glimmer of approval in his eyes.

Jake's smirk faltered, but he quickly recovered. "Charming as ever, I see. I just hope you don't find yourself regretting that boldness."

Felix took a breath, as if grounding himself against the weight of the exchange. "You know what? We'll let our art speak for itself, thanks."

The moment hung heavy in the air, the tension palpable. Lila, seemingly sensing the impending storm, stepped between Jake and us, her expression shifting from amusement to concern. "Maybe we should all just enjoy the night? There's enough room for everyone's talent here, right?"

Jake's eyes darkened, and I could see the gears turning in his mind, but he relented, a hint of irritation creeping into his smile. "Fine, let's see who comes out on top then."

As they turned to leave, Lila paused, glancing back at us with an almost apologetic smile. "Hope to see you both soon. I'd love to paint with you."

As they moved away, Felix and I exchanged glances, both surprised and relieved. "Well, that was… interesting," I said, shaking my head.

"Interesting? That was like watching a train wreck in slow motion," Felix replied, half-laughing, half-exasperated.

"I didn't mean to get so worked up. It just—"

"Made you feel something? That's okay. Sometimes you have to let it out."

"Right," I said, taking a deep breath. "And sometimes, it backfires spectacularly."

Just then, my phone buzzed in my pocket, cutting through the conversation. I fished it out, glancing at the screen, my heart sinking as I read the name. "It's my mom."

"Do you want to take it?"

I hesitated, feeling the weight of the moment. "Yeah, I should."

As I answered, the bar faded into the background, the lively chatter and music dulling to a distant hum. "Hey, Mom," I said, forcing cheer into my voice.

"Sweetheart, I need to talk to you. It's urgent."

I felt the chill of uncertainty creeping back in. "What's wrong?"

"Your dad… he's in trouble again. We might need you to come home."

Panic surged through me, and I glanced at Felix, his eyes wide with concern. "What do you mean? What happened?"

"Just… come home, okay? I'll explain everything when you get here."

The call ended abruptly, leaving me staring at the screen, dread pooling in my stomach. I looked up at Felix, my heart racing. "I have to go home. Something's wrong."

He reached across the table, his hand wrapping around mine with a reassuring grip. "I'll go with you."

I shook my head, feeling the weight of the world crashing down. "No, you don't have to. This is family stuff."

But the determination in his gaze only deepened. "If you're facing this alone, then I'm coming. You deserve someone in your corner."

Before I could respond, my phone buzzed again, a message this time. I opened it, my breath hitching as I read the words. "We need to talk. I'm sorry."

Felix noticed my expression, concern etched across his features. "What is it?"

"Just... a message from my dad," I managed to say, the tightness in my throat making it hard to breathe.

As the bar's atmosphere shifted around us, the vibrant energy dimmed, and the reality of what lay ahead loomed like a storm on the horizon. With uncertainty swirling within me, I knew that this was just the beginning.

Chapter 17: Unraveled Dreams

The fluorescent lights of the hospital waiting room flickered overhead, their sterile hum punctuating the silence that wrapped around me like a heavy blanket. The air was thick with the scent of antiseptic, a sharp reminder of the fragility of life that always lingered in places like this. I could feel the weight of worry pressing down on my chest as I scanned the room, my heart racing with every second that ticked by. My mind raced through a labyrinth of fears as I took a seat in a hard plastic chair, staring at the muted blue walls that seemed to absorb the anguish swirling in the air.

Felix was pacing at the far end of the room, his tall frame moving in tight circles like a caged animal. The worry etched across his handsome face was palpable; his brow furrowed, lips pressed into a thin line. I wanted to reach out, to soothe him, but I felt like a ship lost at sea, the currents of uncertainty threatening to pull us apart just when we had finally begun to find each other again. The moment we'd shared at the café, filled with laughter and tentative hopes, felt like a distant memory, as fragile as the glass of water trembling in my hands.

I took a deep breath, steeling myself against the wave of dread washing over me. Mia, his younger sister, had always been a bright light in Felix's life, a spark of mischief with her unruly curls and infectious giggle. The thought of her lying there, fragile and vulnerable, sent a shiver of fear through me. I could only imagine the weight of the news for Felix. He'd always been her protector, the one who brushed away her worries with the warmth of his smile. But now, that smile was nowhere to be found.

The doors slid open with a soft whoosh, and my heart leapt as a doctor stepped into the room. He had a kind but serious demeanor, and I could see Felix's body tense at the sight of him. I wanted to hold his hand, to remind him that he wasn't alone in this storm, but the fear of what the doctor might say rooted me to the spot.

"Mia is stable for now," the doctor began, and a collective breath seemed to be held in the room, the air growing thick with anticipation. "But she's been diagnosed with a severe complication related to her chronic illness. We're doing everything we can, but it's going to be a long road ahead."

Felix's shoulders sagged, the tension coiling around him loosening only slightly, but I could see the storm of emotions brewing just beneath the surface. I took a tentative step closer, wanting to offer him solace, but the words caught in my throat. What could I say that would ease the pain of uncertainty? The truth was, there was nothing I could say that would make this right. All I could do was be here, a silent witness to the turmoil.

"Long road ahead," Felix echoed, his voice low and trembling. I could see his hands ball into fists at his sides, his nails digging into his palms as if he could anchor himself against the swell of fear threatening to engulf him. "Why didn't she tell us? Why did she hide it?"

The doctor offered a small, understanding nod. "Sometimes, people protect their loved ones by carrying their burdens alone. It's not uncommon."

I felt the sting of tears prick my eyes, the realization hitting me hard. This wasn't just about Mia's health; it was about the silent struggles we all faced, the hidden battles that often raged just out of sight. In that moment, I could feel the bonds of our connection shifting and tightening, woven together by shared pain. I stepped forward, brushing my fingers lightly against Felix's arm, a grounding gesture amidst the chaos.

"Mia is strong," I said, my voice steady despite the tremor in my heart. "She has you. She has us. We'll get through this together."

Felix turned to me, and for a fleeting moment, I could see a flicker of gratitude break through his stormy expression. "I don't know what I'd do without you right now," he murmured, his voice barely above a whisper. The sincerity in his gaze sent a ripple of warmth through me, and I squeezed his arm gently, letting him know I was there, anchored to him, even as the world around us felt like it was unraveling.

The minutes bled into hours, and we remained huddled together, sharing our fears in quiet moments, our whispers weaving a tapestry of hope and despair. Each time the doors opened, my heart raced, praying it would be news of progress rather than setbacks. The waiting room felt like a prison of uncertainty, the clock ticking mockingly above us, each second a reminder of the life that hung in the balance.

Finally, the doctor reappeared, his expression somber but hopeful. "We're starting a new treatment plan that has shown promise," he announced, and relief surged through me like a wave crashing against the shore. "It's a long shot, but it's a shot nonetheless."

Felix looked at me, his eyes glistening with unshed tears. "A long shot," he echoed, and I could see a flicker of hope rekindling in his gaze. In that moment, we were no longer just two people navigating a storm; we were partners, united in the fight for Mia, ready to face whatever lay ahead together.

The hospital was a strange, pulsing world, and I felt like an intruder wandering through its halls of sterile white. Each step echoed against the linoleum floor, a constant reminder of the reality we were grappling with. Felix and I remained in the waiting room, time stretching and contracting like a rubber band, snapping back whenever a nurse whisked by, carrying a clipboard as if it held the secrets to life itself. I caught glimpses of families huddled together, their faces clouded with worry, and wondered how many other stories of heartache and hope were unfolding in this single, bustling space.

"Did you see the way he looked at us?" Felix murmured, his voice low, barely cutting through the silence. "Like we're in some sort of tragic soap opera." He raked a hand through his tousled hair, the movement betraying his mounting frustration. I wanted to reach out, to brush my fingers against the nape of his neck and reassure him that this wasn't a scripted drama, but our messy, unpredictable lives spilling into reality. Instead, I leaned back in my chair, trying to mimic the calm I wished to exude.

"Hey, you're right. Next time, I'm bringing popcorn. I hear the plot twist is quite the kicker," I quipped, forcing a smile. He gave me a sidelong glance, amusement flickering in his stormy eyes, but the humor dissipated as quickly as it had appeared. I could feel the shadows creeping back in, heavy with unspoken fears.

The wait felt endless, and the fluorescent lights buzzed above us like a swarm of angry bees. I focused on the rhythm of Felix's breathing, steady but shallow, and the way his fingers drummed against his knee, each tap echoing his anxiety. I wanted to fill the space with words, to weave a tapestry of distractions, but the gravity of our situation weighed down on us like a thick fog.

Finally, the door swung open again, this time revealing a nurse who looked as though she had just stepped out of a comforting scene from a favorite childhood storybook. She wore a soft smile, though I could see the fatigue etched around her eyes. "Felix? We've moved Mia to a private room. You can see her now."

Felix shot to his feet, the urgency of his movements like a taut string ready to snap. I followed closely behind, our footsteps echoing as we navigated the maze of corridors. The sterile smell of the hospital intensified, mixing with the faint scent of flowers and something sweet from the cafeteria. My heart raced, each beat a drum heralding the unknown.

As we approached the room, I could hear muffled voices, a comforting sound that reminded me we weren't alone in this. Felix paused at the door, taking a deep breath, his body tense as if bracing against a strong wind. "What if she doesn't want to see me?" he whispered, his vulnerability cracking through the bravado he often wore like armor.

"Then we'll leave her to rest," I replied gently, placing my hand on his arm. "But I doubt that's what she wants. She needs you." It felt like a clumsy reassurance, but it was all I had.

He nodded, pushing the door open to reveal a small oasis of calm amidst the chaos. Mia lay in the hospital bed, her curls tumbling around her like a halo, a stark contrast to the dullness of the sheets. She looked small, even frail, the vibrant spirit I remembered tucked away beneath the surface. The sight of her made my heart ache, a tugging sensation that blended sadness with hope.

"Mia," Felix breathed, crossing the threshold with careful steps. I followed, giving them space, but my heart ached to be part of this fragile reunion.

Her eyes fluttered open, revealing a flash of surprise followed by recognition. "Felix?" she croaked, her voice weak but still laced with warmth. A smile broke across her face, a beacon of light cutting through the grayness that surrounded us.

"I'm here," he said, his voice steady now, holding the strength of a thousand unshed tears. He reached for her hand, and I watched as she curled her fingers around his, her grip like a lifeline.

The moment felt sacred, charged with unspoken emotions. "What happened?" she asked, her brow furrowing in concern.

Felix took a deep breath, his voice thick with emotion. "You scared us, Mia. We didn't know you were sick."

Her smile faded slightly, and I could see the weight of secrets pressing down on her. "I thought... I thought I could manage it. I didn't want you to worry," she admitted, her voice barely above a whisper. The honesty in her admission broke my heart. How often do we convince ourselves that silence is the best medicine?

"Worry? You mean like the kind that keeps you up at night?" Felix said, his voice sharp but laced with concern. "You could have told me. I would have been there, every step of the way."

Mia looked down, her fingers fidgeting with the blanket. "I didn't want to burden you," she mumbled, and it struck me how this tendency to shoulder pain alone can isolate us, even from those who love us most.

"You're not a burden, Mia. You're my sister," Felix said fiercely, the passion in his voice igniting a fire in my chest. "And I'm not letting you go through this alone."

Tension crackled in the air, a palpable shift that filled the room with hope. I stepped forward, eager to add my support. "We're all in this together. You've got two fighters in your corner now," I said, injecting some lightness into the gravity of our conversation.

Mia's gaze flickered between us, and a tentative smile broke through the uncertainty. "You two are ridiculous," she said, her voice regaining some strength. "But I think I like it."

The laughter felt foreign but warm, like a sunbeam breaking through clouds. In that moment, we were not just fighting against illness; we were stitching together the frayed edges of our lives, binding our shared pain with threads of love and resilience.

As we settled into a comfortable rhythm of shared stories and laughter, the world outside faded away. The hospital transformed from a place of dread into a sanctuary where we could confront the reality of our lives together.

The laughter lingered in the air like a delicate promise, wrapping us in a cocoon of warmth. Mia, still nestled in her hospital bed, was slowly emerging from the haze of illness that had enveloped her for too long. The way her eyes sparkled as she exchanged jabs with Felix reminded me of summer days spent lounging in the sun, unbothered by the shadows creeping around the edges. I felt a sense of relief wash over me, a balm to soothe the tension that had gripped us since the moment we rushed to the hospital.

"Okay, so what's your game plan for taking over the world once you're out of here?" Felix teased, leaning closer to Mia, his smile transforming his worried features into something more akin to his playful self.

She rolled her eyes dramatically, the movement eliciting a chuckle from me. "Oh, I was thinking of starting with world domination through bubble tea shops. I hear the secret to happiness is tapioca."

"Bubble tea?" I interjected, my voice filled with mock indignation. "You're really aiming high, aren't you? What about unicorn farms or something more impactful?"

"Unicorns are just an urban myth," Mia shot back, her laughter brightening the sterile room. "Besides, if I want a pet unicorn, I'll just summon it from the realm of imagination."

Our banter filled the room, a delightful distraction from the reality of her illness. I leaned against the wall, watching the two of them. This was the light I had hoped for, a sign that things might just be okay. As Mia playfully argued the merits of bubble tea with Felix, I allowed myself to believe in a brighter future for her, for us.

But as the sunlight began to fade outside the window, a shadow of doubt crept back in. The doctors had said it would be a long road ahead, and I couldn't shake the feeling that our newfound normalcy was teetering on the edge of something far more precarious.

After a while, Felix and I stepped outside the room to catch our breath, leaving Mia to rest. The sterile hallway felt uninviting, but it was better than the heavy atmosphere of the hospital room. I watched as Felix leaned against the wall, running a hand through his hair, his expression shifting from relief to uncertainty.

"What if she doesn't recover fully?" he asked suddenly, his voice raw, vulnerability cracking through his bravado. "What if this is just the beginning?"

I stepped closer, closing the gap between us. "Then we'll be here for her," I said, trying to infuse my words with the strength I wanted to convey. "We'll fight together, every step of the way."

He looked down the hall, where the bright lights cast long shadows, and I could see the tension etched into his features. "It's just... I feel so helpless, you know? I thought I was protecting her by not asking too many questions, but now..." His voice trailed off, the weight of regret hanging heavy in the air.

"We can't go back," I reminded him gently. "But we can move forward." I wanted to tell him that it was okay to feel helpless, that it was a natural reaction in the face of something so uncertain. Instead, I leaned into him, resting my head against his shoulder. It felt intimate, comforting—a reminder that even in moments of despair, we were not alone.

"I just wish I could take her pain away," he murmured, his breath warm against my hair.

As if summoned by our conversation, a familiar figure appeared at the end of the hallway—Dr. Patel, her smile warm yet professional. "Felix, can I speak with you for a moment?" she asked, her tone serious.

I felt a chill settle in my stomach. I stepped back, wanting to give them space, but Felix caught my gaze, a flicker of worry crossing his features. "What is it?" he asked, the tension in his voice palpable.

Dr. Patel led him a few paces away, her body language shifting into that of someone who needed to convey important information. I strained to catch snippets of their conversation, but the hospital noise drowned out their words. I felt like a voyeur in a play where the plot was twisting dangerously, and I wasn't sure if I wanted to stay for the finale.

The two spoke in hushed tones, and I could see Felix's expression change, the hope slowly draining from his face. His fists clenched at his sides, and I felt my heart drop into my stomach. Something was wrong. The air around me felt charged, heavy with an impending storm, and I could almost hear the thunder rumbling in the distance.

When Felix returned to my side, his eyes were stormy, a tempest brewing beneath the surface. "What did she say?" I asked, my voice barely above a whisper.

He hesitated, the words seeming to get stuck in his throat. "Mia's treatment plan... it's not working as expected. They want to try something more aggressive, but..."

"But what?" I pressed, the urgency rising in my chest.

His voice cracked, and I felt the tremor in his words. "But there's a chance it could make things worse."

The walls of the hallway seemed to close in on me, and I had to force myself to breathe. "Worse?" I echoed, the word tasting bitter on my tongue. "How can they even think of that? She's just a kid!"

"I know!" he exclaimed, his frustration spilling over. "But the doctors think it might be our only shot. If we don't take it, she could deteriorate even faster."

I felt the floor shift beneath me, the weight of impossible decisions hanging in the air. "And what if she doesn't survive the treatment? It's a gamble."

"Every option feels like a gamble right now," Felix shot back, his voice sharp. "But we can't just sit here and do nothing."

I closed my eyes, fighting against the tears threatening to spill. The thought of Mia going through something even more painful felt like a cruel twist of fate. "What do we do?"

He ran a hand through his hair, a gesture that had become all too familiar. "We support her, whatever she decides. We give her the strength to fight."

Just then, the hospital's PA system crackled to life, announcing the names of patients and their visitors, an echoing reminder of the lives interwoven with ours in this space of healing and uncertainty. The noise brought me back to reality, and I felt the weight of our situation bearing down harder than ever.

Felix's phone buzzed in his pocket, pulling his attention. He pulled it out, glancing at the screen, and his expression shifted again, confusion crossing his features. "It's Mia's friend, Tara," he said, frowning. "She wants to know if Mia's okay. Why would she be texting now?"

"Maybe she sensed something was off?" I suggested, trying to rationalize the sudden communication.

But Felix was already moving, the urgency of the message drawing him in. He tapped out a quick response, but before he could send it, his phone vibrated again, and I could see a flicker of worry cross his face.

"Felix?" I asked, concern lacing my voice. "What's wrong?"

He stared at his screen, his expression shifting from confusion to horror. "It's a video... it looks like Mia."

"What do you mean it looks like Mia?" My heart raced as I leaned closer, peering at the small screen.

"Just... just watch," he stammered, his voice barely above a whisper.

I glanced at the video, my breath hitching in my throat as the image flickered to life. Mia, vibrant and laughing just hours ago, was on the screen, but her eyes were clouded, a raw energy crackling around her. The background blurred, and the words scrawled across the bottom sent a chill down my spine: "This is just the beginning."

A feeling of dread washed over me as the screen faded to black, leaving us in a room filled with unanswered questions and uncertainty. In that moment, I realized that the shadows lurking around us were darker than we had imagined, and the fight for Mia's life was only just beginning.

Chapter 18: A Tenuous Connection

The room was dimly lit, the air thick with the scent of old wood and lingering notes of forgotten jazz. It had been my sanctuary, a refuge from the chaos that seemed to swirl just beyond the threshold. The piano sat there, its polished surface gleaming faintly in the low light, a silent witness to the hours I had spent pouring my heart into its keys. Tonight, though, it felt more like a lonely companion, its chords waiting patiently for me to coax out the melody I so desperately needed to create.

I took a deep breath, letting the weight of the world slip off my shoulders for just a moment. The news had hit us like a thunderstorm, sudden and unforgiving. Mia's treatment was a battleground of uncertainty and hope, and with each passing day, I could see Felix retreating further into the shadows of his own mind. It was as if the more I tried to reach him, the more he clung to his guilt like a lifebuoy in a tempest. His music, once a bridge between us, now echoed hollowly in the distance as he lost himself in its depths.

I touched the keys gently, feeling the cool ivory beneath my fingers. A simple arpeggio danced into the air, fragile yet potent. Each note carried the weight of my longing, of the desire to connect with Felix, to pull him from the abyss he had crawled into. "Why are you so stubborn?" I whispered, half to myself, half to the ghost of the man who used to sit beside me, a glimmer of light amidst my darkness.

The silence that followed was deafening, as if the room itself held its breath, waiting for the storm to break. I missed him—the way he would laugh, how his eyes sparkled when he played, the warmth of his presence that used to envelop me like a well-worn blanket. Now, the space beside me was cold and empty, a chasm that felt as wide as the ocean. I squeezed my eyes shut, summoning the memories that flickered like the faint glow of a candle.

"Hey, genius!" I imagined his voice, teasing me about my relentless pursuit of perfection. "Stop staring at the keys like they're going to bite you. Just play!"

I could almost hear his laughter, a sound that once filled the air like a melody, vibrant and full of life. But now, the laughter was gone, replaced by a heavy silence that weighed on my heart. "Come back to me," I murmured, pressing down on the keys with a force that reverberated through my fingertips.

The music flowed out, raw and unfiltered, a tapestry of emotions woven into every note. I poured my fears and frustrations into the melody, crafting a piece that echoed the struggles we faced together, the unspoken battles that raged behind the facade of normalcy. It was a haunting piece, a bittersweet elegy to the love that felt like it was slipping through my fingers.

As I played, I imagined Felix listening—his eyes closed, his brow furrowed in concentration. Would he hear the desperation in my chords? Would he feel the flickering hope woven into the fabric of the music? I hoped that my vulnerability would bridge the chasm between us, that he would understand the depths of my concern and love.

With each passing moment, I felt the weight of the world lifting, if only slightly. The music became my escape, a means of communication where words failed. I could almost visualize him, standing in the doorway, his silhouette outlined by the soft glow of the streetlamp outside. I could see the way his shoulders would relax as he took in the notes, the way his heart would begin to thaw under the warmth of my song.

But as I played, an unsettling thought crept in. What if he didn't come? What if he remained locked away in his fortress of solitude, too consumed by his demons to hear me? I shook my head, dispelling the dark clouds that threatened to envelop my thoughts. I would not give up on him.

As I finished the final notes, I felt a surge of determination wash over me. This was not just music; it was a declaration, a promise that I would fight for us, even if it meant battling against his own mind. I wanted to be the light that pierced through the darkness he had wrapped around himself like a protective cocoon.

The jazz night was just days away, and as I prepared for it, the pressure began to mount. Would my composition resonate with him? Would he understand the raw, messy love that fueled every note? My heart raced at the thought, the uncertainty dancing in my chest like a live wire.

I tucked my hair behind my ear, my thoughts swirling with anxiety as I gazed out the window into the dusky evening. The city hummed softly below, a symphony of life and motion that seemed to contrast sharply with the stillness inside me. I needed to reach Felix, to break through his walls before he completely lost himself.

The night of the performance arrived, cloaked in an air of anticipation that crackled like static electricity. The small jazz club was a cozy haven, filled with laughter and the clinking of glasses. I took my place on stage, the spotlight warm against my skin. The audience buzzed with excitement, but all I could focus on was the vacant seat in the corner, where I had always imagined Felix would be.

As the first notes filled the air, I poured my soul into the performance. Each chord was a plea, a whisper of hope, and a declaration of love. I played for him, for us, hoping to bridge the divide that had grown so vast. The music flowed, drawing me deeper into its embrace, and with each passing moment, I felt more alive. But would he feel it too? Would my vulnerability be enough to break through the walls he had built so carefully around himself?

I stole a glance toward the door, heart pounding in my chest, wondering if tonight would finally be the night I reached him.

The dimly lit jazz club thrummed with energy, the audience's chatter melding into a soft symphony that filled the air. As I stood on stage, my fingers poised above the piano keys, I felt the weight of their collective anticipation pressing down on me like a velvet curtain. Each tick of the clock seemed to echo in the cavernous room, amplifying the anxious rhythm of my heart. This wasn't just any performance; it was a lifeline thrown into turbulent waters, a desperate attempt to pull Felix back from the edge of the abyss he had been teetering on.

With a deep breath, I let the first notes spill forth, trembling yet resolute. The melody danced like a wisp of smoke, curling and twisting through the air, weaving in and out of the shadows that loomed between us. It was a bittersweet concoction, a mixture of hope and despair that mirrored the turmoil inside my chest. As the music enveloped me, I became acutely aware of the audience fading away. This was between Felix and me—a secret language that only we understood.

I glanced at the door again, the way my heart leapt at every figure that entered, a flutter of hope each time. The last time I had seen him, he had looked so small, hunched over his guitar, his eyes clouded with that familiar storm. Guilt gnawed at him, a relentless beast that refused to let go, and every time I reached out, he had pushed me away with a quiet ferocity that left me breathless. It was infuriating, watching him retreat into a shell, convinced that he was unworthy of love or support, convinced that he was drowning in his own mistakes. But I knew better. I knew the man who could light up a room with his laughter, who could make the air hum with the strum of his guitar. He was still in there, somewhere.

The song swelled, a crescendo of longing and heartache, and I poured every ounce of my emotion into the notes. It was a tapestry woven with threads of our shared memories—the late-night jam sessions where time slipped away, the laughter that rolled through the air like music itself, and those stolen moments that felt infinite in their simplicity. I could almost see him sitting there beside me, fingers dancing along the strings, a playful grin on his face. "You always play like you're running away from something," he'd tease, that glimmer of mischief in his eyes. "What are you so scared of, anyway?"

But I wasn't running away tonight; I was standing firm, rooted in the belief that love was worth fighting for, even when it felt like the ground beneath us was shifting. Each note hung in the air, quivering with the weight of my hopes. I wanted him to hear this, to feel the pulse of my heart echoing in the melody, to know that I was here, ready to weather whatever storm was brewing in his mind.

As I transitioned into the next section of the piece, my gaze flicked to the back of the room. The soft glow of the exit sign illuminated a figure leaning against the wall, hands tucked in his pockets. My heart stopped. Felix. He was there, watching, the faintest hint of a smile playing at the corners of his lips. It flickered like a candle in the wind, hesitant yet undeniably present.

The realization nearly derailed me, but I anchored myself, letting the music guide me. His presence infused the air with a new energy, a spark of hope igniting the embers of my determination. I played harder, the notes pouring from me like rain, each one a plea to bring him closer, to remind him of the connection we shared.

When the final chord resonated through the room, silence enveloped me like a warm embrace. The audience erupted into applause, but my focus remained solely on him. Felix stepped forward, the light catching the shadows on his face, illuminating the turmoil still lurking in his eyes. I could see it there—the guilt, the confusion, but also a flicker of something else, something more vulnerable.

As the crowd continued to cheer, I rose from the piano, heart pounding, and made my way toward him. The distance between us felt monumental, each step heavy with unspoken words.

"Felix," I breathed, finally reaching him. "You came."

"Yeah, well, I couldn't let you make a complete fool of yourself without me," he quipped, but the humor fell flat, a thin veneer over something deeper.

"Is that what you think?" I challenged, my voice barely above a whisper. "That I was just putting on a show?"

His gaze flicked away, and the moment felt charged, like the air before a summer storm. "I don't know what you were doing. I just—" He ran a hand through his hair, frustration boiling just beneath the surface. "I'm not... I'm not okay, and I don't want to drag you down with me."

"That's not how this works," I countered, feeling the heat of my passion rise. "You think I'm going to stand by while you wallow in this? You're not a burden, Felix. You're my partner. We face things together, remember?"

He looked at me then, really looked, and for the first time, I saw the walls begin to crumble in his gaze. "I just didn't want to ruin everything for you."

"Too late for that," I shot back with a wry smile, the tension breaking like a wave crashing against a rocky shore. "You've already managed to steal my heart, and I'm not giving it back without a fight."

A small laugh escaped him, a sound so precious I wanted to wrap it in bubble wrap and keep it safe. "You always were the tenacious one."

"Guilty as charged," I replied, stepping closer. "Now, how about you let me in? I promise not to bite... much."

His expression softened, and the playfulness in his eyes began to rekindle. "You know, I used to think you were just a little too optimistic for your own good."

"And you thought you were too cynical to ever let anyone in," I teased, mirroring his smirk. "Looks like we both have some adjusting to do."

The atmosphere between us shifted, and for the first time in a long while, it felt like we were teetering on the edge of something beautiful—an unspoken promise that perhaps we could still find our way back to each other.

As the sounds of laughter and clinking glasses faded into the background, I could see the flicker of hope lighting up Felix's eyes. He wasn't entirely free yet, and I knew it would take time, but tonight, perhaps, we could begin to bridge the gap. The world felt vibrant again, full of possibilities, and I could almost hear the music swelling around us—a reminder that we were in this together, a melody that would carry us through the darkness ahead.

The moment hung between us, fragile and electric, as Felix's gaze softened, his defenses slipping ever so slightly. I felt a thrill of hope surge through me, but it was quickly tempered by the awareness of the battles still raging within him. His shoulders, usually so broad and relaxed when he played, were tense now, as if he were carrying the weight of the world on his back. The flicker of amusement in his eyes was promising, but I knew all too well how quickly it could vanish beneath a cloud of self-doubt.

"Okay, Miss Tenacious," he said, his voice a low rumble that sent a shiver down my spine. "What's the plan? You think just because you played some pretty music, I'm going to magically fix my life?"

"Not exactly," I replied, crossing my arms and leaning in, my tone playful but earnest. "But I do think you've got some serious skills when it comes to unraveling a song. How about you give me a few lessons on how to help you see that you're not alone?"

He chuckled softly, a sound that wrapped around me like a warm blanket. "Is that how this works? I'm supposed to just sit back and let you save me?"

"Well, I mean, I was hoping for a bit of teamwork here," I replied, raising an eyebrow. "You know, like we did in those jam sessions when we'd trade solos? I played the bright, hopeful lines, and you brought in the heart-wrenching riffs."

"Touché," he conceded, a hint of mischief creeping back into his voice. "But can we just agree that this isn't going to be some sappy duet? I'm still a little rough around the edges."

"Oh, I wouldn't dream of it," I said with a smirk, playfully nudging his shoulder. "More like a duet with a side of chaos and a sprinkle of existential dread."

He laughed, and in that moment, the tension that had wrapped around us began to dissipate. "Okay, chaos and dread I can handle. But seriously, what do I do now? I don't even know how to begin to fix what's broken inside me."

"Start with the things you love," I suggested, my voice softening. "The music, the laughter, us—whatever it is that brings you joy. Let's just take one step at a time. We've both been through hell, but I believe we can find our way back to each other."

Felix ran a hand through his hair, uncertainty flickering in his eyes. "And what if I can't? What if this is who I am now?"

I leaned closer, my heart pounding. "That's not true, Felix. You're so much more than your struggles. You have a light in you that refuses to go out. I can see it, even when you can't."

For a heartbeat, he seemed to ponder my words, the vulnerability laid bare between us like a delicate thread. The laughter had faded, replaced by a silence heavy with unspoken fears. "I'm scared, you know," he admitted finally, the words barely escaping his lips. "Scared of what I might drag you into, scared of what might happen if I let you in."

"Then let me in," I urged, reaching out to cup his cheek, feeling the warmth of his skin beneath my palm. "Let me be there for you. I promise I won't let you fall. Not again."

His gaze bore into mine, and for a moment, I could see the walls crumbling, replaced by a flicker of hope. But then, like a specter rising from the depths, the doubt returned, shadowing his features. "I don't want to hurt you, Mia."

"Hurting me is not a superpower, Felix," I quipped, trying to lighten the moment. "Trust me, I've handled worse. I've survived years of dealing with my own fears. You don't get to decide what I can or can't handle."

A smile tugged at his lips, and for a moment, we were both suspended in a bubble of shared laughter and connection, as if we had been transported back to those carefree days when life felt simpler. But beneath the surface, the currents were still churning, and I knew we had miles to go before we reached calm waters.

"Alright, I'll give it a shot," he said, his voice steadying. "But I'm still a work in progress, and I can't promise that I won't trip along the way."

"Neither can I," I replied, a teasing glint in my eyes. "But tripping could be fun. Think of it as our own jazz improv—unexpected but always interesting."

Just then, the laughter from the bar rolled over us, the patrons oblivious to the small revolution happening in our corner. As I turned to gauge the crowd, a familiar face caught my eye, and I froze. It was Mia, standing just inside the doorway, her expression unreadable as she scanned the room.

"Mia!" I called, waving her over. "Over here!"

Her gaze flickered between Felix and me, a hint of confusion etched on her features. She took a hesitant step forward, her eyes darting back to Felix. "Hey! I just got here. I didn't know you were—"

"I was just telling Felix how much he means to me," I interjected, sensing the tension crackling in the air, a sudden chill creeping in. "He's finally letting me in, so that's a good start, right?"

Mia's expression shifted, her brow furrowing as she glanced between us. "Right. That's great. But, um... are you okay, Felix?"

"Just peachy," he replied, his tone a touch too light, an uneasy smile plastered on his face. "Just having a little chat about how to not fall apart."

"Nothing like a little public therapy session, right?" I said, trying to ease the tension that had settled around us like fog.

Mia's eyes narrowed, and I could feel her assessing the situation with the keen awareness of someone who had navigated her own battles. "You're sure? Because I can stick around if you need me to..."

Felix shook his head, a glint of determination returning to his gaze. "No, I think I've got this. Just some unfinished business, you know?"

Mia hesitated, the protective instinct flaring in her eyes. "Alright, but just remember, I'm here. For both of you."

"Noted," I said, giving her a reassuring smile, though inside I felt a tightening in my chest. I knew Mia's presence would complicate the fragile moment we had just begun to build.

As she turned to grab a drink from the bar, Felix's gaze drifted to me, and I could see the vulnerability flickering back into his expression. "You sure this is what you want?" he asked, his voice barely above a whisper. "To be here, with me?"

"More than anything," I affirmed, my heart racing. "But if you're not ready..."

Before I could finish, a loud crash erupted from the far side of the room, shattering the moment. I whipped around, just in time to see a figure stumble backward, knocking over chairs and sending drinks flying. The chaos spread like wildfire, gasps erupting from the crowd as people turned to witness the commotion.

"Mia!" I shouted, instinctively reaching for Felix's arm as we both turned toward the unfolding scene. Panic coursed through the air, and the once-vibrant atmosphere turned electric with tension.

As I scanned the room, searching for Mia, a sense of dread gripped me. There she was, still near the bar, her eyes wide as she took a step back from the chaos. But in that split second, another figure emerged, slipping through the crowd and heading straight for her.

"Watch out!" I screamed, adrenaline surging through me as I launched forward, heart pounding.

But before I could reach her, everything erupted into chaos, and the world around me seemed to tilt on its axis.

Chapter 19: The Night We Remember

The backstage area thrummed with the low hum of anticipation, a vibrant pulse that reverberated through my bones. Cues and murmurs intertwined, the scent of polished wood mingling with the faint hint of sweat and the overzealous fragrance of stage makeup. My fingers brushed against the worn edges of my guitar, the strings cool beneath my touch, promising a release that felt both exhilarating and terrifying. I could hear the faint echoes of the audience through the heavy velvet curtains, a collective breath held in the anticipation of the evening's performance.

I took a moment, closing my eyes, willing my heartbeat to steady. The world felt sharp and electrified, every sound heightened, every feeling magnified. I remembered the countless hours I'd spent rehearsing in my small apartment, the songs pouring from my soul like a dam finally breaking free. This wasn't just another gig; it was the culmination of a journey fraught with uncertainty and yearning, a chance to reclaim my voice.

Felix, standing at the edge of the stage, looked like a silhouette against the flickering backstage lights. I hadn't anticipated how seeing him would make my stomach flip. There he was, a slice of vulnerability wrapped in a tailored suit, his dark hair tousled in that way that made my heart swell with warmth. His expression was a strange mix of admiration and apprehension, a flicker of hope dancing in his gaze. We hadn't spoken much since the fallout, but I felt our shared history linger in the air, a tapestry woven with laughter and sorrow.

The stage manager's voice cut through my reverie, her sharp tone sharpening my focus. "You're up, Sam!"

I nodded, though my legs felt like they were mired in quicksand. Taking a deep breath, I stepped forward, my heart racing as I crossed the threshold into the spotlight. A sea of faces greeted me, a medley of curiosity and eagerness shimmering in the dim light. The soft glow illuminated their expectant eyes, a thousand stories waiting to intertwine with my own.

As I settled into the center of the stage, I could almost taste the adrenaline. The crowd fell into a reverent silence, as if the air itself held its breath. I glanced down at my guitar, its polished surface reflecting the bright stage lights, and let my fingers find their way across the strings. The first chord reverberated through the silence, a sound that echoed in my chest, igniting a spark within.

I poured myself into the music, each note a testament to the love I had lost and the hope I yearned to reclaim. I sang of summer nights spent beneath a canopy of stars, the warmth of laughter mingling with the cool breeze, and the heartache that inevitably followed. The melody flowed like water, each word a ripple that reached out into the audience, connecting us in a shared experience of longing and resilience.

As I performed, I could feel Felix's eyes on me, his presence an anchor in the swirling tide of emotion. The way he leaned slightly forward, his lips parted in awe, made my heart swell. In those moments, I let go of the past, each note resonating with the truth of who I was and who I wanted to be. I poured every bit of pain and joy into that performance, crafting a bridge of sound that we could both walk across.

When the final note hung in the air, a breathless pause enveloped the room. Then, like the breaking of a dam, applause erupted, filling the space with warmth and electricity. The sound enveloped me like a soft embrace, yet I barely registered it. All I could see was Felix, his eyes glistening, something raw and tender flickering in their depths.

He moved toward me, the crowd fading into a dull roar around us. "Sam," he breathed, his voice thick with emotion. I hadn't heard him say my name in what felt like eons, and it wrapped around me like a familiar blanket.

"Felix," I replied, my heart racing as I stepped closer. There was a magnetic pull between us, an unspoken acknowledgment of all we had navigated, both together and apart. "Did you—"

"Your voice," he interrupted, his gaze intense and unwavering. "It's incredible. I can't believe how far you've come."

A soft blush crept up my cheeks at his praise, yet beneath the admiration lay an undertow of vulnerability, a crack in the facade we had both maintained. I could sense the weight of all the unsaid words, the remnants of our shared history swirling in the air, heavy with significance.

"I'm still figuring it out," I admitted, my voice a whisper. "But tonight felt... different. Like I was finally letting go of the past."

Felix's gaze softened, a hint of a smile tugging at the corners of his lips. "You're not alone in this, you know. I've been navigating my own storm."

The tension shifted, crackling with the electricity of unresolved feelings and the potential for healing. The world around us faded, the audience's applause dwindling into a distant echo, leaving just the two of us suspended in that moment of connection. It was fragile yet potent, a reminder that love, though battered, could find a way back home.

"Can we talk?" he asked, the vulnerability in his voice wrapping around me like a soft embrace.

"Yeah," I replied, my heart pounding as I felt the remnants of our fractured relationship stir to life once more. We had crossed a threshold, and while the path ahead felt uncertain, I could sense that the journey would be worth every step.

The backstage area, once a sanctuary of pre-performance nerves, transformed into a bustling world of celebration. The applause resonated like a heartbeat, infusing the air with an energy that both thrilled and unsettled me. I stood there, caught between the lingering euphoria of the performance and the raw intensity radiating from Felix, who lingered just outside the spotlight, as if hesitant to step fully into my orbit again.

"Sam," he said, and the way my name rolled off his tongue made my heart do an unexpected somersault. I could almost feel the weight of our past pressing down, a tangible reminder of all the times we had danced around each other—too afraid, too proud, too human.

"Let's find somewhere quieter," I suggested, my voice steady despite the whirlwind in my chest. I gestured toward the side door that led to the alley behind the venue, a shadowy realm away from the bustle and noise, where the air would feel less charged and more intimate.

He nodded, his expression shifting from uncertainty to a cautious hope. We slipped outside, the cool night air wrapping around us like a comforting embrace, contrasting sharply with the heat of the performance lingering on my skin. The alley was dimly lit, graffiti art splashed across the walls, a collage of vibrant colors and rebellious messages that somehow felt like a backdrop to our own tangled story.

"I didn't expect you to be this good," he said, leaning against the wall, his arms crossed defensively. There was a twinkle in his eye, a mix of admiration and mischief, as if he were challenging me to defy his expectations further.

"Good?" I shot back, raising an eyebrow. "I prefer 'extraordinarily talented,' thank you very much."

He chuckled, a sound that danced between us, easing the tension. "Fair enough. You really blew me away tonight. I could hear the passion in every note."

The compliment settled between us, grounding me even as my heart raced at the intensity of his gaze. "It's easier to sing when you're not drowning in your own emotions," I admitted, the words tumbling out before I could stop them. "There was a time I felt lost in them, you know? Like I was treading water, just trying not to sink."

He shifted, his expression turning serious. "I've been there too. It's a dark place. Sometimes, it feels like you're fighting against the current, and every stroke you take just pulls you deeper."

I nodded, the heaviness of our shared understanding thickening the air around us. "But tonight, I felt... lighter. Almost like I was floating instead of sinking."

"Because of the music?" he asked, his brow furrowed in curiosity.

"Partly. But also because of you being here." The admission slipped out, raw and unfiltered. "I didn't realize how much I missed having you around until I saw you in the audience."

His gaze softened, the hardness of our past melting away, even if just a little. "I've missed you too, Sam. More than I thought I could."

The words hung in the air, palpable and charged, and I could feel the threads of connection weaving between us. There was an undeniable chemistry, an unspoken acknowledgment that our paths were still intertwined, tangled in ways we couldn't yet understand.

"What are we doing, Felix?" I asked, my voice barely above a whisper. "Can we really go back to what we had? Or are we just setting ourselves up for another fall?"

He hesitated, running a hand through his hair in that familiar way that sent a thrill down my spine. "I don't know. But I do know that I'm tired of pretending I don't care. You matter to me, and I want to figure this out. Together."

His sincerity struck a chord deep within me, reverberating through the very essence of who I was. "Together," I echoed, savoring the word, letting it dance on my tongue like the sweetest of melodies. "What does that even look like?"

Felix stepped closer, the space between us shrinking, the air electric with possibility. "I think it starts with honesty. Not just the good stuff, but the messy, complicated, downright uncomfortable truths. I want us to be real, Sam. No more pretenses."

I swallowed hard, the weight of his words sinking in. "Okay. So, let's start. What's your truth?"

He met my gaze, unwavering. "I was terrified when you told me you were leaving for that tour. I didn't want to be the one holding you back, but it hurt more than I expected. I thought we had something worth fighting for, but when you walked away, I felt like I lost my footing."

His honesty resonated, each word a brushstroke painting a clearer picture of the emotions I had buried. "I was scared too," I admitted, a lump forming in my throat. "Leaving felt like stepping off a cliff. I wanted to fly, but I didn't know if I could. And when you didn't chase after me, it felt like I was falling alone."

There it was, the truth laid bare between us, raw and vulnerable. Felix's expression shifted, the tension in his shoulders easing just a fraction. "Maybe we were both too scared to reach out," he mused, a hint of regret lacing his words.

I reached out, brushing my fingers against his arm, the warmth of his skin grounding me. "We can't change the past, but we can choose how we move forward."

"Together?" he asked again, his voice low, filled with hope.

"Together," I confirmed, a smile breaking through the weight of our confessions.

Just then, the distant sound of laughter and music from the venue floated through the alley, a reminder of the world that continued to spin outside our cocoon. Felix's eyes sparkled with mischief, pulling me from the depths of our heavy conversation. "How about we make a pact? No more talking about feelings until after dessert."

"Dessert?" I laughed, the absurdity of the situation striking me. "You mean to say you're willing to brave the chaos of the after-party just for a slice of cake?"

"Hey, it's not just cake; it's a small slice of redemption. Plus, I hear the chocolate mousse is to die for. And we could use some sugar after this intense therapy session."

I couldn't help but grin at his playful challenge. "Fine. But if they run out of chocolate mousse, I'm holding you responsible."

He held up his hands in mock surrender. "I promise to get you the biggest slice available. Deal?"

"Deal."

As we turned to head back inside, I felt lighter, as if the weight of uncertainty had lifted, replaced with an exhilarating blend of hope and mischief. The night was still young, and the promise of possibilities loomed just ahead, sweet as the chocolate mousse that awaited us.

The after-party was a kaleidoscope of laughter and color, a whirlwind of energy that spilled from the venue into the cool night air. As we stepped back inside, the lively chatter enveloped us, mingling with the intoxicating scent of rich foods and the sweet undertones of dessert waiting to be devoured. My heart raced—not just from the performance but also from the electric possibilities that hung between Felix and me, making the air shimmer with promise.

"First things first, let's secure that mousse," I declared, my playful determination shining through. "I'm not leaving here without it."

Felix chuckled, falling into step beside me. "Lead the way, oh fearless dessert conqueror."

We navigated through the throngs of people, the crowd an unpredictable sea of familiar faces and new acquaintances. As we weaved through the sea of bodies, I caught snippets of conversation—a mix of congratulations and excitement, each word a reminder of how the night had unfolded. It felt surreal, being part of this world where art and connection thrived, but I was acutely aware that my journey had taken an unexpected turn tonight, pulling me closer to Felix in a way I hadn't anticipated.

"Is it me, or is everyone way too cheerful for a Monday night?" I quipped, scanning the exuberant crowd.

Felix smirked, a mischievous glint in his eye. "You'd be cheerful too if you just witnessed a musical revival. This place is buzzing like a beehive in spring. Everyone's here for the honey."

I laughed, shaking my head. "And I thought you were only here for the chocolate mousse."

He feigned shock. "You wound me! I'm here for both the mousse and your delightful company."

We arrived at the dessert table, which boasted a delectable spread of treats—cakes, pastries, and, of course, the promised chocolate mousse. It glistened under the soft lights, a dark, velvety temptation that called to me like a siren song.

"There it is," I gasped, eyes wide as I approached the mousse. "It's even more glorious than I imagined!"

Felix chuckled as I quickly grabbed a plate. "You'd think it was a life-changing experience based on your reaction."

"Maybe it is!" I exclaimed, scooping a generous portion. "You have no idea how many disappointing desserts I've encountered on this journey. This one feels like a victory."

He shook his head in mock disbelief, grabbing a plate of his own. "You and your desserts. If you ever need a sidekick for dessert adventures, I'm your man."

"Is that a promise or a threat?" I shot back, teasingly narrowing my eyes at him.

"Definitely a promise. I wouldn't miss out on seeing you light up like that again," he replied, his gaze softening.

We moved to a quieter corner, settling into a cozy nook surrounded by friends sharing laughter and stories. I took a spoonful of the mousse, allowing the rich chocolate to melt on my tongue, and closed my eyes in bliss. "This is heavenly. I could probably live on this for the rest of my life."

"Maybe I should just buy you a lifetime supply," he joked, leaning back in his chair with a playful smirk.

"Please do! Just imagine the fame that would come with it—'The Chocolate Mousse Muse.' It has a nice ring to it, don't you think?"

Felix laughed, and for a moment, we were just two people enjoying the sweetness of life, the lingering tension replaced by a comfortable warmth. The conversation flowed effortlessly, bouncing from silly hypotheticals to deeper reflections, the walls around us dissolving into an inviting haze of laughter and camaraderie.

But beneath the laughter, I could feel the undertow of unspoken truths, the fragile threads of our connection still weaving around our hearts, binding us tighter with every shared smile and secret glance.

"Okay, serious question," Felix said, suddenly turning pensive, his eyes locking onto mine with an intensity that made my breath hitch. "What happens next for you? After tonight, I mean?"

I hesitated, my heart fluttering as I contemplated my answer. The past few months had been a blur of rehearsals, doubts, and an all-consuming desire to prove myself. "I guess I'll keep performing, maybe work on new music. I've been thinking about recording an EP—something that really reflects my journey."

He nodded thoughtfully. "I'd love to hear that. You've grown so much since the last time we were together. You have this... light in you now."

"Thanks. It feels good to let it shine."

"But what if you want to stay here? In this city? I mean, you could really make a name for yourself."

"Are you suggesting I don't go on tour?" I teased, though his question struck a chord deep within. The thought of staying, of making roots in this vibrant community, was both terrifying and exhilarating.

"Just asking the questions everyone's thinking," he replied with a grin. "But really, Sam, you could create something incredible here."

The laughter faded momentarily, replaced by an uncomfortable weight as I considered the choices ahead. "It's complicated. I have dreams, but... I've also realized how important it is to be where I feel supported. And that might just be here."

He leaned closer, his gaze piercing. "Then don't overthink it. Follow your heart. You've already taken the first step by being here tonight."

Before I could respond, a loud crash interrupted us, and we both turned toward the source of the commotion. A group of rowdy patrons had knocked over a stack of chairs, the sound echoing like thunder in the lively room. Laughter erupted, but my heart raced for a different reason.

As the chaos subsided, I spotted someone making their way through the crowd—someone whose presence sent a chill down my spine. Clara.

My heart dropped as she scanned the room, her eyes narrowing as they locked onto mine. I'd hoped she wouldn't show up tonight. Felix's playful demeanor shifted as he noticed the tension in my posture, and I could feel his concern wrap around me like a protective cloak.

"What's wrong?" he asked, his voice low and filled with unease.

"Just... someone I'd rather not see," I managed, my throat suddenly dry.

Clara took a few steps closer, her expression unreadable but undoubtedly determined. "Well, well. If it isn't my favorite starlet." Her voice dripped with mock sweetness, and I braced myself for whatever confrontation was brewing.

Felix moved slightly closer, a protective instinct igniting in his eyes. "Do you need me to step in?"

"No," I replied, though my voice quivered slightly. "I can handle this."

Clara approached, her demeanor shifting to something darker as she leaned in. "I see you've made quite the splash tonight. I hope it's enough to drown out your past mistakes."

"Funny, I was just thinking the same about you," I shot back, my bravado wavering under her icy gaze.

She smirked, unbothered. "Careful, darling. You wouldn't want to make the wrong enemies in this business."

I felt Felix stiffen beside me, his presence a steady anchor as I faced Clara's unsettling energy. "You don't scare me, Clara," I said, my voice firmer than I felt.

"Maybe not. But remember, every choice has consequences."

With that, she turned on her heel, melting back into the crowd, leaving a lingering tension in the air. Felix turned to me, concern etched across his face. "What just happened?"

I swallowed hard, the weight of her words settling over me like a dark cloud. "Nothing I can't handle. But I think this night just got a lot more complicated."

"Let's not let her ruin this moment," Felix said, trying to lighten the mood, but I could see the worry dancing in his eyes.

Just as I opened my mouth to reply, my phone buzzed in my pocket, the harsh sound breaking through the lingering tension. I pulled it out, glancing at the screen, and my heart sank. It was a message from my manager—an urgent plea for me to call back.

"Everything okay?" Felix asked, noticing my change in expression.

"I... I need to take this," I said, the gravity of the moment pressing down on me. I stepped away, heart racing, but as I glanced back at

Felix, I felt the delicate threads of our connection hanging in the balance, fraying at the edges.

Just before I pressed the call button, I caught sight of Clara again in the distance, her smile now twisted into something predatory. I couldn't shake the feeling that tonight was just the beginning of a storm I wasn't fully prepared for.

Chapter 20: A Light in the Darkness

The hospital room is a blend of sharp white walls and muted beige furnishings, a dispassionate backdrop to the tumultuous emotions swirling within. I sit by Mia's bedside, my fingers wrapped around her delicate, warm hand, feeling her pulse thrumming beneath my touch—a reminder that life persists in the most fragile of forms. She lies still, her small frame dwarfed by the vastness of the hospital bed, yet her spirit is anything but diminished. The rhythmic beeping of the heart monitor seems to echo my racing thoughts, an incessant reminder of time's relentless march.

Mia's eyes flutter open, revealing a mixture of confusion and weariness, a silent plea for assurance in this unfamiliar realm of white coats and sterile scents. I lean closer, brushing a stray strand of hair from her forehead, and she smiles weakly, a fleeting glimpse of the girl who used to dance around the living room, singing at the top of her lungs. "Hey, superstar," I whisper, forcing a bright tone into my voice, though my heart feels like lead. "You're going to be okay. I promise."

The words sound hollow, even to me, but I grasp at them like lifelines. If I can believe it, maybe she can too. I glance over at Felix, who stands at the foot of the bed, his posture tense, shoulders squared as if bracing against an unseen force. His dark curls fall into his eyes, casting shadows that mirror the storm brewing within him. The way he shifts his weight from one foot to the other speaks volumes; he's trying to anchor himself, to summon the strength that seems so elusive in this sterile cocoon of despair.

As the doctors file in—each armed with charts and a clinical demeanor that feels both reassuring and disconcerting—I can almost see the weight of their words settling on Felix's shoulders. They begin to outline Mia's treatment plan, detailing procedures and risks with a dispassionate precision that turns my stomach. I tune in and out, focusing instead on Felix's face, which is a portrait of stoic resolve that occasionally fractures into something more vulnerable—a flinch, a clenched fist, the slight crinkle of his brow. It's a dance between hope and despair, and I want to reach out and pull him back from the edge.

"Mia," I say softly, squeezing her hand, trying to capture her attention as the doctors speak in medical jargon that feels foreign and intimidating. "Remember that time we tried to bake cupcakes and ended up with a kitchen full of flour? You were a flour ghost, and we laughed until we cried." Her eyes flicker with recognition, a spark of joy in the midst of her pain.

"Yeah," she whispers, her voice a fragile thread that pulls me deeper into her world. "We made a mess."

"Exactly! And you know what? Sometimes, life is like that—messy and chaotic, but we make the best of it, right?" I'm met with a weak smile that lights up her face, igniting a flicker of hope within me. "And I promise, when you're better, we'll have a cupcake extravaganza. No flour ghosts this time—just us and the sprinkles."

Felix snorts softly, the tension in his posture easing slightly. "I think I'd rather take my chances with the ghosts. At least they're less sticky," he quips, a hint of his familiar humor breaking through the heaviness. There it is—his charm, sharp and witty, cutting through the gloom like a lighthouse beam in the fog.

The doctors move on to discuss timelines and therapies, their words blending into a hum as I focus on Mia's small hand in mine, imagining the day when she would be dancing again, twirling and laughing, flour dust still clinging to her hair. Felix leans in closer, a hand bracing on the bed, and I catch a glimpse of the concern etched on his face. His eyes, dark and deep, are pools of emotion, reflecting both his love for Mia and the fear of losing her.

"What do you think?" he asks suddenly, his voice low and intense, directed at me but layered with vulnerability. "Can she really get through this?"

I take a breath, steadying myself against the weight of his question. "We have to believe she can. She's stronger than she knows, and we'll be right here with her. You're not alone in this, Felix." The words tumble out, a promise that I intend to keep. He nods, but I can see the flicker of doubt lingering in his eyes.

Mia shifts slightly, a wince crossing her features as the doctors finish their explanations, the gravity of their words hanging thick in the air. I want to shake them, to demand they speak softer, kinder, but I know that isn't how the world works. Life is brutal, and the truth often cuts deeper than any blade. But we are here, and we will fight this—together.

"Do you remember that summer at the lake?" I ask, desperate to shift the mood, to distract us from the looming specter of uncertainty. "The one where you challenged me to that ridiculous diving competition? You thought you were going to win with your cannonball."

Mia's eyes twinkle with the spark of memory, her lips curving into a soft smile. "I totally would have if you hadn't splashed me first!"

"Ah, but that was part of my strategy. Distract and conquer!" I laugh, a bright sound against the sterile environment, and Felix chuckles too, the weight of our surroundings lifting—if only for a moment.

Just then, the door swings open, and a nurse enters with a bright smile that seems almost out of place in this clinical setting. "How's our brave girl doing?" she chirps, bringing a lightness that feels refreshing. Mia's smile widens, and I feel a wave of gratitude toward this woman who's decided to infuse our grim reality with a touch of warmth.

The nurse checks Mia's vitals, chatting softly about the weather outside and how the leaves are beginning to change, the hints of autumn painting the world in golds and reds. As she moves about the room, I find myself leaning back, allowing the mundane rhythms of hospital life to wash over me, reminding me that life exists beyond these walls, full of color and laughter, just waiting to break through.

The nurse bustles around the room, her demeanor a delightful contrast to the sterile atmosphere that has become our constant companion. She hums a tune that I can't quite place but that feels familiar, like a distant echo of happier times. Her movements are quick and practiced as she adjusts the IV, checks the monitors, and jots down notes in Mia's chart, all while keeping up a steady stream of chatter that fills the space with a semblance of normalcy.

"Did you know that this time of year, the leaves turn a beautiful shade of amber? You should see it from the park near my house. It's like walking through a sea of gold," she shares, glancing at Mia with an encouraging smile.

Mia's eyes flicker with interest, a spark of life returning as she imagines the world outside. "Can we go there when I get out?" she asks, her voice barely above a whisper, but it carries a weight of hope that hangs in the air.

"Absolutely!" the nurse replies, her enthusiasm infectious. "We'll have a little picnic, just you, me, and some cupcakes—no flour ghosts this time, I promise!"

A chuckle escapes me, and I glance at Felix, who seems momentarily entranced by this lively exchange. The tension in his shoulders softens, and for a moment, the gravity of the situation feels lighter, as if we've collectively decided to slip into a bubble of warmth that shields us from the harsh realities of the world beyond these walls.

"Mia's got a whole cupcake campaign in the works," I chime in, seizing the opportunity to build on the moment. "If she plays her cards right, she might just end up being the queen of confections."

"Queen of cupcakes? I like the sound of that!" Mia exclaims, her voice growing stronger, infused with determination.

"Your subjects shall bow before you," Felix adds, his voice playful, his earlier tension evaporating like mist in the morning sun. "And I'll be your loyal jester, of course. Someone has to taste test those cupcakes."

"Felix, if you think I'll let you eat all the frosting, you've got another thing coming," Mia retorts, her smile brightening the room more than the fluorescent lights overhead.

As laughter dances around us, the doctor returns, pulling my attention back to the seriousness of our circumstances. He clears his throat, the sound cutting through our momentary escape. "I'm glad to see you all in good spirits," he says, his expression transitioning into one of professional concern. "Mia, we need to discuss the next steps in your treatment."

The shift is palpable. I feel the air grow heavy again as we settle back into the reality we must face. The doctor outlines the options—some promising, some daunting. I can see the way Felix's fingers curl into fists, his jaw tightening once more, as if he's bracing himself for a storm. I shift my focus back to Mia, searching her eyes for any sign of fear. Instead, I find a glimmer of resolve, and it fills me with a renewed sense of purpose.

"Whatever it takes, I'll get through this," she declares, her voice firm, a beacon of strength that radiates from her petite frame. It's a quiet vow, yet it reverberates through the room, giving us all something to hold onto.

"Of course you will," I assure her, hoping my words carry the conviction I feel. "We're all in this together, remember?"

Felix nods in agreement, his expression shifting from fear to fierce determination. "Yeah, we'll be right here, every step of the way."

The doctor outlines a plan, but all I can hear are the words "chemotherapy" and "side effects," and my heart sinks. It's a necessary evil, but the thought of it feels like a punch to the gut. I reach for Mia's hand, squeezing it tightly as the doctor explains the timeline, his voice blending into the background as I focus on the warmth of her skin against mine.

After the doctor leaves, a heavy silence settles over us, punctuated only by the soft beeping of the machines. The weight of our reality hangs like a thick fog, but it's broken by Felix's voice, rich with a familiar cadence that brings a glimmer of light back into the room. "So, who's in charge of bringing the cupcakes to our royal feast?"

"I guess that's me!" I declare, feigning seriousness as I push back my hair, mimicking a grand gesture. "As the cupcake queen, I must ensure we have only the finest baked goods for our princess."

Mia laughs softly, and it's the sweetest sound, a melody that cuts through the heaviness. "You're so going to burn the kitchen down, aren't you?"

Felix leans back in his chair, his eyes sparkling with mischief. "She probably will. I'd suggest we keep the fire department on speed dial."

"Hey! I'll have you know I'm a culinary wizard. I can bake cookies without setting off the smoke alarm—at least, most of the time," I retort, raising an eyebrow at them both.

The warmth of our banter creates a shield around us, momentarily warding off the coldness that lurks beyond our little bubble. We exchange jokes and stories, our laughter rising and falling like waves, a comforting rhythm that feels almost normal amid the chaos of our lives.

But just as the shadows begin to recede, an unexpected visitor interrupts our cocoon. The door creaks open, and in walks my mother, her eyes wide with concern that instantly siphons the light from the room. "Oh, my God! I came as soon as I heard!" she exclaims, rushing to Mia's side, her voice choked with emotion.

"Mom," I say, a mixture of surprise and exasperation rushing through me. "You didn't have to—"

But she's already enveloped Mia in a gentle embrace, tears shimmering in her eyes. "I just couldn't stay away. You're my baby, and I—"

Mia squeezes her hand, a gesture both comforting and grounding. "I'm okay, Mom. Really."

Felix and I exchange a glance, the kind that says so much without words. In this moment, I realize how important it is to have the ones we love close, how they can be both a source of strength and an anchor in the storm. I take a deep breath, the air charged with a mix of hope and uncertainty, ready to face whatever comes next with my beloved little family.

The warmth of my mother's embrace lingers in the air, thickening the atmosphere with unspoken worries and love. Mia leans into her, soaking up the comfort like a flower after a rainstorm. I watch as my mother brushes her fingers through Mia's hair, each gentle stroke a silent promise of protection and care. It's a sight that tugs at my heartstrings, reminding me of the power that love has to heal, even in the darkest moments.

Felix shifts in his chair, glancing between us, his expression an unreadable mix of admiration and uncertainty. "Welcome to the party, Mom," he quips, trying to lighten the mood, his smile faltering just slightly as he takes in the scene. "We were just discussing the merits of frosting versus cake."

"Clearly, frosting reigns supreme," my mother replies, a teasing glint in her eyes as she looks at Mia. "But let's not forget the vital role of sprinkles. A cupcake without sprinkles is like a party without music. It's simply not done."

Mia giggles, the sound like a soothing balm on my nerves. "Definitely! But what if the sprinkles are, like, too many and they take over? Then it's a sprinkle invasion!"

I can see the glimmer of mischief in her eyes, and for a brief moment, it feels as though we've escaped the confines of the hospital, the laughter propelling us into a world where worries don't exist. It's a comforting fantasy, one I wish we could hold onto indefinitely.

But reality intrudes again as the door swings open, this time with a swiftness that feels more like a storm than a gentle breeze. A tall figure steps into the room, their silhouette casting a long shadow over our bubble of laughter. It's Dr. Harrison, the oncologist, his expression serious but softened by the slight furrow of his brow. He glances at my mother, and then to Felix and Mia, pausing as if gauging our moods.

"I hope I'm not interrupting anything important," he says, but there's an urgency in his tone that immediately silences us, the laughter dying on our lips like a candle snuffed out.

"No, no, we were just—" I begin, but he holds up a hand, cutting me off gently.

"Mia, I'd like to talk with you about some new developments regarding your treatment." The room shifts, tension coiling tightly around us. Mia's face pales slightly, and I squeeze her hand tighter, willing her to feel my strength.

"Is it bad news?" she asks, her voice small but defiant, a hint of that fighting spirit we all know and love sparking to life.

Dr. Harrison shifts his weight, his expression grave yet compassionate. "Not necessarily bad, but it's certainly unexpected. We've been running additional tests, and it seems your case is more complex than we initially thought."

My heart sinks. The sterile light of the room flickers as if responding to our collective anxiety. "Complex how?" I manage to ask, my throat suddenly dry.

"There are indications that the cancer is more aggressive than we anticipated. However, there's also a promising clinical trial that may offer a new path forward," he explains, his voice steady, though I can hear the underlying tension in it.

Felix exhales sharply, his hands curling into fists again. "What kind of trial?"

Dr. Harrison clears his throat, clearly accustomed to the reactions that follow such news. "It involves a new immunotherapy treatment. It's still in the experimental stage, but early results are encouraging. We believe it could potentially provide a more effective response to the type of cancer Mia is facing."

Mia's eyes dart from Dr. Harrison to me, and I can see the conflict raging within her—a desire to fight, to embrace hope, and yet the fear of the unknown looms over us like a dark cloud. "Will it hurt?" she asks, her voice barely above a whisper.

"Every treatment comes with its risks, but I assure you, we will monitor you closely throughout the process. The goal is to give you the best chance possible," he replies, his tone soothing yet firm.

Felix takes a step forward, leaning closer to Mia, his gaze intense. "We'll figure it out, Mia. Whatever it takes, we're in this together," he vows, and I can feel the weight of his promise hanging in the air, a lifeline we all desperately need.

"Together," she echoes, her voice gaining strength as she looks back at me, her eyes sparkling with a mix of fear and determination. It's a look that reminds me of the indomitable spirit that has always defined her.

The doctor nods, but I can see the flicker of uncertainty in his eyes. "I'll give you some time to discuss this. It's a significant decision, and I want you all to feel comfortable with whatever choice you make." With that, he retreats, leaving the door ajar, a sliver of reality beckoning us back into its clutches.

Once he's gone, the air feels charged, heavy with unsaid words and brewing emotions. I look at Felix and then at my mother, who wears an expression of barely concealed anguish. "What do we do now?" I ask, my voice breaking the silence like a pebble tossed into still water.

"Do we even have a choice?" Felix replies, running a hand through his hair in frustration. "This trial could be the answer, but it's a leap into the unknown."

"It could also mean a chance for a life that's full of cupcakes and adventures instead of just... this," I say, motioning around the room, my voice thick with unshed tears.

Mia looks at us, her small frame radiating an unexpected strength. "I want to fight. I want to try this trial. If it gives me a chance to get back to the things I love, I can do it."

Her resolve is a beacon, cutting through the fog of uncertainty that has settled over us. "And we'll be right there with you," I promise, squeezing her hand once more, infusing it with all the love and support I can muster.

The weight of our decision lingers in the air as we share silent glances, each of us grappling with the reality of what lies ahead.

Suddenly, the door bursts open again, this time with more force than before. A figure strides in, eyes wide and frantic, and my heart drops as I recognize the familiar face of Ethan, our childhood friend. "You guys! I just heard the news—I couldn't stay away!"

His breath comes in quick bursts, and the gravity of his entrance sends a jolt of unease through the room. "What's going on? Are you okay, Mia?"

But before anyone can respond, he pulls out his phone, his voice rising in urgency. "I have something you need to see. It's about the trial—there's a twist, and you guys won't believe this!"

A twist? The air thickens, charged with tension as we lean in closer, uncertainty swirling around us like a storm. I can feel my heart racing, a drumbeat of anxiety and anticipation. What revelation could possibly await us? Ethan's eyes gleam with something between fear and excitement, and I know that whatever he's about to say will alter everything we thought we knew.

"Ethan, what do you mean? What's happening?" I ask, the words tumbling out before I can stop myself, the urgency in my tone matching the chaos of my thoughts.

He glances at each of us, a wicked smile breaking through the worry. "You need to hear this, but it's not what you think… It's way bigger than you imagined."

And just like that, the ground shifts beneath our feet, the laughter and light of moments before fading into the shadows as we stand on the precipice of an unknown fate, every heartbeat echoing with the weight of what comes next.

Chapter 21: Fractured Bonds

The air hung heavy in the dimly lit room, a cacophony of sound and silence mingling like unwelcome guests at a party. Felix was plucking at the strings of his guitar, his fingers a blur of motion, while I sat cross-legged on the floor, drumming my palms against my knees. The rhythm echoed through the space, but it felt hollow. Outside, a storm raged, rain hammering against the windows, the wind howling like a chorus of lost souls. Inside, we were two musicians trapped in a symphony of worry, desperately trying to harmonize amidst the chaos.

Our jam sessions had become a ritual, a desperate attempt to distract ourselves from the growing shadows that loomed over us. We'd chosen this old garage, its walls plastered with posters from bands long faded from the limelight. The scent of musty wood and lingering paint hung in the air, mixing with the unmistakable aroma of Felix's cologne—a heady blend of cedar and something sweet that lingered like a ghost. Each note we played felt like a step into the unknown, a plunge into the deep end where we could either drown or swim.

Felix looked over at me, his brow furrowed, eyes dark with worry. "You ever think about how we used to do this for fun?" he asked, the words tumbling out like the unstrung notes of a forgotten melody. There was a tightness in his voice, as if each syllable carried the weight of the world.

I shrugged, trying to summon a lightness that had eluded me lately. "Yeah, but now it feels like we're trying to keep the lights on in a blackout." My smile felt forced, but I hoped it would break the tension hanging between us like thick fog.

He nodded, a ghost of a smile crossing his lips, but it didn't reach his eyes. "Maybe we need to turn the lights off entirely. Just play." His fingers danced over the strings, coaxing out a soft, haunting tune that seemed to echo the storm outside.

With each chord he struck, I felt a familiar ache in my chest, a longing to bridge the distance that had crept in between us. I picked up my own guitar, the wood cool against my palms, and joined him in the rhythm. The sound melded together, filling the garage with an ethereal quality that made me forget, if only for a moment, the reality of Mia's condition. She was out there, battling demons far more treacherous than our own, and we were here, tangled in our own fears and insecurities.

We played until our fingers ached, lost in the music, the outside world fading into oblivion. But eventually, as the final note hung in the air, the silence returned, thick and suffocating. I glanced at Felix, whose face was shadowed in thought, brows knit together as if he were piecing together a puzzle only he could see.

"Felix," I ventured, my voice barely a whisper. "Are you okay?"

He let out a breath that sounded more like a shudder than a sigh, and I felt a crack in the façade he'd built around himself. "No," he admitted, the word raw and heavy. "I'm not. I can't shake the feeling that I'm losing her. Every day feels like a countdown." His voice trembled, and my heart clenched at the vulnerability he laid bare.

I wanted to reach out, to wrap my arms around him and tell him it would all be alright, but the truth was I didn't know if it would be. Instead, I settled for silence, letting his pain fill the space between us, a reminder that we were both fighting our own battles.

"Do you ever feel like... I don't know, like we're on a stage?" he continued, his eyes staring into the distance as if he were searching for something lost. "Like we're performing for an audience that's just waiting for us to mess up?"

I thought about it, picturing us there in the garage, strumming our hearts out, waiting for the applause that never came.

"Sometimes," I admitted, "but I think it's the fear that makes the music better, you know? Like we're pouring everything into it because it might be our last chance."

Felix met my gaze, and I could see the flicker of understanding in his eyes. "Yeah," he said, voice low. "But what if it is? What if we don't get another chance?"

The truth of his words settled over me like a shroud. I felt my throat tighten, a lump forming as I considered the possibility. Mia was fighting for her life, and we were here, lost in our melodies, when we should have been doing everything in our power to be there for her.

The tension that had been simmering between us erupted like a sudden storm, raw and unfiltered. "We have to be there for her," I said, the urgency in my voice sharper than I intended. "We can't let this slip away without a fight."

Felix nodded, his gaze intense as if he were weighing my words. "You're right," he replied, the resolve in his voice hardening. "But how? I feel so helpless."

I could sense the frustration bubbling beneath the surface, and I reached for his hand, intertwining our fingers. "We figure it out together," I said firmly. "One note at a time."

For the first time in weeks, a flicker of hope ignited between us. We had our music, our connection, and amidst the chaos, we had each other. In that moment, the world outside faded, and in our little sanctuary, we began to weave a plan—not just for ourselves, but for Mia, our shared heart, our tether to everything we loved.

The storm raged on, but inside the garage, we were crafting a new melody—one filled with strength, resilience, and an unwavering promise to fight together.

The air was thick with unspoken words, a tension that pulsed in the space between us like an unwelcome guest refusing to leave. After our emotional breakthrough, the weight of worry hung over

Felix and me, draping itself like a heavy quilt that smothered any flicker of light. We still gathered in that familiar garage, surrounded by memories of carefree laughter and the promise of music. But now, each chord we strummed felt heavy with expectation, and each note seemed to carry the burden of our fears.

Felix had started showing up later for our sessions, the corners of his mouth drawn tight, eyes shadowed with fatigue. He'd pluck at his guitar absentmindedly, as if the strings had turned into a foreign language he could no longer decipher. I would try to coax the music out of him, to draw him back into the world we'd created together, but the fire that had once sparked between us was now smoldering like a dying ember.

One evening, I decided to shake things up. I arrived early, armed with snacks and an idea. I spread out a picnic blanket on the floor, a vibrant tapestry that seemed too bright for the somber atmosphere. I set out a hodgepodge of finger foods—crackers, cheese, and some slightly bruised strawberries that had seen better days but were still sweet enough to tempt. I lit a couple of candles, the flickering flames casting playful shadows against the walls, hoping the warmth would break through the chill in the air.

Felix walked in, his expression caught somewhere between curiosity and bemusement. "What's all this?" he asked, eyebrows raised as he surveyed the spread.

I shrugged, a grin sneaking onto my face. "Thought we could use a little change of scenery. And, you know, a decent meal. Music is great, but it won't fill your stomach."

He chuckled, the sound a small victory against the heaviness that had settled around us. "True. Though I'm pretty sure if we combined our culinary skills, we'd end up with a disaster of epic proportions."

"Challenge accepted!" I exclaimed, picking up a cheese wedge and balancing it precariously on a cracker before taking a triumphant bite. "Mmm. Chef Mia would be proud."

Felix rolled his eyes, but I could see the smile tugging at the corners of his lips. "If only we could serve that to her right now."

"Just think, once she's better, we could host a cooking show called 'What Not to Do in the Kitchen.'"

We both laughed, a sound so rare and precious in the wake of our worries that it felt like a lifeline. It was a brief reprieve, a moment where the burden of reality lightened just enough to let us breathe.

We settled on the blanket, the food laid out between us, and as we nibbled and shared stories, I felt the distance between us begin to close. "You know, it's kind of nice, this... unpretentious gathering," I mused, a playful tone in my voice. "No fancy restaurant or awkward first-date vibes—just two friends trying to figure out how to survive."

Felix met my gaze, and there was a flicker of something unspoken in his eyes. "Yeah, but we're not just friends anymore, are we? This... whatever this is, it feels different."

I swallowed, caught off guard by the weight of his words. "Are we talking different like a new flavor of ice cream or different like... romantic? Because those are two very different paths."

"Definitely romantic. Ice cream is less messy." He chuckled, but his expression turned serious as he continued. "I just don't know where this is heading with everything else hanging over us. It feels like trying to build a sandcastle during a storm."

I leaned back on my elbows, considering his words carefully. "Sometimes, though, storms bring unexpected beauty. It can reshape what we already have into something new."

He looked at me, the sincerity in his gaze unraveling my defenses. "You really believe that?"

"Absolutely," I said, a sudden surge of conviction fueling my words. "We've been through so much together. Just because Mia is struggling doesn't mean we can't find our own way. We need to keep moving forward, even if it's just a little at a time."

"Yeah, but what if we're moving toward heartbreak? What if I lose her, and then I lose you too?"

His vulnerability cracked open something within me. "Felix," I said softly, reaching for his hand. "You're not going to lose me. Whatever happens with Mia, we're in this together. And that means more than just music."

He squeezed my hand, a spark igniting between us, and for a brief moment, I dared to hope that we could find a way to navigate the storm, not just survive but thrive in spite of it.

We finished our impromptu feast, laughter returning as we swapped stories and silly anecdotes from our past. As the evening stretched on, the candles flickered low, casting a warm glow around us. It was in these quiet moments that the tension slowly began to dissolve, replaced by a tentative connection that felt all the more fragile for its beauty.

Just as we were about to pack up, the sudden shrill ring of my phone cut through the atmosphere, pulling me back to the reality we had tried so hard to escape. It was Mia's doctor. The moment I saw the name on the screen, a rush of panic gripped my heart.

I glanced at Felix, whose expression mirrored my own dread. "I have to take this," I said, scrambling to my feet, the blanket and snacks momentarily forgotten.

"Is it about Mia?" he asked, concern etched into his features.

I nodded, swallowing hard. "Yeah, I'll be right back."

I stepped outside into the cool night air, the storm having passed but leaving the world glistening under a layer of silver moonlight. As I answered the call, a familiar sense of dread twisted in my stomach.

"Hello, is this—"

As the doctor's voice droned on in the background, a sense of foreboding crept in, snaking its way through my thoughts. I could feel the weight of the world shifting, and suddenly, I realized that the sandcastle we had started building was far more fragile than I had ever imagined.

The chill of the night air wrapped around me like an unwelcome embrace, and I paced the cracked pavement outside the garage, my phone pressed to my ear. The doctor's words flowed like a river of ice through my veins, each sentence heavier than the last, each pause pregnant with implications. I could almost hear the muted music behind me, the sound of Felix strumming idly on his guitar, waiting.

"I'm afraid we need to discuss some options," the doctor said, his tone as clinical as the sterile walls of the hospital. "Mia's situation has changed. We can't just wait and see anymore."

I felt my breath hitch, the ground beneath my feet seeming to shift. "What do you mean? Is she...?" The words felt like shards of glass in my throat. I couldn't finish the question, the fear clawing at me like a wild animal desperate to escape its cage.

"She's still fighting, but her body is responding less favorably to the treatment. We need to consider some alternative approaches."

My mind reeled, the world around me narrowing down to that single point of anguish. "Alternative approaches?" I echoed, my voice trembling. "You mean... options we haven't discussed?"

"Correct. I'll need you to come in tomorrow to discuss them further."

The call ended, leaving me standing in a void, the darkness swallowing me whole. I turned to head back into the garage, but my feet felt leaden. I opened the door slowly, the familiar scent of wood and music welcoming me back, yet I felt like an interloper in my own life.

Felix looked up from his guitar, his brows furrowed with concern. "What did the doctor say?" His voice was gentle, probing, and I could see the tension in his posture.

I swallowed hard, the lump in my throat refusing to budge. "We need to talk," I said, my voice barely above a whisper.

He set his guitar down, the soft thud of wood against the floor a stark contrast to the turmoil inside me. "That doesn't sound good."

"Yeah, well, it isn't." I took a deep breath, forcing myself to hold his gaze. "Mia's condition has worsened. The doctor mentioned... alternatives."

Felix's expression shifted, the worry morphing into a deeper kind of dread. "What does that even mean? Are they giving up on her?"

"No! No, they're not giving up, but... they want to discuss new options. I think they're running out of ideas." My voice cracked, and I hated how vulnerable I sounded, how the tears were just a breath away.

For a moment, silence hung between us, thick and suffocating, like the aftermath of a storm. I could see Felix's mind racing, the gears turning as he processed the information. "We can't let this happen," he said finally, a fierce determination hardening his features. "There has to be something we can do."

I nodded, grateful for his strength, even as I felt my own falter. "I wish I knew what that something was."

His jaw clenched, and I could see the turmoil behind his calm facade. "We'll figure it out together. Mia wouldn't want us to just sit around and wait for things to change."

"You really think she'll want us to fight for her?"

He nodded resolutely. "Absolutely. She's always been the fighter in this family. We owe it to her to keep pushing."

Something within me stirred, a small flicker of hope igniting against the backdrop of despair. "So, what do we do? Where do we start?"

"Let's look into everything we can find—research, alternatives, specialists. Maybe there's something out there that can help her."

"Sounds like a plan." I hesitated, then added, "But Felix, we might have to face some tough truths. Not everything we find will be hopeful."

"I'd rather face the truth than live in ignorance," he replied, his voice unwavering. "And I'd rather do it with you by my side."

We began to brainstorm, our ideas tumbling out in a chaotic mix of urgency and hope. The garage transformed into a makeshift war room, filled with scattered papers, a whiteboard I had commandeered for jotting down notes, and half-empty takeout containers that bore witness to our long hours.

But just as our determination grew, the phone rang again, a shrill intrusion that sent a jolt through the air. I fumbled to grab it, my heart racing as I glanced at the screen. It was Mia's hospital number.

"Answer it," Felix urged, his voice tense.

I took a deep breath and pressed the answer button, my pulse quickening. "Hello?"

"Mia's had a change in condition," the nurse said, her voice steady but heavy with gravity. "You need to come to the hospital immediately."

My breath caught in my throat. "Is she—?"

"Just come as soon as you can." The call ended, leaving an ominous silence in its wake.

"Did she—?" Felix began, but I couldn't let him finish. The fear crystallized in my chest, an icy grip that left me breathless.

"Grab your keys. We have to go now," I said, my voice low but urgent.

Felix nodded, a new urgency igniting in his gaze as he rushed to gather his things. "I'll drive," he said, and I could hear the determination in his tone, the way he was ready to face whatever awaited us.

As we jumped into his car, I could feel the weight of the world pressing down, a relentless tide of uncertainty that threatened to drown us both. The streets blurred past in a haze, each red light a reminder of the time we were losing, the time Mia didn't have.

"Whatever happens," Felix said, his hand brushing against mine, a silent promise amidst the chaos. "We're in this together."

I nodded, gripping his hand tightly, drawing strength from his presence. The hospital loomed ahead, its lights shining like beacons in the darkness, and as we parked and hurried inside, I couldn't shake the feeling that we were hurtling toward something monumental—an intersection of hope and despair, of love and loss.

As we rushed through the sterile corridors, the beeping machines and muffled voices around us felt surreal, a backdrop to the drama unfolding within our lives. Each step echoed with the weight of our fears, but somewhere in the back of my mind, a flicker of resolve ignited.

Just as we reached the nurse's station, a doctor appeared, his expression grave. "You're here for Mia? I'm afraid we need to discuss her condition."

My heart raced, and I felt Felix's grip tighten around my arm. "Is she...?"

The doctor hesitated, the silence stretching into eternity, and in that moment, I knew we were teetering on the edge of a precipice, a cliffhanger poised to drop us into the unknown.

Chapter 22: Beneath the Surface

The sun hung low in the sky, casting long shadows across the cemetery, where time seemed to hold its breath in reverence. Each step felt heavy with the weight of unspoken words and memories that danced just out of reach. The familiar path to my mother's grave wound through a tapestry of graves, each stone a silent testament to the lives once lived. I could feel the warmth of the earth beneath my feet, the grass freshly mowed, but somehow it only deepened the chill that gripped my heart. I had promised myself I would come here, but now that I stood before her, the words twisted in my throat like barbed wire.

Her grave was adorned with the vibrant blooms I had chosen, petals bright as my childhood laughter but now wilting under the harshness of time. Each flower drooped, mirroring the heaviness in my chest. I knelt beside the grave, fingers grazing the cool stone that bore her name, each letter a reminder of the life I once knew. "Hey, Mom," I whispered, my voice trembling like the leaves in the gentle breeze. "I wish you could tell me what to do." My eyes stung as I blinked away tears, allowing the ache of loss to wash over me, a familiar wave that threatened to pull me under.

As the sun dipped lower, painting the sky in hues of orange and purple, I felt a surge of vulnerability. "I'm scared," I admitted, the words falling from my lips like shattered glass. "Scared of losing everyone I love. Scared of feeling like I'm never going to be enough." I had rehearsed this moment in my mind a thousand times, but speaking it aloud made it all too real, all too tangible. I could hear her laughter echoing in my head, the way it would light up a room, filling the spaces around us with warmth. But that laughter felt distant now, like an old song playing softly in the background, barely audible above the cacophony of my fears.

With each confession, I felt a piece of the burden lifting, but the weight still clung to me like a shadow. "Felix and Mia..." The names tumbled from my lips, imbued with the love and hope that felt both exhilarating and terrifying. "I want to be there for them, to support them like you supported me. But what if I mess it up?" My voice cracked, and the tears I had been holding back broke free, cascading down my cheeks like a summer rain. "What if I can't keep them safe?"

The world around me blurred as I poured my heart out to her, the vulnerability overwhelming. I could almost imagine her sitting beside me, her hand resting gently on my shoulder, grounding me as I spiraled deeper into my thoughts. "I know you'd tell me to be brave, to embrace the chaos of life, but it's so hard," I continued, the honesty spilling from me like a secret I had kept far too long. "How do I move forward without you? How do I let go of the past while holding onto the love?"

I drew a shaky breath, the air thick with the scent of damp earth and fading flowers. There was something cathartic about this moment, as if each word uttered was a key turning in a lock I had kept tightly secured. I had been wrestling with my emotions, my fears wrapping around me like a vice, squeezing until I could barely breathe. But here, in the sacred silence of the cemetery, I felt the chains loosening, the pressure easing just a little.

The light began to fade, casting a golden glow across the graves, and I knew I had to honor this moment, to let it carry me forward. "I promise I'll try," I whispered, the words a soft vow that felt like a release. "I'll find a way to honor you while living my life fully. I'll be there for Felix and Mia. I'll embrace the moments we have together, the laughter, the love. I'll let them know how much you meant to me, how much they mean to me."

Wiping my tears with the back of my hand, I lingered for a moment longer, allowing the cool evening air to envelop me, a gentle reminder of the world waiting just beyond this sacred space. I felt a flicker of hope igniting within, a quiet determination to embrace the present and weave my mother's memory into the tapestry of my life. This was not a farewell; it was a promise to carry her spirit forward, to cherish the moments that lay ahead.

As I stood up, brushing off my knees, I glanced back at the grave one last time, feeling a shift within me. It was as if I had left a part of my sorrow behind, transforming it into something lighter, something that wouldn't hold me captive anymore. The sky had turned deep indigo, stars beginning to twinkle like distant dreams, and I felt a surge of gratitude for the guidance that had come from my heartache.

With each step away from the grave, I could feel the weight of despair lifting, replaced by a resolve to cherish the present. I needed to make the most of my time with Felix and Mia, to nurture the connections that mattered most, and to embrace life with all its messy, beautiful chaos. My heart swelled with anticipation for what lay ahead, the promise of laughter and shared moments filling the void left by my mother's absence. It was time to live fully, to create memories that honored her while crafting my own story in the process.

The moment I stepped back into the world beyond the cemetery gates, the air felt different—charged with possibility, like a freshly uncorked bottle of champagne, ready to fizz and spill over. The streetlights flickered on, their warm glow wrapping around me like a comforting embrace. I inhaled deeply, the night air rich with the scents of damp earth and blooming jasmine. Each breath felt like a promise I was making to myself, a vow to seize the moments that lay ahead, especially those with Felix and Mia, who were like the sun peeking through clouds on a dreary day.

Turning the corner, I noticed a crowd gathered outside the local bakery. The sweet aroma of freshly baked bread wafted through the air, pulling me closer as if I were a moth drawn to a flickering flame. It was one of those charming little places where the walls were painted a cheerful yellow and the pastries looked like they'd been crafted by fairies. My mouth watered at the thought of their famous lemon tarts, the tartness balanced perfectly with just the right amount of sweetness.

As I pushed the door open, a bell chimed overhead, announcing my arrival. The interior was warm and cozy, filled with the comforting chatter of regulars, their laughter mingling with the clatter of plates and cutlery. I spotted Mia at a corner table, her curly hair bouncing as she animatedly described something—likely one of her many adventures to Felix, who sat across from her, feigning exasperation but clearly charmed.

"—and then the goat literally tried to eat my backpack! I had to wrestle it away from him like I was some sort of animal whisperer!" Mia's voice rose above the din, her eyes sparkling with excitement.

I couldn't help but smile at her enthusiasm as I approached. "I guess you found your calling as a goat wrangler, then," I quipped, slipping into the seat beside her.

"More like a goat wrestle-er," Felix added, his deep voice rich with mock seriousness. "Next thing we know, she'll be launching her own line of goat yoga classes."

"Only if you promise to be my first customer!" Mia shot back, laughter bubbling between them.

"Oh, I'll definitely be there," I said, playing along. "But only if you promise to keep the goats away from my backpack. Last thing I need is a goat-induced wardrobe malfunction."

Felix chuckled, the sound resonating like a warm melody in the busy café. "Now that's a story I want to hear," he said, leaning in closer, his expression both teasing and intrigued.

With the sun setting beyond the bakery windows, the glow from the overhead lights created a cozy haven that felt worlds away from my earlier heartache. We spent the next hour sharing stories, each laugh and silly anecdote weaving an invisible thread that drew us closer. I reveled in the comfort of their presence, feeling the heaviness in my heart gradually lift, replaced by a lightness I hadn't felt in ages.

But just as I began to lose myself in the warmth of our camaraderie, an unexpected figure stepped through the door—Claire, my mother's closest friend and, I'd later learn, a woman with impeccable timing. She entered with a flourish, her bright red coat a stark contrast to the muted tones of the café. Claire had always been larger than life, the kind of person who could walk into a room and make it feel like a party was about to start. But there was something different about her today; her usual exuberance was tinged with an edge of uncertainty.

"Mia! Felix! Oh, and look who it is—the prodigal daughter returns!" she exclaimed, her eyes dancing over to me with a warmth that sent a little thrill through my chest. "I was hoping to find you here!"

"Claire, what a surprise!" I said, trying to mask the slight unease that flickered in my gut. "Everything okay?"

"Oh, darling, it's just wonderful to see you! I brought you something." She reached into her oversized purse and pulled out a small box wrapped in brown paper and tied with twine. "A little something from my latest adventure. I thought you could use a pick-me-up."

My heart sank a little. Claire had always been generous, but the weight of grief hung over us like a storm cloud. "You didn't have to—"

"Nonsense! Just open it!" she insisted, her voice a blend of cheer and insistence that made it impossible to resist.

I untied the twine, my fingers fumbling slightly as I peeled back the paper. Inside lay a delicate necklace, a silver chain adorned with a small pendant shaped like a feather. "It's beautiful," I said, my voice thickening with emotion as I lifted it to the light. "But why?"

"Feathers are a reminder to let go of what weighs you down and to fly," Claire said, her gaze steady on me. "I know you've been carrying a lot, and I thought this might help you remember to embrace the present, just like your mother would want."

The words struck me, and I felt the weight of her sentiment settle in my chest. "Thank you," I murmured, swallowing against the sudden swell of gratitude and sadness. "This means so much to me."

She reached across the table, squeezing my hand gently. "You're not alone, love. You have Felix and Mia. You have me. And we're all here for you, no matter what."

In that moment, I felt the walls I had been building around my heart begin to crack, the barriers I had erected in my mind crumbling just a little. As I looked around the table at my friends, I realized that the bond we shared wasn't fragile; it was a lifeline, something I could cling to as I navigated the uncertain waters of life. We had our own battles to fight, but together, we were stronger.

Felix leaned back in his chair, a playful glint in his eyes. "Well, now that we have the feather of freedom, can we finally decide what's for dessert? Because I refuse to leave this place without trying that infamous chocolate torte."

Mia's eyes lit up, and she exclaimed, "Only if you promise to share! I need a bite of that richness!"

I laughed, feeling the tension of the day melt away. "Alright, but only if we can get a lemon tart on the side. You know, for balance."

The playful banter continued, the laughter wrapping around us like a warm blanket as we dove headfirst into a dessert debate. The evening unfolded in a beautiful tapestry of shared stories and laughter, each moment threading us closer together, reminding me that in the face of loss, love was the strongest anchor I could hold onto. And as I gazed at the glimmer of the necklace resting against my collarbone, I felt a flicker of hope ignite within me, a quiet promise that I would embrace whatever came next.

The evening air was electric with the afterglow of laughter and the lingering warmth of shared moments, but something about the atmosphere shifted as we exited the bakery. The playful banter, which had danced around us like fireflies, dimmed slightly under the weight of the night. Felix glanced at me, his brow furrowed, as if he could sense the faint cloud of uncertainty still hovering over my thoughts. "So, what's the plan now, fearless leader?" he asked, his tone teasing, but his eyes were steady.

I shrugged, pretending nonchalance, but deep down, I felt like a marionette, strings pulled by both hope and fear. "Well, I guess we could go back to my place for a movie? Maybe something light and funny? I still have that ridiculous romantic comedy you love."

Mia's face lit up, her enthusiasm bubbling over. "Yes! But only if you promise to have popcorn with a ridiculous amount of butter. No health food allowed!"

"Fine, fine," I replied, rolling my eyes, though a smile tugged at my lips. "I can't let you ruin your movie experience with healthy snacks."

As we strolled through the now-dark streets, the city felt transformed under the shimmering glow of streetlights, each one a beacon guiding us through the night. The air was crisp, tinged with a hint of autumn, promising change with each fallen leaf. But just as we reached my front porch, the familiar warmth of home wrapped around me like a favorite blanket, a sudden shrill ringing sliced through the cozy atmosphere, pulling me back to reality.

My phone vibrated ominously against the wooden surface of the porch. I glanced at the screen, my heart sinking as I recognized the name flashing there. It was Claire. The cheerful demeanor she had exuded earlier felt like a distant memory now. I hesitated, my fingers hovering above the screen as unease curled in my stomach like a snake ready to strike. "Um, it's Claire," I said, trying to sound casual, but my voice betrayed me, a tremor escaping as I spoke.

"Answer it," Mia urged, her tone now serious. "Could be important."

With a nod that felt more like a resignation, I answered, "Hey, Claire."

"Thank goodness you picked up!" Her voice came through the line, laced with urgency. "I'm so glad to reach you. There's something we need to talk about, and it can't wait."

I swallowed hard, a knot forming in my stomach. "Is everything okay?"

"No, it's not," she replied, and I could hear her pacing on the other end. "I need you to come to my house. It's about your mother's estate."

My heart raced, a whirlwind of thoughts crashing against each other. "Estate? I thought everything was settled."

"It's complicated, and I can't explain it over the phone. Just trust me. I really need you here, and it's important," Claire insisted, her voice now edged with a note of panic.

I exchanged worried glances with Felix and Mia, who stood by, concern etched across their faces. "Okay, I'll be there," I said, trying to sound more confident than I felt. "Just give me a minute to get my things."

Hanging up, I felt a mixture of dread and curiosity swirling within me. "What's going on?" Felix asked, stepping closer, his gaze intense.

"Claire said it's about my mother's estate. Something isn't right," I replied, my stomach churning with unease.

Mia's eyes widened, and I could see her searching for words. "Should we come with you?"

I shook my head. "No. I need to do this alone. I'll be fine." But even as I spoke, I could feel the doubt gnawing at me, a whisper echoing that maybe I wouldn't be fine at all.

The drive to Claire's house felt surreal, each turn and streetlamp illuminating memories of countless visits filled with laughter and warmth. Now, it felt like crossing into a shadowy realm, where secrets lurked just beneath the surface. My hands gripped the steering wheel tightly, knuckles white as my mind raced with questions that refused to settle.

Arriving at Claire's, I parked in her driveway, the house looming ahead like a sentinel in the dark. I could see her silhouette moving behind the curtains, a restless energy that mirrored my own. Gathering my courage, I stepped out of the car, the gravel crunching beneath my feet echoing like a warning.

The door swung open before I could knock, and Claire stood there, her eyes wide and glistening with unshed tears. "Thank you for coming," she breathed, pulling me into a tight embrace.

"What's going on?" I asked, stepping inside, my pulse quickening. The living room was dimly lit, shadows clinging to the corners like secrets waiting to be revealed.

Claire motioned for me to sit down, her demeanor serious as she perched on the edge of the couch, hands clasped tightly in her lap. "It's about your mother's will. There's been a complication… something I didn't know until today."

A heaviness settled over the room, and I leaned forward, anticipation clawing at me. "What kind of complication?"

She took a deep breath, her eyes meeting mine with an intensity that sent a chill down my spine. "There's an asset that your mother didn't disclose. Something she kept hidden from everyone, and it's vital that you understand what's at stake."

"Hidden? What do you mean?" My heart raced, the tension thickening the air between us.

"Your mother had a storage unit. It contains... personal effects, but also documents that could change everything." Claire's voice quivered, the weight of her words settling heavily around us.

"What kind of documents?" I pressed, every instinct in me on high alert.

"Legal documents that might reveal another side of her life, aspects she never shared. I think there are things in there that could affect your inheritance—if not everything you thought you knew about her."

Just then, a loud crash came from the kitchen, followed by the sound of glass shattering. My heart raced as Claire's expression shifted from concern to alarm. "What was that?"

"I don't know!" she exclaimed, jumping to her feet. "Stay here! I'll check it out."

The moment she turned, my instincts kicked in. "No, wait! I'm coming with you."

We moved cautiously toward the kitchen, the tension in the air palpable. My mind raced with thoughts of what might be lurking behind that door. As Claire reached for the doorknob, I hesitated, a foreboding sense of dread settling in my stomach. Just as she opened the door, a figure emerged from the shadows—a tall, hooded silhouette that sent a jolt of fear through me.

"Who are you?" I demanded, stepping forward, adrenaline surging as I braced myself for whatever was about to unfold.

And in that moment, as the figure turned slowly toward us, I felt the ground shift beneath my feet. The world tilted as recognition flashed in my mind, and a voice I hadn't expected echoed through the air, sending a shiver down my spine. "I think it's time we had a talk, don't you?"

Chapter 23: Revelations

The air in Felix's house buzzes with an energy that feels almost electric. It wraps around me, a comforting embrace in contrast to the sterile environment of the hospital where we had spent countless hours together. The dim lighting, punctuated by the warm glow of string lights, casts a magical aura over the room. It's a far cry from the antiseptic white walls that had become my unwelcome backdrop; here, laughter dances through the air like confetti, each note shimmering in a way that makes my heart race. I stand among his relatives, a kaleidoscope of personalities that fill the space with warmth and a kind of chaotic joy that I find myself longing for.

Felix's aunt, a spirited woman with a riot of curly hair, hands me a glass of what she calls her "famous sangria." The fruity sweetness is balanced by a hint of spice, igniting my senses and pulling me deeper into this vibrant gathering. I find myself laughing as she tells stories of Felix as a child—how he would serenade the neighborhood cats with makeshift concerts using a broken guitar. I can picture it vividly: a small boy, oversized in his love for music, surrounded by indifferent felines. The thought brings a smile to my face, a warmth radiating through me that I didn't know I needed.

As I sip the sangria, I catch sight of Felix across the room. He's laughing with his brother, their shoulders bumping as they exchange inside jokes. There's something undeniably magnetic about him, the way he carries himself with a confidence that is both infectious and endearing. In this moment, amidst the warmth and laughter, I feel as if I'm witnessing the best parts of his life—moments he usually hides behind the façade of his stoic demeanor.

Yet, beneath the surface of joy, I sense a subtle tension, an undercurrent that makes my heart flutter uneasily. It's not just the remnants of the hospital's shadow hanging around us; it's something more. I've learned to read the subtle shifts in his expression, the fleeting moments when his laughter doesn't quite reach his eyes. It's during these brief lapses that I wonder if he feels the weight of our situation as acutely as I do.

Just as I'm lost in thought, Felix appears at my side, his smile wide and genuine. "Hey, you," he says, his voice a soft rumble that sends a thrill through me. "How's the sangria? Too sweet, or just right?" He raises an eyebrow, teasingly.

"Just the right amount of sweetness," I reply, matching his playful tone. "You know, if you're trying to distract me from the fact that you've left me to fend for myself among your relatives, it's working."

He chuckles, a sound that seems to resonate in my chest. "I had to give you a chance to bond with them. Besides, I thought I'd spare you from my terrible childhood stories. They'd probably embarrass me."

"Too late," I retort, rolling my eyes playfully. "Your aunt already had me in stitches. I'll be sure to bring a guitar next time we hang out, just to be fair."

"Only if I get to play with you," he replies, leaning in closer. The warmth of his presence is intoxicating, a gentle reminder that there's life beyond the walls of the hospital.

But then, with a quick shift in mood, he steps back, the playful light in his eyes dimming. "Can we talk?" he asks, his voice dropping to a more serious tone. I nod, my stomach knotting in anticipation.

Felix leads me to a quieter corner of the living room, where the laughter fades into the background. The contrast is stark, and I feel the shift in atmosphere settle around us like a heavy blanket. I brace myself for whatever revelation he might be about to share, my heart racing with a mix of excitement and apprehension.

"I've been working on something," he begins, his gaze flickering with both pride and vulnerability. "A piece dedicated to Mia. It's... it's more than just a song. It's everything I feel—everything we've been through."

The words hang in the air, rich with meaning. I can see the passion igniting in his eyes as he speaks, and a rush of admiration swells within me. The complexity of his emotions unfolds like petals on a flower, revealing layers of love, loss, and resilience.

"Felix, that's beautiful," I say, my voice barely above a whisper. "I can't imagine how hard it must be to put all that into music."

He nods, the corners of his mouth twitching into a soft smile. "It's a way for me to process everything. You know how music has always been my outlet. This... this is me embracing all of it—the good and the painful." He takes a deep breath, as if gathering his thoughts like pieces of a scattered puzzle. "I want to perform it tonight."

My heart leaps at the thought. "Here? In front of everyone?"

He looks at me, a mix of determination and uncertainty in his eyes. "Yeah. I think it's time."

A silence stretches between us, heavy yet charged with unspoken understanding. I reach out, placing my hand on his arm, feeling the warmth of his skin beneath my fingertips. "You're ready," I assure him. "Your family will be here for you."

The sincerity of my words seems to resonate with him, and he nods slowly. "Thanks. That means a lot."

Before I can say anything else, he leans in, brushing his lips against my cheek—a fleeting, electric moment that leaves me breathless. It's a soft gesture, but it carries a weight that makes my heart race and my mind spin. I can't help but wonder if this gathering, this moment of revelation, is the turning point we both need.

As the evening unfolds, the sounds of laughter and clinking glasses become a backdrop to the intimate moment Felix and I share. His family continues to buzz around us, each voice blending into a chorus of warmth, yet I can't shake the feeling that tonight is poised on the edge of something significant. Felix's revelation lingers in the air, a melodic promise that hangs between us like a tightly strung guitar string, vibrating with potential.

I'm drawn back to the gathering, glancing at Felix's relatives as they gather near the piano, exchanging animated stories and occasional bursts of laughter. His brother strums a few chords, the soft twang echoing through the room, and I can't help but feel a wave of nostalgia wash over me, reminiscent of long-forgotten family gatherings of my own. I watch as Felix's aunt nudges his mother, both of them sharing a knowing look that implies a lifetime of secrets wrapped up in those shared glances. It's like watching a dance where everyone knows the steps but me.

"Are you ready for this?" I ask, my voice low as I turn back to Felix, searching his face for signs of nerves.

He takes a moment to consider, his brow furrowed. "Ready? Not really. But when is anyone ever truly ready for something like this?"

His honesty pulls a laugh from me, the tension slipping away for a moment. "That's true. I once thought I was ready to try sushi. Turns out, I was just ready to regret my life choices for a solid week."

Felix chuckles, the corners of his mouth lifting in a way that makes my heart flutter. "You'll have to give it another shot sometime. Maybe I'll even join you. I can't promise I'll be any better at it, though."

"Just as long as you promise to wear a bib," I tease, and he feigns a shocked gasp.

We share a comfortable silence, his eyes sparkling with mischief, yet there's an unmistakable depth to his gaze that pulls me in. "I've been thinking about how important it is to let people in," he says quietly. "Especially now, with everything going on."

"Like a worm in an apple?" I quip, trying to lighten the mood, but he catches my eye, and I realize he's not joking.

"More like peeling back layers," he corrects me. "I've spent so long hiding behind my music, my fears. Maybe it's time I let people see the real me."

"Sounds terrifying," I reply, my voice softer now. "But also liberating. It's like jumping into a pool after a long winter."

He nods, the weight of his words sinking in. I can almost see the gears turning in his mind as he contemplates the leap he's about to take.

"Okay," he says finally, determination flickering in his eyes. "I'm going to do it. I'm going to perform."

With that declaration, he strides toward the small gathering near the piano, the moment of truth approaching like a wave building in the ocean. I watch him go, my heart pounding in my chest, a mix of pride and nervous anticipation swirling within me.

As Felix takes his place at the piano, I feel a shift in the atmosphere. The room grows quieter, the sounds of laughter diminishing to an expectant hush. The family instinctively draws closer, their eyes on him, a protective circle that speaks volumes about their support. I can almost see the invisible threads connecting them, binding them in a tapestry woven with love and shared history.

Felix runs his fingers over the keys, testing the notes with a tentative grace that betrays his nerves. "This is a song I wrote for my sister," he begins, his voice steady despite the tremor in his hands. "It's about love and loss, and finding a way to keep going, even when it feels impossible."

The first notes resonate through the room, filling the space with a haunting beauty. Each chord strikes a chord in my heart, pulling me into a reverie of emotions. It's not just a song; it's a piece of his soul laid bare, a mosaic of memories and heartache captured in sound. I close my eyes for a moment, allowing myself to be enveloped in the melody.

With every note he plays, I sense the healing power of music spilling forth. It's a reminder that vulnerability can be a strength, a lifeline to connection that often feels out of reach. I watch his fingers dance across the keys, the emotions etched into his features telling a story of their own. There's sadness there, but also a fierce determination that glimmers like sunlight breaking through storm clouds.

The room is completely still, the silence punctuated only by the gentle cascade of notes. Felix's family watches him, their expressions a blend of pride and grief, a testament to the bond they share. I can see his mother's eyes shimmering with unshed tears, her heart aching with each word sung, yet glowing with the warmth of his bravery.

When he finishes, the room erupts into applause, a spontaneous wave of love washing over him. I can see the relief flooding his features, the tension that had clung to him now dissipating like mist in the morning sun. I want to rush to him, to wrap him in my arms and tell him how incredible he was, but I hesitate, letting the moment settle like a gentle embrace around us.

Felix stands, breathless and vulnerable, a shy smile breaking through as he takes in the overwhelming support from his family. "Thanks, everyone. That means more than I can say," he says, his voice cracking slightly, and the sincerity of his words resonates deeply in my chest.

I approach him slowly, my heart racing, ready to share in this moment of triumph. "You were amazing," I whisper, unable to contain my admiration any longer.

He meets my gaze, the warmth of his smile igniting something deep within me. "I couldn't have done it without you," he admits, and I feel the blush creep up my cheeks at his words.

The room resumes its lively chatter, but we stand apart for a moment, the chaos swirling around us fading into the background. In this bubble, it feels like we're the only two people in the world.

The space between us crackles with unspoken possibilities, and I can't help but wonder if this moment marks a turning point for both of us—two souls navigating the uncertainties of life, perhaps finding solace in one another along the way.

The room pulses with life, laughter mingling with the lingering notes of Felix's performance as his family gathers around him, buoyed by the shared energy of his song. I stand a little way off, a warm drink cradled in my hands, and I can't help but admire the way the light from the string bulbs catches the glint of his hair, transforming him into a shimmering figure. For a fleeting moment, I feel like I'm watching a star take its rightful place in the sky, and I can't shake the sense that I'm witnessing something profoundly beautiful and transformative.

Felix's brother playfully ribs him, his voice a good-natured teasing laced with genuine admiration. "You know, I might just have to add 'songwriter' to my resume. Didn't know you had it in you, Felix!" The laughter erupts again, wrapping around us like a soft quilt, a reminder of the familial bonds that have weathered storms and sunny days alike.

"You'll have to audition first, Liam," Felix shoots back, his grin infectious, and the lightness in his voice pulls at the corners of my mouth. The sight of him here, surrounded by love and support, fills me with an almost overwhelming joy, but beneath it lies a flicker of apprehension. The night feels like a delicate balance between celebration and the reality we can't escape—the uncertainty still looming just outside our bubble of warmth.

Before I can dwell too long on the shadows, Felix approaches me, his expression a mix of exhilaration and disbelief. "Can you believe I actually did that?" He chuckles, a giddy sparkle in his eyes. "I thought my knees would buckle right in the middle!"

"Just think of all those cats you used to perform for," I say, trying to keep the mood light. "They weren't that different from this crowd.

They were probably just waiting for you to throw them a tuna or something."

He laughs, the sound rich and full, a testament to his relief. "At least they didn't boo me. I think my cat-fan base would have been more forgiving, though."

His smile fades slightly, a flicker of vulnerability resurfacing. "But seriously, it felt good to let it out. I think Mia would have liked that. She always wanted me to embrace my music, to stop hiding."

"That's what it's all about, isn't it?" I respond, my heart swelling with empathy. "Living for those who can't anymore, using our experiences to grow and connect."

"Exactly." Felix glances back at his family, who are still buzzing with excitement. "I want to keep doing this. Not just for me, but for her."

As the night wears on, Felix mingles with his relatives, each interaction infused with laughter and love, while I find myself lingering at the edge of the room, a witness to this familial tapestry. It's comforting to watch, yet I can't shake the feeling that something deeper is swirling beneath the surface. The laughter feels almost too loud, the warmth too perfect. There's a fine line between joy and sorrow, and I can sense it wavering, threatening to tip at any moment.

When a hush falls over the crowd, it's as if the air itself holds its breath. A distant siren wails outside, a stark reminder of the world beyond these walls. The energy in the room shifts, a collective exhalation as everyone refocuses on Felix, who seems momentarily lost in thought.

"Let's keep the music going!" his brother suggests, a playful tone creeping back in. "Who's next? I think it's time for a good old-fashioned karaoke showdown!"

The room erupts in cheers, the energy revitalized, and I feel the tension ease again, at least for a moment. Felix's smile returns, and he gestures toward the small karaoke machine tucked away in the corner. "Alright, who's brave enough to go first?"

Before anyone can volunteer, Felix turns to me, eyes sparkling with mischief. "You should totally sing something! Show them your amazing skills."

"Me? You must be confusing me with someone who knows how to sing," I laugh, but there's a thrill in his challenge that sends a rush of adrenaline through me. "The only thing I'm skilled at is karaoke disasters."

"Exactly! It'll be fun!" he insists, his enthusiasm infectious.

I take a deep breath, feeling the familiar flutter of nerves in my stomach. But with Felix's gaze on me—full of encouragement and something deeper—I can't resist the pull. "Fine. Just don't expect anything too spectacular."

As I step forward, I can feel the warmth of their support wrapping around me like a protective blanket. The first notes of a classic pop song fill the room, and I dive in, my voice shaky at first but growing stronger as I lose myself in the music. Laughter and cheers erupt from the crowd, and I find myself smiling despite my earlier apprehensions. There's something liberating about this shared experience, a moment of connection that transcends the struggles we each carry.

Halfway through, as I reach a high note, the doorbell rings, slicing through the atmosphere like a knife. The music falters, the laughter dissipating into an uneasy silence. Felix's brow furrows, and I catch a glimpse of concern in his eyes as he glances toward the door.

"I'll get it," he says, the playful tone now replaced with a sense of urgency.

As he strides away, I try to shake off the sudden chill that envelops me. The warmth of the room feels a world away, replaced by an inexplicable unease that prickles at the back of my mind. I watch as he opens the door, and the moment he does, a shadow seems to fall across his face.

My heart races as a figure appears in the doorway, silhouetted against the porch light. I can't quite make out their features, but the tension in Felix's posture sends a wave of unease rippling through me. I want to rush to him, to bridge the growing chasm, but I remain frozen, a spectator in this unfolding drama.

"Who—?" Felix's voice falters, and I can feel the air grow thick with uncertainty.

The figure steps forward, revealing themselves, and my stomach drops as I recognize the unmistakable look of someone from our past—a ghost I never expected to see again, their presence a storm cloud darkening our precious evening.

"Felix," they say, their voice low and haunting, "we need to talk."

In that moment, the laughter, the music, the warmth of family—all of it feels like a distant memory, overshadowed by the weight of this unexpected arrival. The air grows heavy with anticipation, and I sense that whatever is about to unfold will change everything.

Chapter 24: A Strained Harmony

An unsettling chill filled the hospital room, wrapping around me like an unwelcome shawl as I settled into the plastic chair, the sterile smell of antiseptic stinging my nostrils. I pulled my sweater tighter, trying to stave off the icy grip of worry that had gripped me since Mia's sudden decline. The rhythmic beep of the monitors blended with the distant murmur of nurses and the occasional soft footfall, creating a symphony of unease. I stared at Mia, her small frame dwarfed by the vastness of the hospital bed, a tangle of tubes and machines whirring softly around her. Her pale face was framed by a halo of messy curls, and for a moment, she looked so peaceful, almost ethereal. But the pallor of her skin and the way her body seemed to sink into the mattress told a different story—a story I wished I could rewrite.

Felix paced the small space, a caged animal, his hands stuffed deep in his pockets. The fluorescent lights above flickered intermittently, casting shadows on his furrowed brow. I could feel the tension radiating off him, a palpable wave of frustration and fear. With every turn, he seemed to draw further away from me, retreating into a fortress of guilt that I couldn't penetrate.

"Why is this happening?" he muttered, more to himself than to me. His voice was tight, strained like an over-stretched wire, ready to snap. "I should have seen it coming."

"You can't blame yourself for this, Felix." I tried to sound steady, but my own fear seeped into my words, making them waver. "We had no idea her condition would worsen like this."

He stopped abruptly, pivoting to face me, the anguish in his eyes cutting deeper than any knife. "But I should have. I should have pushed harder, asked more questions. Maybe if I'd—"

"Enough!" My voice cracked, echoing in the small room. "You're not a doctor. You can't foresee every outcome."

But the truth was, I felt the tremors of his doubt. It was there in the way he clenched his fists and in the way his jaw ticked with unrelenting tension. Felix had always been the one with the answers, the one who could navigate the chaos of life with a grace I both envied and admired. Watching him flounder in the face of uncertainty was unnerving, as if the very foundation of our relationship was being rattled by unseen hands.

He turned away, his shoulders tense. "I just can't shake the feeling that I failed her."

I felt a lump rise in my throat, thick and painful, and it took every ounce of strength not to let the tears spill over. The walls seemed to close in around us, suffocating the fragile harmony we'd built over the years. The soft murmurs of other patients and their families faded into the background, leaving us suspended in our own turmoil. I longed to reach out, to pull him back from the edge he teetered on, but the chasm between us yawned wider, filled with unspoken fears and accusations neither of us wanted to voice.

"Mia loves you," I said, my voice barely a whisper. "She wouldn't want you to feel this way. You're her rock."

His expression softened for a fleeting moment, but then the storm returned, darkening his features. "What if I'm not enough? What if I can't be the person she needs?"

My heart ached at his words, the vulnerability laid bare in front of me. I wanted to shake him, to make him see how blind he was to his own strength, but instead, I felt an overwhelming urge to crawl inside his mind, to show him that he wasn't alone in this. "You are enough, Felix. You're doing everything you can. We're all scared, but that doesn't mean you're failing her."

He turned to me, eyes brimming with unshed tears, and for a moment, I thought I saw a flicker of hope. But just as quickly, the flicker dimmed, swallowed by the weight of our reality. "It's so hard to be strong when everything feels so fragile."

"Then don't be strong alone," I urged, my voice steadying as a sense of determination washed over me. "We'll face this together. We can't lose sight of that."

Silence hung heavy between us, thick and almost suffocating. I could see the battle waging in his mind, the clashing of hope and despair, but I couldn't find the right words to bridge the chasm. Instead, I reached out, taking his hand in mine, squeezing it gently, hoping to convey everything I felt through that simple touch.

He looked down, our fingers intertwined like the notes of a melody, both delicate and resolute. "I don't want to lose her, or you," he murmured, the vulnerability in his voice almost breaking me.

"Neither do I," I said, my heart racing. "But we need each other now more than ever. Let's hold on to that."

As he met my gaze, the storm in his eyes slowly began to dissipate, replaced by a flicker of something softer, something that resembled trust. For the first time in days, I felt a glimmer of hope weaving through the darkness, a tiny thread that suggested maybe we could find our way back to each other despite the chaos around us.

Mia stirred in her sleep, a soft sigh escaping her lips, and in that moment, the world felt just a bit more bearable. The challenges we faced were daunting, yes, but together, we could weather the storm.

The sterile fluorescent lights buzzed overhead, casting an artificial glow over the hospital room that felt both oppressive and surreal. Outside the window, nightfall blanketed the world in a comforting shroud, but inside, we were trapped in a relentless cycle of anxiety and uncertainty. Felix sat hunched in the corner, his brow furrowed in concentration, as if willing the walls to yield the answers we desperately sought. I watched him, helpless against the tide of worry that threatened to pull us both under.

In an effort to break the suffocating silence, I picked at the frayed edge of my sweater, trying to distract myself from the gravity of the moment. "You know," I began, forcing a lightness into my tone, "if we keep coming back here, I might just consider moving in. At least I could get a roommate discount on the cafeteria food."

Felix glanced up, his expression a mix of amusement and disbelief. "If we get a roommate discount, then we might as well start a support group for frequent flyers."

A small smile tugged at the corners of his mouth, but it quickly faded, leaving behind the weight of his unrelenting guilt. I could sense the storm brewing behind his eyes, the turmoil that had become our unwelcome companion. "We could start calling ourselves the 'Frequent Hospital Visitors Club'—T-shirts and all," I continued, desperate to elicit a laugh. "I'll design the logo, complete with a cartoon bandage wearing sunglasses."

"I'd prefer a superhero theme," he replied, his voice thick with sarcasm. "Because nothing says 'invincible' like sitting in a hospital gown with your dignity left in the waiting room."

I chuckled, but the sound felt hollow, swallowed by the reality of our situation. Just as I thought we might ease the tension, Felix turned serious again. "This isn't funny, though. Mia's not going to magically get better just because we throw jokes around."

"I know," I said softly, my heart aching at the truth in his words. "But laughter is all we have sometimes. It's our lifeline."

He sighed, running a hand through his hair, the gesture betraying the weariness he was trying to hide. "It doesn't feel like enough. Not when I see her lying there, not when I can't do anything to help."

The weight of his frustration settled between us, a tangible force I could almost reach out and touch. "Felix, you're doing everything you can. Being here for her matters more than you realize."

"Does it?" he asked, his voice barely a whisper. "Or am I just a spectator in this nightmare?"

"I think you underestimate how much she needs you," I replied, hoping to pierce through his doubt. "Mia's always drawn strength from you. You're her anchor."

As if summoned by our conversation, a soft knock interrupted us, and the door creaked open. A nurse with kind eyes peeked in, her clipboard tucked under her arm. "Good evening. How are you both holding up?"

"We're just keeping each other entertained," I said, trying to muster a smile.

She returned the gesture, her demeanor radiating warmth. "That's good to hear. It can get pretty overwhelming in here. Just remember, it's important to take care of yourselves too. Is there anything you need?"

Felix opened his mouth, probably to ask for something ridiculous, but I cut him off. "Just some reassurance that Mia is in good hands," I said, my heart racing slightly.

The nurse nodded, her expression shifting to one of empathy. "She's stable, which is encouraging. We're doing everything we can to monitor her condition. The doctors will be making rounds in a bit, and they'll provide updates."

"Thank you," Felix said, his voice steadier now.

As the nurse left, I turned to Felix, ready to rekindle our previous banter. "So, when they say she's 'stable,' does that mean we can launch a rescue mission to whisk her out of here and back to the land of sunshine and ice cream?"

He gave me a half-hearted grin, but the shadows lingered in his eyes. "If only it were that simple. I wish we could just pop her out of here like a cork from a bottle."

"Just think of the epic adventure we could have—Mia, the fearless heroine, escaping the clutches of hospital confinement." I leaned in, my voice lowering conspiratorially. "We could even throw in a dramatic chase scene. I could play the rogue sidekick."

He snorted, the sound surprising both of us. "I'm not sure how much action you could provide from that chair, but I appreciate the enthusiasm."

As the clock ticked on, our shared humor became a fragile bridge over the chasm of uncertainty. The hours blurred together, each moment stretching and contracting in an endless loop. The faint sounds of beeping machines became our metronome, guiding us through the strange symphony of fear and hope.

Eventually, the door swung open again, this time revealing a doctor clad in a white coat, his expression serious yet kind. "Good evening, I'm Dr. Stevens. I'd like to talk to you about Mia's condition."

Felix and I exchanged a glance, the weight of unspoken dread thick in the air. "How is she?" I asked, my heart thudding painfully in my chest.

Dr. Stevens took a deep breath, and in that moment, the world outside felt impossibly distant, as if it had slipped into a different realm altogether. "Mia's current treatment is showing some progress, but we need to closely monitor her response to the new medications. There are risks involved, but we're hopeful."

Hopeful. The word hung between us like a fragile bubble, shimmering with promise yet threatening to burst at any moment.

"Can we see her?" Felix asked, his voice steady but tinged with urgency.

"Yes, of course. Just keep in mind she may be asleep," Dr. Stevens replied, leading us down the sterile corridor.

Each step felt heavy, the weight of our fears pulling us down as we approached her room. As we crossed the threshold, the soft glow of the bedside lamp illuminated Mia's face, peaceful yet so heartbreakingly vulnerable. She was a warrior resting, her body fighting battles that none of us could see.

"Hey, Mia," I whispered, stepping closer. "We're right here with you."

Felix's fingers brushed against hers, and I could see the flicker of determination reignite in his eyes. It was a small spark, but enough to light our path forward. As the night wore on, the hospital room felt less like a prison and more like a sanctuary—a place where we could confront our fears together, armed with nothing but our love and the promise of hope.

The gentle hum of the hospital's fluorescent lights had become a maddening backdrop, each flicker echoing my own racing thoughts. I stood by Mia's bedside, tracing the outlines of her fingers with my own, feeling the warmth that still radiated from her skin. She was a fighter, I reminded myself, but as the hours slipped by, my resolve began to fray. The quiet moments had turned into a cacophony of what-ifs and worst-case scenarios, each one louder than the last.

Felix lingered near the window, his silhouette framed by the soft glow of the streetlights outside. The way he leaned against the glass made him look small, as if the weight of the world had settled upon his shoulders. "You'd think we'd find a way to keep the lights on in here," he muttered, a hint of bitterness in his tone. "It's like they want us to feel more miserable."

I glanced at him, my heart aching at the sight of his furrowed brow. "I think it's their subtle way of reminding us we're stuck in a hospital. Nothing says 'welcome' like a flickering bulb."

His chuckle was short-lived, the mirth quickly extinguished by the heaviness in his heart. "You'd think they'd at least have a coffee machine that works. I could use a decent cup right now."

"Right? At this point, I'd settle for instant coffee if it means we can stay awake long enough to see Mia smile again." I glanced at Mia, who lay still, her chest rising and falling in a rhythmic cadence that reminded me she was still with us.

Felix ran a hand through his hair, the frustration evident in the way he pulled at the strands. "I just wish I could do more. I hate feeling this helpless."

"Helplessness is the worst. It gnaws at you, doesn't it?" I nodded toward the tiny fern in the corner of the room, a feeble attempt at adding life to the stark surroundings. "If that little guy can survive in here, I think we can too. We just need to keep nurturing the things that matter."

He crossed the room, his expression softening as he looked down at Mia. "I'm trying, but what if it's not enough? What if I'm not enough?"

"Stop that," I said, stepping closer. "You're more than enough for her. You're her compass in this chaos. Besides, if you're looking for someone to blame, I'm the one who brought the instant coffee."

He laughed, a sound that felt like a long-lost friend. "Instant coffee? You'd betray me like that?"

"Only in dire situations. I assure you, I'm still loyal to the cause of decent brew."

Just then, the door swung open, and Dr. Stevens stepped in, his expression a blend of professionalism and warmth. "Good evening. I wanted to check in on Mia. I know this is a tough time."

"Is she...?" Felix asked, his voice barely rising above a whisper, as if afraid to disturb the fragile state of things.

"Her vitals are stable, which is encouraging," he replied, his tone measured. "We've made some adjustments to her treatment. The next few hours will be crucial. I'd recommend trying to get some rest. It's a long journey ahead, and you both need your strength."

"Rest? You do realize we're in a hospital, not a spa?" I quipped, but I could see the concern etched on Felix's face.

Dr. Stevens smiled, a flicker of understanding in his eyes. "That's true, but even the fiercest warriors need to recharge. I promise to keep you updated."

As he exited, the air thickened with unspoken fears. I turned back to Felix, who had retreated to his corner once more, his gaze lost in thought. "What are you thinking?" I asked gently.

"I'm just wondering if we should be preparing for the worst," he admitted, his voice low and vulnerable. "What if this is the beginning of something we can't control?"

"Then we face it together," I said, trying to infuse my words with strength. "That's all we can do. We won't let fear dictate our choices."

He nodded but the tension in his shoulders remained, a physical manifestation of the internal battle he waged. "Sometimes it feels like we're just prolonging the inevitable. Like we're fighting a losing battle."

"Life's not about winning or losing; it's about the moments we share, the laughter we find in the chaos." I stepped closer, placing my hand on his arm, the connection grounding us both. "And right now, that means we need to focus on Mia. She's still here, still fighting."

Just then, the machines surrounding Mia began to beep more rapidly, a jarring sound that sliced through the heavy silence. Panic washed over me as I spun around. "Felix!"

He rushed to the bed, his face a mask of determination. "Mia! Can you hear me?"

The beeping intensified, and I felt my heart race in sync with the rhythm of the monitors. A flurry of nurses entered the room, their movements swift and practiced, but the chaos felt surreal, like watching a storm unfold from a distance. I stood frozen, helpless as the medical team surrounded Mia, their voices a blend of urgency and authority.

"Get the crash cart!" one nurse shouted, her tone slicing through the panic.

The room shrank around me, the walls closing in as I clutched the edge of the bed, willing myself to breathe. Felix's hand gripped

Mia's tighter, his voice steady as he called her name, but the reality of the situation crashed over us like a tidal wave.

In that moment, everything shifted. Time stood still, suspended in a fragile balance between hope and despair. The beeping continued, relentless and unforgiving, and I felt the edges of my vision blur as dread seeped into my bones.

Just as the doctors began to administer treatment, the lights flickered violently, plunging us into darkness for an agonizing heartbeat. "What the hell?" Felix shouted, panic lacing his voice.

I blinked, disoriented, and in that split second of confusion, the door swung open again, but this time, it wasn't a nurse or a doctor. A figure loomed in the doorway, backlit by the faint emergency lights.

"Felix," the figure called out, a familiar voice slicing through the chaos. "I need to talk to you—now!"

My heart dropped as I recognized the voice, the dread coiling tighter in my chest. The storm had returned, and this time, it carried secrets that could shatter everything we had fought for.

Chapter 25: The Thread that Binds

The air inside the small café hummed with the rich aroma of roasted coffee beans and the gentle clinking of ceramic cups. Sunlight streamed through the large windows, casting a warm glow on the scattered patrons who occupied mismatched tables. I was tucked into a cozy corner, a half-eaten scone before me, though my attention drifted far beyond the crumbs. My gaze flickered toward the door, where the bell above chimed each time it swung open. I was waiting for Mia, my best friend and the kind of soul that could light up the darkest room.

Mia had been a shadow of herself lately, her laughter replaced by a solemn silence. But today was different. I could feel the flutter of anticipation stirring in my chest as I imagined her face lighting up when she saw me. I had promised her a small adventure to distract us from the weight of the world pressing down on us. It was a day dedicated to reviving the vibrant hues of our friendship, and I was determined to make it count.

As the door swung open, a gust of cool air swept through the café, and there she was. Mia stepped inside, her dark curls bouncing around her shoulders, and for a moment, I thought I saw the spark of her old self returning. Dressed in a bright yellow sundress that seemed to absorb the sunlight, she radiated warmth. Her eyes, though still carrying the shadows of her struggles, held a flicker of curiosity that hadn't been there for weeks.

"Mia!" I called, waving her over with exaggerated enthusiasm. She approached, a hesitant smile tugging at her lips.

"Hey, sorry I'm late. I couldn't decide between coffee and tea." She plopped down in the chair across from me, her fingers nervously toying with the hem of her dress.

"Coffee, definitely coffee," I said, leaning in conspiratorially. "It's the only way to face the day. Or is it a covert operation to sneak in a double espresso?"

Her laughter danced in the air, a sound I had missed more than I cared to admit. "You know me too well. But I'll settle for the usual this time."

We ordered, and as the barista bustled away, I leaned back, studying her. Mia had always been the kind of person who wore her heart on her sleeve, and right now, that heart seemed buried under layers of uncertainty. "So, are you ready for the grand adventure?" I asked, hoping to peel back the layers and coax out the vibrant woman I loved like a sister.

Her brow furrowed slightly, and the flicker of enthusiasm dimmed. "I don't know, Jess. Everything feels... complicated."

"Complicated is my middle name!" I exclaimed, striking a dramatic pose that earned me an eye-roll but also a hint of a smile. "But we can't let complications hold us back. Remember our plan for Felix's performance next week? We can make it special for him—and for you."

Mia's expression shifted, her gaze drifting to the window where the world outside buzzed with life. "Felix..." she murmured, a bittersweet smile touching her lips. "He's been so supportive, hasn't he?"

"Absolutely," I replied, knowing exactly how much she appreciated his unwavering friendship. "And what better way to repay him than by cheering him on at his show? It'll be like old times."

As if on cue, the barista returned with our drinks, and I took a moment to let her savor the steaming cup. I watched as she inhaled deeply, the scent of rich coffee filling her lungs, and her shoulders relaxed just a fraction. "You're right," she finally said, her voice firming with resolve. "I want to be there for him. I'll go."

"Yes! That's the Mia I know!" I clapped my hands together, a burst of excitement surging through me. "But it's not just about attending. We're going to make this a night to remember."

Mia raised an eyebrow, a playful glint returning to her eyes. "Oh? What do you have in mind?"

"We'll gather everyone who cares about Felix and decorate the venue! We can hang up photos, share memories, and create a space that feels alive—just like our friendship."

She bit her lip, considering my suggestion. "I like that. A celebration of life, despite the chaos around us."

"Exactly!" I leaned in, heart racing at the thought of igniting the spark of joy within her. "We'll remind him how loved he is and how much we've all grown through this madness. It's our thread that binds us, after all."

Mia's expression softened as she considered this, her gaze unfocused as if she were lost in the whirlwind of memories we'd built together. "I do miss those days, Jess. The late-night adventures and the laughter. I feel like I've forgotten how to just... be."

"Then let's reclaim it," I said, a surge of determination fueling my words. "We'll surround ourselves with love and laughter, just like we used to. You and I, we've weathered storms before. It's time we embraced the sunshine."

Mia nodded slowly, her smile returning in full force. "Okay, let's do it. Let's make it unforgettable."

With a plan set in motion, the vibrant atmosphere of the café faded into the background, our thoughts weaving together like the threads of a tapestry, binding us not just to Felix, but to each other. We mapped out our ideas, laughter punctuating our conversation as we imagined the venue transformed into a realm of joy and warmth. Each moment felt like a brushstroke on a canvas, painting a picture of resilience and love amidst the uncertainty surrounding us.

"Alright, then. It's settled," I declared, tapping my fingers dramatically on the table. "Operation Make Felix's Night Unforgettable is officially underway."

Mia chuckled, shaking her head. "You're ridiculous, you know that?"

"Absolutely. But you love me for it." I winked, savoring the moment as the sun dipped lower in the sky, casting long shadows that danced around us.

As the week wore on, the anticipation of Felix's performance grew, buzzing around us like an electric current. Mia and I transformed our afternoons into a whirlwind of preparation, piecing together an elaborate plan that involved more than just decorations. The idea of celebrating not only Felix but also the strength that bound our little tribe together blossomed like the first spring flowers after a long winter. Each day, we worked tirelessly, crafting homemade decorations, sifting through old photographs, and gathering stories that would serve as a tapestry of our shared experiences.

The venue was a cozy, intimate space nestled in a corner of the city, its walls adorned with the kind of character that only years of music and laughter could cultivate. I'd seen it before, a quaint bar that resonated with the soul of local talent, the kind that drew you in like a moth to a flame. The wooden stage, lit by warm fairy lights, had a way of making every performance feel personal, as if the artist was sharing a secret with each member of the audience.

As we arrived one afternoon to set up, I felt the familiar flutter of excitement. "Can you believe we're actually doing this?" I exclaimed, surveying the room. The bare walls called out for color, and the empty tables seemed to yearn for the weight of memories.

"Just promise me we won't turn it into a Pinterest disaster," Mia said, half-joking but with a hint of seriousness. Her brows knitted in concentration as she held up a string of lights, testing their glow against the fading daylight.

"Not a chance. We'll keep it classy. Think understated elegance, with a splash of chaos." I grinned, plucking a photo of Felix from my pocket—a candid shot of him mid-laugh, his curly hair wild against the backdrop of a setting sun. "This guy deserves the best we can give him."

Mia held the photo close to her heart, her gaze softening. "You're right. It's just... I hope he's ready for this."

"Ready or not, it's happening. And besides," I added with a conspiratorial wink, "he won't be able to resist our charm."

The first evening of setup felt like we were stepping back in time, rediscovering the giddiness of our youth. As we draped the string lights around the edges of the stage, the warm glow began to illuminate the space, casting soft shadows and inviting an air of intimacy. Mia rummaged through a box of decorations we had scavenged together, pulling out old tickets, forgotten mementos, and a collection of notes we had written to each other over the years, a testament to our friendship.

"Look at this," she laughed, waving a slip of paper in the air. "Remember the 'complimentary advice' I gave you on how to flirt with Felix?"

I snorted, a laugh bubbling up from somewhere deep inside. "Complimentary advice? More like a how-to manual on how to turn an innocent conversation into an awkward train wreck."

"Oh, come on! You actually used the 'slip him your number in a pizza box' tactic!"

"Desperate times called for desperate measures. What can I say? He was the cheese to my pizza." I leaned against the wall, smirking, but my heart clenched a little as I thought of Felix. The man who had poured his heart into his music while trying to navigate the chaos of life. Would this night help him see how loved he truly was?

As the evening wore on, Mia and I shifted gears, starting to hang the photos around the stage. Each snapshot told a story, a little piece of our shared history woven together like a patchwork quilt. There were moments of joy, tears, and laughter—frozen in time but alive with emotion. As we worked, the room filled with a sense of purpose, a feeling that the night would mean something significant.

"Do you think he'll cry?" Mia asked, her brow furrowed as she studied the arrangement of photos on the wall. "I mean, do you think we might actually make him cry?"

"If he doesn't, I'll be disappointed. It's practically a rite of passage at these kinds of events." I winked, feigning seriousness. "Tears equal success. It's science."

"I like your logic," she replied, chuckling. But then her expression turned contemplative. "You really think this will help him?"

"I know it will. The music will be the heartbeat of the night, but our memories will wrap around him like a warm blanket. It's a reminder of everything he's overcome and all the love that surrounds him."

Mia nodded, the tension in her shoulders easing. "I just want him to feel—feel everything he's held back. He's so talented, yet so burdened. He deserves to know he's not alone in this."

Our conversation drifted into a comfortable silence, the kind that filled the air with unspoken understanding. Just as I began to lose myself in the beauty of the moment, the door swung open, and the sound of footsteps echoed through the room. We turned, startled to see Felix standing in the doorway, his guitar slung casually over his shoulder.

"What's this?" he asked, an eyebrow raised as he took in the scene before him. "Is there a party I wasn't invited to?"

"Just a little surprise for you next week," Mia said, feigning innocence. "You know how we love surprises."

His gaze flickered between us, a knowing smile creeping across his face. "If it involves glitter and embarrassing stories, I'm in. But if you're trying to bribe me with chocolate cake, I'll need a full menu."

I crossed my arms, leaning back against the wall, my heart racing with a mix of excitement and anxiety. "No cake, but plenty of photos. We're decorating your performance like a tribute to your awesomeness."

Felix laughed, the sound rich and genuine, but I caught a glimpse of something deeper beneath the surface. "You two are too much. Seriously, what's the occasion?"

Mia and I exchanged a quick glance, her eyes wide with the thrill of the secret we were keeping. I couldn't help but lean in closer, a conspiratorial whisper escaping my lips. "We thought you could use a little reminder of how loved you are, especially with everything going on. It's a celebration of you and your music, Felix."

He paused, the levity of his expression shifting, replaced by an earnest look that made my heart clench. "I...wow. You really didn't have to do this."

"Too late, we're doing it," I replied, determination infusing my voice. "And trust me, it's going to be epic."

A brief silence settled between us, the weight of unspoken emotions hanging in the air like a delicate thread. I knew then that our plan was more than just decorations and performances; it was a lifeline woven from love, a promise that we would always be there for each other, no matter how tumultuous life became. Felix stood before us, the embodiment of everything we held dear, and together, we were ready to stitch together the fabric of our lives, one heartfelt moment at a time.

As the day of the performance drew near, the air crackled with a unique blend of excitement and anxiety, an intoxicating cocktail that stirred our hearts into a whirl of anticipation. Mia and I devoted every spare moment to refining our plans, but each time I caught her gazing into the distance, I sensed the weight of her unspoken fears. It was a delicate dance we were performing—her uncertainty mingling with my relentless optimism, both of us determined to orchestrate a night that would echo long after the last chord had faded.

The evening before the big event, we gathered in my tiny apartment, a sanctuary strewn with the remnants of our efforts: rolls of colorful streamers, a chaotic assortment of photographs, and enough fairy lights to illuminate a small village. Mia flitted about, rearranging the items with a meticulousness that both amused and worried me.

"Too much blue in this corner," she announced, her voice taking on the tone of a stern art director. "And what's with the random photos of you? This is about Felix, not your illustrious history of awkward hairstyles."

"Hey! Those were experimental phases of artistic expression," I protested, half-heartedly. "Besides, he'll love the nostalgia. It's like a timeline of my questionable choices." I plucked a photo from the pile—me with a frizzy perm that looked like it had been styled by a tornado—and held it up for her inspection.

Mia snorted, shaking her head. "If that doesn't scream 'fearless,' I don't know what does. Just remember, we're going for heartwarming, not horror show."

"Heartwarming it is!" I chirped, tossing the photo back into the pile, and we both erupted into laughter, the tension momentarily forgotten.

As we worked late into the night, the familiar rhythm of our banter filled the space, each exchange a thread weaving us tighter together. Yet, beneath the laughter, a current of anxiety lingered, one that tugged at my heart with every passing hour. Mia's smile was bright, but her eyes told a different story. It was clear that she was battling something within herself, and I feared it would resurface at the worst possible moment.

After what felt like an eternity, the day of the performance arrived, bursting forth with a sun-drenched brilliance that seemed almost unreal. The warm glow of the afternoon sun danced across the venue, casting a golden light over the preparations. The walls were adorned with our handiwork, a patchwork of memories showcasing Felix's journey: photos of him at various performances, goofy candid shots of our friends, and heartfelt notes capturing the essence of who he was to us.

"Looks amazing," Mia said, taking a step back to survey our creation. "I think we've outdone ourselves."

"Agreed! This is basically a love letter to Felix." I paused, my heart racing. "Do you think he'll really be touched?"

"Jess, if he doesn't cry, I'll eat my weight in cake," she declared with a grin, her spirit rising to meet the occasion.

As the clock ticked closer to showtime, we greeted familiar faces—friends, family, and supporters who had all come to cheer for Felix. The energy in the room swelled, a palpable excitement coursing through the crowd like a pulse. Laughter and chatter mingled with the scent of popcorn and the rich aroma of coffee wafting from the corner.

Felix arrived just as the venue began to fill, his presence a breath of fresh air that quieted the noise. He looked around, a mix of surprise and delight washing over him as he took in the decorations. The fairy lights twinkled like stars above him, illuminating the joy in his eyes. I saw the moment he recognized the significance of each photo and note, a flicker of disbelief crossing his face.

"Guys, this is... incredible," he said, his voice thick with emotion. "You really didn't have to go all out like this."

"Of course we did!" I replied, stepping forward. "This is about you, Felix. We want you to know how much you mean to us and how proud we are of you."

Before he could respond, the crowd erupted into cheers, drowning out our conversation. The stage was set, and as he made his way to the front, I felt a surge of pride swelling in my chest. It was a moment we had all been waiting for—the moment when Felix would pour his heart out through his music, transforming the emotions that had weighed him down into something beautiful.

As he began to play, the room fell silent, every person transfixed by the sound of his guitar mingling with his rich, velvety voice. He strummed the first chord, and it felt as though the very air around us shifted. Each note danced through the room, wrapping around us like a comforting embrace. I glanced at Mia, who stood beside me, her eyes glistening with unshed tears.

"See?" I whispered, nudging her with my elbow. "Tears already!"

She smirked, swiping at her eyes. "Shut up. I'm just... emotional. This is beautiful."

The music swelled, and Felix launched into a song that felt like a direct dialogue with his soul. The lyrics poured from him, raw and authentic, and I could see the weight of his struggles lifting with each note. But as the song progressed, I caught something shifting in the air—a tension that seemed to coil within the crowd, a hushed whisper creeping into the otherwise joyful atmosphere.

Just as Felix reached the bridge of his song, a loud crash echoed from the back of the venue, silencing everything in an instant. Heads turned, and I squinted through the dim light to see a figure stumbling through the door, a man in a dark jacket, wild-eyed and panting as though he'd just run a marathon.

My heart dropped. Something about his frantic energy sent a ripple of unease through the crowd. Felix faltered mid-verse, confusion etched across his face as the crowd murmured in surprise.

"Mia, what's happening?" I whispered, my eyes darting between the stage and the unexpected intruder.

"I don't know," she replied, her voice low, anxiety knitting her brow.

The man staggered forward, his gaze locking onto Felix with an intensity that felt almost predatory. "Felix!" he shouted, his voice piercing through the stunned silence. "You need to come with me. It's urgent!"

Gasps rippled through the audience, tension electrifying the air as the man's words hung ominously over us. Felix's expression morphed from confusion to alarm, a flicker of fear crossing his features.

"Who are you?" he demanded, gripping the guitar tightly, his knuckles white against the wood.

"I said, you need to come with me!" the man insisted, desperation lacing his voice. "It's about your brother."

The collective breath of the crowd caught in their throats, an icy wave of dread washing over the room. The world around me blurred, and for a heartbeat, everything froze as Felix's eyes widened in disbelief. I felt the ground shift beneath me, the celebration slipping away like sand through my fingers, leaving behind only uncertainty and the haunting question of what lay ahead.

Chapter 26: The Sound of Healing

The night hums with a palpable energy, wrapping around me like the warmth of a favorite blanket. The club is a kaleidoscope of laughter and whispered secrets, a sanctuary where hopes converge under the soft glow of vintage Edison bulbs that dangle from the ceiling like fireflies captured in glass. I can almost taste the anticipation, sweet and sharp, as I peer through the curtain, my heart thudding a rhythm of its own.

Felix steps into the spotlight, and the room falls silent, a collective inhale as if everyone is holding their breath, waiting for something magical to unfold. He stands there, guitar slung low, his dark hair falling into his eyes, obscuring the vulnerability he usually wears so openly. Tonight, however, that vulnerability is hidden beneath layers of resolve and purpose. I can feel the tremor of his fingers against the strings even from backstage, a silent conversation between him and the instrument.

The first chord rings out, slicing through the quiet like a blade. It resonates, echoes bouncing off the walls, and I swear it catches everyone in its web, binding us together. I can see Mia in the front row, her face aglow with excitement and pride. She's been a steadfast companion, a beacon of light through this tumultuous journey we've embarked upon together. Every strum sends ripples of emotion through the crowd, reminding me of why we're here—to fight, to heal, to reclaim the parts of ourselves that have felt lost in the shadows of doubt and fear.

I glance at the small banner draped across the stage, "For Hope," its letters meticulously painted in cheerful colors, a testament to our shared mission. The night is not just a performance; it's a manifestation of everything we've worked for. As Felix's voice rises and falls, it weaves a tapestry of longing, joy, and pain, each note a brushstroke painting our story on the canvas of this moment.

When Felix launches into the next song, the one that's become our anthem, I can't help but sway slightly, caught in the undertow of the melody. The club transforms into a sea of bobbing heads and tapping feet, and I find myself lost in the rhythm. I can see familiar faces in the crowd—friends who've walked this road with us, their eyes shimmering with unshed tears, laughter bursting forth like confetti at unexpected moments. It's a reminder that we're not just performers on this stage; we're part of something much larger.

In the pause between songs, Felix locks eyes with me, and a knowing smile breaks across his face. It's as if he's inviting me into the magic he's creating, and I can't resist. I step out from behind the curtain, joining him on the stage, my heart racing with the thrill of being part of this shared experience. The audience erupts into applause, and I can feel the heat of their encouragement wash over me.

"Come on, join us!" Felix calls, gesturing for Mia to come up. She jumps to her feet, her laughter infectious, and suddenly the three of us are on stage, basking in the glow of the spotlight. Together, we become an impromptu trio, our voices melding in harmony, blending our fears and dreams into something beautiful. The club is no longer just a venue; it's our sanctuary, our place of healing.

As we sing, I catch glimpses of the faces in the crowd. There's an elderly couple, hands clasped tightly, their eyes sparkling with the kind of love that speaks of decades spent together. A group of friends sway in sync, their laughter ringing out like a bell, a reminder of the joy in shared experiences. Each note we play is a lifeline thrown into the sea of their lives, a promise that healing can come in unexpected forms.

When we finish, the applause crashes over us like a wave, and I feel a flush of exhilaration. We've not only entertained but connected, shared our souls through the medium of sound. The music lingers in the air, wrapping around us, a protective cocoon against the world's harsh edges. It's exhilarating and terrifying all at once.

After the set, the energy remains vibrant, a bubble of laughter and conversation floating through the club. I watch as Mia grabs Felix's hand, pulling him toward the small bar at the back. She leans in close, her laughter bright and clear, and I can't help but smile. They've grown so close, a friendship forged in the fire of our shared struggles, and I'm grateful for the connection they've nurtured.

As I step off the stage, I feel a gentle nudge at my side. I turn to see a little girl, her wide eyes reflecting the sparkling lights above. She clutches a small stuffed bear, its fur worn and faded, but the way she hugs it tight speaks of comfort and love. "You were amazing!" she beams, her words spilling out like candy, sweet and sincere.

"Thank you!" I reply, crouching to her level, my heart swelling. "What's your name?"

"Emma!" she chirps, bouncing on the balls of her feet. "I want to be a singer just like you!"

Her enthusiasm is infectious, a reminder of the dreams we all hold onto, no matter how small or big. "You will be," I assure her, feeling a warmth spread through me. "Just keep singing, okay?"

As she nods vigorously, I can't help but wonder about the paths we take and the connections we forge along the way. The music has given us a voice, a way to express what often remains unspoken. It's in these moments of vulnerability that we discover our strength, that we learn to heal together.

The room buzzes with life, a vibrant tapestry of sounds, laughter, and the gentle clinking of glasses. As I weave my way through the crowd, I'm struck by how easily the barriers between us dissolve in this shared moment. The strains of Felix's guitar still linger in the air, a sweet echo of our collective heartbeat. People huddle in small clusters, their conversations flowing like wine from the bar—a mixture of hope and unfiltered joy.

Mia's infectious energy draws me toward her, and I can't resist the pull of her laughter. She stands at the bar, a radiant figure with her wild curls bouncing like springs, an embodiment of the spirit that this night represents. "Did you see how into it everyone was?" she exclaims, her eyes wide with excitement. "It was like they were all under a spell!"

I lean against the bar beside her, picking up a glass of sparkling water, grateful to have a moment to breathe. "More like a musical fever dream. I half-expected to see someone dancing on tables."

Mia laughs, a sound that slices through the noise. "Maybe we should have encouraged it. It's not every day you get to be part of something so... alive."

A few feet away, a couple of friends are engaged in a spirited debate over which of Felix's songs was the best of the night. Their voices blend with the hum of conversation, creating a harmonious backdrop to the stories being shared. Each anecdote becomes a thread, weaving us closer together as we bond over shared experiences and memories.

"Speaking of alive," Mia nudges me playfully, "is it just me, or is there something different about Felix tonight? He was practically glowing up there." Her voice drops conspiratorially. "Do you think it's because of you?"

I feign a gasp, hand over my heart in mock horror. "Me? Please! I was just trying not to trip over the microphone cord. But I do think he's found his groove. It's like he tapped into something deeper tonight."

As if summoned by our conversation, Felix approaches, his face flushed and his hair a delightful mess. "There you are!" He grins, a triumphant expression lighting up his features. "I thought you two might have run off to start your own fan club."

Mia bursts into laughter, sloshing a bit of her drink in the process. "Only if you promise to serenade us every week!"

Felix rolls his eyes, but the smile on his face betrays him. "As long as you keep promising not to steal the show with your dance moves."

"Only when you stop being so utterly charming!" she retorts, her voice filled with playful challenge. "It's not fair, you know. You get to strum that guitar and woo the crowd while I'm left here admiring your talent from afar."

"Ah, but you're the one who brings the real magic," he says, shooting her a wink that sends her into a flurry of giggles. "Without you two, it's just me and my guitar, and that's not nearly as fun."

A wave of warmth floods my chest as I watch them interact. This camaraderie, this vibrant connection—it's a balm to my soul. For too long, I felt like a ghost in my own life, hovering at the edges of conversations, afraid to step into the light. But here, amidst the laughter and the music, I'm reminded that these bonds we forge can be our greatest source of strength.

As the night unfolds, I find myself gravitating toward different groups, each conversation revealing more layers of our shared experience. I chat with an older gentleman who introduces himself as a retired teacher, his stories of inspiring students echoing the passion I feel for guiding others. "You never know which words will stick," he says, his gaze distant, as if lost in memory. "Sometimes, it's the little things that ignite a fire in someone."

That sentiment resonates deeply, igniting a spark within me. I've always believed that moments of connection, no matter how small, can create ripples in someone's life. The energy in the room, the healing power of music, and the warmth of friendships create an invisible thread binding us all together, a collective hope that shines brighter with each shared laugh and every heartfelt conversation.

As I drift from one group to another, I catch sight of Mia again. She's now sitting at a table, deep in conversation with a woman I recognize from our community. I can't help but smile at their animated discussion, a contrast to the earlier tension that loomed over us. The laughter that spills from their lips is infectious, and I can see the way they light up each other's faces.

"Who knew Mia was a natural at this networking thing?" I murmur to Felix, who's joined me by the bar once more.

"Seems like everyone loves her. She's like a walking ray of sunshine," he replies, leaning against the bar with an easy grace. "And you? You're not too shabby yourself. I've seen you holding court with just about everyone here."

I roll my eyes, though a smile tugs at my lips. "I'm just trying to keep up with you two. It's a challenge, you know."

Felix chuckles, a sound that feels like music in itself. "I think you've got more charisma in your pinky than most people have in their whole being. You light up a room without even trying."

"Flattery will get you everywhere," I tease, but his words settle in my heart like a cherished secret. It's a strange feeling, being seen in such a way, a reminder that perhaps I'm not just a backdrop to the lives of others.

Just then, the music shifts—a slow, soulful melody filling the air, beckoning people to the dance floor. I watch as couples begin to sway, bodies moving in time with the rhythm, a living embodiment of the healing that music brings. Without thinking, I take Felix's hand, pulling him toward the dance floor. "Come on, you can't just stand there!"

He hesitates, a glimmer of uncertainty flashing across his face, but I can't help but laugh. "I promise not to embarrass you too much. Just think of it as another performance!"

With a resigned grin, he allows me to lead him, and we step into the swirling mass of bodies, our laughter mingling with the music. As we sway to the beat, I let the rhythm guide me, embracing the joy of the moment. Here, in the midst of our friends, surrounded by the warmth of shared connection, I finally feel the weight of my worries lifting, replaced by a giddy sense of freedom and possibility.

The dance floor transforms into a world of its own, where worries dissolve into the air, leaving only the music and the moment. I glance around, soaking in the sight of people lost in their joy, their laughter echoing like a promise. Here, under the glow of the lights, we are all just souls searching for connection, for healing. It's a reminder that even in the chaos of life, beauty can be found in the simplest of moments, in the shared rhythm of hearts beating as one.

The music swells around us, a rich tapestry woven from laughter and the soft thrum of bodies in motion. Each pulse of the bass seems to synchronize with the beating of my heart, and I lose myself in the rhythm, the weight of the world falling away with every sway and step. Felix stands beside me, slightly awkward but undeniably charming, and as we dance, his eyes shine with a mix of surprise and delight.

"You know," he says, leaning in closer so I can hear him over the music, "I never pegged you for the dancing type. More of a 'watch me from the shadows' kind of person."

"Maybe I just needed the right encouragement," I reply, twirling away before spinning back to face him. "Besides, it's easier to dance when the whole world seems to melt away."

He grins, that boyish charm flooding his expression. "Or when the world is filled with people who can't dance either. It's an equal opportunity disaster."

The laughter bubbles out of me, and I take a moment to glance around. The dance floor is a sea of swaying limbs, some perfectly in sync, others blissfully unaware of the rhythm around them. Mia is lost in a circle of friends, her laughter ringing out like bells, and for a brief moment, the weight of everything feels lighter. The connection we share, the raw vulnerability that has surfaced tonight, shimmers in the air like a delicate thread binding us all together.

As the song fades, the DJ shifts gears, and the tempo picks up. The crowd erupts into cheers, bodies swaying faster, laughter mingling with the beat. My heart races as I try to keep pace, the energy intoxicating. I'm caught up in the moment, forgetting the worries that usually cling to my mind like stubborn shadows.

But then, amid the laughter and the music, my eyes catch sight of a figure lingering by the entrance. A tall man with dark, tousled hair, standing apart from the crowd, his expression inscrutable. My heart skips a beat, the joyous atmosphere suddenly feeling a touch electric in a way that makes me uneasy. He seems out of place, an anomaly against the vibrant backdrop of friendship and connection.

"Felix," I murmur, my voice barely audible over the thumping bass, "do you see that guy by the door?"

He glances over his shoulder, brows knitting together as he scans the crowd. "Yeah, what about him? He looks like he just stepped out of a noir film."

I can't shake the feeling that he's watching us, the way his gaze flicks from person to person, but settles on us for just a heartbeat longer. "I don't know. I just...something feels off."

Felix follows my gaze again, a hint of concern flashing across his features. "You want to go see what's up? Might just be someone who took a wrong turn on the way to the bar."

"Or someone looking for trouble," I say, feeling a knot tighten in my stomach. "I don't want to ruin the mood, but..."

"Hey, let's check it out together." He takes a step back, his hand sliding into mine as we weave through the throng of dancers. The vibrant colors and laughter dim in my periphery as we approach the man, each step feeling heavier, laden with an unspoken tension.

When we reach him, he turns slightly, revealing a pair of piercing blue eyes that seem to hold secrets I'm not sure I want to uncover. "Can I help you?" Felix asks, voice steady but laced with an underlying edge.

The man smirks, a mix of amusement and something darker playing across his features. "Just admiring the talent," he says smoothly, but there's an intensity in his gaze that sends shivers down my spine.

"Right, well, we're just here for the music," I interject, trying to keep my tone light despite the growing sense of unease. "You know, support a good cause and all that."

His smile widens, but it doesn't reach his eyes. "Oh, I know all about the cause. It's a shame how things can get so complicated." He takes a step closer, his presence suddenly looming. "I'd hate to see anything ruin a beautiful night, wouldn't you?"

I can feel Felix tense beside me, his grip on my hand tightening. "You should probably move along," Felix says, his tone turning steely. "We're not interested in whatever you're selling."

The man's expression shifts, something dark flickering beneath his cool demeanor. "It's not what I'm selling you should worry about, my friend." He glances toward the crowd, his gaze sweeping over the joyous faces, then back to us. "It's what might come knocking on your door when you least expect it."

Just then, a loud crash reverberates from the back of the club, drawing the attention of everyone nearby. The music screeches to a halt, and silence falls like a heavy curtain, anxiety rippling through the room.

"What was that?" I whisper, my heart racing as the tension thickens in the air.

The man chuckles softly, almost condescendingly. "Just a little reminder that some things are best left alone." With a last, lingering look, he steps back into the shadows, leaving me with an unsettling chill that crawls along my skin.

Felix pulls me closer, scanning the crowd as murmurs erupt around us. "We need to check that out," he says, determination etched on his face.

"Should we?" I ask, my voice trembling slightly. "What if it's nothing?"

"It's better to be sure," he insists, and I can see the resolve in his eyes, a fire igniting that I wish I could feel too. "Let's go."

As we make our way toward the source of the sound, the crowd begins to part, revealing a cluster of people huddled around a table that's now overturned, drinks spilling across the floor like a chaotic mosaic. My stomach twists with unease, and I glance back, half-expecting to see that stranger lurking nearby.

"Get back!" someone shouts from the crowd, and I push forward, straining to see what's happening.

And then, in the midst of the chaos, I catch sight of something glinting on the floor. My breath catches in my throat. A silver object, unmistakable and sharp. A knife.

"Felix..." I manage, but my voice falters as panic rises within me. Just as he turns to look, the lights flicker, plunging the room into darkness for a brief moment before the emergency lights cast an eerie glow over the scene.

In that fleeting darkness, the tension thickens, and I feel a surge of adrenaline, realizing that whatever is happening tonight is far from over. A chill dances down my spine as I look around, the laughter now replaced by whispers of fear.

"Stay close," Felix says, his voice low and steady as he pulls me protectively to his side. I nod, but my heart races with uncertainty, the night shifting from a celebration of hope to a chaotic storm of dread.

And as I stand there, gripped by fear and confusion, the last flicker of light reveals that familiar figure reemerging from the shadows, and I know, without a doubt, that the night has only just begun to unravel.

Chapter 27: Broken Strings

The echoes of applause still lingered in the air, wrapping around us like a warm blanket as we stepped off the stage. The bright lights of the performance venue faded behind us, leaving only the soft glow of fairy lights strung along the walls, casting a soft luminescence over the gathering. I clutched my drink, a fizzy concoction of lemonade and something I hoped was more than just the mundane. Laughter bubbled up from our group, a lightness that felt almost absurd now. We celebrated, reveling in our small triumph, a hard-fought victory of the night that danced in the rhythm of the music still thrumming in my veins. Felix, with his hair tousled and an exuberant grin plastered across his face, looked like he could conquer the world. He was the embodiment of joy, and I couldn't help but be swept up in his enthusiasm.

"Did you see the way the spotlight hit me during my solo? I swear it was like the universe had conspired to shine just for me!" he laughed, his eyes bright with a mischief that was unmistakably contagious. I rolled my eyes, but a smile crept onto my face. "Felix, you always think the universe is conspiring in your favor. I'm still waiting for it to throw a little more chaos your way, just to keep you humble."

"You're just jealous of my gravitational pull," he shot back, mockingly puffing out his chest as he twirled around dramatically. We laughed together, the kind of laughter that sent ripples of warmth through the crowd, a moment suspended in time.

But then, like a thundercloud rolling in uninvited, the atmosphere shifted. A sudden stillness washed over the group, and my smile faltered. My heart began to race as I caught sight of Julie, one of our friends, her expression pale and strained as she approached us, her lips pressed into a thin line.

"Hey, um, can I talk to you for a second?" she said, her voice low and trembling.

I felt the smile drain from my face, the air growing thick and suffocating around me. "What's wrong?" I asked, bracing myself, every instinct screaming that this was more than just an ordinary conversation.

"It's Mia," Julie said, her eyes glistening with unshed tears. "She's in intensive care. It's… it's serious."

The words landed like heavy stones in the pit of my stomach. The lightness of the evening crumbled to dust, and an icy dread settled deep within me. I looked at Felix, his face going ashen, the vibrancy we had just shared evaporating into nothingness.

"Mia?" His voice trembled, cracking under the weight of disbelief. "What do you mean, serious?"

"She collapsed right after your performance," Julie whispered, looking as if the words themselves might shatter her. "They took her to the hospital. She's… she's not doing well."

I could see the storm brewing in Felix's eyes, a tempest of fear and confusion battling for dominance. "We need to go," he said, his voice barely above a whisper, but the urgency was palpable.

We rushed through the streets, the warm summer night transformed into a chilling race against time. The laughter and music faded behind us, replaced by the steady rhythm of my heart pounding in my ears. Each stoplight felt like an eternity, each red glow a cruel reminder of how little control we had over the world unfolding around us.

When we arrived at the hospital, the stark white walls and sterile air felt foreign, as if we had crossed into a different realm altogether. The fluorescent lights buzzed overhead, creating an unsettling atmosphere. I gripped Felix's hand tightly as we navigated the labyrinthine corridors, my heart thudding loudly in my chest. The scent of antiseptic hung heavy in the air, a grim reminder of the gravity of our situation.

"Where is she?" Felix demanded, his voice strained as he approached the front desk, a mix of desperation and determination etched on his features.

The nurse behind the counter looked up, her expression shifting from professional to sympathetic in a heartbeat. "Room 302. Please take a seat; the doctors are with her now."

The words sent a wave of nausea rolling through me. I wanted to argue, to demand answers, but all I could do was follow Felix's lead, the strength in his voice trembling like the ground beneath our feet.

We sat in the waiting area, silence enveloping us like a heavy fog. I could feel the cracks forming in Felix's resolve, the way he clenched his hands into fists, his knuckles white against the dark fabric of his jeans. "She can't be... not Mia," he muttered, the disbelief in his voice cutting deeper than I could bear.

I leaned in closer, placing my hand on his arm, trying to anchor him amidst the chaos swirling around us. "She's a fighter, Felix. You know that better than anyone. She's been through so much already; she'll get through this."

He turned to me, eyes brimming with unshed tears, vulnerability laid bare. "What if she doesn't?"

My heart ached for him, the weight of his fear pressing down on both of us. "We'll face it together," I said softly, willing him to believe it, to draw strength from my words. "Mia needs us to be strong for her. Remember all those late-night talks we had? She always said we were her family, her safe place. Now it's our turn to be that for her."

The tension in his shoulders eased just slightly, a flicker of hope igniting in his gaze, though the shadows of doubt still lingered. Just then, the heavy double doors swung open, and a doctor stepped out, a white coat swirling around him like a cape, every bit the harbinger of news we dreaded.

"Are you here for Mia?" he asked, scanning our faces, and my stomach dropped. This was it, the moment we had both been bracing ourselves for.

"Yes," Felix said, standing up as if propelled by some invisible force. "How is she?"

The doctor's expression was grave, but his eyes held a glimmer of something I couldn't quite place. "She's stable for now, but she needs immediate care. There are some complications we're monitoring. You can see her, but please remember, it's critical."

I felt Felix's breath catch, the weight of the world pressing down on him as he nodded, determination mixing with fear in a cocktail too potent for either of us to swallow. We followed the doctor, each step resonating with the reality of our situation, the fluorescent lights casting harsh shadows on the sterile white walls.

As we approached her room, I could feel the tension coiling tighter within me. I glanced at Felix, his features resolute, masking the fear that lay just beneath the surface. I had to be strong for him now, to remind him of the strength they had built together. We were in this together, and I would not let him crumble.

Stepping into the room felt surreal, the bright lights and the soft beeping of machines creating a disorienting symphony. Mia lay there, fragile yet fierce, a warrior in a battle no one wanted her to fight. The sight of her surrounded by tubes and wires was enough to choke back my breath, but I steadied myself, drawing strength from the love and resilience that connected us.

"Mia," Felix whispered, his voice trembling as he moved to her side, the cracks in his facade finally showing. I could see the battle within him, the fear threatening to pull him under. But as he reached for her hand, I could almost feel the warmth of their bond radiating through the cold hospital air. I knew then that even in this moment of uncertainty, the power of their connection would light the way forward, no matter how dark the path ahead might seem.

Mia lay in her hospital bed, a frail figure amid the whir of machines that hummed a melancholic tune. The sterile room felt too bright, the fluorescent lights bathing everything in an unflattering glow. Her skin was pale, nearly translucent, contrasting sharply with the bright blue of the hospital gown that hung loosely on her. I could see the slight rise and fall of her chest, each breath a fragile testament to her fighting spirit. Felix gripped her hand, his fingers entwined with hers as if trying to infuse his strength into her lifeless form. His face, once brimming with joy, was now a canvas of anguish.

"Stay with us, Mia," he murmured, voice cracking as if he were afraid that saying it too loudly would shatter the delicate moment. "You have so much left to do. Remember that time we talked about going to Italy? You promised to show me the best gelato shops."

His words hung in the air, a lifeline thrown into turbulent waters. I watched him, a mix of admiration and heartbreak swelling in my chest. His vulnerability was raw, unfiltered, a stark contrast to the confident persona he wore like armor in front of our friends. The sight of him laid bare like this reminded me of how deeply he loved her, how fiercely he would fight against the shadows that threatened to steal her away.

"I bet you're just trying to distract me with talk of gelato," I chimed in, attempting to inject a note of levity into the heavy atmosphere. "You know she'd never let you forget that hazelnut was the best, even if you did order the raspberry."

Felix turned to me, his eyes shining with unshed tears, a flicker of a smile breaking through his worry. "You know me too well. But she'll come back just to remind me I'm wrong, won't you, Mia?"

It felt like a fragile agreement, a silent pact among us, the three of us intertwined in a moment that was both beautiful and achingly sad. I leaned closer, wishing to breathe warmth and hope into her, even if it was just a fleeting wish.

The door swung open, and a nurse stepped in, her presence a grounding force. "How is she?" Felix asked, his voice trembling as he tore his gaze from Mia to the nurse, a desperate plea woven into the question.

"She's stable for now," the nurse replied, her tone professional yet kind. "The doctors are doing everything they can. It's important for you to stay close. Sometimes, just knowing someone is there can help."

The truth of her words hit me harder than I expected. Here we were, three of us tangled in this web of life and death, desperately hoping for a miracle. I watched as Felix nodded, absorbing the nurse's reassurance like a sponge, the tension in his shoulders easing ever so slightly.

"Do you think she can hear us?" he asked, voice barely above a whisper.

"Absolutely," the nurse replied, adjusting a couple of settings on the machines beside Mia's bed. "Patients often can hear their loved ones, even if they can't respond. Keep talking to her."

Felix resumed his vigil, and I settled beside him, wishing I had the right words to offer. I could see the worry etched into every line of his face, the exhaustion beginning to take hold. "You need to take care of yourself, too, Felix. You can't help her if you're running on fumes."

"I can't," he said, his gaze fixed firmly on Mia. "I can't leave her side. What if she needs me?"

My heart broke a little more at his words. The depth of his love was a double-edged sword, beautiful yet painful. "I get it, but you have to be strong for her. And being strong sometimes means allowing yourself a moment to breathe."

He sighed, the weight of the world resting heavily on his shoulders. "You always know what to say."

"I've had practice," I quipped lightly, hoping to break the tension. "Remember that time we tried to convince Mia to take up skydiving? She practically threw her shoes at us!"

Felix chuckled, a sound that felt foreign but welcomed. "She said she'd only jump out of a plane if it was over the ocean, and even then, only if there were no sharks."

"Smart girl," I said, winking. "She knows how to play it safe."

The lightness of our conversation hovered in the air, fragile yet hopeful. For a moment, we were transported back to that carefree day, where life was simpler, and the most daunting challenge was convincing Mia to trust us enough to leap into the unknown.

Hours slipped by, punctuated by the rhythmic beeping of machines and the whispers of nurses as they passed through the room. Each time the door opened, we held our breath, waiting for news. The waiting felt like an eternity, stretching the fabric of time until it became unbearable.

I found myself drifting into thought, a mixture of memories and fears swirling in my mind. I could picture Mia in the throes of laughter, her voice a melody that filled the room with warmth. I thought of late-night talks under a canopy of stars, dreams woven together, each thread representing a moment that made us who we were.

A sudden rattle of the doorknob pulled me back, and a doctor stepped inside, clipboard in hand. "I'm Dr. Ramirez," he introduced himself, glancing between us, his expression somber. "I need to speak with you both."

Felix stood straighter, instinctively bracing himself for the impact of the words about to be spoken. "Is it about Mia?"

"Yes," Dr. Ramirez replied, his gaze steady. "We've been monitoring her condition closely, and we need to discuss a possible procedure."

The words hung in the air, heavy with implication. I could see the dread flicker across Felix's face as he processed the information. "What kind of procedure?" he asked, his voice strained.

"There are complications we didn't anticipate," the doctor explained, his tone calm yet urgent. "We believe there may be a need for surgery to address some internal bleeding. I want to be honest with you; it's risky, but it may be her best chance."

My heart sank. The very notion of surgery felt like a chasm opening up beneath us, ready to swallow us whole. I could see Felix's expression hardening as he wrestled with the weight of the decision laid before him.

"What if we wait?" Felix asked, desperation creeping into his voice. "Isn't there another way?"

"I understand your concerns," Dr. Ramirez said, his demeanor softening. "But the longer we wait, the more perilous her situation becomes. I won't sugarcoat it; it's a difficult choice, and I wish it didn't have to come to this."

Silence settled like dust in the air, heavy and unyielding. I could feel Felix's tension radiating through the room, the struggle within him palpable. He was caught between the desire to protect Mia and the fear of making the wrong decision.

"Can I have a moment?" Felix finally asked, his voice barely above a whisper.

"Of course," Dr. Ramirez replied, stepping back into the hallway, the door clicking shut behind him.

Felix sank back into the chair, burying his face in his hands. I wanted to reach out, to reassure him, but I felt the weight of his anguish pressing down on me, rendering me almost motionless. The quiet that enveloped us was stifling, a reminder of the fragility of life and the uncertainty that lay ahead.

"Mia is a fighter," I said, my voice breaking the silence like a fragile thread. "She's always been strong. We can't let fear decide this for us."

"I don't know if I can bear the thought of losing her," he admitted, looking up at me, his eyes filled with a mixture of fear and hope.

"We won't lose her," I said, the conviction in my voice surprising even me. "But we have to trust the doctors. They want to help her, just like we do."

His gaze held mine, searching for reassurance, for a glimpse of the strength I hoped to impart. In that moment, I realized that sometimes love meant standing in the shadows, ready to fight for someone else's light. And for Mia, we had to be brave, even when the path ahead was fraught with uncertainty.

The silence in the room felt like an electric charge, a taut line of anticipation that neither Felix nor I dared to break. His fingers fidgeted against the armrest, tracing patterns that only he understood, while I sat beside him, acutely aware of the gravity of our situation. The air was thick with unspoken fears, each breath heavier than the last.

"Do you think she's scared?" he finally murmured, his voice so low I barely caught it.

"I think she's fighting," I replied, though my heart trembled at the thought. "Mia's never been one to back down from a challenge, you know that."

He nodded, the tightness in his jaw easing ever so slightly, but his eyes reflected a whirlwind of emotions—fear, hope, and the kind of love that could tear a person apart.

"I keep replaying our last conversation," he said, his voice a fragile thread in the suffocating silence. "We were joking about that terrible movie we watched together. You remember how she laughed so hard she nearly cried?"

"Of course," I said, forcing a smile. "She said it was so bad it deserved an award for 'Most Likely to Make You Question Your Taste in Film.'"

A small chuckle escaped Felix, and I felt a flicker of warmth between us. "I guess that's the key to her strength, isn't it? She never lets anything get too serious."

Before I could respond, the door swung open, and the doctor returned, his demeanor calm yet serious. "Have you come to a decision?" he asked, glancing from Felix to me, assessing our readiness.

"Is there really no other option?" Felix pressed, determination lacing his words.

"The surgery is the best course of action," the doctor replied, his voice steady. "We can't afford to wait. Every moment counts."

Felix's expression hardened, a storm brewing behind his eyes. "What if something goes wrong?"

"Every procedure carries risk, but we are prepared to handle complications should they arise," the doctor assured us. "The longer we delay, the greater the risk to her health."

I could see the internal battle raging within Felix, his mind racing between hope and despair. I squeezed his hand, offering silent encouragement. "You know what she'd want," I said softly. "She'd want to fight."

He hesitated, his gaze flickering back to Mia, who lay motionless, a fragile figure lost in a sea of white sheets and sterile equipment. The battle raged on, visible in the tension of his shoulders and the worry etched on his face.

"Okay," he finally said, his voice trembling with resolution. "Let's do it. Let's give her a chance."

The doctor nodded, relief evident on his face. "I'll arrange for the surgical team. You can stay with her until they come to take her in."

As the doctor stepped away, I felt the air shift, charged with the weight of our decision. Felix turned to Mia, his eyes softening as he leaned closer. "You're going to be okay," he whispered, brushing his fingers across her forehead. "We're going to get you the help you need."

I watched him, admiration swelling within me. He was being strong for both of them, embodying the courage I wished I could summon for myself. I wished I could shield him from the pain that shadowed his heart, but I also knew that together we could navigate this dark moment.

Time slipped away, each tick of the clock amplifying the tension in the room. Nurses came in and out, checking monitors, adjusting IV drips, their movements a careful choreography that somehow felt invasive yet necessary.

I turned my gaze to Mia, a rush of memories washing over me—the way her laughter filled the room, how she could brighten even the gloomiest of days with a single smile. I remembered our countless late-night talks, our dreams woven together like threads in a tapestry, each one vibrant with possibility.

Felix's voice pulled me back. "Do you think she knows how much we love her?"

I met his gaze, the sincerity in his eyes compelling. "I believe she does. She's always known. It's part of what makes her so special."

Just then, the door swung open again, and a nurse entered, her expression one of calm professionalism. "It's time to take her to surgery," she announced gently, her voice soothing like a balm.

Felix straightened, the weight of the moment pressing heavily on him. "Can I... can I walk with her?"

"Of course," the nurse replied, smiling reassuringly. "Just keep her close to you as we move her. She'll appreciate your presence."

As they prepared to move Mia, I felt an ache in my chest, a longing to shield them from this moment, to curl around them like a protective barrier. But as they wheeled her out, I stepped back, letting Felix take the lead.

"Stay with her, Felix," I called softly, my voice steady despite the turmoil within. "I'll be right here, waiting for you."

He nodded, his eyes locked on Mia, determination etched in every line of his face. "I'll be with her every step of the way," he promised, as if that pledge would somehow tether them together through the uncertainty ahead.

As they turned the corner, I felt a deep breath escape me, a mixture of fear and hope swirling within my chest. The waiting room felt emptier now, the silence almost deafening. I sank into a chair, my heart racing, anxiety clawing at my insides.

Minutes felt like hours, each tick of the clock a reminder of the fragility of life, a countdown to the unknown. I pulled out my phone, scrolling aimlessly, desperate for any distraction from the gnawing worry that threatened to consume me.

And then, the hospital's waiting room door swung open, and a familiar face emerged—Mia's mom, her expression weary but determined. She spotted me and rushed over, worry etching deeper lines on her brow.

"Have you seen her?" she asked, breathless.

"She's in surgery now," I replied, trying to convey the reassurance I didn't fully feel. "Felix is with her."

Her shoulders sagged slightly, but the worry remained etched in her features. "I just got here. I couldn't reach her all night, and when I finally did..." Her voice trailed off, the emotions surfacing as she took a deep breath. "I knew something was wrong."

I reached for her hand, squeezing it gently. "She's a fighter, and we're all here for her. She's going to come through this."

We shared a moment of silence, a bond formed in our shared concern. But before we could say more, the emergency room doors swung open once again, and a doctor stepped through, his expression grave.

My heart dropped, dread pooling in my stomach. "What's wrong?" I asked, my voice barely above a whisper.

The doctor looked directly at me, his gaze intense, and in that moment, I felt the world tilt beneath my feet. "There have been complications during the surgery, and we need to discuss the next steps."

Every muscle in my body tensed, the words spiraling into a vortex of fear. I glanced at Mia's mother, who stood frozen beside me, disbelief etched on her face.

"Complications?" I repeated, the word a bitter taste on my tongue.

"Can we speak privately?" the doctor asked, his tone firm yet compassionate.

I nodded, panic rising as I followed him down the corridor, leaving behind the waiting room and the comforting familiarity of shared hope. Each step felt heavy, like walking through molasses, the uncertainty thickening the air around me.

What awaited us in that private room could shatter everything we had fought for, and I could only hope that whatever news the doctor bore wouldn't take away our last threads of hope.

But as we turned the corner, the doctor's words hung in the air, a dark cloud threatening to swallow us whole. A feeling of dread settled deep within me, a gnawing fear that this was just the beginning of a storm we were unprepared to weather.

Chapter 28: The Final Note

The room was drenched in a twilight hue, the kind that makes shadows dance across the walls, whispering secrets to one another in hushed tones. I perched on the edge of the chair, my fingers entwined with Felix's, feeling the warmth of his hand as if it could somehow channel the storm of emotions swirling around us. Mia lay in the hospital bed, a fragile figure wrapped in white sheets, her breaths shallow and uneven, each one a reminder of the relentless march of time. I had seen her spirit flicker like a candle flame, battling against the inevitable darkness, but now the light seemed to dim, and my heart ached with an urgency that made me want to scream and cry and clutch at the universe until it unraveled.

Felix's eyes were pools of anguish, reflecting a grief so profound that it threatened to drown us both. Yet, within that sorrow, there was a flicker of determination. "She would want me to play," he said, his voice cracking like a brittle twig underfoot. The weight of his words hung in the air, heavy and poignant, and I felt the corners of my mouth tug upward despite the grief wrapping around us like a shroud.

"She would," I whispered back, nodding as memories of Mia flooded my mind—her laughter bubbling like champagne, her smile radiating warmth on even the coldest days. I could almost hear her teasing us, urging us to embrace the fleeting beauty of life, even in moments like this, when it felt like the world was splintering apart. "She always said music was the heartbeat of the soul. It's the best way to say goodbye."

Felix inhaled deeply, the air trembling with unspoken fear and longing. He rose from his seat, a palpable shift in his demeanor, the weight of despair momentarily replaced by a glimmer of purpose. As he approached the corner of the room where his guitar rested, a simple wooden instrument that had witnessed the best and worst of our lives, the atmosphere shifted. It was as if the very air around us held its breath, waiting for the magic that would unfold.

When he plucked the first chord, the sound was tentative, like the first drops of rain against parched earth. I closed my eyes, allowing the notes to wash over me, each one a thread woven into the fabric of our shared history. It felt like a portal, transporting us back to simpler days—the laughter at Mia's favorite café, her enthusiastic debates about art and life, the way she would hum along to Felix's songs, her voice harmonizing with his in a way that felt sacred. The music was a lifeline, pulling us closer to her even as she slipped away from us.

Felix's fingers danced across the strings, each stroke a delicate caress that coaxed the room to listen, to feel. As he played, I opened my eyes and watched the light shift across Mia's face. There was a serene beauty there, a quiet acceptance that made my heart swell with an inexplicable hope. Maybe she could hear him, maybe the music was wrapping around her like a warm embrace, promising her that she was not alone in this final journey.

"Remember that time we all went to the beach?" Felix's voice broke through the melody, and I couldn't help but chuckle through my tears. "Mia dared us to swim out to that rickety old raft, and we were so stupidly brave."

"Stupidly brave," I echoed, shaking my head as the memory flickered to life. "I thought we were going to drown, but she just laughed and splashed water in our faces like we were kids again." The laughter felt like a fragile thread, tenuous yet unbreakable, binding us together.

Felix nodded, a bittersweet smile ghosting across his lips. "She always had a way of making the mundane feel extraordinary. I remember her saying that life was just a series of moments, and we should fill them with joy, even when the world feels heavy."

The guitar filled the silence once more, rich and resonant, as he transitioned into a melody that felt like an aching farewell. It was a haunting composition, one he had written for her long ago, and as the notes cascaded around us, I felt every unspoken word, every ounce of love pouring out into the space. My heart swelled with a mixture of pride and sorrow, knowing that this was Felix's final gift to her.

As he played, the tears fell freely now, an unrelenting tide that mirrored the emotions crashing over us. I felt a swell of gratitude for this moment, for the chance to share in something so raw and beautiful. It was a strange juxtaposition—the pain of loss intertwined with the brilliance of love. I glanced at Mia, her chest rising and falling in a gentle rhythm, and I could almost imagine her smiling at us, urging us to remember her not in grief but in laughter, in music, in the countless memories that shaped our lives.

The melody swirled in the air like a gentle breeze, brushing against my skin and filling the room with an ethereal glow. It was as if time had slowed, each note stretching out into infinity, allowing us to linger in this sacred space just a moment longer. I wanted to capture this feeling, to hold it close and never let it go, but I knew that was impossible. Just like all good things, this moment would eventually fade, yet it would leave an imprint on our hearts, a reminder that love, even in its most fragile form, is the most powerful force of all.

Felix's fingers trembled as he transitioned into the final notes, the air thick with emotion, and I felt a sense of finality wash over us. It was as if the universe itself paused to listen, to honor this intimate farewell. In that shared silence, I reached for Felix's hand, squeezing it tightly, grateful for the bond we shared, even as we stood on the precipice of unimaginable loss.

The last note lingered in the air like a fading echo, a spectral remnant of everything we had shared, everything we would never share again. Felix lowered the guitar, his fingers trembling with the weight of the moment, and I felt the room shift, as if the walls themselves were sighing in relief or perhaps in grief. I could see the light reflecting in his eyes—an intensity that belied the devastation we both felt. He looked at me, searching for something, and I offered a faint smile, though my heart felt like a ship caught in a storm, tossing between hope and despair.

"She always loved when you played that song," I murmured, the words slipping out like a fragile promise. "You know that, right?"

Felix nodded, his gaze drifting back to Mia, whose fragile form seemed to rest deeper into the mattress as if she was surrendering to the melody we'd just created. It was as if she were saying, "Thank you for remembering me."

"What if she doesn't want to go?" he asked, his voice barely above a whisper, laced with an aching uncertainty. "What if she's fighting, but there's nothing left to fight for?"

The rawness of his question struck me like a cold wind, and for a moment, I was paralyzed by the weight of it. It was a terrifying thought, one that no one ever wants to confront: the possibility that love isn't always enough to hold someone tethered to this world. But I remembered Mia's laughter, her insistence that life was about choices, that each day was a canvas waiting to be painted. "She would want to be free," I finally replied, my voice steadying. "To paint her own masterpiece wherever she goes."

Felix swallowed hard, his throat working against a tide of emotion. "I just wish... I wish I could have given her everything. All my music, all my love." His words hung heavy in the air, and I could see the flicker of desperation behind his eyes, a kind of longing that felt both infinite and entirely futile.

Before I could respond, the door creaked open, and a nurse peeked in, her expression warm yet professional, like sunlight filtering through leaves. "I just wanted to check on you both," she said, her voice gentle as a lullaby. "Is there anything I can get you?"

"Just... more time," I blurted out, the plea escaping my lips before I could think better of it.

The nurse's smile faltered for just a moment, but she quickly regained her composure. "I understand. I'll be right outside if you need anything." With a nod, she left, closing the door softly behind her, leaving us enveloped once more in our cocoon of sorrow and memories.

Felix ran a hand through his hair, the movement revealing the tremor beneath his steady facade. "Time," he scoffed, a wry smile curling his lips. "If only we could bottle it up and use it as a potion to keep her here. Maybe then we wouldn't have to face the inevitable."

"Or perhaps we'd turn into hoarders of moments," I teased lightly, trying to coax a smile from him. "Can you imagine? 'Welcome to my home! Please mind the piles of memories in every corner. And yes, that's a cat named Time.'"

He laughed then, a sound that felt like sunlight breaking through storm clouds, if only for a fleeting second. "I'd name the cat Tick. You know, to emphasize the urgency of it all."

The conversation began to lighten the atmosphere, even as it surrounded us like a shadow. But the laughter felt like a temporary reprieve, a distraction from the truth that loomed just outside the door. "What's your plan, Felix?" I asked, my voice turning serious again. "What will you do after this?"

His expression shifted, becoming distant as if he were staring into the abyss of a future he hadn't dared to contemplate. "I don't know," he admitted, his vulnerability spilling out like ink on a page. "Music was always about us—our trio. Without Mia... I'm not sure how to keep writing."

I wanted to reach for him, to wrap him in a cocoon of comfort, but I also wanted to challenge him, to remind him that music is not merely a reflection of what we've lost, but also a celebration of what we've shared. "You know, she always believed in your talent, Felix. She saw something in you that even you couldn't see."

"I wish I could believe that," he replied, his voice barely above a whisper.

"You have to," I insisted, my heart racing with a mixture of frustration and determination. "Mia wouldn't want you to dim your light because hers is flickering. You owe it to her—to yourself—to keep shining."

Felix turned to me, his eyes glimmering with a mix of admiration and disbelief. "You really believe that?"

"Of course I do," I replied, matching his intensity. "You're not just a musician; you're a storyteller. And stories aren't bound by endings. They evolve. They change, just like life. Just like love."

His breath caught, and for a moment, I saw a glimmer of hope sparkle in the depths of his sorrow. "Maybe I could write a song about her... about us."

"Absolutely," I encouraged, feeling a swell of excitement. "Make it a celebration. Infuse it with all the chaos, the laughter, the bittersweet moments. Let it be an anthem of who she is, who she was to you."

Felix took a deep breath, his chest rising as if he were gathering the strength to dive into unknown waters. "I think... I think I'll call it 'Fleeting Moments.'"

"That's perfect," I said, a smile spreading across my face. "It captures everything. The beauty and the heartbreak."

As he picked up the guitar again, I felt a warmth spread through me, the spark of inspiration igniting a flame that had been flickering in the shadows. The first few notes floated through the air, each one a promise that the essence of Mia would not be lost, that her laughter and love would echo through his music long after the final curtain fell. In that moment, the darkness didn't feel so suffocating. It felt like a stage, and we were simply waiting for the lights to come back on.

As Felix strummed the opening chords of "Fleeting Moments," the air thickened with a bittersweet nostalgia that enveloped us like a favorite sweater—worn and comforting, yet frayed at the edges. Each note cascaded like a waterfall, pouring memories into the room, painting vibrant pictures of laughter, shared glances, and unspoken dreams. I closed my eyes, surrendering to the music, allowing it to wash over me and pull me into the vivid tapestry of our past.

"Remember that ridiculous karaoke night?" I interrupted his soulful strumming, the memory bubbling to the surface. "Mia belted out that awful pop song, and you were so mortified you nearly hid under the table?"

Felix chuckled, the sound rich and warm against the backdrop of his song. "I can't believe you'd bring that up. I thought she was going to burst a lung. And here I was, praying she wouldn't hit any high notes."

"She hit all of them," I countered, grinning. "And she made up for your lack of enthusiasm by dancing like a lunatic. If the floor could talk, it would have asked for a raise."

His laughter turned to something deeper, more resonant, as he poured that joy into the music. "God, she had such a way of turning everything into a spectacle," he said, a hint of reverence in his tone. "I think she thought we were all her captive audience."

"Maybe we were," I replied softly, my heart aching with the weight of loss and love intertwined. "And we loved every second of it."

With each strum, Felix seemed to channel more than just memory; he was breathing life back into our shared experiences, honoring Mia not just in sadness, but in joy. The guitar hummed, transforming the sterile hospital room into a sanctuary filled with laughter and light, if only for a fleeting moment.

As the final notes reverberated in the air, I felt an electric pulse of anticipation. "You know," I began, hesitating for just a beat. "This could be the beginning of something new for you. A way to channel all of this." I gestured around us, encompassing the room, the memories, the emotions that hung thick like mist.

Felix nodded, his eyes alight with a glimmer of understanding. "You think so?"

"Absolutely. Mia would want you to keep going, to tell your stories. Your music has always been a part of you. Don't let it fade away with her."

He took a deep breath, his determination shining through the layers of sorrow. "I think I need to do this. Not just for me, but for her. I want her to be proud."

The words hung in the air like a promise, resonating between us. But just as the warmth enveloped us, a cold wave of reality crashed in. Mia stirred slightly, a soft sigh escaping her lips, and we both turned to her. I felt a jolt of panic wash over me as I watched her face twist in discomfort, her brow furrowing, as if she were caught in a dream she couldn't escape.

"Is she—" Felix started, his voice thick with concern.

Before I could respond, the monitor beside her let out a series of beeps, urgent and alarming. The sound sliced through the air, sending a rush of adrenaline coursing through my veins. I shot to my feet, the brief sanctuary we had created now shattered by the starkness of the moment.

"Stay here," I urged, instinctively knowing I needed to alert the nurse, to ensure we weren't losing her right then and there. But as I turned to leave, a flicker of movement caught my eye. Mia's hand, once limp at her side, now twitched slightly, as if reaching for something just beyond her grasp.

"Felix!" I called, my heart racing. "She's—"

But before I could finish, a wave of darkness washed over her, a brief flicker of confusion in her eyes as if she were wading through the murky waters of consciousness. "Mia!" Felix cried, rushing to her side, his fingers wrapping around hers, grounding both her and himself in that moment.

"Mia, can you hear me?" His voice was a mixture of fear and desperation, cutting through the sterile silence. "Please, just squeeze my hand if you can hear me."

In the quiet chaos, I could feel the room holding its breath, every second stretching into eternity. Then, as if she had found the strength buried deep within, Mia's fingers tightened around Felix's, just a slight squeeze, but enough to send a jolt of hope through us both.

"I'm here, I'm right here," he said, his voice trembling as he brushed a strand of hair from her forehead. The monitor continued to beep, the urgency of its rhythm matched only by the frantic beating of my heart.

And then, as if propelled by some unseen force, Mia's eyes fluttered open, revealing a spark of recognition, a flicker of the vibrant spirit we both adored. But there was something different about her gaze—a depth that hinted at experiences beyond our understanding, a flicker of something unsaid that cast a shadow over our relief.

"Mia?" I ventured cautiously, stepping closer. "Can you hear us?"

She blinked slowly, her gaze shifting between us as though trying to piece together a puzzle that had been scrambled. "I... I saw colors," she murmured, her voice barely above a whisper. "So many colors..."

Felix's grip tightened on her hand, his expression a mix of confusion and awe. "Colors? What do you mean?"

"They were beautiful, swirling... like music," she continued, her breath coming in shallow bursts. "But they faded, and now... it's dark."

The room grew colder, the weight of her words settling heavily upon us. I exchanged a glance with Felix, my heart racing with a mix of hope and dread. "Mia, you're safe. You're here with us," I said, my voice firm yet laced with uncertainty.

But Mia's eyes seemed to drift beyond us, searching for something that wasn't there. "I don't want to go," she whispered, and the fragility in her voice shattered the tenuous thread of hope that had begun to weave itself between us. "I want to stay, but I can't... it's pulling me."

"Pulling you where?" Felix demanded, panic flooding his tone as he leaned closer, desperation etching lines across his brow.

"The colors... they want me to follow," she murmured, and I could see a flicker of fear ripple across her features, the kind that made my stomach knot and my heart ache.

"Don't follow them, Mia!" I urged, stepping closer, my voice tinged with urgency. "You're here with us. Stay with us!"

But as her gaze lost focus, the monitor began to beep faster, the urgency in its tone rising like a tide threatening to swallow us whole. Mia's face contorted with confusion and fear, her hand slipping from Felix's grasp. "I can't hold on anymore," she gasped, and in that moment, the fragile thread connecting us to her seemed to fray, the darkness encroaching as she stared into the void, caught between two worlds.

"Hold on!" Felix cried, his voice rising in desperation, but as he reached for her, I felt the world around us tilt, the boundaries between light and dark blurring, and the chaos of that moment spiraled into a dizzying abyss, leaving us grasping for something that was slipping away faster than we could comprehend.

Chapter 29: Embracing the Echo

The rain fell softly at first, each drop a gentle whisper against the windowpanes, but it soon transformed into a furious torrent, drumming a chaotic symphony that drowned out the world outside. I sat on the worn leather couch, a refuge amidst the storm, surrounded by the lingering scent of damp earth and burnt wood from the fireplace. It felt as if the weather mirrored my heart—conflicted, raging, and yet desperately yearning for peace. Felix paced the room, his hands stuffed deep into the pockets of his hoodie, the fabric hanging off him like a comforter draped over a child.

"Is this what grief is supposed to feel like?" he asked, his voice a low growl, frustration bubbling beneath the surface. I glanced up from the flickering flames, their orange tongues dancing as if mocking our turmoil.

"Pretty much," I replied, trying to keep the wryness in my tone from slipping into bitterness. "Like walking through mud, but the mud is your memories, and every step threatens to pull you under."

He huffed a short laugh, the sound unexpected and raw. "Great. So, I'm stuck in a swamp, feeling guilty for even breathing."

"Exactly. You've got it."

I couldn't help but admire the way he tried to navigate his pain with humor, a futile attempt to buoy his spirit in the depths of sorrow. Felix had always been the light in a dark room, his laughter a beacon that drew people in. Now, that light flickered as he wrestled with shadows of what could have been. We were both trapped in a purgatory of memories, haunted by the absence of Mia, her laughter echoing in the corners of our minds like a song half-remembered.

"Do you think it ever gets better?" His voice dropped to a whisper, the bravado slipping away like water through his fingers.

"I think we just learn to carry it differently," I said, leaning forward, resting my elbows on my knees. "Like a backpack that never gets lighter, but you find ways to adjust the straps so it doesn't crush you."

He let out a long breath, staring into the flames as if the answers lay within the flickering glow. "I'm so tired, Jess."

"Me too," I replied, and it was true. The fatigue settled deep in my bones, an unyielding weight that made every day feel like a climb up a steep hill. "But we have to keep moving. Mia wouldn't want us to get stuck, would she?"

Felix looked at me then, those eyes of his—brimming with uncertainty and pain—searching for some form of solace. I held his gaze, a tether connecting our grief, recognizing that the bond we had was forged in shared loss. In that moment, we were two souls wandering a vast, desolate landscape, hoping to find a trail that led us back to life.

As the storm outside intensified, so did our conversation, weaving threads of honesty and vulnerability between us. Each word was a step forward, despite the weight of our sorrow. We spoke of memories—of late-night ice cream runs and spontaneous road trips, moments that once shimmered like gold but now felt tarnished by loss. Yet even in the recalling, there was a flicker of light, a reminder of laughter shared and love embraced.

"Remember when we tried to bake that ridiculous cake for Mia's birthday?" Felix chuckled, a genuine smile breaking through the darkness. "We nearly burned down the kitchen."

"How could I forget? The smoke alarm practically called the fire department!" I laughed, the sound ringing out like a bell.

"Or when Mia decided to take that 'nature walk' in the middle of winter. I swear, she thought wearing sandals was a great idea."

"Fashion over function!" I chimed in, and we both fell into a fit of laughter, the warmth of shared memories momentarily pushing back the chill of grief.

Yet, as the laughter faded, the silence that enveloped us felt heavier than before. I could see the conflict dancing behind Felix's eyes, the guilt creeping back in like a thief in the night.

"I should have been there," he murmured, his voice cracking. "If I had just—"

"Stop," I interrupted gently, a hand reaching out to him, hovering in the air like a lifeline. "We can't keep doing this to ourselves. You weren't responsible for her choices."

"Doesn't feel that way."

I could see the pain etched on his face, each line a testament to the turmoil brewing inside him. "I know. But if you keep holding onto that, it'll only eat you alive. Mia would want you to be happy, Felix. To live fully."

"Easier said than done," he muttered, a hint of defiance dancing in his voice.

"Of course it is. Grief isn't a straight line; it's a winding road with all kinds of unexpected twists."

"I hate that it feels like this," he said, frustration bubbling just beneath the surface.

"I do too. But maybe, just maybe, we can navigate it together."

Felix met my gaze, and for a brief moment, the storm outside receded, replaced by a sense of shared resolve. We were a team, two misfits bound by the memory of a friend who had touched our lives in profound ways. I could feel the walls beginning to crack between us, the weight of grief becoming a little lighter, if only for now.

As the rain lashed against the windows, a sudden flash of lightning illuminated the room, casting fleeting shadows that danced around us like memories. I realized then that the journey ahead would be fraught with uncertainty, but we would face it side by side, learning to embrace the echoes of our loss while reaching for the light that still flickered ahead.

The morning light slipped through the curtains like a shy visitor, hesitant to fully intrude. I squinted against the brightness, the memories of last night's conversation lingering like a sweet, bittersweet ache. Felix had left only moments before, his footsteps echoing in the hall like the ghost of laughter. We'd made plans for today—tentative, like the fragile hope we both clung to, but plans nonetheless.

The aroma of fresh coffee wafted through the air, a warm embrace that coaxed me out of the depths of my blanket cocoon. I slid my feet into the soft slippers that Mia had insisted I keep, her belief that "every day deserves a touch of comfort" ringing in my ears like a mantra. It was impossible to ignore her presence, her essence woven into the very fabric of my life, and even the mundane felt sacred now.

I shuffled to the kitchen, the wooden floor cool against my bare feet, and poured myself a steaming cup of coffee. The rich, dark liquid swirled like thoughts racing through my mind, and I cradled the mug, savoring its warmth. Outside, the world was waking up, birds chirping with the kind of zeal that always seemed slightly too optimistic for my mood. I couldn't blame them; they hadn't lost anyone.

I flipped on the radio, letting the soft strains of a familiar song fill the space, and for a fleeting moment, I lost myself in the music. I imagined Mia dancing in the living room, her arms wide, spinning like a dervish, laughter spilling from her lips. The vision was so vivid that it almost pulled me back to happier times, those sun-drenched afternoons when the world felt limitless and possibilities stretched before us like an unbroken horizon.

The knock on the door jolted me from my reverie, and I glanced at the clock—Felix was early. He had a habit of being punctual, which I found both endearing and a tad annoying, depending on how ready I was to face the day. I opened the door, and there he stood, tousled hair and an oversized flannel shirt hanging loosely on his frame, the kind of look that said he'd rolled out of bed and thrown on whatever he could find.

"Good morning, sunshine," I greeted, my voice teasing as I leaned against the doorframe.

"Sunshine? That's rich coming from you, Miss I-Haven't-Changed-Out-Of-My-Pajamas-For-Three-Days." He shot back, a grin breaking through the veil of grief.

"It's a look, Felix. You wouldn't understand." I waved him inside, the teasing lightening the heaviness that still clung to us like a stubborn shadow.

He stepped over the threshold, and for a moment, the air felt electric, charged with unspoken words. "I brought donuts," he said, holding up a crinkled brown bag like it was a treasure. "Thought we could indulge in some unhealthy coping mechanisms."

"Donuts? That's not a coping mechanism; that's just a lifestyle choice." I grabbed the bag, peeking inside. "Glazed or bust, my friend."

We settled at the small kitchen table, the two of us surrounded by the remnants of last night's conversation—half-formed thoughts and shared laughter. I could still feel the warmth of our connection, an anchor in a world that felt like it was constantly shifting beneath our feet.

As we devoured the donuts, the sweetness coated our tongues and for a moment, I forgot about the dark clouds that lingered at the edges of our lives. We talked about everything and nothing—how Felix had watched a documentary that had supposedly changed his life (though I doubted it), and how I had finally finished that book I'd been stalling on for weeks.

"Do you ever think about what Mia would say if she were here?" he asked suddenly, his voice cutting through the lightness.

"Every day." I paused, swirling the dregs of coffee in my cup. "She'd probably tell us to get our acts together and go on a road trip or something. She always wanted to explore the world."

"Then let's do it." The words tumbled out of Felix's mouth, bold and unexpected. "Let's take a trip, just like old times."

I stared at him, the suggestion igniting a flicker of excitement in my chest. "A road trip? Like a full-on 'Thelma and Louise' situation, minus the cliffs?"

He chuckled, but the moment hung between us like an unresolved chord. "Just a little getaway. We could drive up the coast, stop at some random diners, and pretend we're living our best lives. It might help."

"Help with what? Running away from our problems?" I raised an eyebrow, skepticism brewing.

"Or facing them." He leaned forward, intensity flickering in his eyes. "It's not about escaping; it's about finding a new perspective. We can honor Mia by embracing life, even when it feels impossible."

A thousand objections bubbled in my mind, but there was a truth in his words, a raw honesty that resonated deep within. It felt like a dare, one I didn't know if I was ready to accept. "You really think it could work?"

"Couldn't hurt to try." He shrugged, his bravado palpable yet vulnerable. "Besides, what's the worst that could happen? We get lost and end up at some weird roadside attraction, or worse—get stuck in a car together for days on end."

"Sounds like a horror movie in the making," I replied, but I could feel the corners of my mouth lifting in a reluctant smile.

"Exactly. And isn't that how life works? It's never the easy path." He reached across the table, his hand brushing against mine, a moment of connection that sent a jolt through me.

"Alright, let's do it." I surprised myself with the ease of my agreement, the words tumbling out like a confession. "But if I end up sleeping in the car, you owe me a hotel stay."

"Deal." Felix grinned, and in that moment, I could see it—the glimmer of hope, the beginnings of a path forward etched in the promise of new adventures.

We spent the rest of the morning plotting our route and compiling a playlist, the air thick with anticipation. The heaviness of yesterday began to lift, replaced by the thrill of possibility. And as we made plans, I realized that we weren't just honoring Mia; we were choosing to embrace the echoes of her laughter, to find joy in the memories, and perhaps, to carve out a new narrative in the space she left behind.

The days flew by in a blur of planning and anticipation, each moment stitched together with laughter and a sense of purpose that felt foreign yet invigorating. Felix and I poured over maps and travel blogs, deciding on whimsical stops like a giant ball of twine and a pancake house that boasted the world's largest blueberry pancakes. The mundane transformed into an adventure; every detail was a thread pulling us closer to something beyond grief. The idea of it felt daring, exhilarating, and it breathed life back into our souls, even if only for a moment.

The morning of our departure arrived, cloaked in a blue sky that stretched endlessly above us, its brightness almost mocking the shadows we carried. Felix arrived promptly, sporting a bright yellow beanie that made him look like a cheery cartoon character. "What's with the hat?" I teased, helping him load the last of our bags into the trunk of his old hatchback, which had seen better days but still hummed with a spirit of its own.

"It's called optimism, Jess. You should try it," he shot back, plopping the beanie firmly on his head with a flourish. "Plus, it makes me more visible in case we get lost and need rescuing."

"Right, because a bright yellow beanie will be the beacon guiding rescuers through the woods," I laughed, slamming the trunk shut with a satisfying thud.

He grinned, the sunlight catching the freckles on his cheeks, reminding me of the warmth that friendship could bring, even in the wake of sorrow. "Now we just need snacks, and we'll be unstoppable."

I rolled my eyes but followed him inside, where we meticulously selected every sweet and savory treat that caught our fancy, as if building a fortress against the uncertainties ahead. The grocery store became our playground, filled with impulsive choices—gummy bears, beef jerky, and an assortment of sodas that promised a sugar rush worthy of the wildest road trip fantasies.

"Remember, no crying over spilled soda or melted chocolate," I joked, loading the last of our loot into the cart.

"Deal. But if you spill any of my gummy bears, I can't guarantee I won't cry," he shot back, and I couldn't help but snicker.

With the car loaded and the playlist queued, we finally hit the open road. The engine roared to life, and as we pulled away from my house, a sense of liberation washed over me. The familiar sights of our town faded into the background, replaced by a ribbon of asphalt that beckoned us toward the horizon. The world felt vibrant, alive, and bursting with possibility.

We sang along to our carefully curated playlist, voices blending in a chaotic harmony, laughter punctuating the air like firecrackers. I could feel the tension in my chest begin to loosen, the weight of grief shifting into the background as the scenery rushed by. Trees transformed into fields, fields into mountains, and with each mile, I felt a little lighter, a little more hopeful.

"So, what's our first stop again?" Felix asked, glancing over at me as we navigated a winding road flanked by towering pines.

"A diner that claims to have the best milkshakes in the state. And if they don't, I will raise a considerable fuss until they reconsider," I declared, gesturing dramatically with my hands.

Felix chuckled, his eyes sparkling with mischief. "I can already picture it: 'You call this a milkshake? I've had better from a carton!'"

"Exactly!" I said, laughing alongside him, the absurdity of it grounding us in the moment.

But as the sun dipped lower in the sky, casting golden light across the landscape, an uneasy tension crept back in. It was a gnawing reminder that we were still on a journey through our grief, no matter how far we ran.

After several hours, we pulled into the diner's gravel lot, a quaint little place adorned with retro signs and twinkling fairy lights. The exterior was charming, but the air inside was filled with the smell of frying bacon and freshly baked pie, the kind of aromas that wrapped around you like a hug. We slid into a booth, the vinyl seats squeaking under our weight as we settled in.

"See? This is what life is all about," I said, gazing around. "Good food, better company, and a whole lot of laughter."

Felix raised his milkshake in mock salute. "To the great escape!"

"To new beginnings," I replied, clinking my glass against his.

As we indulged in shakes that were indeed the best I'd ever tasted, the conversation flowed easily, weaving through our past, our dreams, and our fears. We talked about the things we'd do once we truly embraced life again, which felt almost like a secret we were sharing with the universe.

But then, as if the universe had other plans, a commotion erupted near the entrance. The door swung open with a dramatic flourish, and in walked a man who seemed straight out of a thriller novel. He was tall, with tousled dark hair and an air of intensity that set the room on edge. His eyes darted around, taking in the patrons with a sharpness that made me instinctively grip my milkshake a little tighter.

"Is he okay?" I murmured, glancing at Felix, who had gone still, his expression shifting from amusement to concern.

"Not sure," he whispered back, his gaze fixed on the newcomer. The man's presence radiated something unnerving, like a storm gathering just out of sight.

We watched as the stranger approached the counter, his voice low but urgent. I couldn't catch his words, but the waitress's expression turned serious, a flicker of fear crossing her features.

"Should we—?" I started, but before I could finish, the man turned abruptly, his eyes landing on us.

A moment stretched, the air thick with anticipation. I could feel the pulse of the diner quicken, the murmur of conversation fading into the background as if the world had narrowed down to just him and us.

Suddenly, he took a step toward our booth, and Felix tensed, ready to spring into action. "Do you know him?" he whispered, panic creeping into his voice.

"I've never seen him before in my life," I replied, my heart racing.

The man stopped in front of us, his gaze piercing and intense. "You need to listen to me. It's about Mia."

My heart plummeted. The air thickened with dread, a chill wrapping around my spine. "What do you know about Mia?" I demanded, my voice trembling.

"I know what happened to her. And you're both in danger."

As the words hung in the air, the diner felt like it was spinning out of control, the comfort we had found now a distant memory. My stomach dropped, fear clawing at my insides, the echoes of our laughter drowned out by an urgent, suffocating silence.

Milton Keynes UK
Ingram Content Group UK Ltd.
UKHW032321221024
449917UK00001B/88